"POWERFUL AND ENGAGING . . .
The Indians' spirit is strong, vivid."
San Francisco Examiner-Chronicle

"A powerful, beautiful book. Linda Hogan gives us
a true and vivid look at part of a great American
tragedy. I wish everyone would read MEAN SPIRIT
and begin to understand."

TONY HILLERMAN

"Richly textured . . . The strong, vibrant heart of a
people betrayed beats thoughout MEAN SPIRIT. . . .
Linda Hogan has given us, in beautifully spare and
unpretentious prose, a powerful work filled with
characters we come to care for."
The Washington Post Book World

"Superb . . . Sprawling . . . Heartbreaking . . .
MEAN SPIRIT is imbued with a poet's lyricism and
a wonderful sense of traditional storytelling. . . . A
vivid portrayal of suffering and survival, of the
collision of one world against another."
Kansas City Star

"Powerful."

The Der

MEAN SPIRIT

Linda Hogan

IVY BOOKS • NEW YORK

This is a work of fiction based on historical events. Some names of characters remain intact, for historical reference, but the characters and events have been fictionalized by the writer. The landscape and terrain, as well, have been reimagined and recreated for fictional purposes.

Ivy Books
Published by Ballantine Books
Copyright © 1990 by Linda Hogan

C. T. Plimer letter on page 34 was excerpted from *The Underground Reservation* by Terry P. Wilson, University of Nebraska Press, page 143.

Library of Congress Catalog Card Number: 90-134

ISBN 0-8041-0863-3

This edition published by arrangement with Atheneum Publishers, an imprint of Macmillan Publishing Company.

Manufactured in the United States of America

First Ballantine Books Edition: January 1992

15 14 13 12 11

In memory of Carol Hunter,
Osage woman, scholar, and friend

PART ONE

OKLAHOMA, 1922

That summer a water diviner named Michael Horse forecast a two-week dry spell.

Until then, Horse's predictions were known to be reliable, and since it was a scorching hot summer, a good number of Indians moved their beds outdoors in hopes a chance breeze would pass over and provide relief from the hot nights. They set them up far from the houses that held the sun's heat long after dark. Cots were unfolded in kitchen gardens. White iron beds sat in horse pastures. Four-posters rested in cornfields that were lying fallow.

What a silent bedchamber the world was, just before morning when even the locusts were still. In that darkness, the white beds were ghostly. They rose up from the black rolling hills and farmlands. Here, a lonely bed sat next to a barbed wire fence, and there, beneath the protection of an oak tree, a man's lantern burned beside his sleeping form. Near the marshland, tents of gauzy mosquito netting sloped down over the bony shoulders and hips of dreamers. A hand hung over the edge of a bed, fingers reaching down toward bluegrass that grew upward in fields. Given half a chance, the vines and leaves would have crept up the beds and overgrown the sleeping bodies of people.

In one yard, a nervy chicken wanted to roost on a bedframe and was shooed away.

"Go on. Scat!" an old woman cried out, raising herself

half up in bed to push the clucking hen back down to the
ground.

That would be Belle Graycloud. She was a light-skinned
Indian woman, the grandmother of her family. She wore a
meteorite on a leather thong around her neck. It had been
passed on to her by a man named Osage Star-Looking who'd
seen it fall from the sky and smolder in a field. It was her
prized possession, although she also had a hand-written book
by the old healer, Severance.

Belle slept alone in the herb garden. The rest of her family
believed, in varying degrees, that they were modern, so they
remained inside the oven-hot walls of the house. Belle's
grown daughters drowsed off and on throughout the night.
The men tossed. The two young people were red-faced and
sweating, tangled in their bed linens on sagging mattresses.

Belle frightened away the hen, then turned on her side and
settled back into the feather pillow. Her silver hair spread
over the pillow. Even resting outside in the iron bed surrounded by night's terrain, she was a commanding woman
with the first morning light on her strong-boned face.

A little ways down the road toward Watona, Indian Territory, a forest of burned trees was just becoming visible in
morning's red firelight. Not far from there, at the oil fields,
the pumps rose and fell, pulling black oil up through layers
of rock. Across the way was a greenwood forest. And not
even a full mile away from where Belle slept, just a short
walk down the dirt road, Grace Blanket and her daughter
Nola slept in a bed that was thoughtfully placed in their flower
garden. Half covered in white sheets, they were dark-skinned
angels dreaming their way through heaven. A dim lantern
burned on a small table beside Grace. Its light fell across the
shocking red blooms of roses.

Grace Blanket sat up in bed and put out the lamp. It
smoked a little, and she smelled the kerosene. She climbed
out from between her damp sheets. Standing in her thin
nightdress, buried up to her dark ankles in the wild iris leaves
that year after year invaded her garden, Grace bent over her
sleeping daughter and shook the girl's shoulder. Grace smiled
down at Nola, who had a widow's peak identical to her own,
and even before the sleeping girl opened her eyes, Grace
began to straighten the sheets on her side of the bed. "Make

your bed every morning,'' they used to say, ''and you'll never want for a husband.'' Grace was a woman who took such sayings to heart and she still wanted a husband. She decided to let Nola sleep a few minutes longer.

Lifting the hem of her nightgown, she walked across the yard, and went inside the screen door to the house.

Indoors, Grace pulled a navy blue dress over her head and zipped it. She fastened a strand of pearls around her neck, then brushed her hair in front of the mirror.

It was a strange house for a Hill Indian, as her people had come to be called. And sometimes, even to herself, Grace looked like an apparition from the past walking through the rooms she'd decorated with heavy, carved furniture and glass chandeliers. It seemed odd, too, that the European furniture was so staunch and upright when Grace was known to be lax at times in her own judgments.

She went to the open window and leaned out, ''Nola! Come on now.'' She could see the girl in the growing daylight. She looked like an insect in its cocoon.

Nola turned over.

The Hill Indians were a peaceful group who had gone away from the changing world some sixty years earlier, in the 1860s. Their survival depended on returning to a simpler way of life, so they left behind them everything they could not carry and moved up into the hills and bluffs far above the town of Watona. Grace Blanket had been born of these, and she was the first to go down out of the hills and enter into the quick and wobbly world of mixed-blood Indians, white loggers, cattle ranchers, and most recently, the oil barons. The Hill Indians were known for their runners, a mystical group whose peculiar running discipline and austere habits earned them a special place in both the human world and the world of spirits.

But there were reasons why Grace had left the hills and moved down to Watona. Her mother, Lila Blanket, was a river prophet, which meant that she was a listener to the voice of water, a woman who interpreted the river's story for her people. A river never lied. Unlike humans, it had no need to distort the truth, and she heard the river's voice unfolding like its water across the earth. One day the Blue River told Lila that the white world was going to infringe on the peace-

ful Hill People. She listened, then she went back to her tribe
and told them, "It is probable that we're going to lose everything. Even our cornfields."

The people were quiet and listened.

Lila continued, "Some of our children have to learn about
the white world if we're going to ward off our downfall."

The Hill Indians respected the Blue River and Lila's words,
but not one of them wanted to give their children up to that
limbo between the worlds, that town named Watona, and
finally Lila, who had heard the Blue directly, selected her
own beautiful daughter, Grace, for the task. She could not
say if it was a good thing or bad thing; it was only what had
to be done.

Lila was a trader. That was her job at the Hill settlement.
She went down to Watona often to trade sweet potatoes for
corn, or sometimes corn for sweet potatoes. On her journeys,
she was a frequent visitor at the Grayclouds'. Moses Graycloud, the man of the house, was Lila's second cousin. She
liked him. He was a good Indian man; a rancher who kept a
pasture and barn lot full of cattle and a number of good-
looking horses. One day, when she mustered up enough
strength, Lila took cornmeal and apples down to the small
town, stopped by the Graycloud house, and knocked on the
door.

As always, Belle was happy to see Lila Blanket. She
opened the door for her. "Come in. Welcome." She held
Lila's hand and smiled at her. But when she saw Lila's grief,
her expression changed to one of concern. "I see you didn't
come to trade food," she said. "What is it?"

Lila covered her face with her hands for a moment, then
she took a deep breath and looked at Belle Graycloud. "I
need to send my daughter to live near town. We've got too
far away from the Americans to know how their laws are
cutting into our life."

Belle nodded. She knew that a dam was going to be built
at the mouth of the Blue River. The water must have told
Lila this, about the army engineers and the surveyors with
their red flags.

Lila was so overcome with sadness that she could hardly
speak, but she asked Belle, "Can Grace stay with you?"

"Yes. I want her here." Belle put her hand on Lila's arm.

"You come too, as often as you want. There's always an extra plate at our table."

On the day Lila took Grace to the Grayclouds, she kissed the girl, embraced her, and left immediately, before she could change her mind. She loved her daughter. She cried loudly all the way home, no matter who passed by or heard her. In fact, an old Osage hermit named John Stink heard the woman's wailing and he came down from his campsite, took Lila's hand, and walked much of the way home with her.

Grace Blanket had a ready smile and a good strong way with Belle's wayward chickens, but she paid little attention to the Indian ways. She hardly seemed like the salvation of the Hill Indians. And she was not at all interested in the white laws that affected her own people. After she finished school, Grace took a job at Palmer's store in town, and put aside her money. It wasn't any time at all before Grace bought a small, grassy parcel of land. She rented it out as a pasture for cattlemen, and one day, while Grace was daydreaming a house onto her land—her dream house had large rooms and a cupid fountain—Lila Blanket arrived in Watona, Indian Territory, with Grace's younger sisters. They were twins, ten years old, and the older woman wanted them to live with Grace and go to school. Their American names were Sara and Molene. And they had the same widow's peak that every Blanket woman had. They were wide-eyed girls, looking around at the world of automobiles and blond people. The longer they were there, the more they liked Watona. And the more Lila visited them, the more she hated the shabby little town with its red stone buildings and flat roofs. It was a magnet of evil that attracted and held her good daughters.

But the girls were the last of the Hill Indians ever to move down to Watona. Molene died several summers later, of an illness spread by white men who worked on the railroad. Sara caught the same paralyzing illness and was forced to remain in bed, motionless for over a year while Grace took care of her. By the time Sara was healthy enough to sit up in a wheelchair, both she and Grace wanted to remain in Watona. It was easier to wash clothing in the wringer washers, she reasoned, than to stir hot water tubs at home, and it was a most amazing thing to go for a ride in an automobile, and to turn on electric lights with the flick of a fingertip. And the delicate white women made such beautiful music on their pianos that Grace wanted one desperately and put away some of her earnings in a sugar bowl toward that cause.

There also were more important reasons why they remained; in the early 1900s each Indian had been given their choice of any parcel of land not already claimed by the white Americans. Those pieces of land were called allotments. They consisted of 160 acres a person to farm, sell, or use in any way they desired. The act that offered allotments to the Indians, the Dawes Act, seemed generous at first glance so only a very few people realized how much they were being tricked, since numerous tracts of unclaimed land became open property for white settlers, homesteaders, and ranchers. Grace and Sara, in total ignorance, selected dried-up acreages that no one else wanted. No one guessed that black undercurrents of oil moved beneath that earth's surface.

When Belle Graycloud saw the land Grace selected, and that it was stony and dry, she shook her head in dismay and said to Grace, "It's barren land. What barren, useless land." But Grace wasn't discouraged. With good humor, she named her property "The Barren Land." Later, after oil was found there, she called it "The Baron Land," for the oil moguls.

It was Michael Horse, the small-boned diviner who'd predicted the two-week dry spell, who had been the first person to discover oil on the Indian wasteland, and he found it on Grace's parched allotment.

With his cottonwood dowsing rod, he'd felt a strong underground pull, followed it straight through the dry prairie grass, turned a bit to the left, and said, "Drill here. I feel water." Then he smiled and showed off his three gold teeth. The men put down an auger, bored deep into the earth, and struck oil on Grace Blanket's land.

Michael Horse fingered one of his long gray braids that hung down his chest. "I'll be damned," he said. He was worried. He didn't know how he had gone wrong. He had 363 wells to his credit. There was no water on Grace Blanket's land, just the thick black fluid that had no use at all for growing corn or tomatoes. Not even zucchini squash would grow there. He took off his glasses and he put them in his shirt pocket. He didn't want to see what happened next.

When Grace Blanket's first lease check came in from the

oil company, she forgot the cupid fountain and moved into a house with Roman columns. She bought a grand piano, but to her disappointment she was without talent for music. No matter how she pressed down the ivory keys, she couldn't play the songs she'd heard and loved when white women sang them. After several months, she gave up and moved the piano outside to a chicken coop where it sat neglected, out of tune, and swelling up from the humidity. When a neighboring chicken built a nest on the keys, Grace didn't bother to remove the straw and feathers.

After that, she only bought items she could put to good use. She bought crystal champagne glasses that rang like bells when a finger was run over the rim, a tiny typewriter that tapped out the English words she'd learned in school, and a white fur cape that brought out the rich chestnut brown in her dark skin. She wore the cape throughout her pregnancy, even on warmer days, so much that Belle Graycloud poked fun at her. "When that baby comes, it's going to be born with a fan in its tiny hands."

"That's all right," said Grace, flashing a smile. "Just so long as it's electric."

"Say, who is the father, anyway?" Belle asked. But Grace just looked away like she hadn't heard.

After Nola was born, Grace took the child back a few times each year to the world of the Hill society, and while Nola had a stubborn streak, even as an infant, she was peaceful and serene in the midst of her mother's people. As much as the child took to the quieter ways of the Hill Indians, they likewise took to her, and while Grace continued to make her way in life, enjoying the easy pleasures money could buy, not one of those luxuries mattered a whit to Nola. By the time she was five years old, it was apparent to everyone that Nola was ill suited for town life. She was a gentle child who would wander into the greenwood forest and talk to the animals. She understood their ways. Lila thought that perhaps her granddaughter was going to be the one to return to the people. Nola, not Grace, was the river's godchild.

But what Lila didn't know, even up to the day she died, was that her daughter's oil had forestalled the damming of the Blue River, and that without anyone realizing it, the sacrifice of Grace to the town of Watona had indeed been the

salvation of the Hill Indians. The dam would not go in until
all the dark wealth was removed from inside the land.

That morning, as the sun rose up the sky, and Nola was still
asleep, Grace went to the window and called out again,
"Nola. Get up!"

Nola was dark and slender. Even with her eyes swollen
from sleep, she was an uncommonly beautiful girl. She sat
up like a small queen in her bed, with already elegant brown
skin stretched over her thirteen-year-old bones. She climbed
out of the bed, still sleepy, and went indoors. She slipped
out of her nightgown, washed herself, and put on a Sunday
white dress, and after Grace tied the bow behind Nola's thin
waist, they walked together up the road to where Belle Graycloud slept in the middle of her herb garden with a stubborn
golden chicken roosting on the foot of the bed, a calico cat
by the old woman's side, a fat spotted dog snoring on the
ground, and a white horse standing as close to Belle as the
fence permitted, looking at her with wide, reverent eyes.

It was such a sight, Grace laughed out loud, and the laugh-
ter woke Belle.

Belle was indignant. "I knew someone was looking at me.
I felt it. There ought to be a law against sneaking up on
people like that. You gave me a fright."

Nola had slipped away to the house even while Belle talked.
She was looking for her friend, Rena.

"Especially old people," Belle grumbled, rising from the
bed. "Shoo!" She pushed the hen away from her bed.

Grace moved the cat. "Here, let me help you make the
bed." She began to smooth Belle's sheets.

"Leave it," said Belle. "You know the saying. Maybe if
I leave it in a mess, the young men will stop chasing me all
the time." She pushed her dark silver hair back from her
face. It hung like an ancient waterfall. Then she headed for
the house, Grace alongside her. Behind them, the cat
stretched and followed.

In the house, Belle's granddaughter, Rena, was already
dressed. Rena had gold skin, the color of ochre, like a high
yellow mulatto. It gave her, at first glance, a look of mystery.
Her eyes, also, were gold-colored, and her hair. But she was
still a child and she was impatient that morning as she walked

around the creaky floor of the farmhouse, impatient to go with Nola and Grace to cut willow branches, impatient also for Grace to teach her how to weave the willow baskets, how to be that kind of an Indian woman.

In the kitchen, Belle's unmarried daughter, Leticia, took the perking coffeepot off the woodstove and set it on the table. "You sure you don't want some?" she asked Grace.

The girls passed by her in a hurry, and again the screen door slammed. Lettie opened the door behind them and called out, "Do you girls swear you won't soil your good church dresses?" She looked sharply at Rena. "You hear?"

"Cross my heart," said Rena, but she was already halfway down the walk. She looked back at Lettie who was dressed in a house dress and apron, but who nevertheless wore an expensive felted wool hat on her head. It was blue and a net was stitched to it.

"That goes for you, too," Lettie called out to Grace as Grace tried to catch up with the girls.

Grace turned and took a few steps backward before she blew a kiss to Lettie. Then she caught up with the girls. The sun lit her arms. For a change, she was in a hurry and the girls fell behind. Grace wanted to gather water willows and be done in time to put in a rare appearance at church, an appearance prompted only by the presence of a new, handsome man in town, and the only thing Grace knew about him was that he was a Baptist, so she knew where to find him.

Michael Horse drove a gold car. It matched his teeth. That Sunday morning, he was in his shirtsleeves. On his way to church, he drove past three Indian boys who were playing hooky from the House of Our Lord. They sat on a curb, sharing a fat brown Cuban cigar. They called it a stogie and blew gray smoke rings into the summer air. The boys wore lightweight Sunday suits, had taken off their jackets, and their shirt collars were opened. It was sweltering. One of the boys was Ben Graycloud, the grandson of Belle and Moses.

Horse was late for church, but even so, after he parked his car, he stopped for a moment in front of the boys and let them shake his hand the way their parents had taught them to do with elders. All of them were taller than he was. They tried to hide the cigar. Horse pretended not to notice the cloud of smoke one of them fanned with his hat.

There was a blue law on Sunday mornings and the town was quiet. Sinners and saints were in church, nonbelievers still in bed. The streets were almost empty of people, but dark, expensive automobiles were parked outside of the Oklahoma Indian Baptist Church. Michael Horse was proud of the fact that he owned the only gold car in town. It shined bright as a brick of bullion.

Not that the other cars were shabby. On South Street alone there were two powder-blue Ford roadsters with tooled leather seats, five Lincolns, three Cadillacs, and everyone of them belonged to the cash-paying Indians who were singing "Amazing Grace" inside the church.

Horse heard their voices. The congregation had risen up to sing. They rested the backs of their legs against dark pews and fanned their faces, he knew, with paper fans that had pictures of Jesus knocking on the door of a heart.

Horse went in and stood in the back of the church until the singers closed their hymnbooks, and in a rustle of clothing and a clearing of throats, he walked in and sat down in a pew not far behind Moses and Belle Graycloud.

As usual, the church was nearly full. Mixed-blood people were side by side in faith with their darker brothers and sisters. Though they wore dark, American suits, most of the men still braided their hair. Some of the younger women had lightened their hair to a brassy orange with hydrogen peroxide. Some of them wore makeup that was paler than their faces, imitating the white women's pictures in magazines, but Michael Horse wasn't fooled; they were Indians, and even if he hadn't known most all their parents and grandparents—and he did—he would have known by the way their bones moved, by the way they sat or talked, that they were from one of the tribes around Watona. It was in the way a person tilted her head when she laughed, or in the set of shoulders. He would have guessed Ben Graycloud just by the way the boy held the Cuban cigar between his thumb and middle finger like Moses had always done.

Horse was a good judge of people and he had what they called a sixth sense. He was also a dreamer.

At night, asleep, he saw a side of people that was more

true than the poker faces some of them wore in public, more telling than bloodlines, and way more revealing than black suits or blue silk dresses.

He was lost in these thoughts when everyone rose up once again to sing a hymn. Horse searched absently in his shirt pocket for his little round reading glasses until Velma Billy, in the pew behind him, handed him a hymnal opened to page 261, "Rock of Ages." He smiled, "Thank you," and saw how her wire-framed glasses caught a yellow glint of sunlight from the stained glass window, and so did the cross she wore around her neck, resting in the soft center of her bosom. She didn't need the book. She knew the songs by heart.

In front of Horse, Moses Graycloud sang with vigor. He had removed the jacket of his hot, dark suit, and his shirt was damp with sweat. A medal of valor from the Spanish-American War was heavy on his chest. Moses was a very dark man and he was physically strong, even though he limped on damp, rainy days. Beside Moses was Belle. At first glance she looked small, but in spite of her slight stature, she was a giant on the inside, and hard to reckon with.

Horse watched her. Her steel-gray hair was damp from the heat, with loose strands plastered against the back of her neck. The sun came through the stained glass robes of Jesus and touched one side of her strong-boned face and warmed her hair. Now and then, she glanced over her shoulder toward the door, and once Horse caught her eye, and even though she was surprised to see him in church—Horse was not a Christian Indian—she nodded a hello at him before her eyes again watched the door.

Horse could not explain, even to himself, what he was doing in church that morning. Except for the gold car, he was one of the last proud holdouts from the new ways and he didn't want younger Indians to get the wrong idea about how old-timers lived in the world or that maybe he believed in the white man's God, but mostly he was embarrassed to be caught gazing at Belle. Michael Horse had a soft spot for Belle, but he wouldn't have said so.

That morning, the young Reverend Joe Billy was talking about toppling worlds. "The Indian world is on a collision course with the white world," Billy said.

Wasn't that the truth, Horse thought. It didn't even need to be said.

Joe Billy fanned himself with his sermon notes, "It's more than a race war. They are waging a war with earth. Our forests and cornfields are burned by them. But, I say to you, our tears reach God. He knows what's coming round, so may God speak to the greedy hearts of men and move them."

And he had hope, the kind of hope a young Creek Indian had when he'd gone to a seminary back East, in Boston, married a white society woman against her father's will, and returned home determined to save and serve his own Indian people.

Service and praying were in Joe Billy's blood; he'd inherited those traits from his father, Sam Billy, who'd been a medicine man for twenty-three years before he'd converted to the Christian faith.

At least a dozen of the Billy line were in church that morning, Horse noted. Velma Billy, with the "Rock of Ages" fixed permanently in her mind, was Sam's daughter. Joe Billy, Sam's favored son, saying, "So be it, my brothers and sisters." And when he said, "Amen" that morning, his voice put Horse in mind of Sam's.

Horse watched Belle Graycloud's shoulders rise and fall with every breath. He overheard her whisper to Moses. "Something's not right. I think the girls are in trouble."

Moses was what they called a logical man, and no matter how many of Belle's hunches proved true, he was hard put to believe her, so he smiled reassuringly at her and laid his hand over hers. Then the service was over, and the congregation began to spill out of the church, but each and every person stopped at the door and shook hands with the preacher's blond wife.

When it was Michael Horse's turn, she took hold of his hand and pumped it. "Why, hello, Mr. Horse." She sounded musical. Her name was Martha. She was skinny and frail, and sweating from the heat. Her yellow hair was in a tight, damp bun. Horse was shy. He stared down at her small hand. It was the color of the paper he wrote his journals on, all the way down to the pale blue lines of her veins.

"Come back soon, Mr. Horse," Martha Billy called out to him as he went down the step.

Outside the church that morning, Belle was giving her grandson Ben one of the glares that she had been famous for all her life. Ben got up from his roosterlike perch, left the other boys behind, and followed his grandmother.

Horse followed along with them. He was thinking that Belle's bones were never wrong and he'd felt it too, something uneasy in the air that day, like a dry, hot wind starting to blow over the scorched land.

Horse dropped behind Belle, behind her bountiful, gliding hips.

"I'm going straight home," she said to Horse, over her shoulder. "If you want to come, you're welcome."

Horse accepted Belle's invitation. He fell into step with Ben. "You want to ride with me?" he asked Ben Graycloud. Ben brightened up. He looked at his grandmother for approval.

She turned back and was stern a moment. "You sure do smell like cigar smoke," she said with her owl eyes staring sharply into his, then she waved him away and said, "Go on if you're going. Git!" She didn't look back again.

Ben hooted and raced ahead of Horse. By the time Horse reached his gold convertible, Ben was already in the passenger seat, his hat pulled down over his eyes, one leg crossed over the other. He looked like a dandy. If they hadn't known him better, anyone would have thought he was a city boy in gabardine pants.

"Get out," Horse said. He sounded gruff. Ben looked up, surprised, but Horse had a big grin on his face and he was smiling and held up the key. "Slide over," he said to the young man.

Ben slid over to the driver's seat. He turned the car around, and he drove tall and proud past the dressed-up churchgoers while Michael Horse enjoyed the scenery. Maybe it was the light reflecting off the red sandstone buildings that day but people walking on the street looked rosy and golden. White dresses, in the light, were blushing. The men's black suits had a sheen about them, like burnished metal. The sunlit Indian people stood in line outside the stores, waiting for shopowners to turn the "Closed" signs around. Some of the women held red umbrellas above their heads and so they stood in ruby circles of light, scolding their children for playing in the white noonday heat. One Indian woman called to her daughter, "You're going to faint. Get in here." Under the circle of shade, she meant.

There were two dry goods stores in Watona. One of them was painted red. Palmer's Red Store, as it was called, sold yard goods and household things that appealed to the women. The other one was sky blue. The Blue Store sold hardware, hunting rifles, and had a thin, yellowed catalogue on a stand where women could order wallpaper and linoleum. It was also owned by Palmer since the previous winter when the Indian owner disappeared. The last person who'd seen him was John Tate, Moses's brother-in-law. Just before noon, the shopkeepers covered their candy bins to keep children's thieving fingers away, then, at twelve sharp, they turned their signs around. Mr. Palmer, at the Red Store, opened the door with a jangle of keys, and stepped aside to let the Indian women enter. They went into the store, folded down their umbrellas, and fawned over lead-backed mirrors that were filled with their own faces. While older women haggled over the cost of lacquer boxes that played the "Blue Danube," young girls bought paper fans for their friends to autograph and like most Sundays, the men and boys went their own ways into the Blue Store where they bought tobacco and rifles for hunting the last remaining bear and deer. And gunpowder was cheap.

But for Belle, Sunday was the day when she changed the racks in her beehives, cleaned out her chicken coop, or walked along the creek bed, gathering watercress and wild onion. "The earth is my marketplace," she would tell her family, and they understood what she meant for they ate the fruits of her labor.

When Ben drove the gold car up the road to his home and honked, Belle was outside standing beside a large azalea bush. She watched the distant roads where dust flew up as cars zigzagged back and forth across the land.

Horse got out of his car, looking off in the direction she was squinting. There was a bluebird flying, but it was nearly invisible against the blue sky and the dust from the roads. A few cardinals stood out like spots of blood in the distant trees.

"I'll be back," Horse said to Belle, and he went out to

the barn to talk with Moses. Ben remained in the driver's seat, turning the wheel as if he were going somewhere. He imagined he was driving between the many cattle that dotted the pasture.

In the barn, Moses was at work shoeing one of his horses. He held the black mare's leg up on his thigh and cleaned the hoof, then took a nail from his pocket.

"How's your car running?" he asked Michael Horse. He tapped the metal shoe lightly with a hammer. The horse blinked at him with big black eyes.

"Good." Horse looked in the direction of his gold roadster. It ran like a charm.

"That's good. How are your teeth?" Moses breathed heavily, from the effort, and he glanced quickly up at Michael Horse.

"I went to the dentist in Tulsa last week." Horse bent down and watched Moses. "Say, do you need some help?"

"I'm almost done." Moses put the mare's leg down and wiped his forehead with his arm. He didn't mention the other man's bad reputation with horses. He breathed a little heavily. "You've got more money tied up in your mouth than I have in horse flesh."

Michael Horse laughed. "Isn't that the truth?"

They led the mare out of the barn. Moses limped. A hot wind had started blowing. It blew the horse's dark mane over to one side. Moses looked up at the sky. "You say we've still got a week or so before it rains?"

"Maybe two," Horse confirmed.

"The way my bad leg hurts, I'd say it's going to rain today." The dust blew up around them. Moses led the horse over to where Belle was standing. Her hands were on her hips, the breeze blowing her dress against her soft body. Moses clicked his tongue at the mare, but he did it for Belle's comfort more than for the horse, and he watched Belle all the while he patted the black-eyed horse and tossed a gray blanket over its back.

His plan was to ride the horse to the far pasture and set it loose, then walk back to the house.

"I'm going to stop by Mother's on the way back," he told her. That was what he still called the place where his twin sister Ruth lived with her husband, John Tate. She hadn't appeared in church that morning, and that troubled him.

"Here," Belle said, "I'll hold the reins," and she watched while Moses pulled himself up and threw his stiff leg over the horse. He tried to put her worries to rest. He said, "They'll be back before long. It's all right, Belle."

"It's hot for walking," Horse said. "Don't you want me to drive out after you?"

Moses smiled down from the mare. "It's my constitutional," Moses said. "If I stop moving this leg, I'll lose it." He looked elegant and tall astride the dark horse. He was at home. Michael and Belle watched him turn the black horse toward the road.

"What's up?" Michael Horse asked Belle, trying not to sound too prying. He'd been watching her nervous behavior.

"Grace and Nola came by this morning. They took Rena out to cut willows. Then they were going to soak them in saltwater, and be back in time for church." While she talked, Belle fidgeted with a pearl button on her dress. She glanced at Horse, then back out at the road where Moses was becoming smaller. "We haven't seen them since."

Horse was known for his predictions, so when he said, "They probably just lost track of time," Belle took his word for it. "Well then, maybe we should have a cup of coffee," she said. But still she worried. In the kitchen, while waiting for the coffee, she tapped her fingertips on the table.

Horse looked out the window in the direction Moses had gone, as if he were still there. "How is Ruth?" he asked.

Belle also glanced that direction, seeing the road grow small, the path, the distance across the Mill Creek and the dark solid old house where Ruth and Moses's mother had lived out her life, where John Tate moved in after he'd married the single, quiet twin of Moses.

It was only a short while later, as they sat at the table talking, a strong wind came up. It was a "turn wind," the kind that stirs things up for a few hours and then dies down. Earlier that summer, other unexpected turn winds had caused fierce and dangerous sandstorms.

"It looks like a bad one," Horse said. He smelled the air. "Maybe we'd better drive out to see if we can't find Grace."

Belle went upstairs to grab a headscarf and by the time she

told Lettie where she was going and returned, a dark cloud had blown in. It cast a shadow over the land. The wind picked up. It swept through tall dry grasses, hissing.

Horse drove through the flying dust with Belle Graycloud sitting next to him. The wind whipped at her scarf. Nothing was staying put; stray pieces of paper flew up all the way from town, and when they reached the creek, it was already blown full of earth. It rushed, muddy and red, downhill between swaying trees toward where it joined the wide Blue River. Horse parked. Belle got out of the car and called the girls. She crooked an arm over her eyes to shield them from the flying sand. Held up that way, the skin on her inner arm looked soft and vulnerable in the storm around them. Michael Horse gave her a handkerchief to hold across her eyes. He was worried about his paint job. He put the top up on his car and Belle got back in.

By the time they reached Woody Pond, Belle's scarf had blown away and caught on a tumbleweed that rushed across the land. Wind whistled down from the hills, and then just as they rolled up the windows, sharp rain started. It began as a roar moving toward them, then it let up a little as the roaring arrived and passed by them.

Belle and Horse walked against the violent wind, leaning into it. Horse's black pants whipped up against his legs. Belle's hair flew away from her face like seaweed pulled in a furious rip tide. There wasn't a trace of the girls. She cried, "Rena!" from the top of her lungs, but the wind only blew her words back to her. She called again, "Grace!" but there was only the raging sound of the wind and Horse, standing next to her, had not even heard her.

They drove to Grace's house. The sky was the deep lead color of sea. At the front door, Belle beat the brass knocker, but no one answered. Belle picked her way through thorny bushes and peered into the wind-rattled window. Inside, everything was still and peaceful.

Gold angels were on the walls. A crystal chandelier hung from the ceiling. Glass swans sat on the mantle and they were swimming in a marble lake. The silence was like the calm eye of a tornado.

Belle went around back. Grace's bed was standing in the rose garden. The wind had whipped up the sheets. One billowed like a sail against the metal bedframe. Another was flat and wet, spread over several rosebushes nearby.

They were at a loss. The gas tank was nearly empty. They hadn't found a single clue to the whereabouts of Grace, and Horse's gold car was chipped from the flying gravel and debris. Finally, they gave up the search and returned to the Graycloud house.

"I'm sorry about your car," Belle said to Horse.

He smiled at her. "It's okay. I was getting tired of gold paint anyway." He looked in the mirror. "Maybe we should go out to get Moses."

"No. He'll be all right. He'll stay at Ruth's until the storm dies down."

Then she became silent, and at home again, Belle sat down on the steps, pulled her damp blue skirt down over her knees, and didn't bother to protect herself from the rain.

Michael Horse said nothing, but he turned when he heard the door slam, and when Belle's daughter, Leticia, ran out, holding her hat down on her head, screaming out over the wind, "Mama, come inside." She pleaded, "You can't sit out here all day in this weather."

Belle looked at her daughter. She said defiantly, "Who says I can't?" And her hair whipped angrily about her face, but then she gave up, sighed, and with Horse, she followed Lettie indoors.

It was quieter in the house. They shut the door and latched it, but Belle kept watch at the windows, still looking for the girls. Awhile later, Moses, wet and dirty, limped in. "That's a hell of a turn wind," he said, rubbing his sore right leg and hip. "Why didn't you come get me?" To Horse he said, "What did I tell you about my leg and rain? You're losing your touch, old man. You're getting worn out. It's raining like crazy."

"It's true. I think I'm slipping," Horse said. He shrugged his narrow shoulders. It would be better for him anyway if people stopped coming to ask him to find their rings and their lost dogs.

"Why didn't you stay at Ruth's?"

Moses seemed like he didn't want to answer, but said, "Tate had some of his friends over. Ruth was angry about it. I felt like an intruder."

He'd never liked Tate. John Tate was a small, fussy man with only one eye and every time Moses looked into it, he could see nothing warm, nothing human.

Normally Belle would stand up for Ruth and Tate. She'd seen the toll of loneliness on Moses's twin sister for way too many years, but she was worried about the girls.

"I think we ought to get the sheriff," Belle said. She was anxious, but Moses convinced her to wait. His reasons made sense. Grace Blanket was famous in those parts, both as a basket-maker and as an oil-rich Indian who was given to catting around. She had a sweet disposition, a mind of her own, and a fondness for men and drink.

"She's gallivanting around somewhere with a new boyfriend," Moses said. "The two girls are eating gritty ice cream in some man's rumble seat. I can see them now. Their hair is flying straight out behind them in the stiff wind. They're having the time of their lives."

Grace had that kind of reputation. And it made sense, Belle finally agreed, since two nights earlier, Grace had a public fight with her new white boyfriend over another man. That scene, combined with the one Moses's words just painted, allayed Belle's fears. Even Horse agreed that Grace was sometimes brash and reckless, especially if she had a drink under her belt.

"Say, Horse," Moses said. "There's a livestock auction over in Walnut Springs. I have to go over there. Why don't you come along with me?" He opened the icebox and took out a sugar bowl full of cash.

Horse looked at Belle. He was a single man, so he was sensitive to her worries.

"Oh, go ahead," she told them. "I'm sure everything's fine."

"Well, I guess it wouldn't hurt to go look." Horse seemed a little reluctant. He watched her.

"I'll stay here with Mama," Lettie assured them. Lou, Belle's other daughter, and her white husband had gone to Tulsa for the weekend. They were due home later that night.

Belle and Lettie waited. Belle went outside often, to watch. They were both alarmed, though they said almost nothing.

And that night, after the dark set in, the two girls came home. They were alone. They were filthy and their eyes were full of terror. Belle was standing outside, watching the long dark horizon, and still wearing her white apron when they arrived.

What had happened that morning was this: After dawn, before Grace and Nola Blanket walked up to Belle's white bedstead, they passed the oil field. An oilman named John Hale nodded at them. Hale was a lanky white man who wore a gray Stetson hat. He'd been a rancher in Indian Territory for a number of years before he invested in the oil business. He was known as a friend to the Indians. He'd always been generous and helpful to his darker compatriots, but Grace didn't care for him.

Once, feeling Hale's eyes on her, Grace glanced back, quickly, over her shoulder. Hale watched her, but she was a beautiful woman and it wasn't unusual for men to stop and stare, so she thought little about it.

On their way to Woody Pond that Sunday morning, the girls walked a little behind Grace. They whispered to each other the secret things girls share. Nola bent and picked a sunflower. She handed it to Rena. Rena pulled the yellow petals from the flower, looked at its black center, and said, "He loves me."

"Who?" asked Nola.

"How should I know? But it's grand to be loved, isn't it?" Rena smiled.

Grace walked faster. "Hurry! We'll be late for church!" The sun moved up in the sky. They had another mile to go. But the girls didn't keep up with her and they lagged farther behind and there were more distances between Grace and the girls than just that stretch of road; there was a gap in time between one Indian way of life and another where girls were sassy and wore satin ribbons in their hair.

They turned and walked up the red dirt path to the pond. Grace gave each of the girls a small knife. "Cut those thin ones." She pointed to the willows she wanted for her baskets, and in their chalk-white dresses, the girls bent and pared them off, then handed the cuttings to Grace. She put them, one at a time, neatly in the sling she carried looped up over the padded shoulder of her dress.

It was hot and the white sun had risen further up the sky

when Grace heard a car. It wasn't unusual for whiskey peddlers to drive past Woody Pond on Sunday mornings, nor was it odd for drivers on their way home from the city to stop there and rest.

The car kicked up a cloud of dust. When it cleared, Grace saw the black Buick. She smiled at first, thinking it belonged to Moses Graycloud, and that he was picking them up because they were late for church, but then her hand froze in the air.

The men in the car turned their faces toward her, as if something was wrong.

They talked while they watched her. She thought she saw a pistol, then thought she must have imagined it. The driver seemed to be saying "No" to the other man, and they drove in closer, still arguing. Hale was driving. Grace didn't know the passenger. He was a broad man with dark hair. She looked at them, then moved behind a tree. They turned the car around and drove slowly away down the road, but Grace remained nervous and watchful. "Hurry, it's getting late," she urged the girls. She glanced back toward the car. The girls worked faster. The sun was hot and the bees sounded dizzy, and then the car returned, and again the men's eyes were on Grace.

When the car braked, Grace panicked and held still, like a deer in danger, rooted to where she stood. Even the air became still, and not a hair on Grace's head moved as she stood still and fixed, a hand poised on the branches in the sling at her side. In desperate hope, she looked around for other Indians who might have been at the pond searching for turtles, or a Sunday morning rabbit hunter. But they were alone, and the girls felt Grace's fear, like electricity, rising up their skin, up the backs of their necks.

Nola looked around. "What is it?" she started to ask, but without turning toward her, Grace hissed at her, hoarse with a fear so thick that Nola dropped down to the ground. She hardly breathed. Grace scanned the oaks and hilly land. "Don't move!" she told the girls. "Whatever you do, don't follow me."

The car went by and turned around another time, with the men still looking, and in a split second before it returned, Grace whispered dryly, "Stay down. Stay there." Then she dropped her sling on the ground and ran, crashing through the bushes, away from the pond, toward town.

The girls fought their impulse to run. Even their own breathing sounded dangerous to them.

Grace was an easy target, and she knew it, but she wanted to, had to, lure the car away from the girls. She hoped and prayed she could turn and cut through rocky land a car couldn't cover, but the Buick followed her down the road, and when she ran faster, the car speeded up. Then she saw the rocky land and with relief, she veered off and cut through a field, and even from where they hid, the girls could hear the car turn and follow, grinding across the summer grass. The driver struggled with the dark steering wheel over stones and clumps of earth. In spite of her fear, Nola rose up to look, stood just enough to see her mother kick the shoes off her feet and race into the forest. As Nola watched, Grace disappeared in the dark green shadows of leaves and branches.

Rena was crying. She pulled Nola close to earth, tugging at her skirt. "Stay down."

The car braked, and Nola peered over the brush to see a man jump out. The driver remained inside, though, and the motor idled. Then in day's full light, a gunshot broke through air. Like a stone cracking apart, something falling away from the world.

The girls lay flat in the shallow water, hidden in the silty pond between the reeds. Nola covered her eyes with one of her muddy hands, but it was too late, she had already seen her mother run barefoot across the field, followed by the black car, and in her mind's eye she saw her mother wounded.

The car doors slammed shut. The girls heard the car begin to grind and jam once more across the field. They pressed themselves deeper into the marshy pond, still and afraid. Only their heads were out of the muddy red water. They barely breathed. Nola dropped her knife and searched the silt frantically, with shaking fingers, until she found it and held it tight and ready in her fist. Then the wind began to blow, hot and restless, drowning out the sound of the car. The men had propped Grace's body between them as if she were just a girlfriend out for a Sunday drive. They drove up to the pond where water willows were quaking in the wind, and when they lifted the woman out of the car, both of her dark braids came loose and fell toward earth. The wind blew harder. The men placed Grace's body behind a clump of wind-whipped black bushes, then they straightened their backs, turned around, searched for Nola.

Nola could barely hear them speak over the sound of wind.

"I thought you said the girl was with her."

"She was."

Nola held her breath. She heard nothing else, for a sudden gust of wind whistled across the water and rattled the cattails. The girls were afraid to look. They heard the men search among the rushes, close to where they remained paralyzed with fright, but by then, the girls could not tell the difference between wind and the men's hands pilfering through the reeds.

The turn wind, a current from the south, blew grit up from the ground. The hillsides stirred with dust devils. Branches broke off the older trees.

As the hot wind quickened, tree branches began to creak. The storm drowned out the sound of the car and when the men drove away, the girls did not hear them. A mallard moved across the pond and took cover, hiding as the girls hid, in the blowing reeds.

A short while later, the car returned. Its motor sounded like the wind. The girls were sure the men were searching for children in Sunday dresses. One man got out and walked through the wind-swept grass toward Grace Blanket's body. From between the reeds, Nola could almost see his face. The wind blew his jacket open and away from his shirt. Behind him the trees bent. He placed a pistol in the dead woman's hand. Nola caught another glimpse of him. She couldn't tell who he was. She had never seen him before. He opened a bottle of whiskey and poured it on Grace Blanket's body, and the wind blew the smell of whiskey across the pond. The girls held their breaths while the man buttoned his dark jacket and laid down the empty bottle. He got back in the car and it rattled off toward town, erased by a storm cloud of dust.

The girls were drowning in the heat and wind of the storm. They didn't hear the sound of Michael Horse's gilt-colored car, nor did they hear Belle call out their names. They heard only the howling wind, and when it finally died down, they heard the horrible flies already at work on the body of Grace and then the afternoon sun turned red in the west sky, and then the long day was passing and the frogs began their night songs, and then it was night and the stars showed up on the surface of the dark pond. Nola crawled out of the water and up the bank of the pond on her elbows and knees. She half crawled toward her mother's body. Rena followed, shivering even in the heat. Her thin-skinned hands and feet were cracked open from the water. And in the midst of everything, the moon was shining on the water. Grace was surrounded by black leaves in the moonlight, and the whiskey smell was still thick and sickening. Grace was twisted and grotesque and her head turned to the side as if she'd said "No" to death. In her hand was the gun. The girl stood there for what seemed like a long time. She laid her head against her mother, crying, "Mama," and wept with her face buried in the whiskey-drenched clothing.

"Come on," Rena pulled Nola back into the world of the living.

Nola started to take the pistol. "Leave it," Rena told her, so Nola reached down and unclasped the strand of pearls from her mother's neck. With Rena's arm around her, she walked away, then looked back, hoping against all hope that her mother would move, that her voice would call out the way it had always done, "Come here, little one," but there were only the sounds of frogs and insects.

Rena took Nola's hand. They walked toward the Grayclouds' house, hiding themselves behind bushes or trees. The muddy weight of their dresses dragged heavily against their legs.

That night, the lights of fireflies and the songs of locusts were peaceful, as if nothing on earth had changed. How strange that life was as it had been on other summer nights, with a moon rising behind the crisscross lines of oil derricks and the white stars blinking in a clear black sky.

At the dark turnoff to the Grayclouds' house, sweet white flowers bloomed on the lilac bush. The mailbox, with its flag up, was half hidden by the leafy branches. The house, too, looked as it always did, with an uneven porch and square windows of light. The chickens had gone to roost for the night, and they were softly clucking, and out in the distance, the white-faced cattle were still grazing, looking disembodied.

When they passed through the gate and neared the front door, the girls saw something white at the azalea bush. They were startled. They stopped and stared, thinking at first it was a ghost. But then the ghost in its white apron stepped toward them and said, ''Where's your mother, child?'' and the ghost became solid and became Belle Graycloud. Between sobs that night, Rena tried to tell the story of what had happened, and before the loss of Grace turned to grief in the old woman, Belle raised her face to the starry sky and thanked the Great Something that the girls were alive.

Neither Belle nor Lettie Graycloud could sleep that night. They were still awake when Moses returned home from the livestock auction in Walnut Springs. He was wearing a new straw hat. Belle heard him whistling as he led a new palomino pony—they were the fashion that year—through the dark lot and into the barn.

She opened the door and called his name.

''I'm coming,'' he said from the darkness, then she saw him in the light from the house. He walked through the door and set his hat on the table. ''What is it?''

She told him about Grace.

Moses was stunned with the news. He sat down heavily in a chair, and slumped over the table. He covered his face with his hands and was silent a long while, then he asked, ''Did they see who did it?''

Belle shook her head. ''All they know is that they drove a car like ours.'' She sat beside him. Her eyes were swollen.

He said, ''Belle, I'm so sorry.'' He had doubted her. Then he said, ''Black Buicks are everywhere.'' He took a deep breath, stood up, and put the new hat on his head.

Belle was alarmed. ''What are you doing?''

He answered slowly. ''I'd better go talk to the sheriff.''

She put up her hand to stop him. ''I don't think you should.''

He was puzzled. ''Why not?''

She hesitated. She was weary and hoped she wasn't making a mistake. ''Because, Moses, the killers didn't see the girls. I'm afraid that if they knew there were witnesses, they might come looking for them.''

He turned it over in his mind, then took his hat off and, without an argument, he sat back down and rubbed the grit off his face.

Belle put her hand over his. She fingered one of the scars that crossed his knuckles. They sat that way, in silence for a while, Moses deep in thought, Belle too shaken to say more.

Then Moses pulled at one of his dark braids and said, ''It was probably a lover's fight.''

Belle studied his face. Moses was trying to push away his fear. It made her twice as cautious, as if to make up for him. ''And if it wasn't?'' she said, but before he could answer, she was on her feet. She took a pistol from a cabinet. It was a small handgun, one she used to frighten coyotes away from her nervous chickens. She loaded it. Moses said nothing.

Upstairs, the girls slept in Lettie's bed. It was hot. In the dim light of the lamp, they looked vulnerable in the large bed. Lettie watched over them. She also held a pistol. She straightened the sheet tenderly over them and smoothed the hair back from their damp faces. She wanted to hold them, to offer solace, but their breathing was deep and the waking world was dangerous, so she left them to the gift of sleep.

After a while, Belle relieved her of her watch, and the old woman set up her own silent vigil over the girls. But Lettie was overwhelmed with a feeling of loneliness, and around two in the morning, she returned to the bedside of the girls. She looked haggard. She wore a dark, worn robe. ''Go on now, Mama,'' she said. ''You need rest.''

But Belle made no attempt to leave the room. ''I can't sleep anyway,'' she said. Lettie was insistent, though, until Belle pulled herself up from the chair and went down the hall to her own room. She was restless, gripped in a hot fear, afraid for Rena and Nola.

She sat at the mirror. Out of habit, she brushed her long silver hair while she thought. In the dark, sparks flew and snapped through the air around her. She was sure something was afoot. She put the brush down.

Moses seemed to sleep. Through hell and high water, Belle thought, he always slept, and she was angry at him, but then she noticed that his breathing was uneven. He turned over.

Belle rocked herself in the rocker and gazed out the window. The floor creaked. She was watchful as she looked into the dark. She wanted to read the deep night and decipher the story of what had happened to Grace Blanket. She believed it was a plot since Grace's land was worth so much in oil. All along the smell of the blue-black oil that seeped out of the earth had smelled like death to her.

Belle climbed into bed beside Moses and tried to sleep. The old wood house settled and creaked. It was too hot. The sheets felt stiff against her skin. She climbed out of bed once more, and crept down the staircase. The furniture downstairs was dark and heavy, with ominous silence living in the shadows. Belle checked the latches on the doors.

Moses pulled on his pants and followed her downstairs. In the kitchen, he poured water into a glass and carried it over to Belle. "I'll stay up," he said. "You go rest."

She smiled at him. His wide chest looked soft beneath his undershirt. She laid her head against his chest briefly, long enough to hear his heart, and then she went back up the stairs.

Moses sat at the kitchen table in the darkness. He was waiting for his daughter, Louise, and her white husband, Floyd, to return home. By now, he thought, they were drunk and driving in from the city. The thought made him angry. He put his elbows on the oilcloth.

Once, before dawn, when the house made a noise, Belle climbed out of bed and in her big dressing gown, she looked out the window. In the gray light, she could have sworn a man was standing at the edge of the berry grove. "Moses!" she called down to him, but by the time Moses reached the window, the man was gone. She went down the stairs and peered out the window. He followed. She tried to convince him. "Someone was there. I saw him."

In the bedroom, Lettie Graycloud sat beside the sleeping girls. She held the pistol on her lap. She was uncomfortable with the weapon, but the murder, even if it had been a crime of passion like her father thought, had struck too close to home. A cool breeze from the window blew in across her face and hair.

In the first red light of morning, both girls breathed softly. Exhaustion had overcome even Nola's grief. But her face, almost overnight, had begun to look somehow hollow and older. Her skin was tight across her bones. Gazing at her, Lettie felt the first pain of her own loss, the first ache of missing her friend, Grace Blanket.

Lettie studied Nola's dark skin, the widow's peak, the distant quality that had once prompted Lettie to remark to Grace that if anyone's prayers were going to be heard in this life, she knew Grace's would.

Lettie's mind went back to the time when Grace had first traveled down from the bluffs above Watona and moved into the Graycloud house. Grace and Lettie became fast friends. They'd lived together in this same room, slept in this bed as their bones grew longer. They'd whispered together at night, and now here was this girl, the same bone, blood, and skin as Grace. Lettie felt overwhelmed with love for the girl, whose dark, slender hand hung peacefully over the side of the bed.

But then, as the room lightened more, what Lettie saw frightened her. At first, she thought Nola was awake and staring at her, like a person half-dead, gazing into her own watching eyes. But Nola's eyes stared through Lettie and beyond, looking through the ceiling and roof to some far distant point in the sky. While some part of her was awake, was looking perhaps at the other world, the one where her mother had gone, the rest of her slept. She breathed deeply and evenly, and she did not so much as blink her open eyes.

Lettie looked away. She felt clammy. She went to the window. Another day of heat was blowing in. Already the ground was dry, and dust filtered into the room. Lettie leaned over to feel the thin breeze of air. That was when she saw him. The man stood in front of the house. Without changing her position, Lettie raised the pistol to the window and aimed, but even as she did, she noticed that his legs looked rooted to earth, and he stood like one of the Hill Indians, as if he'd never lived among white people or their dry goods, or the cursed blessing of oil. His face was smooth and calm. Instantly, Lettie knew he was from the same band as Grace Blanket. She lowered the gun back down to her side and buried it in a fold of her robe as if she were afraid it would fire against her will. She knew, somehow, that he was there for Nola, to help her.

The man raised his eyes. Lettie wanted to step back, out of the light, but instead she remained in full view of the watcher, and for a brief moment their eyes met. He was one of the sacred runners from the hills. Lettie felt calm in his gaze, but as she looked out the window he seemed to vanish from her view.

Behind her, Rena began to stir. She opened her golden eyes and looked at her aunt's red and blue scarves that hung like flames on the wall above her. At first Rena thought they were burning, they were on fire, and she gasped awake, full of fear, and fought her way out of the tangle of hot sheets.

Outside, the rooster crowed and the little dog, Pippin, ran toward the road, barking at Louise and Floyd. The couple walked past the watcher without seeing him. Lettie heard their footsteps on the gravel, then the opening door and voices downstairs, and then the sound of high heels clapping up the stairs.

The door sprang open. Louise rushed into the bedroom. Rena smelled the whiskey on her mother's breath. She pulled away, remembering Grace's body and the odor of whiskey that had drifted across the pond, but Louise held tight to the girl, asking over and over, "What happened?" and saying "I can't believe it. I just can't believe it. My God." Her shrill voice woke Nola. The girl turned over in the bed, then sat up like a ghost. She was damp with the heat and with shock. Her eyes were black and haunted-looking, with dark circles beneath them. Looking at the ash-pale girl, Lettie felt a chill wash over her skin. Even Louise went silent. The air seemed to go out of the room.

After Louise took Rena back downstairs, Lettie could think of nothing to do, so she dressed Nola in one of her own dresses. "Raise your arms," she told her.

Nola did as she was told, and lifted both arms above her head. Lettie pulled the blue, too-large dress down over Nola's head. "Turn around now, honey," she said. Nola flatly obeyed. She stood vacantly as Lettie pinned the back of the dress to fit her limp and silent body.

Then, out of daily habit, while Nola stood in the poor-fitting woman's dress, Lettie took a dark blue hat off one of the hooks on the wall and settled it on top of her own thick black hair. She always wore a hat, it was her custom. She pushed the hat pin through her hair, and while she looked in the mirror she saw Nola's expression change. A look of surprise passed over Nola's face as she caught sight of the watcher outside. She ran over to the window and looked out, her face pitiful and broken. The watcher looked up. Lettie felt the whole room fill with sorrow, but she took the girl's cold hand and led her from the curtained square of light, and said to Nola, "Stay away from the windows. It's not safe." But something tugged at the girl and she pulled out from Lettie's grasp and went into the hall. Lettie followed behind her in through the door of Belle's room. Nola pulled aside the curtain and looked out. Down on the ground, near the berry grove, was another one of the watchers.

There were four altogether. They had come in the night.

Michael Horse was the last person in Indian Territory to live in a tepee. That morning he was sitting outside on a rock watching the fire. It was an important fire. It had descended from the coals of his ancestors. Their lives still burned in the eternal flames. When Horse wasn't there to look after the fire, someone else, usually a woman named Ona Neck, watched over it and made sure that the coals never burned out. The task of firekeeper had been handed down to Michael Horse through his mother even before the Osage Indians had bought land in Oklahoma and moved there from the Neosho River in Kansas. That was in 1861. It was the same year that, in another part of Oklahoma, Belle Graycloud had been born.

As soon as Michael Horse thought of Belle, he knew she was walking toward him. That was the way his gift worked.

And only a moment later, he heard her walking up the Crow Hill road toward his tepee. The fire smoked. He stirred it.

Belle sat down beside him and was quiet a moment. "Are you all right?" She studied his face.

"Why do you ask?" He stared into the fire.

"I wondered if you had any visions or nightmares the last few nights."

He made a little pile of the coals. "Should I have?"

Belle was quiet for a while, then she spoke softly. "Grace was killed yesterday." She let her words work on Horse. "The murderers put a pistol in her hand and poured whiskey on her to make it look like she'd gotten drunk and shot herself.''

He looked at her with dark, sad eyes. "How did you know this?"

"Nola saw them. Not enough to know who they were." She looked through the flames of the fire. "They drove a black Buick."

Horse stared off into the hot sky. Two crows called out to each other.

"It's bad," said the old woman, then she covered her mouth with her hand as if to keep herself from saying more.

Horse said nothing, and Belle took away her hand and went on, "It's so strange, you know. We act like it's any day, like our daily chores are planted in us with long roots, like a devil's claw in a field of wheat. You'd think time would stop when someone gets killed. But the house settled all night, and creaked, and this morning I set a platter of eggs on the table, Moses drank his tea, and Lettie came downstairs wearing one of her hats.''

Horse stirred the fire while he listened to Belle. He knew she was using words as a road out of pain and fear. When she was quiet, he stood up. "Wait here," he told her, and he walked up the road toward Ona Neck's place.

Belle watched him walk away. She saw his sharp shoulder blades through the thin and faded cotton shirt.

When he returned with Ona, the old Mrs. Neck looked fatigued. With ancient dry hands she pushed loose strands of hair up into her hairnet. "The fire again?"

He nodded.

"That's what I thought. What happened this time?"

"Grace Blanket's been killed," he told her.

"Everyone's always getting killed," Ona said. She nodded at Belle. Carefully, she sat down by the fire and took a long needle out of the bag she carried. Her hands were shaky.

Horse went through the open flap into his tepee and took his diaries out of a cedar box and put them in his car. He knew that Ona looked through his things when he was gone, and he was a private person.

At the Graycloud house, Louise and Floyd talked with Moses. Like Moses, Louise thought it was a lover's quarrel. She searched her mind, trying to remember the names of men Grace had been seeing. "It could have been anyone," she finally said, and that was true enough since Grace was beautiful. But even more than that, marriages with Indian women benefited white men financially. An Indian agent in Watona, Oklahoma, frequently received letters such as the one that Michael Horse kept in his diary in the cedar trunk:

Dear Sir:

I am a young man with good habits and none of the bad, with several thousand dollars, and want a good Indian girl for a wife. I am sober, honest industrious man and stand well in my community.

I want woman between the ages of 18 and 35 years of age, not a full blood, but prefer one as near white as possible.

I lived on a farm most of my life and know how to get results from a farm as well as a mercantile business. Having means it is natural I want some one my equal financially as well as socially. If you can place me in correspondence with a good woman and I succeed in marrying her for every Five Thousand Dollars she is worth I will give you Twenty-Five Dollars. If she is worth 25,000 you would get $125 if I got her. This is a plain business proposition and I trust you will consider it as such.

The women were business investments. Another white man, when asked what he did for a living, said by way of an answer that he'd married an Osage woman, and everyone who listened understood what that meant, that he didn't work; he lived off her money.

Louise paced restlessly. She looked at the Indian man standing outside the house. "Jesus. What's he doing here?" She stood back from the window, out of the watcher's view, while she peered at him.

Floyd, Louise's husband, was a tense but likable man from Joplin, Missouri, and he was in all ways the opposite of Louise. While Lou wanted to rely on what she called "White man's logic," Floyd imitated Indian ways. He had proudly taken the Graycloud name when he married Louise, and he wore his fine blond hair in a ponytail down his back. "He's here for Nola," Floyd said to his wife.

"For Nola? Why?" She was impatient with him.

"She needs protection now. With Grace gone, Nola is one of the richest, if not the richest, Indian in the territory."

Louise had not thought of this herself and she looked even more alarmed. "We've got to get her out of here."

The screen door slammed. Alone, Belle entered the kitchen. Horse had stopped a moment and exchanged a few words with the watchman who stood guard in front of the house. They knew each other. Horse had stayed in the hills as a younger man, and knew most of the families at the settlement.

"We're going to keep her here," Belle said, without giving Louise a chance to argue over the girl.

"But every fortune-seeker in the country will come around here wanting to rub elbows with a rich Indian girl," Louise said.

"It's settled, Lou. She's staying."

"She could live with Sara. Sara's her blood kin."

"That won't do. Sara just barely takes care of herself. And if it's some kind of scheme, Sara's not safe either."

"Scheme? What scheme?" Louise said, sounding more upset.

"Isn't that why you don't want her here?"

Without listening, Louise added, "Why can't Nola go away with those men." She pointed outside. "And live with the Hill Indians? One of them is probably her father, anyway."

"She can't, Louise." Belle was firm. "We can't let her go. There's a new law. All the Hill children under sixteen have to go to boarding school down in Custer, Oklahoma."

Louise still didn't understand, but Belle was tired of her daughter's arguments, and of how she rejected everything Indian, and as she herself had said, "I love everything European," but even so, she didn't trouble herself with the new laws and ordinances. She couldn't be bothered even when they affected her own children. But according to this recent law, if the families resisted, the children would be made wards of the state and removed permanently from their homes. In other tribes, Belle knew, the authorities had hunted down hidden children and taken them, lifted them up, screaming, from the ground, and carried them away from their families so that they would learn the cultured, civilized ways of the Americans. Belle gave her daughter the cold eye. "Even if Nola was just a bone in a pen of hungry dogs, I couldn't leave her there. Here, at least, we can watch over her."

Louise bit her tongue and remained silent, but she was going to take her children and move at the first chance.

Horse was still there that morning when a gray truck pulling a horse trailer bounced up the dirt road. It was driven by a young French-Indian who had only one name. Benoit. Benoit was a horse-breeder with green-gray eyes, light olive skin, and dark shining hair that he brushed straight back from his smooth forehead.

Benoit was Lettie's lover. He was also, through an arranged marriage, the legal husband, by white law, of Sara Blanket, Nola's aunt, but the entire Graycloud family forgot this discreet arrangement in the heat and tragedy that surrounded them. And Moses had forgotten about the red horse Benoit carried in the horse trailer, a stud that he had rented for his mares.

Benoit parked close to the barn and opened the door of the horse trailer. He caressed the horse's red, sweaty hip. The horse was a blood bay named Redshirt, an energetic stallion, seventeen hands in height, and lean-muscled. It spoke to Benoit as he opened the back of the trailer.

Horse stood at the window and watched Benoit unload the horse. From the moment Benoit led Redshirt down the ramp and tied him to a fencepost, the dark red horse burned like a fire in the sun. Benoit put a clean white cloth over Redshirt's back, went back to the truck's cab, drove closer to the house, and walked in carrying a gray hatbox. It was a gift for Lettie, and it was tied with silver ribbon. Like Louise, Benoit did not see the watcher even though he passed beside him.

He knocked on the door. Redshirt whinnied from the fencepost. He was a jealous and demanding horse.

Moses had forgotten all about Redshirt even before the tragedy of Grace's death. Just a day earlier, he'd taken his last brood mare out to join the others that were pasturing in the far range. All he had left in the barnyard were two work-horses and the new palomino from Walnut Springs.

Benoit was a frequent visitor. He did not need an invitation. He entered the kitchen, looked around, and the smile vanished from his lips. The misery was thick enough to cut with a knife. He looked from face to silent face, then he asked, "What's wrong?"

"Benoit," Belle said, "Benoit, it's Grace. She was killed yesterday."

He stared at her in disbelief.

Belle wanted to say more, but she said only, "Nola's safe, but she's in shock." Belle poured Benoit a cup of coffee in silence. "We're going to keep her here." He sat down but didn't touch the coffee. He was still taking in the weight of the facts.

He went so pale that Belle thought he would faint. She put some rum in his coffee.

"Where is she?" Benoit asked.

"Nola? Follow me. She's in Lettie's room."

The young man followed her up the stairs to the second floor. Young Ben Graycloud went up behind them. When they entered the room, Lettie stood up. She was tired. She gave Benoit only a glance. She brushed down her skirt and glanced helplessly toward Nola. The girl looked baleful and gray. Except for her hairline, she barely resembled the girl she'd been just the day before. Even her face had changed shape, it seemed to them. Benoit stared at her. And Ben Graycloud, who'd loved Nola for ten of his fifteen years, didn't say a word, but he felt his heart swell in fear when he saw the far-off look in Nola's eyes.

"It's shock," Belle said. "She doesn't even know we are here." As they went back down the stairs, Belle related parts of the story that she had gleaned from the girls the night before, about how two men in a black Buick had chased Grace into the forest, killed her, then left her body behind a leafy bush, drenched with whiskey.

Down in the kitchen, Benoit's jaw tightened while he listened. He was a man with a short fuse and his shock was giving way to anger. He began to pace back and forth across the floor. He stood up and started for the door. "I'm going to get the sheriff," he said.

Belle grabbed his arm. "You can't do that. As far as they know, there aren't any witnesses." She spoke more softly, "Besides, Benoit, you are too angry. We can't let you stir things up."

As soon as she said it, Benoit's eyes grew soft, but he was still agitated. "How are you going to find the killers if witnesses don't talk?" But he calmed down and promised Belle that he wouldn't talk to the sheriff or anyone else until after Grace's body was found, but his face had a pinched look, and he unbuttoned the top button of his shirt as if it had grown too tight. "Okay," he said after a moment. "Okay. But sooner or later, I'm going to get to the bottom of all this."

When Benoit settled down, Moses went outside to speak with the watcher. He spoke Creek to the man; it was a language they knew and used with traders. He asked the man how they had known Nola Blanket was there.

"The screech owls told us," the man answered.

"I believe them," Belle said, and her gray eyes grew even more suspicious that something dangerous was unfolding, something the ragged gray owls already knew.

"That's a lie," Louise said. "You old people are superstitious. How do you know that man out there isn't the killer?"

Floyd believed the runner, but he didn't want trouble with Louise, so he went out the door, saying it was his day to work the Blue Store, where he was a clerk when he wasn't helping Moses with the cattle and horses.

Louise started to turn her anger on Floyd, but instead she said calmly, pleadingly, "Don't go, Floyd. Rena's just seen a murder."

Floyd looked apologetic, but he went out the door, started up the car, and headed for town.

Louise watched him drive away. Her face sagged. "He always leaves when I need him."

For the first time since he'd been there, Horse spoke. "I heard those owls myself. I was sure something had happened." Horse didn't know the language of the owls, but it didn't surprise him that the watchers understood it. They still remembered the older ways of animals.

When Horse returned to his camp later that day, he drove

Ona Neck the short distance home. When he returned, he poked at the hot coals and gazed at the flame. It was nearly invisible in the hot, sunlit air and the waves of heat reddened his skin.

He tried to think. He wanted to put together the broken edges of things. A few of the Indians were beginning to awaken with dreams of danger. That was why Belle Gray-cloud thought something large was transpiring around them. Velma Billy had dreamed a freezing white snow covered her body and had gone to Michael Horse to ask him the meaning of such a dream. Ruth Tate, the strong and beautiful twin sister of Moses Graycloud, had also visited Horse and said she remembered a dream of fiery stars that fell to earth and when they landed, everything burned.

Bad dreams were as common as gas fires at the drill sites, as ordinary as black Buicks. Many people had brought their dreams to Horse, and he reminded them all that earth was being drilled and dynamited open. Disturbances of earth, he told them, made for disturbances of life and sleep, but he wondered if he might be wrong. He'd made a mistake on the dry spell, after all, but the truth was that in half a year there had been seventeen murders in just their small booming cor-ner of Oklahoma. A month before Grace's death, an Indian man was shot by his wife. She didn't go to jail for the crime because it was common knowledge that he was a drunk, a wife-hitter, and a molester of girls. Then, another man, an Indian railroad worker, was found beaten to death near the oil workers' makeshift housing settlement right after oil had been found on his land. There were no suspects. Not long after that, a white rancher said he found an old Indian man butchering his black cow and he forced the man to drink lye. Then there was the tragic case of three children who disap-peared from family picnics. Their bones had been found several weeks later in Sorrow Cave up in the bluffs. Seth Eye, an oil worker who went crazy after drinking canned heat, was said to have kidnapped and eaten the children. He was found in Sorrow Cave, surrounded by the children's shoes. A gold locket that belonged to one of the girls hung over a rock. Every day there were new violent acts reported in the newspapers. The day before a man was shot for tying his horse near cars. The world had gone crazy.

Insanity was no stranger to boom towns, and that's what went through the minds of Watona people when they heard that Grace Blanket had been killed, or had killed herself, and why her death didn't strike a new chord of fear with most of the citizens. They'd witnessed those recent years of violence, when roughnecks and swindlers had arrived to seek their fortunes in Watona. There were newer kinds of thieves than had been visible before, and these thieves wore fine suits, diamond stickpins, and buffed their fingernails.

Belle was one of the danger dreamers, but like everyone, she reminded herself that the new, greedy people were crazy in the face of money, and even though she had looked for a pattern to the earlier deaths, she'd finally been convinced that they were random murders, part of the madness cropping up like Johnson grass in dry, barren towns that grew rich overnight, part of what happened in poor old places where some gambler struck paydirt. In these places, everyone knew, the worst citizens of the underworld rose up to stake claims.

Horse himself hardly dreamed at all those days. The dynamite blasts at the drill sites had made him restless and weary. Second sight, it was a known fact, was easy to lose when new shiny cars honked on the dirt roads, and fine china plates were being thrown up in the air and shot down like clay pigeons. He was coming unstrung, losing both his vision and his feelings, and because of this he agreed with Moses that Grace Blanket was a woman who catted around. That was the only plot that existed, he told himself.

The Indian people wanted, with all their hearts, nothing more than to be left alone and in peace. They wanted it so much that they turned their minds away from the truth and looked in the other direction, and even Horse, who was known for his divinations, saw it coming only a little at a time.

Later that same Monday, a dove hunter happened across the body of Grace Blanket, went to town, and reported to the sheriff that a drunk Indian woman had killed herself out at Woody Pond. The sheriff, a man named Jess Gold, and the undertaker drove out in a hearse to pick up the woman's body. The undertaker said, "Isn't it a pity that a pretty girl would shoot herself? And in the heart to boot?"

The deputy wrapped the gun carefully in cloth. If foul play was called into question at a later time, the evidence would be there.

As it turned out, the mortician couldn't tell one Indian woman from another, so Benoit was called in anyway, to identify the body of his sister-in-law. Since Benoit was part French and lighter-skinned, the Americans usually thought he was more like them than were the other, darker Indian people, so occasionally he was called on to help with contracts, negotiations, or for purposes of identification. The undertaker didn't know Grace Blanket was related in any way to Benoit, and when he said again, to Benoit, that it was a pity the woman shot herself, Benoit stalked out of the funeral home and went straight to the sheriff's office.

The office was housed in the red stone jailhouse.

Benoit stood in front of Jess Gold's desk. "Look, I've just seen her. I know she wasn't drunk. Someone drenched her with whiskey."

"What's the point, Benoit?"

"I think we should have an investigation."

"Benoit," Sheriff Gold said. "She had a fight just Saturday night. I saw it with my own eyes. We cited her for disturbing the peace." He ruffled through his papers and pulled out the report. "Don't go getting on a high horse about this, Benoit. I know she's your wife's sister, but she was real worked up. I'm surprised she didn't take a few men to the graveyard along with her."

"What about witnesses?" Benoit said, trying to remain calm. "Did you wonder about that?"

"No one's come forward. If there were witnesses, they haven't talked as of yet."

Benoit eyed him suspiciously. He sensed that if he breathed a word about the black Buick, he'd be in over his own head, so he turned, still red-faced, and walked away from the jail in frustration. Whoever shot Grace in the heart wanted it to look like suicide, even though suicide had never been a way out of life for Watona's Indian people.

Despite Michael Horse's prediction of dry weather, it rained again on the day Grace Blanket was buried. Since Horse was usually known to be right, the funeralgoers had not prepared for the torrents of rain water that rushed to earth. Some of them, even in their sorrow, couldn't help pointing out to Horse that it was raining, as if to remind him of his error. "I know," he said more than once to the mourners as they stood together beneath a crowded canvas lean-to.

The pounding rain fell in heavy sheets to the earth for several hours, splashing mud on pant legs and skirts before it finally stopped and the grievers placed gold rings and beads in Grace Blanket's coffin before it was lowered into the muddy ground. Wet clods of earth, mixed with corn kernels according to custom, were shoveled on top of the casket, and the wet clay was tamped firmly down on top of it. A heavy marble tombstone, a winged angel, was set in place above Grace's body. The angel's left arm was raised and her finger pointed west.

When the people arrived home and found their outdoor beds once again soaked through with rain, they complained about Horse's predictions. "He's getting forgetful," they said. "Or maybe he's getting too old."

Then they returned to their grief and kept their houses dark.

Several days later, from her house, Ona Neck heard the loud cawing of crows and went to the door to see what was wrong. The black, oversized birds were circling the graveyard. Ona mumbled to herself, took out her walking stick and made her way along the rolling Blackjack hills toward the cemetery.

As she reached the graveyard, Ona saw that the fine marble angel that marked Grace's resting place had been overturned. Its west-pointing arm was pointing straight up to the sky at the crows who dived after the corn that had been worked into the soil. Ona felt faint, it was a hideous sight, but she walked the rest of the way to the gravesite. From the distance, she thought the wet ground had settled, but when she reached the site, the casket was upended on the ground where it had been opened and left vacant. She frightened the crows away. Nothing remained, not the body of Grace, not the beads, gold, not even the medicines that had been buried inside the coffin for the woman's journey to the other world.

Mrs. Neck sat down on the damp earth and tried to catch her breath, and before she even knew it, she was weeping.

Her scrawny knees drawn up, she bent over and cried into her skirt, then wiped her eyes on her hem and thought about what should be done. If she reported the theft, it would mean that the sheriff, deputies, and all the others would learn that Indian people buried valuables with their dead. In no time at all, the entire cemetery and old burial grounds up on the hill would be looted, and the Indian people, who respected the sanctity of death, would be up in arms, so Ona decided to keep it a secret, and to put the coffin back in the ground herself, somehow, and cover it up. With her bony hands, she pushed at the coffin to see if it would fall back into the hole. The ground was still muddy so the box began to slide, and so did Ona, but she managed to stop herself, whereas the coffin crashed the rest of the way down into the hole in the earth.

Ona, muddied, went home to get her shovel and a rope. Her hands were shaking, but amazingly, when she returned, she summoned up enough strength to shovel a few feet of soil into the hole before one of the Billy boys came by. He was out shooting birds with a slingshot. "Come and help me," Ona ordered the obedient boy, and he nodded a yes at her. "The ground must've settled," she told him.

"No," he said, biting his lip and shaking his head. "There's been looters out here again."

"Oh?" was all Ona said, and together they looped the rope around the angel and pulled it almost upright. Ona was huffing and Jack Billy's face was red, but he was a strong, muscular boy and the angel was somehow replaced, though its accusing finger pointed south, not west. "Now promise me you won't tell a soul that the ground had settled there," Ona commanded.

"Why's that?" he wanted to know.

"You know how superstitious the other Indians get. They say if the ground settles over a body, the land will be haunted, you know." She peered at him.

"I never heard that."

"You're Sam Billy's son. No one wants to scare you."

But he insisted. "It was looters, I swear. I've seen it before."

That summer, with the record high temperatures, heat waves rose up visibly from the hills. Along the roads, a number of trees lost their green summer leaves a little at a time, and they were filled with the exposed white cocoons of ravenous bagworms.

In some ways, as autumn grew near, life continued on as before, except that the girls slept in Lettie's brass bed surrounded by her peacock-colored hats and scarves and everyone was afraid and watchful. Nola was slow to recover from her mother's death. Her face reflected her tragic and violent loss. She still slept with her eyes wide open, not letting her guard down even in the darkness of night with the watchers posted outside and the Graycloud women taking turns beside her silent bed like armed sentries.

Lettie set up a cot in a little, almost private, cove in the hallway. She slept there on the nights when Belle or Louise took their turns at staying with the sleeping girls, and often, at dawn, when the hall shadows doubled, Lettie would wake in states of panic and fear.

No one felt safe, but there was nothing they could put a finger on, and that state of being in the dark made the situation even worse. The family grew suspicious of everyone. Even at home, there were new silences in the house. Floyd wired outdoor lights at both the front and back doors, and when he sold his mason jars full of Tulsa liquor, he paid keen attention to the careless words of drunks, to see if any of them might let something slip about the murder.

Moses complained about all this "fear business," but he went to town more often than he had before Grace's death, pretending he needed supplies. At the Blue Store, he'd pore through bins of nails and listen to men discuss how Grace Blanket's body had been found. According to one, she was covered with a striped horse blanket. Another said she was stark naked when she shot herself in the heart, having gone insane with unrequited love. After Moses heard the men's stories, he'd go to the Red Store, buy an umbrella or a sack of dried beans, and listen to the women say wasn't it a shame that Grace Blanket brought this on herself by gadding about with men every Saturday night and hadn't they all known she would come to a bad end?

And there were the watchers for the Grayclouds to contend with. One stood near the sunny berry grove where Belle kept her beehives, one at the edge of the barn fence, one on the

west side of the house, and the one in front who, in the
sweet perfume of honeysuckle, sometimes closed his eyes
and listened to the hum of bees and the scurry of mice
moving to and from the barn. They were an ethereal four-
some. Each time the tenants of the Graycloud house peered
out at them, the watchers looked darker in the tenacious
heat and light of the summer sun. Still, at other times they
could have been nothing more than a trick of the eye. And
they never spoke, even to one another.

Belle fed the four watchers, but she never saw them eat.
All Belle knew was the food disappeared off the blue plates
she left outside on the dry grasses.

One day, in that late and still-hot summer, Belle noticed
a number of dead bees on the ground near her hives. It was
the productive season for her bees, the time when they
brought in wildflower pollen, so Belle was concerned about
the loss of these drones. A disease called Foul Brood was
going around. That afternoon, Belle had put on her boots, a
canvas coat, and a hard-brimmed, veiled hat. It was white,
like the coat. She pulled on her leather work gloves as she
walked outside to change the racks of honey in her beehives
and to check for signs of the disease. But between the intense
heat of the weather and her heavy bee clothing, Belle had
pulled only one rack out of the hive when the world spun
around her and went black, and the gray-haired woman collapsed on the ground with a swarm of bees covering the chest
of her coat, moving, swarming together like they were all
one life and all of one mind.

She was fortunate that the watcher was there. He rushed
to her side, and before he removed her hat, he replaced the
queen bee in the hive so that the others would follow. Then,
when they had swarmed away and settled back down to their
sweetness, he unbuttoned her hot coat and lifted up the white
veil that swept across her wide, dark face. Belle came around
enough that she walked into the house, held up by the man.
His touch was soft. She looked toward him and smiled
weakly.

Inside, Lettie and Louise fretted over their mother.

Ruth Graycloud Tate came by several times to check on
Belle. She brought food. She was calm and beautiful, often
just smiling a bit rather than talking. Belle loved this twin of

Moses. She was happy to have her there. Her presence was strong and peaceful. They packed ice around her and washed her face off with cool water. They wrung out the washcloth and wiped her forehead. Finally Belle's color returned, but this bout of heatstroke accounted for a new family rule. Because the weather was "hot as an oven" out there, and because of her own collapse, Belle insisted that every member of the household nap in the middle of each hot summer day.

"They do it in Mexico," she said, so even Floyd, who worked in town, put a siesta sign in the window of the Blue Store at lunchtime, drove home, and lay down on the bed wearing nothing but his wide-legged shorts over his pale skin.

One hot day Benoit arrived to drive Lettie to Grace Blanket's abandoned house. Lettie had asked him to help her collect Nola's clothing and board up the windows. It was around four o'clock and the hot sun had slipped down the sky. Lettie had put a sheet and pillow on the slat wood floor of the hallway, where it was cool, and she'd fallen soundly asleep until Benoit's loud knock on the door woke her.

"I'll be right there," she called out to him. The nap had left her exhausted. She rinsed her face with cold water and dashed cologne on her wrists and neck, but she was still in a lazy fog when she went downstairs.

Benoit waited in the shade of a tree until Lettie came out, then he opened the truck cab door for her, leaned over and kissed her flushed cheek. She smiled at him, still arranging the light blue hat on her head. Her face was slightly swollen from sleep. "Lord, isn't it hot?" She rolled a paper and fanned herself. She asked, "How's Sara?" and pulled a strand of hair off her neck and pinned it.

"She sends her love," Benoit said. He smiled, his head cocked to the side a little. Then he backed the truck all the way out into the main road. "You smell good."

"It's gardenia."

Benoit took Lettie's hand in his own while he drove toward town. Lettie glanced at him, at his profile. His rich-colored skin was sweaty enough to shine. She wanted to taste his salt.

"How can you look so good in this heat?" she asked him.

"We've been cheating the weather." He adjusted the rearview mirror. "We're using electric fans."

Lettie leaned her head against the back of the seat. Her friend Sara was more modern than any of the Grayclouds, except Louise. "I'm trying to talk Mama into buying one," she said.

Sara liked all the conveniences of the present day. That was what Lettie most envied, not that Sara was legally married to Benoit, but that they had a radio and electric fans. Besides, the term "legal" only meant it was a marriage recognized in the name of white law and not necessarily recognized by Indians. The Indian people knew that it had been financially necessary for Sara and Benoit to marry since Benoit's mother was French, and that meant he would have been outside the tribe without an Osage Indian wife. And for Sara, Benoit was company, a friend, a strong man who could help her both with lifting her in and out of her chair and with the house.

In reality, however, Benoit and Sara were like brother and sister. And, as Benoit put it, he had enough love to go around for both women. And then some. Sara was in agreement with this. He gave her all the friendship and care she needed. It was love, they both said, but not romance. With Lettie, it was different. Benoit could barely refrain from touching her, and even driving to town that afternoon, he wanted to hold her close to him. He ran a fingertip across her cheek. She touched it with her lips and moved closer toward him.

Lettie and Sara were friends, doubly bound together by their mutual love for Benoit. It was an uncomplicated arrangement, but in those times it was an affair that would have been misunderstood by the townfolks who didn't know a thing about love without possession. And though the white people never bothered themselves about the private lives of Indians, some of the mixed-bloods were staunch and upright citizens, and they had assumed that Sara, the more cultured of the two women, stayed at home, miserable in her cane-seated wheelchair, waiting for Benoit to grow tired of Leticia Graycloud's plumed hats and satin blouses. But he never did, and eventually the gossip had worn thin.

Lettie fanned herself with the folded newspaper, and she fanned some of the air at Benoit as he drove through the stifling heat. They went to the Red Store, bought cold sodas, and visited with Mr. Palmer for a while beneath the silver painted ceiling fan.

"You sure are putting on the dog these days," Palmer said as he eyed Benoit's white embossed shirt. He gave Lettie a piece of the licorice he remembered was her favorite. "And you're still keeping the milliners in business, I see."

Lettie laughed good-naturedly. "I sure am."

When they reached Grace Blanket's house, it was overgrown with weeds. Lettie went slowly up the porch stairs. Her footsteps sounded hollow. She unlocked the door, pushed it open, and stopped cold, staring at the cool, shimmering opulence of Grace Blanket's home. It was an icy palace of crystal, and European to the ceiling, even though Grace herself had never cut her long black braids, and had preferred moccasins to the spool-heeled shoes she wore that last Sunday on her way to church. Grace, with her placid dark face, had lived surrounded by rooms of cut glass, and despite the lightness of that glass, the entire house felt heavy and ghostly to Lettie, and despite the outside heat, the house was cold as a cave, and silent.

Lettie felt jumpy. There was an uncanny presence of Grace sitting in the rose-flowered rocking chair, she thought, and just then, the chair began to rock, just a trifle, from the warm air blowing in through the open door.

Lettie hurried up the staircase to Nola's pink bedroom. The chilly vacated house made her tense. She looked back over her shoulder at the rocker as she ran up the stairs and gathered the first armload of Nola's clothing and anything else she could find, a pearl-edged mirror, a doll with yellow hair whose eyelids opened and closed.

Downstairs, Benoit began to shut down the house, began to nail boards across the windows.

Lettie shut the bedroom window, and before she pulled the curtain closed, she saw the empty bed sitting in what had been the rose garden. The sheets had blown off it and were rumpled and dirty on the ground where they'd been caught in thorns from the rosebushes. The mattresses were dusty. Even at a distance, Lettie could see that the bed joints were beginning to rust. The wild irises Grace kept weeded from her garden had persistently begun to overtake the domestic roses. The piano was there too, farther out, by the old chicken coop. The varnish was blistered and peeling off the wood. Lettie heard Benoit's hammering knocking on the hot day.

Lettie made several trips down to the car, still keeping an eye on the rocking chair. She emptied Nola's drawers and closet. The hammering rattled chandeliers and they tinkled and swung back and forth above Lettie's head, and threw little rainbows of colored light on the walls. And then those western windows and their afternoon sun were covered with wood, closed in with nails.

The last thing Lettie took from the house was Grace's typewriter. Horse would like it, Lettie knew. He'd put it to good use. She set it down on the porch, then she went to the garden and picked the four remaining tomatoes off the vining plants.

The boards Benoit nailed up would never keep determined looters at bay, he knew, but it would slow them down.

Benoit took off his shirt and hung it from the front door-knob. Suddenly, he was overcome with the sorrow of his task. It seemed to him that putting boards over the windows was like closing the eyelids of the dead. He sat down on the stoop and looked out over the land, at the green post oaks and the thorny bushes along the road. He thought he saw a woman, Grace, walking slowly, as was her way, along the red road that disappeared into the hills, but the rising heat shimmered up from the ground and the mirage vanished.

Benoit began to suffocate in the thick air. His face was wet. He couldn't tell if he was crying or if the salt he tasted was sweat. He reached over and grabbed a sleeve of his shirt and wiped his face with it while Lettie carried the last bundle of Nola's things from the breakable house and placed them in the back of Benoit's gray truck.

At the truck, Lettie wiped her own forehead with her arm and placed a mother-of-pearl music box that contained a little diamond ring on the car seat. She put a heavy cloth bag on the floor. It held a pair of beaded moccasins and leggings. The typewriter she placed on top of that stack. She was over-heated, but she went back to help Benoit. She held a piece of wood up to the window. Benoit hammered a nail into it and she felt the pounding in her hands and bones, and then Benoit lowered the hammer and looked at Lettie. He wanted to tell her how sad he was, but she looked inside his gray-green eyes, said, "I know," and touched his hand before he had a chance to speak. She stood quietly beside him.

Benoit moved stiffly, took his shirt off the doorknob, shut the door, removed the brass knocker, and nailed the final piece of wood across the doorway. Inside the house, something crashed to the floor and shattered.

WASHINGTON, D.C.

It was early morning. Already hot and humid. Stacey Red Hawk, a Lakota Sioux, turned over in his bed. For a minute he thought he was home, at his mother's house. He could hear the chickens out back pecking in the dust, and he smelled the snap of bacon from the kitchen. His little sisters were sitting on chairs looking at the sleeping Stace, and he could feel their presence, their black manes of hair and loose-fitting cotton dresses. He opened one eye, beginning to smile at the girls before he realized he was in Washington, D.C., at the Boston Apartments and Rooming House for Men where a sign in the window said, "No Women," in large letters.

He got dressed and went down the long, dark hallway of the rooming house. The boarding house smelled stale, but outside, the sun was just coming up. The trees were filled with green leaves and nesting birds, and last night's moon was still in the sky.

He stepped out on the small balcony at the end of the hall and he offered tobacco to the four quarters of the earth. He'd been instructed by the elders to always remember the earth and the spirit people, especially now, when he was so far away from home. At a distance, it was easy to fall away from the old ways. They hardly seemed real in the midst of noise and hurry.

Stace was a keeper, a keeper of tradition, and a carrier of the sacred pipe of his people, but he seemed so far away from all that now, so far from Eagle Butte, South Dakota, that his earlier life felt like little more than a dream, a half-hidden memory.

He missed South Dakota, but he believed he could do more for his people in Washington than he could do at home where so many of the young Indian men had been broken that a cop's sole job was to keep them from killing each other as they relived the heritage of violence that had been committed against them.

It had been two years since he'd stepped off the bus and walked the two miles out to the Old Post Road where his mother had stood by the turnoff, waiting for him.

"How did you know I was coming?" he'd asked her.

She was a big woman, and warm. She held him close and kissed his face, then smiled into his eyes and said only, "The bus was a little late today."

He'd laughed.

"I should have never let you work for the police," she said later as she watched him eat toast with her berry preserves. "You want more eggs?"

"No. I'm fine."

"I never should have let you." She shook her head.

As he washed his face at the Boston Apartments, Stace was caught up in memories of home. He dressed. He put on a black jacket. He wore it buttoned, even on warm days. It was his habit. He came from the cold north. Beneath it he wore a white shirt with wide sleeves, and he wore a hat with his long hair tucked up inside it. He carried a briefcase.

He was thinking about home as he walked to work. He was thinking about how he should fill up his hard suitcase with shirts for the men at Eagle Butte and Manderson, pack up his own few things, and go to where the dry golden heat was just settling on the rolling Dakota hills.

He walked up the steps to his office and placed his hat on the coatrack. His braids fell out down his back. He took off his jacket, then straightened his hair.

A voice interrupted his thoughts. "I said, Stace are you in there?" It was Levee. His partner. Dr. Levee. An investigator who'd abandoned a slow, new medical practice to work for the U.S. Bureau of Investigation. He had been good at forensics and had a soft voice that encouraged his patients to tell him about their private lives.

Stace looked up.

"You're in there, then? I thought for a minute you'd abandoned your body."

"I was just a few miles away." Stace smoothed down his shirt and sat down at his desk.

"Home again?" Levee leaned energetically over the desk and looked Stace Red Hawk square in the eye. "Try this one on," he said. "Indian Territory." He sat down.

"Oklahoma?"

"Right."

"I'm hard at work on the Wyoming case."

"I think you might want to know what's going on down there."

"No. I've got no desire to know." Stace added, "Anything."

Levee leaned back and waited as Stace looked through a stack of papers.

"Okay. What is it?" Stace was suspicious. He'd heard about what Indians still called Indian Territory. It was where every outlaw and crook used to hole up and be safe from the law. Now there were new thieves, those who bought and stole Indian lands.

"Well, let's see. It's not solid yet. There's murder. What looks like insurance fraud. That's where I come in. Life insurance. We have a letter from a medical doctor there. It says he's done a few physicals for life insurance. The insured died under suspicious circumstances. A dozen or so. Maybe connected. Maybe not. There's oil, lots of it, and all belonging to Indians. Land theft. The usual." He paused before he added, "Most of the victims are Indians." Levee knew this last bit of information would interest Red Hawk, who always wanted to rescue his dark brothers and sisters who were constantly under siege by the Americans.

"How come you never tell me when Chinese are involved? What am I, the resident Indian?"

"Don't complain." Levee looked out the window, put a hand in his pocket and jingled his change. "Besides, I'm the resident doctor."

"But that's a profession."

"Anyway, look at this picture." He placed a photo in front of Stace. "That's Grace Blanket. Suicide they say. But I doubt it. She was killed, or I think that anyway. This one over here is her daughter." He put another picture in front of him.

"She's a very beautiful girl."

"Yeah, and she's probably in trouble, too." He looked at

Stace. "Oil money, you know. Grace Blanket was the richest woman in the Territory."

"So, are we being sent in?" Stace raised a questioning eyebrow.

"No."

"Why not?"

"It's not our jurisdiction."

"Maybe we should check on it anyway."

Levee smiled as he went out the door.

In Watona that autumn the temperature dropped by only a few degrees. The leaves that had not been eaten away by hungry bagworms turned red. There was a hint of fall in the air, a slight odor of decay, but the hot weather had not broken.

It was payment day. Indian people, even from other, smaller towns, were heading for Watona, which in English meant "The Gathering Place." They drove in from the hills and plains to sign for their royalty payments and lease checks. The dust rose like smoke above the busy maze of roads as cars traveled over them, then settled back down on trees and on the polished furniture inside farmhouses. It was a busy day, one when money would change many hands.

Those people who drove past Grace Blanket's boarded-up house grew silent on her stretch of road. The house was stark. The boards nailed across the door looked as if part of the world had closed down forever. The bed outside was naked and rusting apart in what appeared to be a bramble field. Knotted weeds climbed up the bed legs and springs.

In spite of the shuttered house, the drivers half expected to see Grace sitting on the steps, squinting toward the sun, waving the way she did, a smile on her lips, her hand shielding her eyes from the light, or to see her bent over the flowers she had coaxed into bloom.

Up the road from Grace's sunburned roses, was an enormous crater a gas well blowout had made in the earth. It was fifty feet deep and five hundred feet across. This gouge in the earth, just a year earlier, had swallowed five workmen and ten mules. The water was gone from that land forever, the trees dead, and the grass, once long and rich, was burned black. The cars passed by this ugly sight, and not far from there, they passed another oil field where pumps, fueled by diesel, worked day and night. These bruised fields were noisy and dark. The earth had turned oily black. Blue flames rose up and roared like torches of burning gas. The earth bled oil.

The workers moved rapidly across the dry land, like swarming bees. In the office, John Hale, the tall and lean oilman, tallied up the books. Every quarter, when Indians were paid their oil royalties, most found themselves still in debt, owing the stores, the court-assigned legal guardians, and some of them obligated to bookies and bootleggers. That meant they'd sell off a few more acres of land and Hale was always ready with a quick offer and fast cash. A geologist had mapped out the underground for Hale and a few other men. The maps pictured the locations of oil pools. If he could just keep going a little while longer, Hale was certain he could make his fortune in oil.

Hale's girlfriend, a young woman named China, looked out the window at the cars and dust, then settled back down in a chair and twirled a strand of her platinum hair while she read the newspaper.

In his narrow boots, Hale walked away from the file cabinet. He had lived among Indians since he was a boy, and they knew and trusted him. He'd been called, jokingly, the "King of the Indians," both because of his service to the tribes, and because he'd reigned over the cattle grazing land he'd leased from Indian landholders. He was one of the first men to bring cattle to the Indian Territory. They were a good investment. Hale had hired Indian men to help him cut, burn, and clear their own land. He introduced new grasses, and they swept over the earth, the bluegrass, which fattened cattle quickly, and the Johnson grass, that had roots so strong they spirited away the minerals and water from other trees and plants, leaving tracts of land barren-looking. Moses Graycloud called it "Hale Grass." The Indians were happy to learn business ways, but before long they had no choice themselves but to become meat-eaters with sharp teeth, devouring their own land and themselves in the process. Some of them renamed the grass "Hell Grass."

"I don't believe for a minute that Indian woman killed herself for love," China said. She didn't look up from the paper.

Hale glared at her. He asked, "Why not?"

"Shooting herself. Women don't shoot themselves. You ever hear of that?" She had an Arkansas accent. "They drink poison, maybe, or drown themselves, but they don't use guns." She looked up from the paper, and watched him pace across the floor. "Did you ever know of a woman to shoot herself?"

He watched the workers out in the field. His jaw tightened. "You wouldn't use a gun. But she was an Indian." He lit a cigarette and glanced over her shoulder at the paper. "How old is that paper?"

"It's this week's."

"Wasn't that suicide a while back?"

"But they're not so sure it was suicide. It says it might be murder. It says here they're going to dig her up and examine her body."

Hale returned to the window, watching the cars go by. He saw the black Buick of Moses Graycloud pass by.

That payment day Michael Horse drove his newly painted silver car. He kept some distance behind Moses. He wanted to avoid the gravel flying up from the tires.

Horse wasn't a man for the fast life of town, but Ona Neck had told him that her son would be there that day with herbs and bear grease he'd brought back from a medicine man in Arizona, so Michael Horse, who really preferred a life apart from others, at least that's what he said, drove past Grace Blanket's house, past the crater in the earth, and past the town limit sign. The sign, he noted with pleasure, had once again been vandalized. Talbert, Oklahoma, was covered with red paint, and WATONA was written over it in large black letters. For the Indians it was still the gathering ground, and not some banker's hilly red stone town.

Horse planned to get some cash at the council house for Ona's boy and he wanted to chew the fat with men who were in town that day collecting their oil lease payments.

On his way up the steps to the council house, he heard the children up at the encampment. The boys teased the girls. The girls laughed and screamed.

Most of the men were down at the Indian Agency building, standing in long lines to collect the cash percentages they and their wives received from oil and cattle grazing leases. Some of them were wealthy from only the small two or four percent royalties and interests the companies paid. But even with such a spare tithe, the oil company owners resented having to pay the Indians for the use of their land, in spite of the fact that the Indian people had purchased it themselves. The owners thought the Indians were a locked door to the house of progress. And even more than that, they disliked the way Indian people displayed their wealth, driving showy red and cream-colored cars, wearing bright clothing, and joking back and forth about dollars and cents. And they didn't know what to do with their money. One of them, an old Osage man named Jim Josh, a man who loved plants, was said to have bought several useless claw-footed bathtubs even though he lived in a shack with no running water. Others were even more extravagant about squandering their money. It wasn't unheard of for an Indian to buy a new automobile because the old one was stuck somewhere out in the mud. Or, for instance, they always pointed out how the dead woman, Grace Blanket, had put a grand piano outside for roosting chickens.

Michael Horse parked his roadster and was covering his journals and diaries with a canvas tarp when he saw John Stink out of the corner of his eye. Stink was a big man. He walked up to Horse, smiled, and extended his gigantic hand. Horse smiled back and he clasped the man's dry, warm hand, then they walked away with Horse's arm stretched around the large, scar-faced Osage man. Stink dwarfed Michael Horse, and as they walked together, he smiled happily down at the smaller man.

The older people loved the good-natured John Stink, but the younger Indians ignored him. It was easy enough to do, since he had grown mute from a childhood disease and no longer tried to communicate with anyone he didn't already know. At one time Horse and Moses had taught him to write, but Stink decided he was happier without communicating and gave up his studies with the other men. He wore a red babushka on his head, which made him look silly and seem eccentric to the young. Stink had money, but shunned it, and he lived up on Mare Hill, above the golf course, with his many mongrel dogs who followed him everywhere he went.

Stink opened a paper sack and offered Michael Horse a cookie. Horse, who didn't have a taste for sweets, was polite, so he reached in, took one out, and bit into it with his gold teeth, while the dogs wagged their tails faster, begging him for a treat. He dropped a piece. They rushed toward it.

Also in town that day were the eagle hunters, but since it was during payment time, no one noticed them, nor did any of the Indians know that the oilman, Hale, had sponsored an eagle hunt, and that the marksmen from the East had traveled across the continent in plush new trains in order to shoot eagles out of the balmy Oklahoma sky.

The hunters were invisible among the crowds of merchants that filled the streets. They blended in with the con men who sold lottery tickets and the hard gamblers who brought in their own yards of green felt on which to deal their slick cards.

During all the quarterly pay periods white "naholies," as some of the Indians called them, arrived to sell their wares. They were laughingly called "scalpers" because their markup was so high. And the darker people joked about the white men's heavy eyebrows. It was hard for the newly rich Indians to take their wealth seriously and most were more than happy to buy any and all of the gadgets the scalpers sold from their rickety tables and stands, no matter how much the prices had been marked up. The women bought red and pink satin ribbons, black patent leather shoes, and expensive jeweled watches they pinned on their dresses. The men bought bow ties and Gillette razor blades, and carried bags full of trinkets to the children back up at the camp.

The eastern eagle hunters had never seen such Indians as these and they postponed their hunt until after payment time in order to watch the well-dressed men and women who came from miles around. Most of the Indians were Osages, though there were some Creeks and Seminoles, and a few Chickasaws. They set up tents and tepees on the first rise of the wide, rolling hill above town.

The hunters watched the tribal people drive through town in new Lincolns, wearing large Stetsons on their heads, their shoulders wrapped in colorful red and black blankets. The hunters were amused that the women camping up on the hills

had set the outdoor tables with Bavarian china, linen table-
cloths, and full services of silver.

Earlier that morning, the Indian men had shot a squealing
pig. It was scalded and cooked, then served up on the linen-
covered tables along with platters of venison, oven bread,
and as usual, the coconut macaroons everyone loved so well.

The women sat together that day, gossiping about what a
shame it was that their daughters were growing up and rushing headlong into the new ways, heading for Denver, Colorado, to look for husbands they believed were good enough
for them. A group of full-chested women sat in a row on a
bench. They said, wasn't it a disgrace that their sons were
acting just like boomers, drinking too much and dressing
like all the dandies, and they talked about the suicide of
Grace Blanket. One said, "I don't believe it, do you? She
always had a good time and a big smile. Why would she kill
herself?" A tall woman with lead-gray hair took the other
side of the argument, shook her head sadly back and forth,
sat stiffer on her perch, and said, "That's what happens when
you drink too much and troll around for men." She looked
righteous.

While the women talked, the men played cards for high
stakes and one of them could be heard praying out loud, his
eyes closed, his voice rising, "Please sweet Jesus let me
break even."

At the red-stone tribal council building, people milled
about catching the news, their voices a low hum inside the
building. One woman, an Osage, wore a mink coat despite
the still-warm autumn weather, and the heat forced her to
keep waving a palm fan before her flushed and sweating face.

John Tate was there that day. He was Moses Graycloud's
brother-in-law and a photographer. Tate appeared at all sig-
nificant events in the territory, standing behind the three-
legged stand that held his camera, his head covered with
black cloth, his one good eye seeing everything through glass
lenses.

Moses avoided both the little man and the camera that
brought the world into a different focus. Moses made his way
over to Horse. They exchanged a few words of greeting, then
Moses searched out his name on the posted list of royalty
recipients. The list was printed with the surnames and tribal

enrollment numbers of each Indian, and the dollar amount of payment they were to receive. Moses, who received his money from grazing leases, not from oil, followed his name across the page with his index finger. His payment was minimal compared to the Indians with oil, only two thousand dollars, but it was a decent income. It kept his family in food and supplies.

The pay tables were set up along two walls, and the clerks from Washington stood behind them counting their cash. They had narrow, pallid faces. The Osages believed that the climate in Washington was unhealthy and poor, since the clerks were so sickly looking. And the people loudly discussed the Washington men in Osage, speaking back and forth across the room, as if it were the only revenge they had for the wrongs that had been done to them. "Look at that one with the jaw like a goat," one of the women would say, "No, not that one. I mean the one by President Harding's picture." All the heads would turn and the clerk counting the money thought they were looking at the picture.

The government workers called out the names of payees. That morning, in innocence, they called, "Grace Blanket," and the bustling roomful of dark-suited Indians in braids and large hats became still except for the click of John Tate's camera. For a silent moment, everyone half expected to see the beautiful, black-haired Grace walk out of the throng of people, wind her way through the crowd, and sign for her annuity. They missed her. Just hearing her name reminded them. Also, word had gotten out among most of the younger Indian people that her grave had been vandalized, and that frightened the people into a deeper silence, as they thought how the naholies wouldn't leave them alone even in death, and that their afterlives were bound to be haunted by money-hungry people who weren't above turning over the red clay earth and tombstones that marked the final homes of Indians.

When one of the clerks cried out, "Camp," and a mixed-blood man walked over and signed for his cash, the chatter started up again, with relief. At another table, an uneasy clerk made a mark on his list and called out three names at once, "Deermeat, Graycloud, Hunka shi pa!"

Moses stepped up to the table and repeated his name. The clerk fixed him with a watery stare. "Where's your Certificate of Competency?'' He looked over every inch of Moses's body, down to the red dust on his boots.

Moses took the paper from his shirt pocket and he slowly unfolded it. He handed it to the man.

"Okay, Graycloud, put your thumbprint right here." The clerk had a plug of tobacco tucked in his thin cheek. He pointed to a dotted line. Moses wrote his name in the beautiful script he had learned in school, and the sullen clerk cast a glance over his shoulder at the guard from the sheriff's office. They were prepared for trouble, and they were tense, afraid of the dark people. They had ideas about Indians, that they were unschooled, ignorant people who knew nothing about life or money. But whenever an Indian didn't fit their vision, the clerks and agents became afraid. That was why Michael Horse, who was witness to what happened next, always remained silent in the presence of the men from Washington. If they knew he kept a journal of all the events in Watona, and if they knew he had translated three languages back and forth during the Boxer Rebellion in China, they would have found a way to cut him down to the size they wanted him to be, and he knew it. Not that all of them were bad. Far from it. Nevertheless, Horse was afraid to even let them see that he had three gold teeth because he knew some of them were so greedy they'd find a reason to pull them out of his head, so he kept his mouth closed and his ears wide open, and what his ears heard that day, he didn't want to believe.

After Moses wrote his name, the clerk counted two hundred dollars into his open palm, turned a page in his book of accounts, looked over Moses's head, and called out above the voices, "Henderson!" He sounded exasperated.

But Moses didn't turn away. His deep voice even sounded calm when he said, "That's not the full amount due to me, Mr. Smith."

The clerk ignored him, but he said, "Where is the rest of my money?" He sounded more demanding.

Smith, the clerk, fidgeted a moment, then he said quietly to Moses Graycloud, "They changed the regulations." He paused, then went on. "You're a full-blood Indian, Graycloud. According to the rolls here." He pointed at the piece of paper. "Full-bloods only get part of their money. You're getting ten per today.'' He looked Moses square in the face, and he looked so full of resentment that Moses almost missed the fear. But the room went cold with it. In the background, a surly clerk in a white shirt piped up and said to another one, out loud, "Hell, some of them buy three cars. We don't even have that kind of money, and we're Americans.''

James Josh, the man with the claw-foot bathtubs, was at another table where another nervous clerk pushed a paper in front of him for a thumbprint or X, but Josh paused to listen, and the other people also listened, even those who pretended not to hear, waiting to see what Moses would do next. Their own responses depended on him. Moses was a man of good sense and they all knew it, and it was likely they would follow his lead when they took their turns in the payment line. One of the guards touched his pistol, but despite the implied and obvious threat, Moses made no move to leave. "Who made this regulation?'' he wanted to know.

The clerk realized that Moses had no intention of leaving without his money. "We don't have any say in the matter,'' he said to Moses. He looked resigned. "The Indian Commission changed the rules.'' His hands were shaking. "There's nothing we can do here. I'm sorry.''

Everyone knew those words were the truth. The room was silent with only the shuffling of a few shoes, a cleared throat. Many of them had taken up their needs and losses with the government. Some of them had even gone to Washington, D.C., to talk with the president who refused a hearing with them.

When Moses spoke again, he sounded reasonable. Not an ounce of the anger he felt filtered into his voice. "In the spring you told us our people with white blood only received part of their money since they are part white. And not entitled. Now you are saying that we full-bloods get only part of our money since someone we never see believes that we mismanage it? The government is doing this, right?''

Every Indian in the room had heard this argument and knew it by heart. Sometimes there was even a grain of truth to it, but no one thought it should matter how they spent their money. They knew only that the courts used that argument against them, assuming they were like children and without a nickel's worth of intelligence.

"Is that right?" But Moses never finished all of what he wanted to say. The clerk became alarmed, and when he spoke to Moses, it was hard to tell if he was offering advice out of fear or if his words were a threat, but he again told the truth when he said to Moses, "If you carry on that way, Mr. Graycloud, the judge will declare you an incompetent."

With this mention of the competency commission, Moses knew he was beaten, and so did all the others. The courts had already named at least twenty competent Indian people as incompetents, and had already withheld all their money until they were assigned legal guardians.

Moses became silent and turned away, even though his heart was racing in his angry chest and he wanted to scream at them, who were they to judge?

Benoit stood in the back of the room, listening, and then he pushed his way through the crowd. Red-faced, he began to yell at the clerk. "What did you say? Say that again."

"It's all right, son," Moses said to Benoit. He put his hand on Benoit's arm. "It's all right." He tried to calm the younger man.

The guards stood at attention.

Benoit's body was taut. "It's not all right." He looked at the clerk. "What the hell are you talking about? Last time you said mixed-bloods got less. Now you say full-bloods can't have all their own damned money?"

The clerk was afraid. He nodded at one of the guards.

John Tate photographed the angry young man.

"It's all right, Benoit." Moses turned Benoit's shoulder with his hand, turned him away from the table.

"It's not! It says two thousand right there on that sheet of paper." He stepped over and snatched the list off the wall. "Who carries out their orders? You do." He glared at the clerk, but Moses and another man managed to push Benoit toward the door. Moses looked back to be certain they were safe.

Benoit was close to tears. "They're stealing our lives! We've got to fight them. Why do you just take it?"

The crowd parted to let the two men through. Those who were there to collect their payments turned their eyes downward, feeling ashamed of something they couldn't even name.

One of the guards raised a rifle toward Benoit and Moses.

The guards knew the situation could explode at any time, but the Indians knew, from history itself, that it was a smart thing to keep silent on the affairs and regulations of Washington, to be still and as invisible as possible. They might be cheated, but they still had life, and until only recently, even that was not guaranteed under the American laws, so they remained trapped, silent, and wary.

All that was why Horse, the diviner and translator and the keeper of accounts, had moved far away from town and set up camp on Crow Hill, and even that wasn't far enough for him, he thought that day, as he watched his people, already bent down from the weight of it, accept still another swindle.

Moses led Benoit out the door. "Not a word of this to Belle," he said, steering Benoit by his elbow.

Benoit was frustrated. "Why not?" He pulled away from Moses.

"It's not worth it." Moses felt his anger rise again, directed this time at Benoit.

Benoit stalked away from him. He was young and temperamental; he had to walk away, even from Moses, had to take his anger to a silent place and study it so he wouldn't turn it back on his own people. He went around a corner and was gone.

Moses watched him leave, his shoulders high and tight. But even with the anger on the streets that day, cash and liquor flowed like happiness. People paid on their debts to the stores and the blacksmith, and Moses, pushing down his anxiety, went to the Blue Store and, as if he could afford it, he ordered grain for his horses and blue linoleum for Belle's kitchen. Then he went to the Red Store where he stood beneath the ceiling fan and began to feel sick and shaky.

All around him in the store that payment day, women bought skillets and tortoise-shell hair combs, and men bought felted beaver hats and cameras they used outside the store to photograph their wives. The women posed on the street in lovely dresses, gold bracelets, and their black straight hair burned orange with waving lotion, hair that surrounded their dark Indian faces like false haloes.

Mr. Palmer waved at Moses. "Come over here, Moses," he called. Moses was a good customer and he always paid on time. "Here," he said. "Try one of these José Merego

cigars." He opened a gilt-covered box and took out one of
the rich dark stogies. "Tell me you don't think these are fit
for the chief of police." He handed a cigar over the glass
counter to Moses.

Moses only smoked after his evening meal. Palmer knew
that. "I'll let you know how it is." Moses thanked Palmer.
He put the cigar in his chest pocket. "I want to buy that blue
vase over there." Palmer took it off the shelf. "And I want
that umbrella." He pointed up at the ceiling to a yellow one.
It hung from the ceiling like an open flower.

With a hook Palmer latched on to it and maneuvered it
down from the ceiling. "Why do you Indians use so many
umbrellas?" he asked Moses as he closed it down.

"The wind," said Moses. "The wind turns them inside
out."

"Oh," said Palmer, as if he understood.

Moses paid cash for the umbrella and the Persian blue
vase, and while he stood at the register watching the numbers
rise up in the glass window, John Stink walked up behind
him and placed one of his huge, warm hands on Moses's
shoulder. Moses, as down-spirited as he was, knew it was
Stink, just by the size of the hand, and he began to smile
even before he turned around, though it was only his mouth
that smiled. His dark eyes were filled with sadness.

Moses finished what he was saying to Palmer, that it wasn't
just the umbrellas that were inside out, but "the whole world
and everything in it." Then he turned and looked into the
eyes of old, mute John Stink.

John Stink bought a bag of cookies for his dogs. Two of
them, scraggly and hot, had managed to sneak inside the
store. Stink offered them a cookie now and then while
he made signs with his hands that Moses understood. And
he avoided the eyes of Palmer, who didn't allow dogs in the
store.

Moses scratched the dogs' mangy coats and told Stink that
there were stray humans who would probably like those
chocolate coconut cookies. Stink threw back his head and
laughed, as he often did. His teeth were bad.

Stink pointed up to the encampment and raised a questioning eyebrow at Moses.

"Yes. I'm going. I might as well. Things are pretty bad

here today.'' He wanted to pass on the news of what had happened in the council house, though word had probably already gone around.

They walked together up the hill, followed by the pack of mongrel dogs. Moses opened the new yellow umbrella and the two Indian men walked inside its yellow shade.

Most of the Indian families had been up at the encampment for several days, long enough to settle in and establish a work routine. The women scrubbed dishes with Oxydol soap in a tub while the men served food. Moses and Stink sat down at one of the long white tables. Moses could see by the mood that the other Indians already knew what had happened. One of the boys, serving coffee, touched Moses's arm, a gesture of solace. The dogs sat behind them with hopeful eyes, looking at the venison and ham.

Two of the eagle hunters sat at the table across from Moses and Stink. The hunters ate hungrily, then quickly pushed away their empty plates, lit their pipes, and watched the Indians.

In town that same day, Hale made a deal with an older Indian man named Walker. Walker owed Hale for three breeding horses and some cattle, but because Walker was a full-blood Indian and did not receive the full amount of his annuity, he couldn't pay off the debt. Hale, who'd arrived in town to order new drilling equipment, on hearing that Walker was broke, came up with the idea of taking out a life insurance policy on Walker. That way, he told the older man, he could collect later when Walker died, and he'd call it even for now. Walker thought it was an excellent arrangement and he signed the agreement with Hale, and since the policy required a physical examination, he accompanied him to the doctor's office.

"They didn't get full payment today," Hale said by way of explanation to Doctor Black. "This way, he won't have to pay me back. It works out fair and even."

Walker sat beside Hale and nodded his agreement.

The doctor looked at them through the top of his bifocals. He looked at the paper. "You want me to sign this." His voice was flat. He gazed off, squinting out the window.

"He's healthy as a horse."

Doctor Black, Benjamin was his first name, took his
glasses off his face. "Walker," he said, "go in that room
and take off your shirt. I've got to listen to your heart." He
pointed to the door. Walker obeyed. Then Black took a sip
of his coffee. He looked at Hale, then looked out the window
at the crowds of people on the busy street, the fast business
of oil money changing hands, hawkers selling Indian people
useless baubles, and white men collecting on their debts. He
didn't like any of it. He'd written a letter to Washington. The
last two Indians who died had insurance policies. One of
them named Hale as beneficiary. And Hale had a lien on the
property of the other one. But in D.C. they'd told him there
wasn't enough evidence. And it was outside their jurisdiction.

Black didn't like it but it was the times. What could he do,
confront Hale, ask him if he were guilty of murder? He
couldn't go back to the sheriff. If he told Walker, that would
only increase the danger, if there was any, for both of them.
If not, he'd be liable. He could say that Walker didn't qual-
ify. But if his suspicions were true, it wouldn't make a difference; they'd find another way.

He turned back toward Hale. The younger, thin man
seemed confident.

Resigned, Black put his cup down on the desk, went into
the examining room, and listened to Walker's heart. He removed the stethoscope from his ears. "You feeling good,
Walker?"

"Damn good, doc. Damn good."

That autumn night after payment, a peyote ceremony was
going to take place in the arbor at Twin Forks Road. Also, a
carnival had been erected just outside the Watona town limits. The Pentecostal Brethren set up their own tent, as always,
as close to the carnival as they could get, hoping to catch
stragglers that passed by and save their souls. All three events
customarily accompanied payment times when the town was
richly populated with Indian people whose pockets were full
and whose tired spirits longed for renewal.

At the Graycloud house, the calliope music filtered in the
open door and windows, but Belle made no mention of the
carnival to Nola or Rena. It was best, she thought, that

the girls continue to stay out of sight from any free-wandering hustlers or possible killers, and besides, she told Lettie, the carnival lights attracted hordes of large, black-winged autumn moths. All in all, she thought it was an unpleasant, if not a dangerous, place to be, and a waste of time and cash. But Lettie wanted to go. She argued with Belle, "All we've done since Grace's death is sit around here waiting for something else to happen."

Louise overheard the raised voices from the kitchen. "Go ahead," she told her sister. "Mama's superstitious is all. For her, everything is a plot."

But Belle's face remained stubbornly set, and then Benoit drove up and Lettie said she was going anyway, and as she was leaving, she smiled at Lou, and checked the tilt of her green hat reflected in the window.

Belle went up to her room. From upstairs, she saw Lettie and Benoit, wearing his good silver concho belt, walk out to the truck, turn on the headlights, and drive away. She sat before the burning sacred heart candle, a cross, and an eagle prayer feather. She could hear the sounds of the shooting gallery from her room. She cried and prayed, then she wiped her eyes and went out into the hall.

Nola sat on the edge of Lettie's hallway bed in the dark blue light of evening. The girl winced with the sound of every gunshot that was fired at the live pigeons and ducklings in the shooting gallery. Belle went to her and held the girl's head to her heavy breast.

For that one night, Benoit and Lettie vowed to each other that they would forget the past. As the truck's gears shifted, so they tried to shift their own thoughts. Lettie looked out the window at the passing landscape. She could feel the motor of the car through her legs, could feel the stones in the road, the potholes. Benoit concentrated on turning the wheel and directing the truck to the smoothest places in the road. By the time they arrived at the carnival grounds, they pretended to be in unusually good spirits. Benoit parked his gray truck out on Beeline Road, and they walked together through dried, worn-out grass toward the carnival lights. "It looks pretty," Lettie said. Benoit agreed.

The carnival was attended by Indians, oilmen, cowboys,

and young people who looked for excitement of the senses. There were sideshows, including a Seminole Indian woman snake handler who wore a boa constrictor around her neck like a mink stole, and a two-headed girl who had been born in Watona the year of the Dawes Allotment Act in 1906, and had been sold to a traveling circus ten years later. A famous rope twirler and professional cowboy named Fraser was there doing tricks with a rope he'd set on fire. He wore a black satin shirt, black pants, and if it hadn't been for the burning circle of hemp that was suspended and circling midair like a hellfire halo, and the way it lit up his hand and made ugly shadows on his long-lashed face, he would have blended invisibly into the dark night.

Lettie saw him from the Ferris wheel and she reached for Benoit's hand. They stopped, suspended for a minute at the top of the wheel, swinging, and looked down over the colored lights and the pigeon shooters. The wheel stopped long enough that they could see the large-winged dark moths Belle had warned them about. The moths flew into the colored lights, large as birds. Their motion added to the noise of the carnival was dizzying.

Just beyond those lights, whiskey peddlers sold their goods. In the first circle of darkness, Floyd Graycloud, Belle's son-in-law, had set up shop with the best, highest-priced moonshine in Oklahoma Indian Territory. There was a crowd around his table. Lettie could see the men's white shirts moving in the darkness. And the dry leaves were falling from autumn trees and scurrying across the fields and roads like hurried animals, and farther out, stars filled the sky.

The Ferris wheel moved and stopped again.

Lettie saw Ben walk past his father's liquor business. Ben pretended not to see his father. He walked on, into the night. As she watched him, Lettie felt a sudden surge of panic. She wanted Ben to be afraid, to stay away from places that held danger.

Benoit touched her chin. He smiled gently into her eyes. "Just one night, remember? One night without sadness."

He put his arm around Lettie. When they came round to the bottom, they gave another ticket to the Ferris wheel operator and rode again. But Benoit thought he saw Moses Graycloud down on the ground walking. He leaned forward.

"Isn't that your father?" He pointed at the man. Graycloud was just beyond the lights and people, walking past a group of men who were shooting craps beside a dim lantern.

Lettie followed Benoit's gaze. "Yes." She watched Moses. "He's thinking. His mind thinks Mama's is just suspicious, but his heart believes her. So does mine."

Then, while they watched, Moses disappeared into the same darkness that swallowed Ben.

Benoit started to remind her of their one night of happiness, but then he went silent, for he himself was thinking of poor Nola who had lost her color. A sense of dread filled him. The Ferris wheel dropped down and stopped again. Just before they reached the bottom, Lettie leaned against Benoit's muscled shoulder and looked out, feeling protected by the arm he put around her and by the starry night. They didn't see John Tate take a photograph of them. Then the wheel turned and they were stopped at the bottom, swinging just above the ground.

The young couple walked arm-in-arm through the corridor of game booths, past the real fur bears that hung on hooks beside the Kewpie dolls with red-painted cheeks and black lashes. Lettie and Benoit stayed away from the shooting galleries, where a dime bought three shots at live birds. The Indians didn't approve of this practice and their numerous complaints about such cruelty had gone unheeded.

At the bottle toss, with the strain of music in the background, Benoit stopped and winked at Lettie. He said, "I'm going to win you a doll." He threw the rings toward the necks of bottles but he missed every blue glass bottle, and Lettie knew that Benoit, an excellent shot, was having as much trouble feigning joy as she was.

They passed by a fortune-teller's tent. The woman sat just inside the door at a little red table. She was around fifty years of age, and had sharp, dark eyes. The woman, a Cajun from Louisiana, stared at Benoit's belt with its silver coins and hammered silver conchos. Something inside her heart began to talk. "Something's wrong," she said out loud. "Come here, lady." She beckoned to Lettie. "The spirits want to tell you something. Come over here."

With a large gesture, the woman pushed her hair back and

went into a powerful trance. More quiet now, she said, "I hear them now. They say, there's flying feathers. Flying wood. Things are flying apart."

Lettie stopped and listened, but Benoit wanted to leave. He felt itchy. He put his hand on Lettie's sleeve. "Let's go," but Lettie brushed him away. She wanted to hear what the spirits were saying through the dark-eyed woman.

The fortune-teller went on. Her eyes were closed. "Beware. Beware. The crocodile doesn't harm the bird that cleans his teeth for him. He eats the others but not that one."

As soon as she had spoken those words, she opened her eyes and her palm for money.

Lettie opened her bag.

"What did she tell you?" Benoit started to argue, but Lettie brushed him off and took out two coins. As she held the money over the woman's palm, she was startled. The woman's hand had no lines in it. Lettie paused. She looked at the hand, then up at the woman, meeting her eyes. Then, without speaking, she paid the woman and walked away with Benoit.

Benoit wanted to make light of things. He joked, "She's probably got northern fur trapper blood." He half smiled and looked at Lettie, but she was preoccupied, and the mood of false happiness had dropped away. Both of them were silent as they walked on through the autumn night.

They drove out to a distant side road, turned off, and parked the truck beneath a leafless tree. It was still warm, a kind of lazy autumn heat, so they left the windows down. Benoit slipped his arm around Lettie. She rested her head on his shoulder. Neither of them saw or heard the black Buick that pulled up behind them with its lights switched off. Benoit was still thinking of the fortune-teller.

"Look at the stars," said Lettie. "There is one for every person born. Did you know that? It lights up when we're born and when we die it goes out."

Benoit moved close to Lettie. He began to remove the pins from her hat.

She reached up to stop him. "No, don't," but it was too late. He lifted the hat off her hair while he kissed her, and then, in a startled voice, he said, "What's this." He pulled away from her. "What in the hell are you doing with a knife under your hat?"

At first, she felt like laughing, but it was just her nerves and she looked at him, deep and serious, and she said, "I don't feel safe."

"A knife in your hat's going to make you safe?" He took hold of her shoulders and turned Lettie to face him directly. "Look, Leticia." He used her formal name. "What happened to Grace was that she played around with too many bottles and too many men. Your dad says so. Even Michael Horse thinks so."

Lettie looked away, into the darkness.

"Besides," he said, "what good's a knife going to do you up on your head?"

"You don't believe that about Grace. None of us do. You saw my father. You saw him looking around, looking for signs and traces of what happened. It just makes it easier to try to believe it was Grace's fault. It's easier to swallow that way."

Abruptly, Benoit changed his tone and took her into his arms. "I know. But tonight, remember?" He kissed her. He ran his hands down her shoulder and across her back. "Tonight we are happy." He touched her hips, as if he were smoothing down a wrinkle, but then he touched her thigh, and he pulled back once again, as if burned, then examined the lump he'd found there. "A gun? Christ Jesus, it's a gun."

Lettie began to cry.

On his way to the ceremony, Moses walked past the revivalist's green tent. Pentecostal preachers appealed to the lost, cash-filled Indian souls who had been suffering from spiritual malnutrition. Inside the tent, the faithful prayed with closed eyes. Oil lanterns burned through the green canvas walls, so that from a distance the tent looked luminous, like an emerald, and the mostly mixed-blood people inside were sweating and weeping and wiping their eyes with white handkerchiefs. It was here, in religion, that all their sorrow came out. Moses could hear the Indian preacher speak, "And when the spirit touches us, there won't be any more danger here on earth," said the evangelist. "No mean spirits walking this land, no smallness in people, no heartaches, no sorrow, nor any pain.'' Moses knew the man's arms were raised up before the sad adults, and he heard the congregation cry out, ''Amen,'' and in that word they were bound together.

Moses walked on past the pumping oil wells farther down the road. A white sign, visible even in the dark, read ''Indian Territory Illuminating Oil Company,'' and then, past that, the land stretched out beneath the dark hand of night, and from the peyote tepee in the hilly, rolling country, Moses could hear the drum. It calmed him. It was the song of a deeper life, the beating of earth's pulse. He stopped on the road to listen before he made his way through the dark to join his people.

Earlier that same evening, Michael Horse had left his tepee and walked across the land. He traveled by foot, collecting medicinal plants and sassafras. He carried two bags. By the time he reached the peyote ceremony, the bags were filled with herbs. As he neared the lodge where the ceremony was going to take place, he saw Moses standing still on the night road, listening to the drum which was named ''The Life of the People.''

Horse called out from the dark trees. ''Moses! Where's your car?''

Horse's voice brought Moses out of his reverie. He answered, ''I've been thinking. I always walk when I'm thinking.''

''Oh, I see. What about?'' Horse stepped out of the shadows.

''I don't know yet,'' Moses said. They started off together the short way to the tepee.

Horse joked with him, ''Neither do I.''

''Well, when you figure out what I'm thinking, will you let me know?''

They both laughed.

The other members of the Native Church were already there, and when Moses and Horse arrived, they all entered the tepee and sat in a circle on the earth. Some of the people gazed with sad faces into the fire. Some were already praying and their eyes were closed. Others were saying what fine ham was served at the encampment above town that payment day. ''It really hit the spot, didn't it?'' a woman asked Moses.

He nodded. But his mind was elsewhere.

Moses's twin sister, Ruth Tate, sat directly across from him. They looked alike and they'd been known to have that link between them that is common to twins. They'd had it since birth. If Ruth fell down, Moses would feel the same pain, the same scraped knee. If Moses lost one of his beloved horses, Ruth would stop by his place and say, "What's wrong? I feel sad."

Ruth had a rich, warm voice which she seldom used and black gentle eyes. She was given to chills and female complaints, so she kept wrapped, as she did at home, in a dark blanket, even with the slow autumn heat and the fire she was sitting before. The other people had wondered about Ruth when she married the busy little photographer, John Tate. They seemed ill-suited to one another. Opposites in all ways. But the marriage seemed solid and Ruth had been lonely for many long years.

Moses looked at his sister. The light softened the bones of her face. She looked, as Horse had once described her, "Indian from the heart out." Her hair was deep black, her skin smooth and brown.

Reverend Joe Billy of the Indian Baptist Church was what they called the road man. The road man shows Indian people the path of life, takes the stones out of their way, and maps out the spirit's terrain. Joe Billy's face was rubbed with red clay and yellow ochre, the elements of earth. He wore a red scarf around his neck. His eyes were closed and he was praying, but he was a different man than the one who wore the black suit on Sunday mornings. And even his prayers were different, deeper somehow, more heartfelt, more physical as if they came through the body and not just the mind. He stretched wet buckskin across a small drum, and when he arranged the holy sage all the talkers became silent.

The people prayed and cried that night. The drummer beat the drum. Joe Billy shook the gourd rattle. Every person lit a cigarette, ate the cactus that was their teacher and their healer, and blessed themselves with the smoke of sage.

Young Ben Graycloud sat on one side of his grandfather, his skin fresh and young, and his eyes squeezed shut. On Ben's other side was a veteran named Keto. It was already late when Keto prayed. This was his prayer:

Now I'm a good Indian, and the best true American on
earth. I salute the flag. And I was in the world war.

The listeners nodded and said, "Hmmm." It spurred Keto
on.

But what happened here, I want to know. The judge asks
me if I'm happy in my marriage and I tell him I am. He
says do I know the difference between a five dollar bill and
a twenty. I say that I do. Then they tell me I'm feeble. I
can't handle my own money, they say. They assign me a
guardian. He's a lawyer. Now, I know lawyers are good
men. Some of them even went to the war. But this lawyer
buys me a big house. I don't want a big house. I tell him
I want to stay in my home where I was born and where
my sons were born.

"I understand," said Joe Billy, softly.

So this lawyer moves his own things in that house, even
his wife. Well, holy spirit, please look into this for me.
It's just not right. And forgive me for speaking in English,
but like I said, I'm a true American. I went to their war. I
fought in it.

After Keto's prayer, everyone was silent, pondering his
words and their truth. They felt defeated and walled in by
what was around them. It was nearly midnight. It seemed a
long while before Ben began to pray. He wanted to pray in
the Osage language, but he began awkwardly and Joe Billy
put his hand on the boy's knee and said, "Son, the heart's
words are all that's important in the ears of our creator."
And Joe Billy thought how it might have made Keto feel bad
to hear a younger Indian, a mixed-blood, speaking the tribal
tongue that Keto had not himself learned.

Ben prayed. "Grandfather," he said, "I don't have a good
feeling these days, either. Ever since Grace Blanket was killed
I've been afraid. And now with us having to go away to
school."

But then, suddenly, in the middle of Ben's prayer, an explosion shocked them upright, jolted them wide awake. It rocked the earth like it had been split wide apart.

"Jesus!" Reverend Billy cried out. "What in the hell was that?" His eyes were alert. At the same moment, both Moses and Ruth made for the door flap to go outside and look, but Keto, who worked in the oil fields as a roughnecker, told them, "It's a new well blowing out at the drilling site," and his explanation made sense to everyone, so they settled back down. Ruth wrapped the blanket tightly around her.

"Go on, then," Joe Billy said to Ben, when he'd sat back on his heels. He touched the boy lightly on the thigh.

"We've had awful hard times," Ben said, and his words seemed strengthened by the shock of the blast. And everyone knew he didn't mean his own bad times. "They put us on this godforsaken land and no one knew what was underneath it, but even with all this oil and money, it seems we can't come out ahead."

"Amen," said one of the listeners.

"Some of us have broken all apart, like the earth just did."

"Mmm-hmm," said some of the listeners.

"I'm tired of those landmen coming round to tap the earth for oil." Ben thought a moment. "We have so much pain, it's on our faces and in our eyes. It's in the clothes we wear," and his words went straight as an arrow to everyone's hearts. They were moved and touched. One of the women began to sob. Michael Horse's throat went tight. Moses covered his face with his aging hands, and thought how his grandson had a man's good heart and a man's strong words and he was proud at the same time that he was miserable under the weight of their history.

Ben grew suddenly uncomfortable, like one who had not expected to reach so far with his words. "That's all. That's all I have to say."

It was quiet a long time, except for the crying and sniffling of people in the dark circle. Ruth's tears ran down her face, and Moses felt them as his own. The faint roar of the gas fire could be heard burning in the distance.

After a while, Joe Billy said, "That was a good prayer, son." The darkness engulfed them.

Joe Billy added, with humor, "For English that is."

The listeners caught the joke and laughed a little, wiped their eyes, and felt better.

The eagle bone whistle was blown four times and a water cup was passed around the thirsty circle of people.

The same explosion that had shocked the praying people jolted Lettie and Benoit into upright positions. The sky south of them went red from the fire, and when that sudden blazing light filled the horizon, they saw the Buick parked behind them. The light outlined the blue-black shape of the hood and caught the gleam of metal.

"Give me that gun!" Benoit grabbed the pearl-handled pistol and cocked it as the driver of the Buick started the car, turned on the head beams, and passed slowly alongside Benoit's truck.

Lettie locked the car door from inside. But the car disappeared down the road.

"Jesus, I'm jittery." Benoit tried to laugh, but it caught in his throat. He started the engine and drove back to the main road.

"That was a Buick, wasn't it?" Lettie sounded suspicious.

"That doesn't mean anything," he said stubbornly. "Buicks are a dime a dozen. Even your dad drives one."

By the time Benoit and Lettie reached the Grayclouds' residence, the firelight had settled down.

Belle was outside the house. All the windows on the south side of the house had been broken out by the midnight blast and she was gauging the damage, picking up the few splinters of glass that had fallen outward.

"I'm sick and tired of oil drillers," Belle said. "They burn the poor birds right out of the sky."

The watchers were standing on the south side of the house, talking among themselves.

"Nola woke up twice with nightmares," Belle said to Benoit. "Rena's still crying. The chickens fell off their roosts. We won't have eggs for months. Cups fell off the shelves and broke." She worked quickly.

Benoit helped pick up the sharp splinters of glass. The indoor light reflected off the broken edges. There was a faint smell of burning trees.

It was nearly daylight when Benoit left for home. Belle

and Lettie were cleaning the floors. Belle watched him drive away. "He's a good man," she said to Lettie. "He treats you and Sara like queens." She squatted down and swept the floor with a hand broom. Lettie held the dustpan for her mother and Belle swept the broken glass into it and added to Benoit's list of attributes that he was good to his mother when she was alive and that he was a clean dresser even though she herself didn't really like the new styles he favored all that much.

In the first hint of dawn, as Benoit neared his home on South Fremont Road, he thought he'd taken a wrong turn. He was tired, and though he was sure he recognized the landmarks, three cottonwoods were there and the mailbox was out on the road with his name written on it, something was wrong. He slammed on his brakes and stared. He tried to gather himself to think, tried to understand what he saw. Where his house had been, there was only a pile of smoking embers, and gray ash had settled over the grasses. He was stunned, and when he opened the truck cab door, he almost fell out, then he pulled himself up in that weightless, absent way people move when they are unable to believe their own eyes.

A water truck was there, still pouring water on the rubble. It steamed and hissed. Gray smoke rose up and there was a stench in the air.

Benoit's mouth was locked open. The remains of his house were nothing but smoking embers. Only a single Greek statue stood unbroken, but even that statue had been blackened on one side from the heat and smoke of the explosion.

"Oh God," Benoit cried out. The life seemed to go out of him. "Oh my God."

From behind the statue, the sheriff walked through the ash toward Benoit. "Benoit," he said. "Don't move, Benoit."

Even without the command, Benoit was stock-still, looking at the ruins of his home. Then he began to run toward the smoldering house, but the sheriff grabbed his arm. Benoit fell out of his grasp, fell down to his knees, crying again, "My God," and he put his face against the devastated earth, and it was covered with ash. He did not pull away or struggle when Sheriff Gold took his arm again and put the handcuff on his wrist.

"Sara?" Benoit called out, like a question. "Where is she?" He looked at the sheriff.

"Benoit, I got witnesses," Jess Gold said.

"What?" Benoit went cold.

The sheriff handcuffed his other wrist and led Benoit toward the car, talking all the while like he was talking to a wild animal, saying, "You know I got no choice, Benoit. It's my job. You know I'm your friend."

He put Benoit in the back seat, and as he drove toward town the sky became lighter. A rooster crowed in the distance. Benoit, his face smudged dark, saw the devastation. A mattress was in an oak tree. A shoe was in a bush. A pair of glasses were on the road. Songbirds began to sing.

The sheriff watched Benoit's stunned face in the rearview mirror. He studied the gray-green eyes, the face that had gone sweaty and pale, the dirty smooth forehead and fine, wide lips. Benoit's hair was still in place, combed back from his face. His stunned eyes took in his broken world. The debris had scattered for over a mile. Books, once his, lay on the ground with their spines broken open, their pages and printed words open to the sky. Shoes he recognized had landed what seemed like half a mile away. He saw one of his own black leather brogans. A pillow had lost its feathers. Splintered wood found a resting place in trees. The arm of a statue was in a creek and Benoit saw it lying there open-handed, relaxed, as they crossed the bridge. Then it was all gone, as if the blast could not pass over the water, and soon they were in town, and the sheriff parked his car in front of the jail.

Through some miracle, Mrs. Inman, Sara's housekeeper, had been thrown clear of the fire. She'd landed in a hedge of bushes and survived with only minor injuries and burns.

Michael Horse, who really wanted nothing more in all the world than to be left alone to his silences and prayers, and to tending the fire, went to Tulsa to visit Mrs. Inman in her hospital room. He was keeping a journal of the fire and the arrest of Benoit. He had come to agree with Belle, that there was danger and that there was a conspiracy and like her, he suspected everyone. He wrote a page on every person he thought might have had a reason to put the nitro fuse in the coalbin of Benoit's house. He even included Lettie in his list of possible suspects, since he knew that she wanted to marry Benoit, had even wished it aloud on past occasions.

The day after the fire died down, Michael Horse returned and sifted through the ruins. He found a silver ring which he took home and held in his hand, waiting for the story that metal might tell. But he heard nothing and thought the heat of the explosion must have killed the tale that lived in the metal.

The dreadful fire and Benoit's arrest filled up several pages of Horse's diary. He wanted to go to the courthouse and find a map that sketched out who owned the lands that adjoined those of the Blanket sisters. He was sure Nola was in trouble, or would be anyway, when she came of age. But for now, Benoit was legally heir to the fortune.

Horse wrote down that he'd seen Lettie and Benoit on the Ferris wheel together early the night of the explosion. Lettie, he knew, would be forced to remain silent about their tryst since the law would certainly think Benoit was a sharp corner in a lover's triangle, and if they knew the situation, Benoit's guilt would double in their eyes. In his journals, Horse named the peyotists who'd been at the prayers. He thought he could rule them out.

When Horse arrived at the hospital, Mrs. Inman looked weak and pale. She was without her glasses, so she squinted at him while they talked. The area around her eyes had been protected by her glasses and was unburned and white, while the rest of her face was red and tender.

Sara had been antsy that night, Mrs. Inman said. "But it was the grave-robbers that concerned her. You knew about them, didn't you?"

Horse was surprised. This was the first he'd heard, even though he lived not far from the cemetery. His breathing grew shallow. "What do you mean?"

"Grace's grave. Ona Neck found it opened. It upset Sara real bad. She talked about it for weeks. It was just too much for her."

Mrs. Inman went on, "We heard a noise around midnight. Sara wheeled her chair over to look outside the window. She thought it was an old tabby cat that had been hanging around. She'd worried about it.

"It's funny," she said, "but when I opened the window a little wider, the black summer moths and insects flew inside. They floated toward the lamplight. I thought, how lovely they are. How beautiful. They were large as birds. They looked like they were swimming. And then, just as I saw them, there was the loud blast."

It had broken her eardrums. The house was torn apart and Mrs. Inman herself was thrown. She landed, burned and bruised, in the bushes some distance from the house. Half conscious, she heard the roaring fire consume the earthly world of Sara and Benoit.

Horse went down the hospital steps. In his car, he sat at the wheel, writing in his journal. No matter how Michael Horse wrote it, the only person with a motive might have been Benoit. Benoit was the one who was sure to inherit Sara's wealth. And though Horse knew deep in his soul that Benoit was innocent, he understood how the sheriff saw his way clear to accuse the young man of not just one, but two counts of homicide, adding Grace's death to the tally. Because of the inheritance alone, the sheriff was convinced he had enough evidence to convict Benoit of the murders.

When he was finished writing, Horse put his face in his hands and closed his eyes. The silver ring was still in his pocket. But it remained silent.

Belle's allotment land adjoined the land of Moses on one side. Her land was "without improvement," as they called it when a person left the trees standing and didn't burn off the brush or put in a fence to contain their property. A creek ran across the land. It was called Mill Creek, and it was low that fall.

A few mornings after Benoit's arrest, Belle sat beside the creek, sprinkled tobacco on the water, and prayed for the spirit world to show her a way through the hard times that were falling again on the Indian people. She prayed for Lettie, who, like Nola, had taken on the face of sorrow and was in a confused mental state. And Lettie slept, pale and absent, in the long hallway's blue light. Belle checked on her periodically. Each time, she found Lettie curled up like a child, her rich black hair falling across her face.

Belle was constantly occupied with her thoughts. At first

she believed it would be unwise for Lettie to visit Benoit. Her presence at the jail might add to the evidence against him and even implicate Lettie. But that day at the creek, when Belle thought more logically about the situation, she realized that white people rarely concerned themselves with Indian matters, that Indians were the shadow people, living almost invisibly on the fringes around them, and that this shadowy world allowed for a strange kind of freedom.

So, later that night, after Belle had prayed at the creek, she dreamed of a way to visit Benoit. In her dream, she saw a woman in a "tear" dress. It was her own grandmother, she supposed, from the straight, way the old woman stood.

Tear dresses were what the women wore during the removal of the Chickasaws from their Mississippi homeland. As they journeyed west, to Oklahoma, the women had been permitted to carry nothing sharp, no knives or scissors, not even their tongues; nothing with the potential for being a weapon against the American army that herded the uprooted, torn-away people from their beautiful, rich woodlands in the south. Because they had no scissors or knives, cloth was torn by their blunt teeth and ripped apart by their hands. The resulting straight lines and corners of cotton were fashioned into dresses. Those women who survived renamed the dresses, calling them "tear" dresses, meaning "to weep and cry."

When Belle woke the next day, she opened the trunk where she kept her finest things and sat before it, looking at her blue tear dress a while before she put it on. Then she took out Lettie's Osage clothing, woke her and helped her to dress. "We're going to see Benoit," she told her daughter.

In the streets, everyone stopped to look at them. They were a spectacle. Belle carried a woman's drum. Lettie wore the ribbon skirt and blanket shawl of her father's people. They carried tomatoes to Benoit. And the appearance of the two women pleased the spectators no end. They liked to romanticize the earlier days when they believed the Indians lived in a simple way and wore more colorful clothing than the complicated Indians who lived alongside them in the modern world. They believed the Indians used to have power. In the older, better times, that is, before the people had lost their land and their sacred places on earth to the very people who wished the Indians were as they had been in the past.

They walked past gamblers and drinkers, past Indians and whites who sat on the dry grass and popped open champagne bottles and drank the sweet liquor from cut crystal glasses.

In the middle of Main Street, the well-known cowboy and trick roper, Fraser, stood twirling his rope. He held it in white-gloved hands for a group of cheering onlookers. This day, he wore a spotless white hat and a red satin cowboy shirt with sequins sewn on the back and chest. His golden spurs— he wore them low—were roosterlike on his boots. Fraser had performed his rope tricks before King Ludwig of Belgium, the Queen of England, and for passengers on luxury liners between the continents.

In the shabby town, he alone looked brilliant. His clean white gloves stood out in the streets full of dark people in dark colors. But when the two Indian women passed by him, he stopped twirling his rope and watched them until they turned the corner toward the jail.

When Belle opened the door and entered the sheriff's office, Jess Gold stood up to greet her. Belle fixed him with her clear, honest gaze, put her hands on the desk and said, "It looks like you're in for a busy night. Whiskey's flowing like water out there, and all the bad dirty money's changing hands. There's a crime round every corner. Just waiting for you."

The sheriff laughed at her words. "Yeah, everyone's flush," but while he spoke to Belle, whom he'd known most of his life, his gaze wandered to the elegant sloe-eyed Leticia. He looked her up and down, from the moccasins she wore to the silver comb in her black hair. Her face looked thin and tired.

"What can I do for you women today?"

Belle shifted the drum under her arm. "We need to see your prisoner, Benoit." She eyed the sheriff and pulled herself up a little taller. "It's about his soul." She willed herself to disarm the man. "You know how we are about those things," she said and he knew she meant Indians.

The sheriff laughed. But then he turned serious. "You know, it's a hard thing, to lock up a man like Benoit."

"I understand," said Belle. She looked at him kindly. Jess

Gold took his keys off a hook. He led the women down a hallway to a cluster of cells.

Inside one of the cells, Benoit paced the floor. They were shocked at his appearance. His skin was pale and drawn across the bones of his face. His eyes were red-rimmed. He was thin, his silver belt was loose, and he smelled sour. When the sheriff unlocked the door, Benoit didn't so much as look up.

Jess Gold left, and Belle and Lettie sat down on the cot and watched Benoit. They heard the keys go down the hall. "He's got the keys," Belle said.

"What's that supposed to mean?" Lettie asked her.

Belle said, "I don't know. It just came to mind."

They tried to disguise their feelings about seeing Benoit in such poor condition. Lettie went to stand beside Benoit. She touched his arm.

"There's witnesses," Benoit said. "How could someone see what didn't happen?" The smell of burning, he thought, remained on his clothes. He had been struggling, in vain, to put things together, to make of events a pattern he might understand. He joined together a burned shoe with Sara's living foot. He'd matched up the mattress in the oak tree with his own sleeping body. He tried to pull it all back together again, as if he could rebuild his life, as if he could step backward in time.

Belle began to beat the drum.

A white man named Walter Bird was in the next cell, but since he was a prisoner and outside the law, Belle wasn't concerned about whether or not Bird heard snatches of the conversation between Lettie and Benoit. But Lettie wasn't so certain, and from time to time, she nervously looked the prisoner over. She kept her voice low. The sickly appearance of Benoit gave her strength, as if she could make up for his miserable condition.

Belle sang a song from her tribal home, a low-pitched song, full of sadness, the purpose of which was mostly to keep the sheriff from overhearing the conversation.

Lettie whispered to Benoit, "Who are the witnesses? Did they say?"

Benoit shook his head.

"Benoit, no one believes you did it." She caught his gaze

just a moment before he turned his face again to one of the little windows that were too small to allow a man to escape from prison. For a moment it looked like some of his fight had returned. "I was set up."

Belle's song filled the jail with a sweet, lonely melody. It reached Jess Gold, filling out report forms in the office. He put down his pen and listened to it.

"Benoit," Lettie said, "we heard that someone put in a claim for Sara's money." She watched his eyes well with tears on hearing Sara's name. Sara's picture, from his wallet, was beside the picture of Lettie on the sink. "I tried to find out who it was," she said, "but the clerk left me standing at the counter, went away, and came back with a lawyer. The lawyer asked why I wanted to know."

Benoit looked at her. "What did you say?"

"I told him, I want to file a claim."

Belle drummed louder, and began to sing, "Jesus loves the little children, all the children in the world, yellow, black, and even white, they are precious in his sight."

"The lawyer said to me, 'You're an Indian. You can't file a claim. Indians are not citizens and this claim would go through a United States court of law.'"

Benoit looked out through the window again. Lettie put her hand on one of his tense shoulders. "Even so, the court is going to appoint you a lawyer."

"I want to hire my own."

"You can't. Your money's tied up until you are acquitted."

He turned to face her directly.

She explained in a calm-sounding voice, "A husband suspected of murdering his wife can't lay a finger on their property. Besides, we're not legal, Benoit. The law doesn't apply to us." She glanced toward the cell that held Bird.

"You mean no one will represent me because they think I'm guilty?"

"No, that's not it at all."

"One of their own lawyers? That's justice?"

Belle closed her eyes. She drummed, and sang louder, over their voices.

"But I was framed!" He whirled away, angry, but then the sheriff returned and said their time was up, and Belle and

Lettie followed the sheriff down the passage. Lettie turned back, once, to look at Benoit.

Benoit watched them leave. Their wide dresses were square and solid like those of his grandmother, evicted from her land, exiled from her world, and this added to his misery, the whole history of his people. He sat down on the cot, bent with fatigue, feeling broken as a horse beaten with a stick by its rider.

The thing about D.C., Stace thought, was that it was a swampland. If it had not been for the persistence of the American government and the constant cutting back of the land, their world of marble and stone would be overgrown by all the green life that wanted to reclaim this place. As it was, he could see the plants grow taller each day. The recent infestation of Japanese beetles had not even decimated the vegetation. It was strong and alive. As everything on earth was alive, even earth itself.

He folded a letter and put it in his pocket. It was from Lionel Tall, one of the strongest of the Lakota medicine people in South Dakota. Tall was an intelligent man. He didn't read or write English, but he kept up with events throughout the world, particularly those relating to indigenous people. "Moccasin telegraph," the people joked, but the truth was, he traveled frequently and was always in touch with people about the problems in Indian country.

Tall's letter had been dictated and was written in an unfamiliar hand. Lionel Tall wanted to know if Stace had learned anything about the murders in Oklahoma. His letter stated that Indian people believed an innocent man was being held for the murder of two women and that the man had few rights, at least by interpretation of the law in Indian Territory, had not even been charged, and he wondered if Stace was looking into the situation.

They had heard, Tall said, that the Oklahoma state governor had sent in a special investigator in response to several requests, that the investigator had been arrested for taking bribes and then had been pardoned by the governor. The released man was known to have a prison record, and to have committed at least one murder before he worked in the governor's office. All of this added validity to the people's suspicions. Now, he wrote, one of the dead women's bodies was going to be exhumed to determine if it was a murder instead of a suicide. If so, charges would be brought against the man named Benoit.

Stace wondered if the letter had been opened and resealed, since it was sent to his work address. He examined the glue along the edge of the envelope.

Stace went to the window and looked outside. People walked past the building on the street below. They'd all been working late, as he had. It was the custom in Washington. It was beginning to get dark. His office light was on. He could see his own reflection in the window, and behind him, the file cabinets. He looked at himself in the glass. He was wearing the rimless glasses he wore when his eyes grew tired from reading reports. He ran his hand along his jawline. He needed a shave.

Ballard barged into the room. He was a large man with thick hair. He was the section chief, in charge of undercover operations. He walked briskly and with authority and set a stack of papers on the end of the desk. "Red Hawk." He sounded brusque.

Stace turned around.

"A new assignment for you. Arizona. A coal company," Ballard said.

Stace knew what Ballard meant. They'd had a special meeting that afternoon. But he interrupted "What about the governor's investigation in Indian Territory?" Stace asked. "Do you know anything about it?" It wasn't only the investigation he wondered about. He wondered why the people at the bureau were so sure that Grace Blanket was murdered that they would order an exhumation through the federal marshal in Oklahoma. According to the evidence, it was still suicide. And why weren't they looking into the explosion that killed her sister?

Ballard lifted an eyebrow.

"There was a special investigation," Stace said.

"If there was, I haven't heard it. Where do you get these things?" He sat down. "Besides, you can't call every hint of crime a conspiracy."

Stace looked at the large wide-shouldered man. Ballard's

white shirt was smudged with newsprint. But Ballard only shrugged.

"When it comes to Indians, we're always like gleaners, going in after the harvest is done."

"We can't do anything until there's a crime on Indian land. It's not our jurisdiction." He walked toward the door, paused, and said, "You always think no one's competent but you. The law down there's on it, Stace."

Stace looked carefully at Ballard. Ballard was sharp, he was known as a smooth operator. He'd pushed his way into other cases, his best talent being force. And he was above the law, or beneath it, Stace sometimes thought. He'd been known to fabricate evidence just to get involved in a case he had strong feelings about.

"What would you do if they weren't Indians?" Stace asked. He looked directly into the older man's eyes.

Ballard shrugged. "Nothing. Just like now." He looked back at Stace. "A word of warning. Don't get emotional about this, Red Hawk." Ballard went out into the dim hall and closed the door behind him.

Stace Red Hawk sat behind his desk until night fell and the streets were nearly empty of people. Then he took off his glasses, put on his black jacket, pushed his hair up into his hat and went down the dark hallway to the street.

There is a saying, that time heals all wounds, but time did not heal those who mourned the loss of Grace. Everyone missed her, and even if time could knit the wounds of sorrow, no scar tissue had woven itself across the gaping loss.

Nowhere was that wound more apparent than at the Gray-cloud house. Even when Nola was awake, she seemed asleep. She cried softly through the nights, dreaming of her mother. Something inside, a voice or a memory, buried deep, spoke to her and she answered, talking to what seemed like merely thin air to the others around her, but Nola said nothing to any of the skin and bone people in the household. Sometimes her own sobbing woke her. The women still watched over the dark, open-eyed girl who lived somewhere between the worlds of spirit and body. And the four watchers still surrounded the house.

Nola was even worse on the day that the old Indian people

went to the graveyard to witness the exhumation of Grace
Blanket. While no one told her about it, she felt that something was wrong.

Though Horse had heard about the grave looting from Mrs.
Inman, few other people knew about it. And only the elders
knew about the exhumation. It was too grisly for the younger
people, so on the day Grace's casket was to be lifted back up
above the ground, Horse stood alongside the other elders as
the ground with its few sprouts of corn was broken open. He
was concerned about the reaction to the missing body. Belle
Graycloud stood beside Moses. She wore a black shawl. Jim
Josh was on the other side of her, and his face was thin and
worried. And standing among the oldest people was Ona
Neck, who believed she was the only one who knew the
coffin was empty, except for Jack Billy.

Ruth Tate arrived late. Moses heard the car door slam. He
turned and saw his sister walking toward the burial ground.
She was followed by Tate. Tate looked awkward, carrying
his tripod and large, heavy-looking camera.

Moses put his hand on Ruth's arm and greeted her before
he turned and walked toward Tate, whose neck was thrust
forward like a turtle.

"No photographs," Moses said. His glance at John Tate's
face did not waver, but it chilled Moses to look at the small
man. He didn't like anything about him, not his hiding beneath the black curtain and behind the glass camera eye, not
how the little man ran horses without mercy until some of
them fell, not how he'd married Ruth and moved into the
home that had belonged to the Graycloud family.

"You go on home," said Moses. "I'll take Ruth home
later."

Tate carried the camera back to his car. Moses watched,
then he returned to the others, still standing, watching the
scene between Moses and his brother-in-law. They watched
Moses walk back toward them.

The people prayed and offered cornmeal. It was not a good
thing to disturb the dead. Above them, the water-filled clouds
passed through the sky. One of the oldest men offered tobacco and the smoke rose up toward the clouds.

As the ground was opened, the witnesses kept their eyes
lowered. Nor did they watch the undertaker open the lid.

They didn't want to see the face of death. But when the sheriff
said, "Hell," and turned away, and faced the trees along the
far horizon, they looked up and saw the empty casket. One
end of it had been shattered, as if it had fallen. There were
only a few clods of earth inside it, not a body, not the beads
or gifts Grace had been given for her journey to the world
beyond this one. Belle stared at the horrible sight of the missing dead. Her first thought was that someone had dug up the
body in order to hide the evidence. Moses thought that perhaps Grace's body had been taken to that museum in Con-
necticut that had bought up bodies and moccasins and baskets
only a few years earlier from local graverobbers.

Because they could think of nothing else to do, the box
was returned, let down on ropes.

Belle, Moses, and Ruth all rode home silently that day,
drove slowly away from the six feet of emptiness they left
behind.

That autumn, Nola was still without speech. While Ben and
Rena went off to Indian school, Belle kept Nola home in
order to keep an eye on her. The girl still slept with her eyes
staring beyond the heavens, and she was given to fainting
spells. Doctor Black had come to see what he could do for
her. When he found nothing wrong, he concluded that she
was anemic. He prescribed beef liver cooked in an iron skillet, but Nola turned up her nose at anything besides chocolate.

The Talbert Indian School was nearby, in town, and when
the children first began to attend, they were allowed to go
home on weekends.

On their first weekend home, Belle was happy to see them,
even though they already looked pale and less vibrant. She
wanted to know about school.

"They believe in single file," Ben said, as if that would
tell her everything she needed to know about the place, and
it almost did. Then he went upstairs and knocked on the door
of Nola's room. There was no answer. He opened the door
a crack and saw the girl's reflection in the mirror. She was
sitting, her hair loose around her shoulders, framing her small
face. He went inside, pulled the chair up to the bed, and

opened the box of French chocolate creams he'd bought for her.

That Friday night Nola devoured the candy in one sitting, and while Belle reprimanded Ben for giving in to the girl's whims, and while Nola was rocking herself with stomach pain, the town of Watona filled up with people. There was going to be an auction the next day. Drill sites would be bid on, and the town bustled. Young men stood on easygoing corners with their hands stuffed in their pockets. Men wore beautiful new snakeskin boots. Women with bobbed hair danced on the streets and twirled their long strands of cultured pearls. A white man and a black woman were married in the light of a lamp post with two dogs for witnesses. The justice of the peace inked the dogs' paws and stamped their prints on the marriage license while the newlyweds kissed. Three giggling Indian women in furs shared a jug with two young men. An old British woman, locally called Buckskin Liz, wore burlap and braids and carried a cat that was dressed in a formal black suit.

Jim Josh, the elderly Indian who was known for growing fine gardens, picked his way through the crowds to join the narrow-eyed Louise Graycloud and her white husband Floyd in the Dreyer's speakeasy where the Victrola played scratchy blues music and women, dressed to the nines, shook their shoulders and nearly danced away from the tables while their men ignored them.

Louise Graycloud looked as young and fresh as her daughter, Rena, that night. She smoked a cigarette, and she smiled at Jim Josh when he sat down at the table across from her. He wore a flannel shirt and suspenders. He yelled across the table to Louise, "Did you hear that I bought a car?"

"It's about time." She blew smoke out of her nose. "Your legs have been on the fritz as long as I can remember." She smiled and added, as an afterthought, "I didn't know you drove."

"Oh, I don't. You'd never get me behind a steering wheel."

Before she asked why he'd bought the car, Walker, the one whose heart was sound, joined them at the table, bringing along his usual bottle of orange soda pop.

Louise smiled up at Walker. "Hey there. Did you hear about Jim Josh's new car?"

Walker's voice was deep. "It's wonderful, isn't it? Everything is wonderful." He smiled. He felt good. He was debt-free. He asked Jim Josh, "How's your lumbago?"

Louise blew smoke up toward the ceiling. Floyd looked around the room, counting up how much whiskey and rum was being downed. He ran a business tally in his head, estimating that fourteen bottles were open on different tables.

"Did you hear about Tex Younger?" Louise leaned across the table. "The showman, you know. He found three missing Indian girls."

"No, I didn't hear that." Josh looked at her eyes. She was glancing about the room.

"They'd all been gone over a year and given up for dead. Some white man stole them." She sat up straight. She looked at Josh. "All of them were pregnant with his babies. They were only eleven and twelve years old. He was trying to wait for the statute of limitations to run out so when he went to court for the land papers, he wouldn't get charged with the kidnappings." She took a drink and tapped Floyd's arm. "Are you listening?"

"That's awful," Floyd said.

"Awful? Is that all you can say?" She sounded drunk. "It's the shits."

"Things are a mess," she said. "And Benoit's house, too." She looked at Jim Josh for confirmation, then sadly shook her head and looked down.

Walker joined in the conversation. "It's a bum deal."

Jim Josh nodded. He finished his drink, then stood up to leave. He said good-bye to Louise and hobbled in his shining black army boots in the direction of the unpainted shack where he lived by himself. He was relieved to get away from the smell of whiskey and smoke and the stories of true misery that were told over drinks. His wife, when she was alive, said he wanted flowers without their thorns, and it was still true, and though he'd had his own lion's share of misfortune, he was a cheerful man, even with his aches and sore bones.

As he walked home in the dark, Jim Josh sang a trail song. The last buzzing and creaking of insects out in the autumn fields stopped a moment. Everything, even the trees and land, listened to the old man's beautiful song.

That night, Michael Horse was halfway to town, thinking about the world that lived in fire when he heard the trail song. The song gave him a chill that went deep into his heart, and he knew it was Jim Josh. No one sang like Jim Josh.

Horse had a mission for going to town. More than one, really. Earlier, he'd had a terrible dream about an Osage man named John Thomas. In the dream, Thomas was shot beneath the famous auction tree in town, the tree where oil rights were going to be leased and bought and sold the next day.

Horse had knocked on Ona Neck's door and told her the dream.

She shook her head. "It seems like everyone's always getting hurt," she said, but she got right in the front seat of Horse's car and let him drive her the short distance over to his tepee so she could watch over the people's burning fire.

Horse's other reason for going toward town, the one that had prompted him to get a little shut-eye earlier in the evening, was the poker game. He was a mediocre player, but he loved the game, and the other men were always more than happy to deal him in since his powers at prophecy and divination never applied to his own life, especially as far as cards were concerned. So he planned to warn Thomas that he was in danger, then sit in on the game. Maybe he'd even take Thomas with him, he thought, so the men could all watch over him.

He drove slowly. As he rounded the bend in the road, the singing James Josh appeared in his car lights. Horse braked the car.

Josh walked up to the car. "Would you give me a lift home? My feet are killing me."

Horse opened the door for Josh, turned the newly painted car around, and drove back the way he'd come to Josh's shack. Just outside the door of Josh's house, Horse saw the shiny new car. It was yellow. "What's that?" Horse was surprised.

"Are you going blind or something?" Josh looked at Horse. "It's a car." Then, as if reading his mind, Josh said, "It's just for looks." He opened the car door, but before he stepped out, he asked Horse, "You ever hear of Edison, Thomas Edison? I've been reading about him. He's the guy who invented the electric light."

"That's good to know," Horse said. He was anxious to leave.

"He changed the world." Josh's eyes gleamed. "Say, why don't you stay a spell and let me fix you a cup of sassafras tea." He bent down and peered in the car at eye level. "It's fresh. I just dug the roots."

"Not tonight. I've got to go find John Thomas."

"Oh, I know him. Lives out on the flats, don't he?" said Josh. "Did you have a vision about him?"

Horse didn't want to say. He was anxious to leave, but he tried to sound cordial. He said, "Moses Graycloud's having a poker game in his barn. Do you want to go?"

"I'm getting too old for poker. And anything else that takes place after dark."

Horse laughed. There was time to reach Thomas, he was certain, since he'd dreamed of him far away on a path, but Horse was still anxious to leave, just in case. He said good-bye and drove away toward Watona.

When he arrived in town, the streets were filled with people. Most of them were from other places. They were talking and shouting and laughing, but Horse drove straight through Watona and out to the other side of town to look for Thomas's house. He was sure he knew where it was, but he drove and turned around and drove the roads again without finding the little brown place that was situated in a grove of pecan trees.

When he returned to town, Horse saw Floyd and Louise half staggering out of the speakeasy. Floyd was a friend of John Thomas, Horse remembered. He stopped the car and beeped the horn. "Floyd," he called out to get the young man's attention.

Their arms around each other, Floyd and Louise left the tangle of people and walked over to Horse's car.

"Floyd, aren't you a friend of John Thomas?"

Floyd nodded. He looked happy.

"Have you seen him tonight?"

"He was in the speakeasy earlier. Why?"

"I have a bad feeling about him. I think he's in danger."

Louise was saying something. Floyd could barely hear Michael Horse over the voice of Louise. "Come again?"

"John Thomas is in trouble."

But Louise was still talking drunkenly about Tex Younger and the kidnapped Indian girls he'd found near the border. Her clothes looked rumpled.

Horse tried to talk over Louise's voice. "Floyd, do you know how to find him? I have a warning for him."

"Yeah. Sure. I'll go out there right now, on the way home. I've got Moses's car."

Louise stopped rambling. She looked closely at Horse and said, "Say there, haven't your predictions been mighty wrong of late?"

"Don't mind her," Floyd said. "She's got too much under her belt."

"Hey!" Louise yelled out. "Wasn't your car gold?"

"Don't miss Thomas," Horse said to Floyd. He drove away. He was satisfied that Floyd, whose word was always good, would warn the Thomas boy that he should lay low, but even so, he went out looking for Thomas one more time. He drove back out to the pecan groves. Again, there was nothing there. It was as if the house had vanished. He drove through town again and took a few other side roads.

After Horse left Floyd and Louise, a young white man rode past the couple on a unicycle. His hat blew off his head. A gust of wind carried it right past Louise. The Indian woman who was with the cyclist—everyone could tell she was one of the Billy girls—laughed and chased the hat. She put it on her own straight hair and pretended she was smoking a cigar. A dog yapped and chased her. Everything was in motion, and when an enormous truck, full of oil equipment, passed by, everyone stopped to watch it. It was headed out toward the Phillips lease. The people cheered and waved as if it were J. P. Getty himself until the red taillights were no longer visible, and then they remained at silent attention, and when they turned back from watching where the truck had gone, they saw John Stink's dogs whining and acting strange, with their ears laid back. The excited dogs were a knotted mess of tails and muzzles.

"What's going on?" said Floyd, but as soon as he'd asked

the question, he saw that John Stink had collapsed in the dead center of his agitated dogs.

The man on the unicycle took one gander at old Stink's body, dropped his wheel, and ran to Doctor Black's house.

The doctor came right away, the young man just behind him, carrying the doctor's leather bag with its smelling salts and needles.

The dogs growled at the doctor a moment before they realized he meant well, then they stepped back out of his way and allowed John Stink's body to be examined.

"There's no pulse," the doctor said. He held a mirror to Stink's nose. He listened for the heartbeat. "I'm sorry." He looked up at the crowd. He shook his head. "I'm sorry." But again he listened to Stink's chest. Then he pronounced the old man dead, and when Stink was carried away to the morgue, the dogs followed his body.

Louise, in her drunkenness, sat on the curb and began to cry about who would take care of the dogs. She cried so hard, Floyd comforted her by saying that he would do it. "I will," he said. "Don't cry, honey. I'll take bones from the butcher shop up to Mare Hill every day. I'll do it."

"Are you sure?" Louise looked tender. She stopped crying.

"Yes. I'll take care of them."

"You sweetheart." She smiled into his eyes while he helped her up to her feet.

They walked to the car and Floyd drove home.

The oilman, Hale, remained in Dreyer's speakeasy late that same night. A man named Mardy sat beside him. Mardy was a rough-looking young man whose pink scalp was visible beneath his thin, wheat-colored hair. He hardly ever spoke.

"Walker is suicidal," said Hale. "I talked to him today. He said he wanted to kill himself."

Mardy shook his head as if to say what a shame it was how people let themselves give in to worry that way.

"I tried to talk him out of it," said Hale. He pursed his lips. "But he's hell-bent on it. If he commits suicide, you know, his life insurance won't be any good."

"That's a shame." Mardy shook his head again.

"It sure is." Hale was still a moment, watching Mardy,

letting his words sink into that pink scalp, then he asked Mardy, "Do you still like that Buick?"

Mardy said, "Don't I." He shook his head, thinking of himself driving the clean black Buick. It rode like a dream. "She's a great car."

"I think we can scratch each other's backs here." Hale leaned toward the young man and told him his plan. They had to rush, he said, before the man committed suicide and invalidated the insurance policy. It wasn't really murder, Hale convinced the rosy-cheeked young man, since it was just a matter of time before he was going to kill himself anyway. Hale said that really it would be a kindness to the poor unhappy Indian who wanted so much to die and be put out of his unhappy, lonely life. "After all," Hale said to Mardy, "Poor Walker has nothing to live for in all the world but a good swig of whiskey now and then."

Mardy said, "It's such a shame."

When Horse arrived at the Grayclouds' barn he tried not to worry about John Thomas. Floyd was trustworthy. Besides, the stinging words from the drunken Louise still rang in his ears. He himself began to doubt his prophetic abilities. And there was nothing more he could do.

The barn smelled strongly of horses and hay. The men were happy to see Michael Horse carrying his bag of coins. The younger ones stood up from their seats and shook his hand and nodded. The older ones met his eyes. They held back their glee that he was joining them. His presence gave them a better chance of winning or at least of breaking even. Then they settled back to the game. The lantern light threw long shadows across the barn.

Horse had borrowed money from Moses by the time Floyd stepped into the barn. Floyd looked nervous. He stood by the door. His blond hair had come free of its ponytail. He'd been drinking, and he held his hat in his hands. When Horse saw him, he knew something was wrong. He had a sinking feeling. He was certain that Floyd had come to tell them he'd found the body of John Thomas.

"Moses?" Floyd said to his father-in-law.

"Yeah." Moses turned toward him.

"Moses, can I talk to you?"

Moses went over to the door. "What is it, Floyd?" He could see that his son-in-law was extremely unhappy, and he smelled the whiskey on his breath.

Horse tried to listen to what Floyd was saying.

"Moses, it's John Stink. He died tonight."

Moses stared at him in disbelief. "What?" His eyes searched Floyd's face. "What happened?"

"I don't know. We thought maybe he had a heart attack. But someone said he might have been poisoned."

When Moses sat back down, he looked so pale that the other men laid down their hands and asked him what was wrong, and he said, "Stink died." Moses wanted to throw in his hand.

"It won't do John Stink no good if you suffer, Mose," said Ona Neck's boy. "We should finish out this game, at least."

Horse wondered if his dream had been about John Stink instead of John Thomas. But they played out that hand silently and then some of them dealt themselves another. What else was there to do, they reasoned, as they began to talk about old Stink. They wouldn't have been able to sleep no matter what. But they held to silence for uncomfortable periods of time, and by the end of the night, Horse was in debt to Moses, and Moses had bet a cow, a prime breeder, and to his relief, he didn't lose it.

By the time they cashed in their chips, it was morning, and Moses felt like crying as he locked the barn door, went into the darkened house, and up the stairs.

About that time, John Thomas drove at breakneck speed into Watona. He was drunk. His black hair was uncombed. His shirt hung out of his pants. He left his car engine running while he chased furiously through town yelling, "I know who killed Grace Blanket," and throwing silver dollars through the store windows, breaking the glass. He wept and screamed. He tore at his shirt like a madman. The people who lived in town closed their windows and pulled down their blinds, out of fear. John Thomas fired a gun, or at least someone did, and then, except for the idling of Thomas's car, the town went silent.

Floyd, who was home in bed with Louise wrapped around him in an alcoholic stupor, sat bolt upright in bed. "Oh, no!'' he cried out. In all the chaos that night, he had forgotten about the warning for John Thomas.

"Oh, honey, don't worry about it." Louise held him tighter. She reminded him that Horse hadn't been on the money with his predictions for quite some time.

"I can't be sure of that," said Floyd. She tried to kiss him, but he moved away, pulled on his pants and, against her will, he drove out to the flats in the dark of night.

Floyd remembered how to reach the small brown house, but for the life of him, he could not find it. Finally—he must have driven past it several times—he found the place. The door was wide open. Floyd went inside. There was an empty bottle on the table, and a stack of papers and magazines, but Thomas wasn't in, and even his car was gone, so Floyd left a note on the table, then turned around and drove to town. He drove on the streets for an hour or so, until finally he found Thomas's car. It was still running and abandoned beside the road. The keys were in the ignition, and the door was unlocked. Floyd killed the motor, walked around the streets for a while, then he gave up and returned home.

A heavy silence was in the air when the hot sun rose that next morning. Floyd, who hadn't slept well that night, was taking Ben rabbit hunting and camping some distance away. They planned to be gone for a few days. When Floyd's friend from the Blue Store pulled up and honked, the two of them climbed into the back seat of the car. Floyd talked mostly about the death of John Stink, but he was thinking about John Thomas.

The burial of John Stink occupied the minds of only a few people. It was an urgent matter, especially with the heat, since at that time the mortician still respected Indian customs which meant that Stink hadn't been embalmed, and his body was beginning to decompose. However, it seemed like the old man was still somewhat warm when Joe Billy prepared the body for burial. He washed the heavy old man, and rubbed him with sage and meal. The coffin was painted black, as was the custom, and late that afternoon, when the worst of the heat had subsided, Reverend Billy returned to the funeral home, wrapped John Stink in a long winding sheet and, with the three young pallbearers he hired for the task, took

the casket to the church on a wagon pulled by four white
horses.

Because of the heat, only a few people attended the funeral. Jim Josh was in pain with swollen feet, so he didn't
show up, and most of the other people remained at home
suffering from the weather, spraying cold water on their skin,
and chewing ice they chipped off ten-pound blocks that sat
in puddles of water. None of the younger people knew Stink
anyway, personally, that is, though they knew he was a dog-
loving hermit who liked cigars and who lived on a hill above
the golf course with his dogs. They'd passed him now and
then, and seen his pots and pans hanging from tree limbs.
There was a rumor that the old man was a millionaire, and
in fact, so many newspapers carried the tale of his money
that John Stink's legal guardian received hundreds of letters
with offers of marriage from women all over the country.

The funeral took place late that afternoon when the sun
shone through the stained glass window of Jesus and his
lamb, and cast light across the wooden pews. Belle and Moses attended. Belle was calm and silent. Moses studied the
bones and wrinkles of Stink's lifelike old face one last time
before the big, mute man was gone forever from his sight.

The three young men were there only for the pay Reverend
Billy had offered them to be pallbearers. They sat in the last
pew. They were uninterested in both the goings-on of the old
Indian ways and the newer Christian ways.

Martha Billy stood behind her husband. Her blond hair
was pulled back into a severe bun. Even in the heat she wore
a black dress that was buttoned all the way up her neck.
Moses saw that her eyes were red from weeping. Those swol
len eyes endeared her to Moses. He had always believed that
Martha had icy distances beneath her handshaking sweetness.

John Stink's dogs also were there, sitting like sentinels in
the rays of gold light that fell over them inside the church.
They sat on their bony haunches and were attentive.

Moses would miss the man who'd worn the red babushka
on his head, old Ho-Tah-Moie, which was Stink's real name.
In English it meant Roaring Thunder. John Stink, or rather
Ho-Tah-Moie, had contracted a childhood disease that had
spread from the weak, coughing settlers to the Indian popu-

lation. Earlier, the Indians had called it the "Pig Sickness," thinking that the settlers' pigs were instrumental in the spread of the disease, but later it was named scrofula. It was a form of tuberculosis, and it was characterized by skin lesions and swollen glands. The illness was accompanied by a decaying smell, which was why the agents from Washington had renamed the man "John Stink."

"And so now we commit back to earth this man, John Stink, whose real name was Roaring Thunder, a child of God," said Reverend Billy. "He's a man who lived close to God under that tree up there on Mare Hill, a man cursed by disease and loved by dogs." The reverend paused, searching for words to describe the man he'd never known very well, and he added, "He was a kind man," which was true, and was also the highest compliment one Indian could pay to another.

Then the white horses pulled the black coffin away from the church. By that time, a red light was falling on the land. Reverend Billy held the reins. Next to him sat Belle and Moses. While they sang, Moses held the drum and beat out the slow rhythm of a mourning song. The young pallbearers in the back did not know the song, so they hung their legs over the end of the wagon, listened, and watched the road rush by beneath their scuffed boots.

Belle had been torn that day between wanting to see John Stink return to his mother the earth, and her worries about Nola. Her concern for the girl won out, and so Belle had asked Joe Billy to take her only as far as the turnoff toward her home. When he stopped there, he asked, "Are you sure I can't take you up to the door?"

"No. This is fine." She climbed down from the wagon. She looked back as if to reassure him. "It's fine, really," and in her dark dress she walked away. She turned once and looked back at the black casket rattling across the earth.

When Belle reached her house, the watchers were standing in the first evening light. Belle nodded at them as she walked up the path. She wondered about them, when they slept, or if, like horses, they rested on their feet. Though she knew the Hill People, these men were strange to her. Their ways were kept secret. Belle was perplexed by their mysterious presence, though she admitted that they lent a feeling of safety to the house.

Inside the kitchen, Belle chipped ice into four glasses, filled them with water, and took them outside for the watchers. The last of her honeybees were flying around the vines near the door. She could hear them.

Belle went heavily up the dark staircase and into the room where Nola slept. Lettie sat beside the girl. Nola was no longer vomiting, but she was bony and gray, asleep in the bed with her face turned to the wall and the whites of her eyes exposed. The room smelled closed in. Belle went to the window to see if it would open wider, and from the bedroom window she caught a glimpse of the slow white horses carrying John Stink's black casket up the cemetery road. Stink's dogs followed.

The wagon passed the Christian cemetery first, with its angels and lambs. The sky was red. The oak leaves were dry. Once, the wagon stopped for a slow group of migrating turtles. It was their last journey before they would dig themselves beneath the ground and hibernate. They crossed the road, with the dwindling sun on their shells. When the last turtle was safe, the men drove on to the older burial grounds. Moses and Joe Billy were still singing the deep, slow song, and as the sun lowered, the shadows of the horses grew longer on the ground. Behind the dogs, a coyote began to follow.

The burial mounds marked the place where the ancestors turned to dust. The men removed their hats in respect before they took shovels from the wagon and opened the hallowed ground. Moses spread tobacco on the earth. The first sounds of evening insects joined with the sound of shoveling. There was a deep fireline between hills and sky.

In the old days, people were buried seated, facing east, with stones piled over them. An opening was left, like a window, in front of the dead person's face. It allowed the travelers in death's world to see the dark road they had to follow. By 1922 that tradition was forbidden by American law; the Americans were afraid of the invisible lives of germs and bacteria that claimed human flesh as their own territory. But the Indians found ways to put the old customs together with the new, and that evening the men dug a deep, narrow hole that would allow the casket to stand on end. Then, they removed the coffin lid, tied Stink in with a rope, and slid the casket in so that John Stink was standing and facing east.

Reverend Billy unfolded a square of red cloth and from inside it, he took out an eagle feather. While he waved the feather across the gravesite and prayed in Creek, the men stood, looking down. When he prayed in English, they all said, "Amen," and set to work piling up the mound of stones. They left a little opening, and before they got back in the wagon, Moses and Joe Billy looked in at the old man's closed eyes. They said good-bye, speaking to him through their hearts.

It was dark. Moses lit a lantern. As the men drove the wagon away, Joe Billy noticed that the dogs were not following. "Kuma," he called out to a large one. "Come here." He whistled. He held the lantern off to his side in order to see them. A few of the dogs went over to Billy, their tails between their legs, but when the wagon started once again toward town, the dogs returned to the mound and lay down on the ground, and before the wagon had gone even a few more yards, they began to whine and scratch at the earth as though they were going to dig up old John Stink's body. One large dog moved a stone aside. The alarmed men stopped the wagon. They were afraid the dogs would expose the face of John Stink, and that the coyote, who watched from beyond the mounds, would gnaw Stink's head down to bone, or that grave-robbers like the ones who had stolen Grace's body would make off with the remains of John Stink.

Joe Billy got down from the wagon. "Kuma!" He walked toward the dog. But this time not even one of the dogs came forward. They skulked away. One of them growled at him. He called again and slapped his thigh and tried to cajole them, but he was forced to give up. Still, in order to protect the old man, Joe Billy went over to the mound and rolled some larger stones across it, stones the dogs couldn't move, and then he drove the wagon away through the night with no trail of dogs following behind it, just the sound of horse's hooves and the lantern light on their white rumps.

Even in the dark, it was still hot. The frogs were chirping in the distant water. From the direction of the graveyard, the riders heard the coyote wail. Once again the wagon passed by the stone angels. Their wings spread white and eerie in the moonlight. Moses held the lantern. Its light fell along the sides of the dirt road.

Not that far from the cemetery, in the light of his lantern, Moses caught sight of something that looked like a man's figure lying curled up beside the road. "Stop!" he said and he jumped down and examined the body. Moses's hands were shaking. The black-haired man was on his stomach, face buried in the ground, his shirt tangled around him. Moses bent down for a close look. "Oh hell," he said. "It's John Thomas."

Thomas had been shot through the neck. The wound was a horrible and violent gape in the man's throat.

The young men leapt out of the wagon. At first, being young, they only wanted to see the face of death, but then, with a heavy sadness, they loaded Thomas into the wagon, and they rode back to town, carrying the still body, in silence. They passed by oil fields and the black woodlands, passed by farms and white-faced cattle, and by a bed where moonlight flooded the sheets, and it was when they rode past the sleeper that they saw the red glare in the sky and smelled heavy smoke, and the snorting horses smelled it and began to shy. Their instincts tugged them to return to the graveyard, to run away from the hot tongues of fire that were by now fully visible rising up from the horizon. The coyote that had followed the funeral procession began to howl, and in the distance, toward the fire, another coyote answered. The men in the wagon looked at each other. Moses's face was lit up in the lantern light. Joe Billy, looking at Moses, said, "What's going on?" as if Moses might have an answer, a key to some of the events transpiring around them, but he just shook his head.

From the house, Belle Graycloud watched the fire blaze above the burning trees. She was nervous. She would turn from the window, then go back to it, her breathing quick and shallow. The fire burned closer. She heard the mournful sound of coyotes. The land pulled into itself, and the air was tense and restless. Birds were screaming in their nests. Belle's skin prickled with fear.

The fire spread rapidly. Volunteers from Watona drove

water trucks to the burning groves. They watered down blankets and laid them over the ground, but it was already out of control. It moved along like a snake with a will of its own, finding its way around the roads and across the water to another stand of trees where the crackling, blowing embers ignited the ancient forest that had been there since long before any living person could remember. And Belle knew what was burning and she feared the loss of animals and plants that were housed only in that place.

By then, the volunteers hoped for no more than just to stop the fire before it reached the plains where it would sweep furiously through autumn grasses and on out to the oil fields, and beyond to the homes that were built of dry wood. They worked rapidly, digging trenches and furrows and wetting down the outer edges of forest.

From the front porch Belle watched the brown rising smoke obliterate the moon and stars. She heard the roar of the fire coming closer and the sparking smell filled her nostrils, and she knew she had to act before it came too close. She called out, "Lettie!" and before Lettie could run down the stairs, the older woman had already run out to the well, filled two buckets with water, and run with them out to the dry hay that was at close range to the fire. The four watchers joined her, running across the land with buckets and throwing water on the sides of the barn. Lettie filled buckets at the well. Her hands were shaking. Rena watched in horror. "Rena!" Lettie screamed at her, and the girl jumped, then joined them, and half filled one of the buckets.

"Where's Louise?" Belle screamed at Lettie.

"I don't know," Lettie yelled back as she ran to the barn to lead the horses closer to the house. The horses were tense, their heads pulled upward, rearing, their muscles rippling. All of them were drenched in sweat and heaving, with burning, tearing eyes.

The fire continued to burn for some time, like a torn, ragged edge of red cloth moving along the horizon, and then, miraculously, it turned a corner and began to die down. The watchers talked loudly among themselves in the old language no one else understood, and Belle stopped pulling the buckets of water up from the well. She wiped her forehead with the hem of her skirt. She sat down. Lettie, exhausted, leaned over the well. Rena began to cry. The horses whinnied.

That was when they heard it, heard the great eerie sound, the frightening loud shrill of crickets, it had to be, a song so loud and resonant it was heavy as water around them, and it contained the night in its shriek.

Belle looked around her, trying to find the source of the noise, and then from the upstairs bedroom Nola screamed. Belle bolted inside, followed by the others, and when she reached the stairs she saw them, thousands of dark crickets that moved like a single mind up the staircase, as though they were on a path. Belle ran up the stairs, crushing some of them as she went. When she reached the bedroom, the black insects were swarming over Nola's sobbing body. The girl was pressed against the wall, paralyzed with fear. She looked tiny and afraid, and tears were running down her face.

Belle was horrified; the crickets filled the room like a spreading dark stain of blood. The shrill sound of them hurt her ears. She brushed them away while Nola wept, half crazy, her thin body racked with sobs. Belle took hold of Nola and shook the crickets off the hem of her sleeping gown. Lettie ran upstairs, shaken, past Rena, carrying a bucket of carbolic acid mixed with water, and she sprinkled it on the jumping crickets who shriveled with pain and ran crazily back down the stairs to escape. Belle untangled the insects from Nola's thick black hair. They fell out, down the girl's shoulders, and scurried away, and Nola went into a frenzy, as if she'd been broken all the way through her body to her bones. She beat her fists on the bed and tore her sheets. For a moment, she looked demonic, possessed. Belle was afraid of her and jumped back, and then Nola took the pistol off the chest of drawers and aimed it at her own forehead. Belle ran for the gun, knocking Nola out of the way and the pistol fired through the window, shattering the glass. Then it was still, and even the crickets were shocked into silence by the blast.

Nola collapsed on the floor, crying. Belle knelt at her side and smoothed the girl's hair back from her forehead. "It's all right," she said, soothing the weeping girl. "It will be all right." She held Nola against her chest and closed her arms around her. A history of fear and sorrow had come undone in the child. Belle caressed the girl's black hair as she held her tight and rocked her.

One of the watcher's knelt down beside Belle and Nola. He put his dark hand against Nola's sobbing back. Almost immediately, the girl stopped crying and she turned to him. For a long moment, their eyes met. Nola became still and the taut muscles of her face softened. The man had kind eyes. He looked at the girl and she returned the gaze.

Belle could not decipher what was spoken in that glance, but it seemed to her a life had been exchanged, a shared world of grief and love, and in that instant Belle thought this man was Nola's father, the man whose identity had been kept secret. She looked at him and their eyes also met and spoke.

That night, Nola's sorrow began to drop away. For the first time since her mother's death, she slept peacefully with her eyes closed. Now and then she woke up, walked to the window, and looked out at the watcher.

It was late when Moses returned home. He was weary and smudged with ash. The pallbearers had stopped along their way to help fight the fire, he told Belle. "What's even worse than all that burned ground, we found John Thomas on the cemetery road. He was dead. A gunshot wound."

When Louise came home that night, she was drunk and giddy. Belle met her at the door, and with a fierce eye said, "I am never speaking to you again as long as I live."

"Why, what did I do?"

"The world is falling apart and all you do is go to parties."

That night, after the men who buried John Stink went to their beds tossing and turning with visions of John Thomas's bloody throat, the mongrel dogs at the gravesite whined and pawed away at the earth. One dog scratched a hole in the ground. Another pushed a stone away from the mound, and from inside the grave, John Stink felt the rock thump earth. He began to work his arms out of the ropes that held him. If Houdini could do it, the old man thought to himself, so could the soul of old Ho-Tah-Moie. He struggled free of the rope, and he moved earth until finally one of his hands found its way through to air where it was licked by the happy dogs.

The dogs were the only witnesses to the miraculous return of John Stink. They were overjoyed that their master rose up from the grave, and when the old man's pockmarked face emerged, they yapped and licked him, and with their aid, Stink managed to pull himself up out of the coffin, climbing up the rope, using it as a ladder. Resurrected, he examined himself. His hands were raw, the thick nails broken. He was dressed like a ghost, all right, in a winding sheet. His joints ached. But for a man who had just been in death's handhold, he was in fairly decent shape.

Something burned in the air. Hellfire, thought the old man, wondering if this place was hell. But something was not quite right. This world with its brimstone was a silent place. The dogs' yelps did not reach John Stink's ears. The insects didn't sing. Stink clapped himself on the head about the ears, and shook his head back and forth, but it was to no avail. He could hear nothing, not even so much as his own heartbeat. The world of the dead was a silent place.

He examined the opening he'd climbed through. It was, indeed, too small for the emergence of a mortal man. He sat on the ground in the midst of his dogs and tried to remember what had happened. He was in Watona, he recollected, and had just caught a glimpse of Louise Graycloud when he went dead and black. He looked his body over. He wasn't shot, so it must have been heart failure that killed him, and now here he was, a ghost, destined to wander a soundless limbo. He guessed that in the spirit world men had no need to hear what they had left behind on earth.

So this is what death was like, he thought, as he wrapped the white sheet tighter around his naked body. Out of habit more than anything else, he started out for his home up on Mare Hill above the golf course.

Stink was already wiser, he thought, since now he knew that spirits wander freely among the mortals on earth. Now he understood why his dogs used to bark at what he'd thought was nothing and why they chased after shadows no living person ever saw. They had vision keen enough to see the dead.

The dogs, who couldn't tell the difference between ghosts and mortals, wagged their tails and followed Stink home. He was surprised that he still wanted a cigar.

* * *

An unsuspecting Michael Horse was asleep in his tepee when Jess Gold and a deputy woke him.

"What can I do for you there, Jess?" Horse asked as he climbed out the open flap. He arranged himself. He straightened up his stiff shoulders and brushed a few loose ends of hair back away from his face.

"We need to ask you some questions," the sheriff said, and right away Horse had a bad feeling. In bits and pieces, a dream about his own capture and imprisonment came back to him.

The sheriff opened a pair of handcuffs.

"What's going on?" Horse asked the question matter-of-factly. Although he knew Gold, he was afraid that if he resisted the lawmen or showed his fear, they would injure him. Jess Gold handcuffed him. The deputy went inside Horse's tepee and returned with a rifle and a handgun, which he thought to be murder evidence. Inside, also, he'd found a gas mask from the Great War and a trunkful of useless notebooks. And then, to Horse's horror the deputy began to kick the fire out. Horse's reaction was so strong that the sheriff, who wanted to be sympathetic to Indian people, told his deputy to stop, then he went over to stir the coals himself, thinking Horse had hidden something in the fire. He turned over a burning log, then poked about in the center of the coals.

"It's not my fire," Horse said. His voice sounded calm.

"What do you mean?"

"I only tend it. This is the fire of the Indian people."

Sheriff Gold looked into Horse's face. Horse looked serious and the expression in his eyes was so sincere that the young sheriff said, "Okay, Horse, but I have to arrest you. What should we do about the fire?"

"I do not know why you are arresting me, but if you will go over to Ona Neck's and bring her back here, she will stay with the fire until we straighten this thing out."

"All right." The sheriff left Horse with the deputy and drove off.

Horse asked the deputy why they were arresting him.

"For the death of John Thomas."

The sheriff returned a short while later with Ona in the car.

"Everybody's getting thrown in the calaboose," Ona said as she got out of the car. Her lips were set tight and she looked resigned.

On his way to town, Horse, not realizing the trouble he was in, was more worried about his predictions than about his situation with the law. His premonitions seemed to be getting him into trouble of late. In the past, when he foretold a tornado, the Indian people hid in their potato cellars and played cards by lantern light until the storm passed over, and they'd always followed his tips on mule races and lightning strikes, but since he'd been off about the weather, they hardly paid him any mind at all, and now there was the death of John Thomas to contend with. Even though he hadn't been able to find the man, Horse felt guilty that he'd trusted Graycloud's son-in-law to pass the warning along while he himself had played poker.

Jess Gold placed Horse in the cluster of cells on the other side of the building from Benoit, in the women's side of the jail. Horse was tired and was distressed about being arrested, and he wanted to sleep, but he had quite a reputation, and the women that had been arrested that night, two of them for impropriety, were happy to have the old seer in their midst and they plied him with questions. "How many children will I have?" one of them asked him. Another asked, "Will I go to New York or will I strike oil?"

"Yes, you'll all be rich and famous," he said through the bars. "Now let me sleep."

Since Michael Horse was a hermit, no one might have missed him or known he was in jail if it hadn't been for Belle Graycloud.

That next morning, early, when the charred earth still smelled like smoke, Belle had dragged herself up from her bed and gone to Watona to deliver eggs to an old woman who lived by the railroad depot. She carried with her a bag of mints for Jim Josh, and a parcel of books and playing cards for Benoit.

On her errands, she walked rapidly past the depot, at her usual pace, but then something stopped her in her tracks. Belle stood dead still a moment, turned and looked again at what she hoped was an error of vision. What met her eyes was a truck filled with eagle carcasses. They were golden brown birds, with the blue-white membranes of death closed over their eyes. For what seemed like a long time, Belle stood rooted to the spot. Her marrow went cold. She stared at the dead, sacred eagles. They looked like a tribe of small, gone people, murdered and taken away in the back of a truck. The hunters were busy beside the truck, counting the eagles.

There were three hundred and seventeen carcasses in all.

Belle hardly remembered what happened next, except that she dropped her eggs on the road, threw down her bags, and ran toward the truck, yelling at the men.

At first, they tried to humor her. She was unmoved by their smiles. She was insane, they thought. She screamed, "You naholies! What have you gone and done this time?" She began removing the dead eagles from the truck. She placed one on a plot of grass. She was crying and talking in a language they didn't understand. They tried to stop her, but even three men could not hold her back. She was ruining the eagles they planned to sell, undamaged, as souvenirs.

"They're just birds," one of them said, trying to reason with the hysterical old woman, but at his words, she became even more agitated.

"What have you done?" She charged at them like a goat and she kicked at their legs. She broke a window out of the truck and when she pulled her bare hand back, it was bleeding from the cuts. Again, the men tried to pull her away but again she charged them, screaming and attacking, until they were forced to hold her down on the hard ground. She wailed and cursed while they held her. She spit in their faces and hissed as they talked over how to keep the pesky old woman from assaulting them and their cargo. Finally, two of them wrapped her in wool blankets, her arms at her sides, and rolled her up tight. Then they tied the entire blanket roll with rope, lifted her up, and drove her to the jail. Only her face was exposed and she continued to spit and scream at them like an old witch, her lead-gray hair tangling around her face.

One of the men was considerate. He had picked up the three eggs that hadn't broken, the bag of mints, books, and the deck of playing cards. He left these with the sheriff for the wild old woman, and then the men drove back to the truck and continued to pack the eagles in paper, ice, and

woodchips for the long journey by train to taxidermy shops
in New York, London, and Philadelphia.

Jess Gold shook his head at Belle. She was still on the
floor, wrapped up in the blanket. Her hair was wild around
her face and her sharp eyes glared up at him. "I don't know
what to do with you," he said to Belle, and when he unrolled
her from the blankets, he jumped back, afraid she would
strike out.

"I don't know," he repeated. He shook his head again.
Belle hadn't exactly committed a crime. She was a public
nuisance, maybe, or a disturber of the peace, and even though
he'd heard rumors that she was hell on wheels if you crossed
her the wrong way, it wasn't her customary behavior. "I just
don't know," he said again.

Belle jumped up to her feet. "Arrest me!" she said. "I
dare you." But the mild-mannered sheriff didn't want to lock
the old woman up, so instead he sent word to Moses that
Belle had attacked some hunters, and if Moses really wanted
a wildcat like Belle enough to come pick her up, he could
have her. "It wouldn't surprise me one bit if he leaves you
here," Jess Gold said to Belle. "And you sit in that chair
and don't budge an inch until he gets here, you hear?"

By accident, or providence, Belle saw Michael Horse being walked across a small courtyard that morning at the jail.

Horse was conducting his morning prayers. Since one of
the deputies, Willis, was half-Indian himself, and since Gold
wanted to treat them well, they were lenient about the religious practices of Indians.

Despite the sheriff's orders to remain motionless in her
chair, Belle ran over to the door and cried out, "Horse! What
are you doing out there?"

He blinked at her.

"Say, what's going on?" She walked up to him, the sheriff
close behind her.

"I foresaw the death of John Thomas. Now they think I'm
the one who did it."

Belle turned to the sheriff. "You ought to know better than
that."

By the time Moses arrived, she had calmed down, her
hand was wrapped in gauze, and she walked around the of-

fice rumpled and with disheveled hair. She looked like the devil, at least that's what the sheriff thought.

That chance meeting was probably what saved Michael Horse. When Moses arrived, the first thing Belle told him was that Horse had been arrested for the murder death of John Thomas that had occurred on Monday night.

"About what time did the death occur?" Moses asked the sheriff.

"I can't say. Maybe between midnight and two."

"Well, Horse played poker with us until at least four that morning." Unlike Belle, Moses remained calm in a crisis, so the sheriff was inclined to listen to him.

"Are you sure?" the sheriff asked.

"Yes. I'm sure. He drew the dead man's hand, aces and eights, somewhere around two. You know why they call it that, don't you. It's what Wild Bill Hickok had in his fist the night he was killed."

"Just answer my question. Can you prove that Horse was there?"

Moses thought a minute. "Yes, I have IOU's right here. His hands are clean." Moses reached into his pocket and took his wallet out. The IOU's were dated and they were written unmistakably in the fancy Asian calligraphy Michael Horse had perfected during the Boxer Rebellion in China twenty years earlier. The deputy, looking over the sheriff's shoulder, said, "Yes, that's Horse's writing, all right. I recognize it from the papers in his trunk."

The sheriff studied the artistic script, and he said, "All right, if you two swear by it." He thought it unlikely that Horse would leave.

The deputy returned with Horse.

"But don't you go anywhere," the sheriff told the old man, as he handed him back his guns, and he swore to him that from now on he was going to watch his every step.

As they left the jail, Moses, by force of habit, handed Belle a red umbrella. By habit of her own, she opened it. A fiery circle of red light bathed her face and she looked young, and that look went straight to Horse's heart. He tried not to show the pang of love he felt for her.

She sat beside him in the car. He noticed that her clothes smelled as they always did, earthy and fresh. Horse hadn't heard about the eagle hunters yet, and he felt sort of cocky that poker and Belle GrayCloud had saved his life. He stole a sidelong look at her, but he spoke to Moses, "I guess I have no choice now but to make good on those notes." The two men laughed. They were relieved. But Horse was already thinking about how he was going to pack up his tepee and cooking pots and his trunkful of journals, put them in his car, and move far away from the human world, move to where no mortal soul could keep a watch on him or hear any words of prophecy that he might speak. He wanted to live closer to the land. And he wanted to escape the bad feeling in Watona these days, or "Talbert" as the naholies were calling it. All this was in his head before he noticed that Belle was unusually silent and did not look quite right, and then he saw the bandage on her arm. "What were you doing in jail, anyway?" he asked her.

Moses answered for her. "She attacked some hunters." It wasn't unusual for Belle. She'd put up quite a fight for bears not long ago, though she hadn't been arrested for it. "Again," Moses added. "I'm proud of her."

Belle was silent. She could find no words to say what had to be spoken.

"What happened to your hand?" Horse asked, but when she tried to find a language that would tell what she had seen, she began to cry like a child, and while she cried, she told them about the eagles.

Moses hardly believed his ears. He slammed on the brakes. "What did you say?"

Belle cried harder. Her eyes were red and swollen. Both men stared at her. And when it sank in, what she was telling them, they were livid with rage and with fear. Moses looked at her a good long time, his jaw tightening. "Where are those hunters?" He sounded so calm that Belle was afraid.

"I'm warning you, Moses, don't interfere. The law's on their side."

"Where are they?"

She hesitated, then said, "They were at the depot."

"The law is on their side because it's their law." He turned the car and headed for the train depot.

Belle put her hand on Moses's arm and left it there while he drove. As they neared the depot in the still, heavy heat, they could see the hunters working in their shirtsleeves. They piled the eagles into wooden boxes. The boxes contained dry ice. When they lifted the wooden lids, smoke rose up, erasing the hunter's faces. In that wisp of gas, they looked foreign and strange, like visitors from another world, a world that eats itself and uses up the earth.

The three of them stayed inside the car. They watched the men wrap eagles in burlap and place the wrapped carcasses on the woodchips above so the ice would not sear the valuable feathers. The windshield was dirty.

Moses's face went dead and empty. Belle's eyes turned silver as knife blades, and Horse looked smaller than usual. None of them said a word. There was nothing that could be spoken, with the rage and pain falling like lead through their bodies. It pulled them down with it. They rolled up the windows of the car, as if the glass would protect them from the hunters and their strange world.

Without a word, Moses backed up the car, turned and drove home on the red road. They drove past Grace Blanket's boarded-up place. The rusted bedframe sat forlornly outside the empty house.

When Moses pulled up outside his own house, Benoit's lean horse, Redshirt, was standing alone and all ablaze in the corral beside the barn, the sun on its coat. Horse waited for Moses to walk Belle to the door, and while he waited, he absentmindedly watched Redshirt pace back and forth. But his mind was on other things.

Moses left Belle in the care of Lettie and Louise. They were alarmed at how bad she looked. They didn't know about the eagles.

"Is she sick?" Lettie asked her father.

"I'll explain later," he said on his way out the door. He looked at Belle once, to be sure she was all right.

"Go on now," she told him. "Take Horse home. And stay away from the train station." She looked meek and tragic. But the moment Moses drove away, she went on a rampage in her house. She stomped into the kitchen and took a burlap bag off a hook and ran up the stairs. Louise and Lettie exchanged glances and followed her.

"What are you doing?" Louise demanded.

Belle ignored her daughter. She was in her bedroom. She

packed the sacred heart of Jesus candle inside the bag, a bundle of cedar and sage, a vial of holy water from the sacred spring, and an eagle prayer feather.

Lou repeated her question. "What are you doing? What happened to your hand?"

But Belle was a headstrong woman, and not to be deterred, and in the sharp silence, Louise noticed too, that the older woman dragged her leg.

"Why are you limping?" Louise asked.

Belle said nothing.

"Does it hurt?" Louise grew shrill. "Answer me. What's going on?"

But Belle didn't answer.

Louise went downstairs and brought up a cup of hot coffee for her mother. "Why's she mad at us?" She asked Lettie, as if the old woman couldn't hear. "God, she's stubborn."

"It's not us. She's just mad."

Lou put the coffee on the prayer altar in front of Belle. "Here, drink this." Belle rifled through her bureau drawers. "The books say it's good for shock. After accidents, Mama."

Belle looked Louise in the eye, then turned and said to Lettie, "Tell her it's too hot."

Louise went back downstairs.

"What is it, Mama?" Lettie wanted to know.

Louise returned a while later with a glass of water.

"Tell her it's too cold," said Belle. She limped back and forth across the room. She packed a cardigan sweater in the bag. Before the girls could ask her why she needed her sweater, she went downstairs, through the kitchen, and down the other set of steps into the dank potato cellar.

Up on Crow Hill Moses and Horse walked over to where the skinny old woman, Ona Neck, fanned the smoke of the fire.

"Did you know George Washington never told a lie?" she asked them.

Moses shook his head. "No, Mrs. Neck, I didn't know that."

Ona scrutinized their faces. "Say, what's wrong with you two?" They didn't answer. She examined their eyes. She asked Horse, "How'd you get out of the clink so fast?"

Horse stirred the fire, but didn't answer.

"What were you in for anyway?"

"I'll drive you home," he told her, ignoring the question.

Beside him in the car, Ona looked in his direction and said, "You know, I'm with you."

"What?" He glanced at her.

"Hey! Watch where you're going, son."

"Sorry." Horse turned his attention back to the road.

"I agree with you, Benoit looks guilty as all get out, but he didn't do it. Someone wants to pin it on him."

Horse looked at her. "Been in my things again, huh?"

"It's nothing I don't already know." She looked out the window.

Horse glanced in the mirror, like he expected to see the world behind him grow open and clear. "Who do you think did it?"

She looked at him. "I don't know."

When they reached her house, she had trouble getting out of the car. Horse went around and took her hand. "I'm getting too old and sore to watch that fire, Horse. You're going to have to look around for some younger person."

Horse nodded, then helped her through the door and to a chair. She collapsed in it.

"Can I get you anything?" he asked.

"No. I'm all right now."

When Horse returned to his tepee, Moses was staring into the fire. He didn't look up. "Go get some paper," he said.

Horse hesitated a moment. "What for?"

"We're going to write some letters."

Horse went inside and opened the trunk. The smell of cedar wafted out. Ona Neck had left his papers in a mess, but underneath his diaries, he found the good parchment and the little bottle of India ink he had made from lampblack, and he took them both back to the fire.

Moses dictated a letter. Horse wrote it down. It read:

Dear Mr. President Harding,

I am just an Indian and with a different way of viewing things from the Caucasian's way. But I am bothered by events that have taken place here in our Indian Territory.

A group of hunters came from the east and by their count 317 eagles were taken from our skies.

The eagles are our brothers. Their loss hurts us. The bear is no longer with us, nor is the wolf. And it goes without my saying that you know how the buffalo were massacred.

We do not have a desire to see our fellow creatures gone from the world. We are small and surrounded by your people, but for all our lives we lived here and none of the animals were wasted this way by our Indian people.

Is there not a way you can find to make a law about the hunting of these birds?

I thank you. May you be rich with money and strong in your mind.

"How does it sound?"

"It sounds good," said Horse. He thought a while. "But I'd rather beat the hell out of those men."

"You're not alone in that. Then they'd hang you up for sure. Okay. Here's another one."

Dear Mr. President,

There's been some murders here in Indian Territory. It's even been in the Tulsa newspapers of late that a plot is under way against the Indians with oil money. One good young man is being held in connection with two of the killings, and we here know that he is innocent. There have been 3 recent murder deaths and 17 before that, just in this one year alone. We are asking if you will investigate these crimes for us.

"How does that sound?"

Horse read it back.

"Okay then, you sign this one."

"Why me?" Horse asked.

"I don't want him to think I'm asking for too much."

It made sense, Horse thought, so he signed it. He wrote two copies for safekeeping.

Moses folded the letters into his pocket alongside Horse's IOU's and drove away.

Horse stayed before the fire all night. In it he could see a buffalo eye. The fire smoked and snapped. It rose up to the other world while the living trees above it looked on at their end.

Belle was true to her word about never speaking again to Louise, and she refused to leave the potato cellar. From time to time, her daughters checked up on her, opening the cellar door and peering into the darkness. Each time they cracked the door, they found her sitting beside the tub of lye soap, staring at the jars of canned chicken, candlelight flickering on her face. Once, Louise opened the door all the way and warned Belle, "You shouldn't burn a candle in the pantry, Mother. The books say the flames use up all the oxygen."

Lettie stood beside Louise. "Tell your sister I'm in my holy cave, and shut the door," Belle said. And finally, the young women gave up on Belle and went back to the work of tending and comforting Nola, who'd been startled back to life by the infestation of crickets. She had weeping spells and was bad-tempered, but they were relieved at her anger, it was so much better than nothing, even when she accused Rena of stealing her little diamond ring. They were relieved that the terrible, silent starings were over. But the conflict had just begun.

Louise warmed milk for the girl. Lettie rubbed the girl's skin with oil.

Later that afternoon they heard Belle singing from under the house. She sang a slow song in a deep voice. They felt her misery rise, up the stairs, up through the wood and ceiling, clear up, they hoped, to sky's heaven.

By the time Moses mailed the letters to Washington and returned home, Rena had exiled herself to the barn, hidden among bales of hay. Louise and Lettie had fought over whether warm milk was more soothing to a mourning girl than blessingroot tea, and when Moses walked in the front door, Louise told him that Belle had locked her "holy cave" from inside, that Nola was locked in her bedroom, Rena was hiding in the barn, and that Lettie had gone to bed in Moses's room with a sick headache.

His heart ached from the loss of the eagles, and still no one had told Louise about them, but Moses couldn't speak of it, and the tension that had been rising in his chest all day long exploded. "What do you want me to do about it?"

Louise turned away in a huff, ran upstairs, slammed the door of her room behind her, and sat on the bed tapping her right foot, her arms crossed over her chest until she heard the car drive up to the house and she knew Ben and Floyd were back from rabbit hunting. She opened the door and she went down to the kitchen.

They were tired. Floyd was paler than usual. He was sitting at the kitchen table, his orange hat in front of him. He claimed that he and Ben had seen the ghost of John Stink.

Ben verified his father's words. "It was there." Ben's eyes were wide. "I saw it too. It was wearing a sheet." It was standing off the road a ways, he said.

The driver of the car had laughed when they'd first seen John Stink. "You've either been hanging around Indians too long or you've got the d.t.'s." But when he adjusted the mirror and caught sight of the large man walking the road in a white shroud, followed by what could only be the dogs of hell, they were so ugly, he sped up so fast that the tires left black skid marks on the dirt road, while John Stink's ghost remained there, watching them and shaking its head as if it were in dismay about the careless young drivers and what the world that he had left behind was coming to.

Always the practical one, Louise asked, "How many rabbits did you bag?" But the men had been so shaken they'd left their rabbits in the car.

From the cellar, Belle yelled up at them, "No wonder his ghost is roaming around. What with all the eagles being killed, who could rest in their graves!"

"What's she doing down there?" Floyd asked. He looked at his wife.

"What eagles?" Louise asked.

By October Sara Blanket's pumpkin vines had stretched out their silver leaves, and the orange fruits were visible. Her corn, though sparse and lanky, had survived. Benoit was still in jail and people continued to find pieces of Benoit and Sara's blown-apart life. A mattress remained at the top of a tree and some hawks had built a nest in it. One of the cattle grazers who leased Indian land filed a lien against Benoit's estate for the cost of a calf that had been hit on the skull and killed by a flying cast iron skillet. Treasure-hunters traveled in from far and wide to search the land for possessions that had blown free of the explosion. A silver cuff link was found beneath the steps of a farmhouse a quarter mile away. One man, out scavenging the woods that autumn with a war surplus metal detector, found a nightgown hanging neatly over a tree limb. It was his wife's size. He took it home.

Several chickens that had died on the night of the forest fire from what was thought to be smoke inhalation, were later found to be full of wood splinters that had blown through their bodies during the blast. They were stuffed for posterity and sat on the curio shelf at the Blue Store next to a jar that held a pig fetus with eight legs. It was known as the spider pig and had attracted a lot of attention, so the souvenir-hunters stopped at the store to look at the pig and chickens.

And that fall John Stink's ghost, still walking around, found a box of expensive cigars that had been thrown clear of the blast. He took them to his campsite above the golf course.

Floyd and his friends had been only the first of many people to spot the ghost. Not long after that, two men notified Reverend Billy that the ghost was picking golf balls out of a sand trap on the golf course. There were so many rumored sightings of Stink's restless spirit that the Indian people made it a priority to find a way to put the old spirit at rest before winter set in. The bodies of Indians were at a premium for displays across the country and in Europe, so it was likely that the same grave-robbers who'd stolen poor Grace Blanket's human remains had also auctioned Stink's body off to one of the museums in Kansas City or Columbus, leaving his unhappy spirit to wander the land, still smoking a cigar.

The traditional people held ceremonies for John Stink and the Indian Baptist Church held prayer meetings for the soul of the old man, but they did not succeed in putting his spirit at rest. Finally it was decided that the only way to make peace with the ghost was to find his body and return it to the grave. But until someone could figure out how to do that, they kept the man's hungry soul supplied with coconut cookies. And Floyd Graycloud held to his promise to feed the dogs. Each day he stopped at the butcher shop and took a bag of bones and fat to the mongrels on Mare Hill. Most days, the ghost of John Stink nodded at the long-haired white man. From time to time, Floyd left a cigar and a bottle of whiskey for the ghost. Once he saw it cleaning its fingernails with a jackknife.

And, Stink himself, with all the food, cigars, and dogs, thought perhaps he'd gone to heaven.

One day, as John Stink crossed the street, he saw Rena Graycloud. With her almost-orange eyes, she looked in the old ghost's face and smiled. He thought for a moment that she could really see him. But her mother jerked her by the hand. Stink didn't hear her say, ''You want to get an evil eye? You'll pee in the bed if you look at a ghost.'' Louise dragged Rena across the street. The girl glanced back over her shoulder at the lonely old spirit. He did look awfully pale, Rena thought, and not quite solid.

That night, as her mother had predicted, Rena woke up with a cold wet spot beneath her in bed. Nola, who slept beside her, smelled the acid odor and when she woke, was upset that the urine had touched her nightgown. She humiliated Rena by saying, ''You're a big baby.''

Louise worried about Rena's wet bed. Since Stink's spirit had been around, there were reports of ghost sickness among children. Wetting the bed was only a first sign. Louise had considered herself modern. She never paid attention to medicines the old people used for curing disease, but this was close to home, so she knocked on the cellar door, and called down the stairs to Belle, ''Come up here, Mother. We've got some things to talk about.''

Belle did not respond to Louise.

Louise opened the door a crack and pleaded. ''Please?''

Belle shut her eyes tightly in the candlelight and said nothing.

Later that day the straw bosses out at the oil fields hosed down the dry October grasses to prevent another fire. The last one, started by the eagle hunters' smoldering pipe tobacco, had come close enough to frighten them. The mist from their hoses made rainbows in the autumn air, and it was through those colorful mists that the school nurse and the man from the Indian Agency appeared at the Grayclouds' house to discuss Nola's absence from school. They stood uncomfortably on the porch steps and knocked on the door. Louise answered the knock. ''We need to see Mrs. Graycloud,'' the man told Louise.

She opened the door wide. "Come in." The nurse looked around the living room, taking in the doilies and photographs of Indians who wore United States military uniforms.

Louise knocked on the cellar door. She called down the stairs. "Even if you aren't going to speak to me, Mama, you better come up here and talk to the Indian agent about Nola."

Ben stood behind Louise. He added, "Grandma, the school nurse is here." Hearing Ben's voice, Belle knew she wasn't being tricked. She blew out the candles and limped up the stairs. She ignored Louise as she hobbled across the kitchen, tapping the floor with her cane.

The school nurse, a tall, kindly-looking young woman, and the man from the Indian Affairs office stood directly in front of Belle. They dwarfed her. She looked up to meet their eyes.

"Mrs. Graycloud," the man said. "It's a law now that we have to enroll Nola in school."

"I can't let you do that," Belle said. "It's not best for the girl." She told them that Nola was given to nightmares, which was true, and that only recently had she begun to speak after the death of her mother.

"We've heard what's been going on," the nurse said, "but we want to examine her ourselves."

"If she goes to school, she'll only make the other girls cry." That was true enough. Nola bickered with everyone, quarreling from morning till night. She sat on a chair in the kitchen, her black hair hanging loose and stringy while she barked out orders: "Louise, do the dishes," "Ben, comb your hair." If the Grayclouds hadn't known her before her mother's death, they would have disliked her immensely. As it was, there were times they wanted to strike the belligerent girl who had always before been so quiet and sweetly composed.

Belle's arguments fell on closed ears, and when the agent ordered Nola down the stairs for an interview, Louise unhappily went to the bedroom and brought the girl back down. Nola's long black hair was braided neatly down her back. She was silent. Belle imagined that through their eyes, Nola was an intelligent young woman who might have been anyone's model student.

"Can you read?" the nurse asked Nola as she listened to the sound of her heart through a stethoscope.

"Yes."

Belle wished they could hear the sound of a broken heart through the cold metal instrument.

"Can you do arithmetic?"

"No," said Nola.

Belle couldn't help herself. She interrupted. "She's anemic." Her face was tense.

"We'll see that she gets liver every day." The nurse looked in one of Nola's ears. "She seems normal and even bright for an Indian girl," she said sweetly.

Belle pulled out the most important of her arguments. "I don't think Nola will be safe at your school. Here, at least, we keep watch over her."

"Safe from what?" She looked at Belle as if the old woman were a crazy liar and Belle was silenced. These people had no sense of the danger that surrounded, even suffocated, the lives of the Indians. Why should they, Belle thought, their lives were not at stake.

She could tell by their faces that both the nurse and the Indian agent believed all the problems might lie with the old gray-haired woman. They'd heard she lived in a pantry and that she had been picked up by the sheriff for attacking the eagle hunters that were recently in town.

That last, the attack on the men from the East, didn't rest well with any of the authorities around Watona, but it especially disturbed the school nurse, who had gone to the movies with one of the hunters and knew him to be a clean, refined gentleman who used a silver toothpick to clean his teeth.

The Indian agent signed an order stating that Nola would have to appear at school on Monday morning or she would be picked up by the sheriff on Tuesday and taken all the way to the Indian boarding school in Custer, Oklahoma. He impressed on Belle that his was an order by law. The old woman looked defiant but said nothing. She knew she was defeated.

The next Monday, Moses loaded Nola's trunkful of clothes into the car and drove her to the Watona Indian School.

* * *

Benoit rolled over on his side. He wanted the comfort of sleep to take him away. There was a deep uneasiness in the whole territory. He felt it. He couldn't sleep, and he only rarely ate. Most of his time was spent looking out the window and smoking cigarettes. His fingers had turned yellow. His mental health seemed fragile, at the point of breaking, and no one wanted to worry him with the details of what was going on outside the jail. But he felt, in his bones, that something was deeply wrong. He turned over again. It was almost dark.

Walter Bird, who occupied the cell next to Benoit, was having tooth trouble. His jaw was swollen and he complained so loudly that Benoit finally got to his feet and called out angrily to the deputy, "He's disturbing the peace. Can't you do something?"

The deputy went into the block of cells to talk to Bird. Benoit heard the man say, "This is one hell of a bad tooth."

The deputy went back to the office, and later that day the sheriff returned and took his prisoner to the dentist in Tulsa. Dr. Bennet, the dentist, traveled from town to town, but for emergencies patients visited his office in the city. From the little windows in his cell, Benoit watched them leave. Peering out, he thought at first that he saw a black Buick pass by. He pressed his face closer to the bars and tried to see who was in the automobile, but he saw nothing. Still, he remained at the window much of the night, wondering if the car would return.

It was late when he saw Jess Gold drive Bird up to the jail in the county sheriff's vehicle. Bird's jaw was back down to normal size. Benoit returned to his cot and pulled the blanket up over himself. He tried to give up his suspicions, and finally he fell into an exhausted half sleep on the cot. Beside him was the tinted, rosy-lipped photograph of Sara. The glass had been removed, in case he wanted to hurt himself.

Walker's body was propped up against the leafless auction tree. For two days, those who walked past the tree thought he was drunk, but finally one of them notified the sheriff's office that the man was dead and the undertaker's hearse picked up the body. Doctor Black was called in to determine the cause of death.

For all appearances, in this case, it looked like the dead

man had swallowed an overdose of wood alcohol. Black noted that there were bruises on the arms, possible signs of a struggle. Something was amiss and he knew it. He stopped by to talk to Sheriff Gold. He said he was alarmed over the recent deaths. "I think Walker was forced to drink the alcohol," he told the sheriff.

Jess Gold was concerned. "Why do you think so?"

Doc Black told him about the bruises and the bleeding from the nose. "Will you look into it?"

"Yes. We'll get right at it."

"Besides," Black added, "Walker was a sober man if I ever saw one."

"I'll take a look. But you know, these Indians aren't like us. They dress pretty. You know? They drive good cars. But under it all, they're still different. Half savage maybe. Well, what I'm trying to say is that even a sober one might take up drinking."

Black was thoughtful a moment. Then, as if he hadn't really heard, he said, "You know, I would suspect Hale if he wasn't such a good citizen around here. Did you know he had a life insurance policy on Walker?"

"No." The sheriff stared into Doctor Black's face. "No, I didn't know that." He got up from his seat at the desk, and walked over to the window. "I don't know. He's always helped out the Indian people here. But it's possible, I guess."

Black thought the sheriff was behaving in a peculiar manner. He thought the sheriff didn't want him to know he too was suspicious of Hale, but then he thought perhaps the sheriff knew something. It all crossed him wrong. And the more he thought about it, the more uneasy he became.

That night he wrote another letter to Washington, D.C.

Stace Red Hawk sat across the table from the young, mixed-blood Indian reporter named Charles Wilson. Like Stace, Wilson was always ready to help his own, but he'd been put in charge of the society pages, attending all the Washington galas, writing up who was present, what they wore and how many courses were served up on china plates. Squab, pheasant, fine wine from Marseilles. So this was his chance to expose the crimes against Indian people and get put up an echelon at the paper.

He leaned anxiously toward Stace Red Hawk and listened to what he said about the doctor's letters, the missing body of the Blanket woman.

"When this breaks, it's going to start a fire," said Wilson.

"I know it. But let's just hope Ballard sends us out."

"Ballard's probably getting paid in oil money."

Stace looked at Wilson a moment, as if he believed him, then said, "No, I don't think so. He's honest. He just doesn't stick up for our people. Not like he would if white people were getting killed."

"Well, I hope this story does it for you." Wilson stood to leave, put a hand in his pocket and jingled his coins.

A few days later, the last leaves were red on the trees in Washington, D.C., and the dry ones scurried about as if they were still alive.

"That's it," said Stace. He put the *Washington Post* down on the desk beside Doctor Benjamin Black's letter and leaned back in his chair. "We've got to go in there."

Philip Levee put his glasses in his shirt pocket. "On what grounds? We still haven't got a case."

Stace's face darkened. He sat forward in his chair again. "On the grounds that people are dying right and left." He spoke with authority. He was Levee's senior.

Outside, the breeze shook the fiery red leaves from the trees.

The federal agents in Washington had already received two more letters. The letters were written in the same hand, but they were signed by two different men who called themselves Moses Graycloud and Michael Horse. Since the names seemed to be false, the letters were thought to be untrustworthy. But by the time Doctor Black wrote a second time, there were even more, and numerous news articles about the events in Indian Territory. Now, even the *Boston Globe* carried a headline, "Oklahoma Scene of Suspicious Deaths," and the *Tulsa Times* ran another story suggesting that there was a conspiracy against Indian people. Radio station WFAF in Dallas went on the air with almost daily commentary about Oklahoma's Indian Territory. Not only that, but Grace Blanket's coffin had been pulled up empty. That didn't set well with Red Hawk. He was certain that the empty coffin was the work of a murderer.

Stace stood up in front of Levee. "Look, these stories are attracting a lot of attention. Maybe we can't act on this situation yet, but we can still investigate it." He was trying Ballard's own kind of argument to justify his impatience to get down there and end the crime spree. "With all this publicity we've got no choice but to get to the bottom of these murders."

"If they are murders, you mean." Levee stood up to leave. He looked at Red Hawk. "What I can't figure is how the *Post* got this info." .

Stace straightened up his body and he looked calm, but as he spoke, he heard the tension in his own voice. "Me either. But we both know that if they weren't Indians being killed, Ballard would have half the bureau out there already." But just then Ballard himself opened the door and called Stace and Levee into his office. They went in and sat down around the table. The pages of the *Washington Post* sat before Ballard. He drank from a bottle of Coca-Cola, set it down on the table, and said, "Okay, okay, I agree with you that something's going on. I've been looking over these cases." He pointed toward a stack of papers. "There's one name that crops up in several of them. It's a man named Hale." He looked at Levee. "I've talked with our letter-writing doctor down there. Didn't have a choice now that it's in the news." He cast a hard look toward Stace. "I'm setting it up for you to take over his practice," he said to Levee. "I hope all this doesn't screw up our investigation."

"But I don't want to practice medicine." Levee's face looked strained.

Stace wondered why Ballard was so slow to get the picture. He knew exactly what was happening. He'd seen it before. Large number of murders in the Badlands. All Indians, all with something the settlers wanted, or with a lien filed against their property. But now, this time, he was an angel of the federal government and he was able to intervene in Indian affairs and he believed he could help the Indian people. And Oklahoma seemed a dark burial ground if there ever was one, outlaw country through and through.

"What gets me is that murder's so common down there that no one even gets riled up," Stace said.

Levee was still protesting, "I don't want to do it." Ballard ignored him.

After Ballard left, Stace looked over the papers once again. Grace Blanket, dead of bullet wound to the heart. Sara Blanket killed in explosion. John Thomas, gunshot wound. At the request of the United States Bureau of Investigation, the Oklahoma courts had sent along information on every death that had occurred within the year. Two men recently dead of alcohol poisoning, both ruled suicides. There was a sheet on John Stink. He had died of natural causes. His body, like that of Grace Blanket, was missing.

It was getting dark. Stace locked the door behind him as he went home. As always, the guard at the door checked Stace's briefcase to be certain that he carried no files of documents out of the building.

When he reached his apartment that evening, Stace took off his hat and let his jet black hair fall down his neck. Then he removed his white starched shirt and took the papers from where he'd sheltered them between his belt and his chest. Bent over the table, he began reading in the light of a lamp.

He read again the account of Grace's death: *Grace Blanket is survived by her sister, Sara, and her daughter, Nola.*

"Nola Blanket," Stace said out loud, haunted by the dark, brooding eyes in the photograph.

When she arrived at school that Monday, Nola Blanket wore a simple skirt and blouse. The dormitory matron brought her a uniform to put on before she went to class. But the first thing Nola did was open her trunk and put on an Osage skirt with ribbons and a pair of moccasins, and when she went into the schoolroom dressed in traditional clothing, all of the other students set down their pencils and stared at her. A smile crossed the faces of the Osage girls, but their grins disappeared quickly beneath the steely gaze of the headmistress. From that first day onward, though no one would say it, Nola became something of a hero to most of the other children. Her anger and defiance spoke for all of them. She alone stood up for what they feared to say and do.

"Go back to the dormitory and take these clothes off," the teacher told Nola.

Nola's face set in harder lines. She left the room, walking very straight and tall. After the class had settled down to reading books, she returned, wearing nothing but her slip. The room filled up with the murmuring voices of the children. And the school nurse, who had seen Nola in the hall, dashed into the room and immediately whisked her out the door. "What do you think you're doing?" she said between her teeth when they were out in the hallway, but Nola went limp as a rag doll and sat on the floor, allowing the nurse only to drag her, by her lifeless arms, down to the office. "Someone come here and help me with this bag of potatoes," the nurse called into the office.

"Let go of her," the headmistress ordered the nurse. Mrs. Seward was a sharp, emotionless woman. The nurse obeyed her command. But Nola leaped up, full of energy. She ran to the end of the hall and broke out a set of windows with her hands. Then she hit her own head against the wall, and the scene was so violent, and the girl screamed so loudly, with her face red and tears falling down her cheeks, that all the other students could not be kept back from running into the hall to see what had happened.

Rena started to cry in fear. She was afraid for what would happen to her beautiful, half-crazy cousin and it was so terrible a distraction that the headmistress, after some consideration, decided she would make a special case for Nola, "temporarily," as she emphasized to the other employees, and within two days Nola became the exception to every school rule, even fingernail inspection.

As if it weren't enough that Nola wore her own clothes, the four watchers in the schoolyard disturbed the students and teachers. The watchers examined every person who entered the double doors of the school. Sometimes one of them could be seen up close, peering into a classroom window like a shadow, his hand shielding his eyes from the light.

The watchers were trespassers, according to Mrs. Seward. Each time she saw them, she called the sheriff, but by the time the sheriff's car arrived, the men had vanished. The deputy soon became tired of being on call for the prim, thin-lipped woman. He was sure she was seeing apparitions. He began to appear only occasionally in response to her calls, taking his own "sweet time," as she accused him of doing.

For her, the presence of the Hill Indians was a source of dismay, even of fear, but the children at the school felt quite the opposite. They were thrilled by the men's presence. They thought the Hill men were "real" Indians, unlike themselves, who didn't live in tepees or cook outside. And the children were even more delighted that each time the authorities arrived, the men were gone. They didn't say so out loud, but they rooted for the Hill men and felt strengthened while Mrs. Seward began to suffer with debilitating migraine headaches.

Nola was in trouble, but she took all her punishments without complaint. She worked extra hours in the kitchen for refusing to make her bed. She peeled potatoes to make up for causing arguments between the other children. She cleaned the schoolroom floors for saying to Mrs. Seward, "If school makes me as stupid as you, I don't want any part of it." Soon Mrs. Seward's headache was so severe that Doctor Black was called. By the time he arrived, she had changed her mind about the dress code and taken Nola's clothes away, dragging the trunk into the office herself. She had screamed at Nola, "I've given you an inch and you've taken a mile."

Dr. Black found Mrs. Seward in the office, her hands over her face. "There is something seriously wrong with my head," she told him.

"Yes," he said, taking her temperature. "I think I can tell you exactly what's wrong."

Certain her time on earth was limited, she waited for the bad news. She slumped and turned her sad eyes toward him.

"I've seen these cases before," he said kindly. "You're in a snit."

"A snit?" She felt humiliated.

He went on. "I don't want to know what it is, but you're probably going to have these headaches until you get things straightened out. Up here, I mean." He tapped his head with a finger.

But Mrs. Seward's headaches continued, as did Nola, the holy terror who refused to tie her long mane of hair back from her shoulders or put on her blue school uniform, but the worst offense finally occurred when Nola, dressed only in her underslip once again, was caught holding hands with Ben Graycloud.

Nola was punished for that encounter, but Mrs. Seward made a plan right then to get Ben sent to another school. The matrons forced Nola to kneel on dry beans in the kitchen. This she did without a word of complaint, although the beans bruised her knees badly and in places the skin broke open like the skin of a bruised and overripe apple.

The morning after the bean incident, Nola tore the uniform they had issued her into strips and used them to bandage her knees. Then she rummaged through the house matron's bureau drawer and put on a simple gray skirt and the woman's favorite brushed wool sweater, went to class, and sat with her bandaged knees showing. The wounds made the school matron feel guilty, so she said nothing about the pilfered clothes Nola wore.

But that morning, Mrs. Seward arrived in the classroom with a cat's grin on her face, and said sweetly to Nola, "Your guardian is here to see you."

"I already have many guardians," Nola retorted, but there was a moment's hesitation, a slight tremor in her voice, and then she saw the distinguished-looking man standing in the doorway, and for the first time since she'd been forced to go to school, she looked small and frightened. She lost her haughtiness. Suddenly every other child in the room was grave and silent; they knew what it meant that Nola was assigned a guardian by the court. Their hearts went out to her. They were afraid. Several of them looked out the window to see what the Hill men were doing.

Nola was shaking, but she went to the door and out into the hall to meet Mr. Forrest. The other students rose up from their seats and followed.

Mrs. Seward loudly clapped her hands. "Sit down!" she ordered, but the children ignored her. Her head began to throb.

Mr. Forrest was a tall, well-dressed man. His hair was white at the temples and smelled sweet, of hair oil. He introduced himself to Nola and told her she needed to go with him to sign papers at the courthouse.

Nola knew enough not to resist. She accompanied him, while the other students watched, down the school steps toward the car. She looked pale and small, but held herself as straight as she could. The motor of the car was idling. A young man sat on the running board. He wore a jaunty cap. He stood up when Nola approached, and he opened the car door for her. He had a boyish face, even though he looked like he was around eighteen years of age.

When he closed the door, Rena cried out. No longer was Nola the overbearing girl Rena had come to think she was. Nola was again her friend. Rena ran toward the car. As it started up the road, she ran behind it, running as fast as her legs would carry her, crying, with her arms stretched out in front of her, pleading, "Stop! Please stop."

A teacher ran after Rena, caught up with her in the middle of the road, and tried to hold her back, but Rena twisted away from her grasp and ran like crazy toward the car, screaming after them. She was frantic. Her face was red. She cried, "Stop!" and just as the young man in the cap heard her and looked back through the window, the teacher caught up with her and struggled to carry her back to the school grounds. By then the children were all disturbed. They were speaking Osage and Creek among themselves, all talking in the forbidden languages about how the white-haired thieves and murderers had taken one more person away to their world.

The teacher was bewildered by the students' behavior. "They act like animals going to slaughter," she said as the nurse, with her arm around Rena's shoulders, took the girl to the infirmary to be sedated.

All that afternoon Rena sobbed. Her face was swollen. Even her hair was moist.

The young man in the cap who had looked back at Rena was Mr. Forrest's only son. His name was Will. Willard John Forrest, to be exact. On the way to the courthouse his full attention was turned on the beautifully dark girl who sat beside his father. He scrutinized the loose black hair that covered her shoulders. A small diamond glistened on her narrow brown finger, just below the knuckle. He gazed at the girl's straight eyelashes, and just when he leaned forward and caught sight of the bandages on Nola's knees, his father slammed on his brakes so hard that Will was knocked off balance and had to catch himself by grabbing the back of Nola's seat.

They had not gone very far.

"What the hell," the older Forrest said. He started to get out of the car, taking a pistol from his pocket. Nola turned to see what the trouble was, and as Mr. Forrest opened the car door, she saw one of the watchers standing nearby. "What do you want?" she heard Mr. Forrest ask the Indian man.

The watchman was silent and while the two men looked at each other, unable to break through one another's worlds, Nola opened her car door and stepped outside. She spoke to the Indian man in a language the white man had never heard. As she talked, another watchman emerged from the brush.

Nola turned to Mr. Forrest and said, "Put your gun away." And for some reason he didn't quite fathom, the attorney did as the girl instructed. He would later wonder why, but in that moment he felt her strength. There was something in her eyes. He didn't know what it was exactly, but he obeyed. And for Nola, the single act, that of putting the pistol back inside his coat, cost Mr. Forrest his authority over her. She saw his weakness. She would remember it.

In spite of his misgivings, the attorney drove the car once again, silently and slowly, toward the courthouse.

"Who are they?" Will asked the girl.

"They're my guardians," she said. She looked over her shoulder at the young man in the cap. Without blinking, she looked him directly in the eye. "Under our law." Her voice was low and quiet. Those last three words carried a weight with them. Will sat back and was quiet. But then he leaned forward again. "What did you tell them?" He looked at her dark eyes.

Nola lied, "I told them you were safe." But what she'd really said was that these two men were lightning-crooked and were probably going to steal her land, but that they wouldn't hurt her until after they'd had a chance to swindle her. That would take time, she told them, since the workings of the government were slow and cumbersome even for the Americans.

After she spoke, Will Forrest sat back in his seat and thought how his father had done as she told, and how also the two Indian men had paid her so much respect. He watched her again. He was enchanted by even the blue bandages wrapped around her knees. He thought there was something a little wild about her. He thought he could love her.

Mr. Forrest turned left and drove up the small hill to the courthouse. Then he parked and the three of them went inside the square building. Inside, Nola glanced up at the paintings on the high walls where naked Indian women offered grain and meat to the white men around them, and one of them rode on the back of a buffalo.

It was around two when Nola signed the last of the papers, and on their way back to the school, Mr. Forrest took Nola and Will to the Regis Café for chocolate cake. Nola, who still loved chocolate, didn't eat a bite. She didn't want to lessen her stature by eating sweets like a child, even though she craved them. Will watched Nola, but every so often he caught sight of one of the guardians, visible behind the lettering on the window. He thought the man looked a little like the girl. He wondered how the men had kept up with them and what they wanted, and if they were dangerous.

When they left the café Nola's cake hadn't been touched. The clean fork was still beside it. They drove slowly, past the horse trader as he and his bedraggled animals clopped along the road.

Ruth Tate sat across from Belle Graycloud in the warm and cozy Graycloud kitchen. Her own house no longer felt comfortable to her, in spite of the fact that she and Moses had lived in it for so many years.

Ruth had a sadness about her, Belle noticed. Not like the loneliness she'd worn before marrying Tate just a few years ago, but a kind of given-up quality.

It was hard for Belle to place John Tate and Ruth together. Tate was a weak man, held up in a way by the inner strength of Ruth. He loved to capture Ruth on film, through the camera, but he didn't seem to love her living presence, in public at least. They seldom went anywhere together, but when they did, he never walked at her side.

"How is Nola?" Ruth asked.

"Tough. She's tough." Belle thought she heard the sound of horses outside. She stood up and went to the window.

The sound of the horses' hooves were muffled in the dust.

Moses stood by the barn, watching the horse trader's wagon approach. Several horses were tied at the sides of the wagon, stringing along beside the driver. It was late and the dust was red in the setting sun. The horses looked dark and mysterious as they trudged along.

The trader would not return to Watona until the next spring, so Moses hoped to sell some of his horses for enough hard cash to last him over the winter. He'd been able to sell off six of his prime, pedigreed holsteins, and two of his black Angus. His barn and pastures looked bereft of animals and the money from those sales barely made up for what he hadn't received at payment time. Still, he knew he was fortunate to have livestock to tide him over until things could be straightened out with the Indian Agency because large numbers of Indians had been moved from their homes and relocated in tar paper shacks on the outskirts of Tulsa.

The trader stopped near Moses. "Ho there. Hoo," he said to the horses.

The trader had red hair and sandy freckled skin. He got down from the wagon and beat the dust from his hat by hitting the brim against his dirty pants. "Hey there, Moses. You have any horses to trade?" He tilted his head at an angle.

Moses shook his head. "Listen, I need to talk to you. I have some horses left. Not many. I don't want to trade them. I want to sell them outright." He did not see Belle. She stood beside the house, a paper bag held to her chest, watching Moses and the trader.

"Well," the man was hesitant. "You know I can't pay top dollar, Moses. You'd do better selling them off around here."

Moses stood by the wagon. Inside it were saddles and blankets, bits, bridles, and the man's bedroll. "It's a hard, hard time, McMann," Moses said.

"You're not telling me nothing new. You should see them down south of here. The land's dead. They're boiling rocks for soup." He looked up at the clouds in the sky. "I'll tell you what I can do for you." He pointed to a colt that was tied to his wagon. "This one's too young to travel. What if I leave him with you. You can sell him later. I'll take those two quarter horses of yours. I'll pay you a hundred each. Now, I know they're worth more, but I can't go it."

Ruth joined Belle at the window. They watched Moses

take the cash from McMann and help him tie his two best cutting horses to the wagon. Then Moses walked toward her. He was looking down, tired and bent, and when he looked up and saw her, he said only, "You saw?"

"Yes, Moses, but I knew it anyway." She placed her hand on his arm and held it there. After a while, she said, "Will you drive Ruth home and give me a ride over to the Billys? I want to talk to them about all of this."

"You go," said Ruth. "I want to stay here tonight."

Belle studied Ruth's sad face. "All right. That will be good." She smiled into Ruth's dark, watching eyes. She could see that Ruth didn't want to go home.

When Martha Billy answered the knock at her front door, she shook the old woman's hand and led her inside. In silence, Martha prepared a frying hen. The grease sizzled. She listened to what was said between Belle Graycloud and Joe Billy.

"You look worried, Belle," the young preacher said. Joe Billy had known Belle all his life. She'd been his father's apprentice, and as a child young Joe Billy had followed them on their searches for healing herbs.

She looked him in the eye with her clear gray gaze. "I am. A man named Forrest is Benoit's defense lawyer. The same man is Nola's guardian."

"I heard. It doesn't seem right to me, either."

"What do you make of it?"

"I don't know. It troubles me, Belle. The whole thing troubles me."

Belle knew he meant the murders. She nodded at him. "Plus Benoit. They aren't doing a thing for him. He's already convicted in their minds. We've got to get him out of there." Belle saw old Sam Billy reflected in his son. She missed the older man. She was lonely for him, especially now when it seemed they were in such great difficulty. For years she'd gone to healings with Sam Billy where she'd sit quietly on a chair, trying to be small so as not to invade the solitary world of the sick. Sam Billy had been a practitioner of bat medicine, one of the strongest traditions of healing.

Martha set the table. As they ate, Belle tried to make small talk. "The potatoes were good this year," she said. And, "Do you think we'll have an early snow?"

"How's your family?" Martha wanted to know.

"Ben's acting too old and smart for the Watona school. He's being sent away to school. Haskell in Kansas. It's a school for Indian boys. I've fought it. But they won't give."

"I'm so sorry to hear that." Martha sat down. Then she stood up again. "Don't you want some more chicken?" Martha asked. "Here, have this breast."

"I don't need it," but Martha had already placed the chicken on Belle's plate. "When's he going?"

Belle noticed how thin and pale the young woman's arms looked. They looked vulnerable. "When he turns sixteen."

Bat medicine had been on Belle's mind of late. As she'd dwelt in her cellar, she realized she had to seek all the forms of help that she could muster, all the "powers," as they'd come to be called. But she didn't mention it to Joe. She was hoping that as the son of Sam Billy, he would be able to help them to know part of the medicine.

After dinner, Belle put her elbows on the table. "We've got to find a way," she said. They knew exactly what she meant.

Martha handed Belle a clean hankie. She was used to being the preacher's wife. It came natural for her. She thought Belle might cry.

"I know." Joe Billy put his hand on Belle's arm. "It's killing my faith, all of this. I hardly believe in my own sermons anymore."

Martha listened. She knew how troubled Joe had been. He sat up nights in his office and spent days pacing the floorboards of the house. But what she didn't know was that many a night while she slept, Joe Billy prayed in his study, holding his father's bat medicine bundle in his hands. He felt it speaking to him. It was urgent, he knew, even though he didn't understand what was being said from inside the leather bag. Something was stirring in there.

Martha, in fact, didn't know there was such a medicine bundle. Probably she would have been alarmed if she'd known that her Christian husband was listening to the spirit world of bats, was praying to a different realm than she had ever known. But she'd slowly come to believe there were other ways besides her own.

It was getting late and Belle looked tired. Martha opened the cedar trunk and took out a quilt for the older woman. Then she made up a bed for Belle Graycloud. While she was gone, Joe Billy said to Belle, "I've been thinking about the bat medicine."

"So have I."

Joe Billy lowered his voice so Martha wouldn't hear. "I've been dreaming of Old Sam"—that's what he called his father—"standing in Sorrow Cave surrounded by crystals and sleeping bats."

Belle nodded slowly.

That night, after Belle laid her head down on the pillow, Joe Billy tossed and turned in the next room. Finally, he tiptoed into his study and closed the door quietly behind him. He took the medicine bundle out of the drawer. The skin that covered it was dry and hardened, like parchment. He sat in his worn chair, placed the bundle on his lap and closed his eyes. He heard what he thought were warnings stirring beneath the surface of his skin, beneath the floors of his house. He fell asleep.

The next morning, when the sun began to rise, Martha Billy put on a shawl and opened the door to the study. She saw her husband asleep in the wooden chair. His head dropped forward, and in his hands he held a leather pouch. Inside it, Martha could see that something was moving. The sight of it bumping and turning in Joe Billy's hands startled her and she drew in such a frightened breath that Joe Billy woke and looked from her blue eyes to the moving bundle that he held.

"What's in there?" Martha asked.

He blinked at her and all he could really say was, "It's the older world, wanting out."

On Neck watched over the fire as Michael Horse packed his worldly goods into his silver roadster. He planned to head for the other side of the bluffs, past the Blue River, over the flatlands, and on toward the Coffee River. He packed his coffeepot and the chest of papers. No matter how far away he could go, he thought it would never be far enough. But just before he reached the Blue, the road dwindled away to nearly nothing and turned into a rocky path. He'd forgotten the land was too rough for a car. He hadn't accounted for that. And now, with practical matters in mind, he realized he would also need gasoline from time to time, so he hid his tepee and cedar box a ways off the last remnant of the road, turned around, and drove back toward town.

As he drove, he hatched out a plan. He was going to trade his car for the horse, Redshirt. He wanted the strong-legged horse. It could get him where he wanted to go. It was probably the only horse in the territory that could drag along a cedar chest filled with papers.

Horse parked his car in front of the Graycloud's house and shined it with a cloth. Then he went to tell Moses his plan.

"I can't do it, Horse. You know I would if he were mine, but Redshirt is Benoit's stallion." Moses shook his head. "He's not mine to trade."

But Horse had kept his eye on that red stallion for some time, and now he had a strong need for it, so he didn't give up. "You could sell the silver car," he said, "and use the cash for a new gas stove or something for Belle."

But Moses still didn't go along with it. He looked down at the ground and said, "I just can't."

"Or you can keep it," Horse said, "and get Belle some driving lessons."

At the thought of Belle Graycloud driving the car, the two old friends smiled. They recalled the day she'd clearly stated her love of riding like a blanket Indian in the back seat of a convertible while Moses drove. She loved the old Indian ways and a plain life, but when she arranged herself like a queen in the back of a car, she fought with herself not to grin from ear to ear. The wind on her face was part of her joy. The larger part was the way white people stared at her as the car passed by. They stopped in their tracks with their mouths hanging open while they looked at the braided driver, and her fat spotted dog yapping at them from the dignified woman's lap as she stared straight ahead.

Horse didn't say it, but he was certain Redshirt was a better horse than Man O' War, who conquered Aqueduct in 1920. He changed the terms. According to his next plan, they would borrow each other's transportation for a short time.

And finally he won Moses over, and with great difficulty Horse got the bit in Redshirt's mouth, threw a blanket way up on his back, and mounted him, with Moses's help, by standing on a stump. He was breathing hard by the time he finally got on the back of the horse. Then, leaving behind his roadster and keys, Horse rode Redshirt back up to where he'd left the trunk and tepee. The horse had a good, long stride, and the old man felt young again on its back.

When Michael Horse reached the place where he'd left his things, he put his belongings on a makeshift travois behind the horse. Then, with dismay, he realized he could not mount the tall stallion without a rock or stump. He led the stallion over to a tree, climbed up a branch and tried to throw his leg over Redshirt. He failed to get on. So he walked alongside the horse, the lead rope in hand. They walked toward the bluffs.

It was nearly winter when one day Belle Graycloud came up from the cellar and found her daughter Lettie sitting at the table, her elbows bent, her chin resting on her hands. She was gazing out the window at the silver car in the yard. The sky was cloudy.

Belle carried her candles and feathers, and she was followed by her dog, Pippin, who shook the musty smell of potatoes out of his fur and looked relieved to move upstairs and away from the underworld of the house.

"I heard voices here," Belle said.

Lettie turned to her mother. "It was the sheriff."

"That's what I thought." Belle sat down across from Lettie and stared out the window with her. The light from the sky looked blue on Lettie's arm. Belle touched that light. "He asked you out?"

"Yes." Lettie looked disheartened.

"You want some tea?" Belle asked Lettie. She stood up and put a kettle of water on the woodstove. It was hot in the kitchen.

Lettie shook her head, no. She had sorrow in her eyes.

"How many times does that make that he's been here?"

"I don't know. Why do you ask?"

"I've had a thought. I've been thinking you should go with him. He's very sweet on you."

"No, Mama," Lettie said. But Belle went on as if she hadn't heard. "Next time he asks, say you will. See him as much as you can. Maybe you can find out something about Benoit. Or at least urge him to bring the case to trial."

"Do I understand, you want me to spy?"

Belle looked at her. "I guess you could put it that way."

Lettie said nothing. But now that she had a plan of action underway, Belle did not return to the root cellar in order to think.

On the following Friday evening while Lettie was upstairs pinning her dark hair up beneath a blue velvet hat, Sheriff Jess Gold arrived to find Belle sitting on the couch, stiff and polite.

Jess, holding his hat in one hand, seemed very young that night. And he was overly gracious. "How do you do?" he asked Belle.

Belle, who'd known him much of his life, almost laughed out loud at his politeness. But she avoided his eyes.

Upstairs, Lettie looked at herself in the mirror. Her eyes were beautiful, even puffy. She powdered her nose and went downstairs, trying not to show the despair she felt. The sheriff held a bouquet of yellow roses. He knew how much Indian women loved roses. He handed her the flowers and he removed his hat.

"They are beautiful," said Lettie, but her voice sounded strained. She went to the kitchen to find a vase.

"It's good to see you again," Jess said to Belle, then he went on stupidly, "You know, two people I never thought I'd see in my jail were you and that Michael Horse." He went on, "And there you both were on the same day."

Belle's eyes turned icy.

"I suppose anyone could make a mistake now and then."

She interrupted him. "I didn't make a mistake," but then Lettie returned carrying the yellow roses in a dark blue vase. The scent filled the room. She had slipped a single rose through the buttonhole of her black woolen jacket, and it brought a pleasant warm color to her face. Up close she smelled of gardenia. She kissed her mother and as she leaned over her, they exchanged a brittle glance. Then Lettie and Jess Gold walked out into the moist air. Belle went to the

window and watched them walk past Michael Horse's roadster. It was parked at an angle and covered with dust.

"Isn't that Michael Horse's car?" she heard the sheriff
ask.

"Yes. It is. It was Horse's." Then she let the subject drop.
Jess Gold opened the door for her.

As they drove toward town, Jess announced, "I'm buying
a piano."

Lettie looked at him. "I didn't know you played." She'd
never thought of him as a gentleman, but now she could see
it, even though she knew he was trying to impress her.

"Just by ear. I don't read music."

She felt sorry that she was using him to get information
on Benoit. It was dishonest. She looked out the window as
they drove. It was damp. The window steamed up. She said
nothing.

When they reached the Bijou theater, Jess Gold parked his
car on the street. Dark, heavy clouds were moving from the
west toward town. The air already smelled of rain. Other
drivers were outside putting the cloth tops up on their con-
vertibles, looking west, reading the rolling clouds that spelled
thunder.

"At least it keeps the dust down," Jess said, and Lettie
nodded in agreement. The other people watched the unlikely
couple with curiosity.

At the door were several old mongrel dogs. They looked
like Stink's. They were curled, thin and bony, on the walk-
way and sure enough John Stink's ghost sat alone in the back
row of seats, an umbrella laid across its knees. Young Will
Forrest, unaware of the restless spirit who sat nearby, was
pining away in another seat for Nola Blanket. Several cowboys sat together in a single row. They shared a bottle between them while they complained noisily about drunk
Indians, although the ones in the theater were still sober.
They complained about the large Stetsons the Indian men
wore until finally the Creeks and the Osages were forced to
remove their hats and put them on the empty seats in front
of them where they worried about them throughout the show.

John Stink did not hear the complaints. He was unruffled
by his loss of hearing and he was grateful he could go to the
movies for free, since it was a good place to rest and get out

of the rain. One of the Billy girls, at the box office, hadn't charged him for a ticket. In fact, she hadn't even seen him at all. He thought it was something of a miracle that he'd come part way back to life, even as a ghost, and been able to dig himself out of his grave. With the help of his dogs, of course.

Rudolph Valentino seduced women while everyone watched closely. Larger than life, Valentino and Fairbanks at the Bijou had changed the love lives of people around Watona. Indian women were just plain out disgruntled with their men. Some of them even compared notes with each other, and suddenly after years of marriage, they complained to their husbands, "Why don't you do it like this? Valentino does," until the men were persuaded to go see exactly what it was the women wanted them to do. Then they would go home and bend their wives over backward, hold them up from falling and, pressed close together, look into their eyes until they both laughed out loud.

That night, Sheriff Gold took Lettie's slender, darker hand and held it in his own. Her long fingers were cold, the palm of her hand dry. In the back of the theater, Will Forrest, alone, imagined his arms were around the narrow shoulders of the beautiful Nola Blanket.

When Lettie returned home that night, she went to her room and closed the door. She drew the heavy curtain closed. She took a deck of playing cards from the bureau drawer and spread them across the blue silk they were wrapped in.

She wanted to learn what the future held. In every spread of the cards, she turned up both the ace of spades and the queen of diamonds. Then she smoked the cards with cedar smoke, and thought hard about how to decipher them. Death. An old woman. A matriarch. Maybe her mother.

The next time Lettie visited Benoit at the county jail Jess Gold smiled at her as he helped her off with her jacket. He hung it on the wooden coat tree behind the door. "Good to see you."

"You too. How are you?"

"Just fine." She felt nervous. She stammered out, "I have these papers. My father sent them for Benoit. He has to sign them." She showed him what looked like legal papers, just briefly. They were horse auction records.

"Sure." He looked into her face. He was a little shy.

She felt guilty as he led her through the corridor but when he opened the first set of doors for her, she smiled at him, a wide, friendly smile.

When they reached the cell where Benoit was imprisoned, the sheriff let her in, but he remained standing by the door with a smile on his face, still looking at her. Her hands grew clammy. "It's private," she told him. "I'm sorry, Jess. It's business." She thought she saw a bit of ice in the sheriff's eyes, but he only looked embarrassed.

"Oh, sure," Jess Gold said, and he nodded politely at Benoit and started to walk away. "Just call out if you have any trouble."

Lettie listened to the keys jangling in Jess Gold's hand as he walked away. Then she heard a door close behind him, and it was silent. She turned to Benoit. "Where's Walter Bird?"

"At the dentist," Benoit said.

She looked around the cells. They were rarely empty in this wild country, but no one else was there that day, or at least no one was visible. She put her arms up around Benoit's neck and held him close. Her heart felt large and broken. She held him tighter. She felt his sharp ribs. She touched the knots of his spine. They closed each other in, holding with a desperate sorrow that was filled to the brim with need and loss. It was comfort they wanted. Lettie wept in Benoit's thin arms, and he held her back and looked at her face and touched her black hair. Then he said gently, "We have to be careful," and he looked around, then stepped away from her.

"You're not eating." She took his hand into her own. Even his fingers felt thin.

But Benoit was thinking of the murders and how he'd been framed and his jaw muscles tightened.

"You have to start eating. You need your strength."

"What have you heard?"

She knew he meant about the murders, about his own imprisonment, about anything at all that might begin to piece together the fragments of their broken lives or get him out of there. "Nothing, Benoit. There's nothing yet." She knew she could not tell him that a man claimed he was Grace's legal husband. The agency had tracked down a justice of the peace who signed the papers. The woman didn't match Grace's description. He was just one of many fortune-hunters. And Lettie needed to keep this from Benoit. For his own safety. Something inside him was desperate. She saw it poised, ready to leap. She made herself remain silent.

"Have you heard anything about a trial?"

Before she answered him, he went on, "They assigned me a lawyer named Forrest. What do you know about him?" His face was tight.

"I don't know, Benoit. I just don't know." She looked pale and hollow, but she said nothing that would alarm the underweight man. She avoided his gray-green eyes. They were made sharp and wide by his loss of weight. "I'll see what I can find out."

But at home, Lettie said to her mother, "I can't stand it! My God. He hasn't even been charged and they say he's guilty. And there's no place we can go. Not even the governor is honest. And the sheriff has said nothing. He doesn't know a thing. I'm sure of it."

"Has he said anything at all?" Belle's voice was calm.

"No. Nothing. He asked if I'd seen anything on the night John Thomas was killed."

"Anything about Nola?"

"No. He said he wondered if she'd gone to the pond that day with Grace. That's all."

"Maybe he was fishing for information."

But there was something else about the sheriff's office that disturbed her. It wasn't just the pictures of wanted men on the wall, but the geologist's yellowed maps of the Oklahoma Indian Territory with their estimates of where oil might exist. Like prophecies, they were, like divining where one black stench of oil might flow into another.

She covered her face with her hands, "They are going to send Benoit up, I'm sure of it."

That night, Lettie decided that she was going to search for the fortune-teller who had told her that things were going to fly apart. The woman's words had come to pass. Lettie felt certain the woman would know who had committed the recent crimes.

When she told Belle about the fortune-teller, Belle said, "How do you think it might help?"

"I don't know. Maybe she'd know something that would shine a light on what's going on."

"Then you should try it," Belle said. She went down the cellar stairs and when she returned, she carried a Ball jar of money, both bills and change.

"Here, take this."

"What's it for?" Lettie asked.

"Just use it. I've been saving it against hard times."

Michael Horse sat looking into the dark and muddy Coffee River. Behind him, the people's fire was burning its eternal flame. He had moved the coals successfully in a moss-filled metal box. He listened to the water. Redshirt stood silent beside a wind-gnarled tree. The old man could feel Redshirt out there, but he hadn't seen him. The horse had gone wild, it had rubbed itself out of its harness, and the old man had been unable to catch him. The bats were out there too, and Horse could hear their last whistling, diving flight before they found their way into caves for the winter. Suddenly he wanted the old ways back. He wanted the white people gone, wanted to turn time around as if it were the steering wheel of his roadster.

When the train doors opened on that auction day, gentlemen offered their hands to the ladies and helped them down the steps of the trains. Geologists and rock hounds arrived with their wives. The women carried flowered bags. There were engineers and oil executives with briefcases. John Tate, the small man with a monocle, was rushing by in a hurry, looking for passengers. And Stacey Red Hawk, who said he was a Lakota traditional healer, stepped down from the long train and asked Tate for directions to the Stanley Hotel. Like most of the traveling medicine men, he wore black slant-heel cowboy boots and carried with him a long cedar box, a small black suitcase, and a buckskin bag that held his most special medicines. He wore his hair braided and had a red scarf tied about his neck.

Stace saw the men, women, and children milling around the giant elm that was known as the auction tree. It was in the shadow of this tree that all the oil business was transacted.

The air was brisk and with the colder weather, many of the local Indians wore mink and bear fur coats as they greeted the trains that arrived from the east coast. Photographers from city newspapers took their pictures and their faces would appear, as they had before, on the covers of national magazines with such headlines as: "Oil Rich Indians Lease Out Land." John Tate was among these, had left his camera standing as he invited geologists to come stand before it and have their faces recorded for posterity.

Merchants had arrived in town the previous day and set up shop on the streets of town. With their scarves wrapped around them, their arms folded across them for warmth, they sold everything from new-fangled bottle openers to maps of the stars that were painted with radium flakes and were guaranteed to glow in the dark. Stace walked along the street, examining their wares. Because of his appearance, the people stared at him with curiosity, at least until he looked back at them, and then they turned away. His presence made them uneasy. They could see he had some depth, some dimension they had never entered, a way of knowing that made them feel he could see inside them.

He walked to the Stanley and checked in at the front desk.

In his room there was a desk with three drawers, a good window, a straight-backed chair. He didn't bother unpacking his bag. He splashed water on his face and went back down the stairway and out into the crowded street.

At twelve sharp the auction began. The younger Indian men thought it was a wondrously funny thing that Indians who wound up living on the dry, untillable, scorched plots of land had turned out to be rich with oil and gas. They sat on chairs in the front row, waiting for the auctioneer to begin. They were wrapped up in coats and blankets. They nudged each other, laughing about the large sums of money being spent on black oil that trickled beneath this worthless earth. This time, at last, they were coming out ahead. They thought it was about time.

That morning, Moses had sold some Herefords to grass leasers. With the money in his pockets he walked through town. He bought staples for winter. He purchased canned goods, dried beans, and flour. Then he paid the electric company for the light that flowed into his house through black, narrow wires.

Moses placed the packages on the front seat and went over to sit with some of the older men on a bench. They remained in the background, watching the proceedings with mixed feelings. Then from beneath the biggest elm tree in Watona, the auctioneer began to pound a block, and spit out words like a crow with a split tongue, and the oilmen looked hungry.

Even from there, they could see the derricks out at the Indian Territory Illuminating Oil Company. Landless men labored out there. They worked for John Hale, the oilman, who kept watch over them in their steel-toe boots as they pulled the great chains back and forth and, inch by inch, drove the pipes down and into the earth. The sound of metal grated against metal out there. Gas rumbled under the ground like earth complaining through an open mouth, moaning sometimes and sometimes roaring with rage.

Hale himself was in town that day. He stood out, even in his plain brown coat, with his gray hat and his long legs. He wanted to talk to John Tate, the small man who wore the monocle, the husband of Ruth, Moses's no-nonsense twin sister. When Ruth saw Hale approach her husband, she managed to get in his way, quietly blocking his path. She had been watching him with her rich brown eyes. She stood squarely in front of Hale. She didn't trust him. She kept her eyes on his. "Lots of wealth beneath this old earth," she said in a throaty voice. Her words had an edge to them.

Hale nodded at her and said, "Yes, ma'am," and tried to move away from her. "Excuse me." He was already looking in the direction Tate had gone.

Tate moved quickly. He was carrying his tripod. He was in a hurry.

Ruth didn't move aside for Hale, nor did she let him out of her gaze. "We gave up our better ways for this oil business."

"I'll bet you did, Mrs. Tate," Hale said. He looked over her head. "Now if you'll excuse me."

She believed that he was dishonest. They'd done cattle business together in the past, and things just never came out right for her. She couldn't really prove it. It was just a feeling she had.

Finally, Hale saw Tate and made his way around Ruth. John Tate was setting up a camera and talking to one of the geologists who'd mapped out the oil pools. When Hale approached, the geologist turned back to the auction, as if he didn't want to talk with the thin man.

Ruth watched her husband and Hale walk toward the parking area. A chill rose up her spine. She thought there was something cold in the man. She watched the men light up their cigarettes. Her husband was fidgety. She went to stand beside her brother, Moses, and reached him just as Jim Josh, who never missed an auction, hobbled over on his sore feet. He nodded at Ruth, then put out his hand to Moses. "Say," he asked Moses. "Do you think Belle would come by my place and take a look at my sore feet?" He pointed to his shoes.

Moses had forgotten. "I'm so sorry, Josh. I will bring her by tomorrow."

"Maybe she has an herb or something," Josh started to say. His words were drowned out by the roaring of the crowd. Both men and Ruth turned to see what all the commotion was about. The young Indians in the front row were laughing and slapping their thighs. The bidders and spectators yelled and threw their hats into the air. The auctioneer yelled again, "Sold to the colonel for one million eight hundred thousand dollars," and the words were greeted with more hoots and shouts.

Moses could hardly believe his ears as the young men whistled and toasted one another with their champagne. It made him sad. He didn't know why. "Why don't I drive you on home?" he said to Josh. Then he looked at his sister. "Ruth? You want a lift?" He saw John Tate taking their picture. He turned his back toward the camera.

Ruth did the same, saying, "No, I think I'll stay."

James Josh bowed politely to Moses. "I thank you," he said as he touched the end of one of his braids. "But don't you want to stay at the sale?"

"No." Moses started in the direction of his car. "I've had enough." Josh followed him. When they reached the car,

Moses moved the packages off the seat to make room for Josh.

Josh was still talking about his sore feet. "They've been like this ever since the war. One of them, that is."

Josh went silent until they reached Josh's place. "I'll bring Belle out tomorrow," Moses told him as he let him out of the car.

Moses returned home that day with his arms full of presents. They were wrapped in silver paper. The sunlight reflected off the wrapping paper and when Rena, home from school, caught sight of it, she ran out to meet her grandfather. Moses smiled. They walked past the hobo who was splitting sweet-smelling wood, and past one of the watchers who seemed to blend like smoke into the background sky.

Rena was overjoyed with the porcelain doll her grandfather brought her. Nola was gracious about it, but she preferred perfume. Belle opened the package of German chocolate, and Nola looked at it so hungrily that Belle put the candy out on a plate for the family and pretended not to pay attention to the way Nola ate it. For Lettie, Moses had brought a red hat. A white wool blanket was for Floyd and Louise and Moses bought one of the maps of planets and constellations for Ben to take with him to Haskell, and that night when darkness fell across the sky, the Grayclouds pinned the star map to the wall and turned off all the lights. They oohed and aahed over "the way of the milk," as Moses translated it from French. In the darkened living room, they finished the chocolates and looked at the small sky on their wall. They felt safe and comfortable for a while, living beneath the way of the milk and above the rich water and minerals of earth.

In town, Stace Red Hawk sat in the darkness of his room and looked out his window. It was the highest priced oil sale in history and Watona was filled with partygoers. A piano was wheeled into the town square and women danced on the streets, holding fox fur neckpieces up like beloved dance partners. The white members of the Rotary Club were dressed up as make-believe Indians. A hypnotist had entranced a handful of very serious Indian people to believe they were chickens and they goose-stepped and clucked at each other without so much as a smile on their faces. They believed they had beaks. They believed they had claws. They believed they had feathers. They believed they were safe.

Stace watched two young Indian men. They leaned against a tree and watched the festivities. They shared a bottle. One of them was Jim Josh's nephew. He had been a survivor of the capsized Titanic in 1912. He returned to Watona now and then in order to hit his elderly uncle up for money. He would be gone within the week. The other was a young man, Calvin Severance, who was proud that he had the distinction of surviving Carlisle Indian School in Pennsylvania. "That's every bit as bad as a shipwreck," he told Silas Josh. They laughed over the comparison, but there was an element of truth in it. Carlisle had been a school well-known for its Indian football team as well as for athlete Jim Thorpe. It closed down in 1918. While it was in operation, Calvin Severance had escaped from the school by stowing away in the baggage car of a westward bound train. At school, Calvin had been hung by his thumbs as punishment for "insolence." The result was that his skin and nerve had torn away from the bone. He lost the use of his thumbs. Because of that, he held the bottle tipped up between his palms, the way an infant would drink.

While the two men talked and drank, the ghost of John Stink passed through the streets. The Indian people believed Stink's ghost was visible only to Indians, since they were the only ones who made room for it to pass. The spirit was accompanied, as usual, by the dogs that Floyd had been feeding every day.

The ghost and its dogs had passed by Floyd that auction night, and he gave the ghost a bottle of bathtub gin. Floyd had already sold an entire carload of whiskey, gone home to put up another batch, and gone back to the little stand of trees just outside of town. When he returned, he called out "Milk and honey," and the buyers gathered around him in the lantern light. One old Indian woman in a red dress and wool blanket was playing a gambling game with sticks and shells. She had a stack of silver coins on the little table in front of her. She'd been winning every wager. She cut the stack with her withered, dry hands and asked for three bottles of Floyd's famous whiskey.

By ten o'clock the jail was full. Floyd's business was at

least partly to blame, what with the young men staggering around and the women putting their hands in the men's pockets. In the crowded jail, Walter Bird's cheek was swollen up again and he was rocking with pain, waiting for someone to reach the dentist. "Give me some whiskey and pliers," he said. "I'll take it out myself." While he complained, the state police brought in a man named Mardy. He was booked for driving a stolen Buick. The police had stopped him out on Fremont Road. They asked him where he'd gotten his car. He explained that it was given to him in payment for work.

"What kind of work?" the officer asked.

Mardy had been apprehensive, but he didn't want to provide information that might incriminate Hale, his employer. "Is there a problem with the car?"

"No. The car's just fine. But there's a problem with you stealing Buicks."

The man named Mardy was confused. "It ain't a stolen car."

"Okay. Then who gave it to you?"

"I can't tell you that."

"That's just what I thought." The blue-shirted officer handcuffed Mardy and took him to the county jail for holding. Mardy was certain Hale would bail him out, so he went quietly and without a fuss. He sat inside the cell next to Benoit and he was quiet as the sheriff opened the door to take Bird to the dentist on an emergency call.

Not long after that, Cal Severance and Jim Josh's nephew were booked for being drunk and placed in the cell with Mardy. They stared through the bars at the man they'd known all their lives as a fancy-dressing Indian. They'd heard he set a nitro fuse in the coalbin of his own home, but they couldn't believe it. Benoit had a reputation for being a decent, law-abiding man.

"Benoit! It's me, Calvin Severance." Calvin hardly recognized the emaciated face of Benoit.

Benoit glanced up, but his eyes didn't quite take in the face of Calvin. "Yes," he said. "I remember you."

Calvin whispered to the man closest to him. "What's he in for?"

Benoit had already turned his attention away. He was watching the street. A singing woman passed by wearing a diamond ring on every finger. Her song made Benoit restless. He wanted to get out. A wave of anger rose up in his chest.

"Murder."

China, Hale's girlfriend, was booked about midnight. She was probably a minor, she looked so young. She was arrested for causing a disturbance when she removed her satin shirt, held it over her head like a parachute, and jumped off the hotel balcony.

Since there was a lack of space in the jail, and her legs weren't broken, she was held in the cell next to the two Indian men and Mardy, a white man with sandy hair. She also watched Benoit. Like everyone else, she had heard about him. She thought he looked too pathetic to be the criminal he was made out to be.

Benoit ignored her and stared out the window. Two men in opera hats passed by. They were discussing the mule races.

"China? Why do they call you that?" Cal Severance asked the towhead. Her skin was smooth and white as paper, and her eyes were pale blue. "They must have drilled an oil hole clean through earth to come up with that name," he said. His friend, Josh's nephew, laughed.

She looked him in the eye. "That's what they did, all right." He was shocked by the clear blue gaze she fixed on him. "And when I looked up from the other side of that hole in the earth, I saw all you rich Indians and I said to myself, I'm going to emigrate right now." She looked at Benoit. "Say, do you have a cigarette?"

"Here. I have one," said Calvin. "Why do they call you China?" He looked interested in her. He lit the cigarette awkwardly, with useless thumbs.

"Honey, you don't think I'd lie, do you now?" and the Indian men were silenced by her toughness, by what was hidden beneath her angelic white face and the words her soft voice spoke. She blew smoke toward the ceiling of the jail.

"Hey, how'd you get to keep that match?" one of the other drunks asked Cal.

Late that night, most of the older, more traditional Indians gathered in the hills to have a sing. Many men wore the black wool blankets that were beaded with an American flag and a golden eagle. These were called Honor Blankets. They had become a tradition for Indian veterans of the World War after a woman named Mrs. Lookout made one for her husband, Fred Lookout. Pretty soon the other veterans all wanted one. She had a waiting list forty men long. They wore their blankets wrapped around their shoulders and when Joe Billy walked up the hill to where the sing was taking place, he thought they looked like a dark range of mountains.

Billy held his wife's hand. He let go when they reached the singers. He nodded and spoke with the elders, then he left Martha at the sing with the breathing mountains, at her insistence. It was getting so that she preferred the Indians to her own kind of people. Joe Billy left her there and made his way back to town to talk with Doctor Black.

Joe Billy and Doc Black were friends, or at least they had something akin to friendship. They talked about things with each other. They liked to philosophize.

Joe Billy knew the doctor would be busy that night, what with injuries and alcohol poisoning, but he wanted to talk to him about Walker's death. It was his first chance to do it, and he thought maybe he could help the doctor out by comforting and quieting the drunks.

"There might be a birth tonight," said Doc Black to Joe, "if one patient will deliver on time. But she's an opium user, and it seems like all their children come late into the world. They don't want to be born." He put a stack of clean towels away. "I don't blame them one bit."

A young man who had gotten into a fight came in. The doctor glanced up at Joe Billy. "Fix me a cup of coffee, will you? Put some brandy in it." The doctor drank brandy in his tea as well. He took two stitches in the young man's skull and the man left, carrying an ice pack on the back of his head. Doctor Black said, as if he'd read Joe Billy's mind, "Yes, I examined Walker. He died of alcohol poisoning."

"Alcohol poisoning?" repeated the Reverend.

"Yeah." The doctor stretched his arms behind his head and leaned back in his chair. He had the defeated look of an honest man in a world gone wrong. "There's a lot of bad moonshine around these days. I see it all the time." He didn't say much more. He'd heard from a man in Washington that he should remain silent, completely silent about the suspicious circumstances of Walker's death.

"But he didn't drink."

"I know."

"Well, don't you think he might have been murdered?"

"I can't say, Billy. Stranger things have happened than an old teetotaler drinking bad alcohol."

But Joe Billy could see a bit of doubt in the doctor's expression. He asked about Hale, the oilman, taking out an insurance policy on Walker.

"He did. It sounds strange to me, too." Then he was quiet a long while before he said, "In any other time or place it would sound strange, I should say. But here, business is business. I don't understand it. It's a different kind of law at work here. Nothing's wrong when cash is at stake. Hale told me Walker owed him money. That was how they wanted to settle it. Walker agreed to it."

"You know Lettie Graycloud, don't you?" Joe Billy asked.

"Yes, what of it?"

"Well, she said she saw Walter Bird on the street that night." Black squinted at Billy. "He's in jail, isn't he?"

"Yeah. What do you make of it?"

"I don't know, Billy."

It was noisy outside. From the office, they could hear the piano. Joe Billy was about to say more, but just then the doctor jumped up from his chair and looked out the window at a bandanna-wearing scarred man. "I'll be damned. Isn't that John Stink?" Outside, the streets were full and busy. Stink disappeared in the crowd.

"It's his ghost," Reverend Billy said. "Robbers stole his body out of the grave. His spirit's been wandering about ever since."

"That's impossible." The doctor stepped out the door and scanned the streets for Stink, but the dead man wasn't there.

Just then a man holding a rag up to his bleeding forehead stepped toward the door, and another fellow came in to ask for help out on a farm where a woman was delivering a baby, and Doc Black briefly tended the head injury, then packed up to go to the birth, all the time wondering who was posing as Stink and what they had in mind. "You want to wait here?" he asked Joe Billy.

"No. I left Martha up at the hill."

The doctor said nothing more. He put a sign on the door that read "Please be seated and wait."

Joe Billy walked away in the clear dark night. He walked back up the hill to where the people were singing deep and low. From outside the circle of firelight, he saw Martha. She was singing with the older folks and she was more beautiful than ever before. He stopped and looked awhile, then walked the rest of the way there. He sat beside her on the ground and held her hand. The deep low singing took him in.

The days grew shorter. Pecan trees were barren. The last leaves blew off oak trees in wintery breezes that stirred at night. Rains came and went. Moses remembered this time to tell Belle that Jim Josh was suffering pain in his feet and legs, and she packed some herbs into a paper bag, wrapped it with string, and Moses drove her out to the shack where Jim Josh lived. Josh had been waiting. He limped out to the car to meet them, but before Belle could even ask about his feet, he said proudly, "Come on around here. I got something to show you." They followed him across the yard, picking their way between old bedsprings, oil drums, and rusted farm implements that cluttered the grounds. Chickens scurried away. Cats and dogs got up and moved aside.

Josh's ten new polished bathtubs were lined up side by side on a square plot of ground. In several of the lion-clawed gleaming white tubs, corn was growing. It was in a sunny spot and each tub was covered with glass.

"Come over here if you want to really see something," said the old man. He emphasized "really." He led them to the new car. Inside it were pots and wooden boxes full of tomato plants. Red tomatoes were growing plump on vines. They pressed against the car windows like they were in a crowded hothouse.

"The temperature is perfect for Beefsteak tomatoes," said Josh.

Belle grinned at him. "I knew you'd figure out what to do with that car."

Moses opened the door of the car and picked a tomato. Josh watched as he ate it. "Best tomato you ever ate, isn't it?"

Moses agreed.

Inside the shack where Jim Josh lived, there were yellowed calendars on the wall. Josh had crowded a new baby grand piano into the small room, and it was surrounded by old, beat-up furniture. On it sat a new fiddle, the five unused electric lamps with wire still wrapped around them, and a kerosene lamp that Josh actually used. In the corner stood a few new rifles and a number of leather-bound books, including Shakespeare.

"I brought you some herbs for your stomach," Belle said. "But I want to look at your feet while I'm here."

"Oh, yes." Josh sat down and removed his old shoes while Belle watched. "They're all swollen up," he said. He pulled down his thin black silk socks. His ankles were bony and pale.

Belle looked at his missing toes. Two had frozen off when he was a boy and the temperature had sunk down to zero for two weeks. Jim Josh, caring for his sick mother, had walked to town for food. When he returned and warmed his feet, he removed his shoes to find that the toes had broken off his foot and remained in his shoe. For a while, it looked like he might lose his entire foot, but old Sam Billy had used a poultice from mallow plants that drew out the black poison.

In spite of his missing toes, Josh had slipped through an army physical and done a brief stint, along with Horse, in China's Boxer Rebellion. While there, he lost two other toes. He still had phantom pain, he said, but at least his feet matched.

"What you need on those feet is hot camphor, good wool socks, and bigger shoes," Belle told him. "Your shoes are too small."

He was skeptical. "These are the same size they gave me in the army."

"Well, they made a mistake."

"The military doesn't make mistakes." He looked at Belle's stern face. "Okay, okay," he said as much to please her as to help himself. "I'll try it. What if I bought some spats to go along with them?"

"Suit yourself, just so long as the shoes are bigger."

He put his shoes back on. "Here, let me get you some tomatoes." He went out to the car, opened the car door and picked a bag of tomatoes. From inside, Belle heard the door

shut. Jim Josh returned, gave her the tomatoes, and the Grayclouds drove home just as a light rain began misting the
windshield.

It was this same rain falling a few days later when Will Forrest drove his new car up the muddy red road to the Indian
school and sat inside it, watching for Nola to appear in the
schoolyard. He knew the children went outside after lunch
every day, regardless of the weather. It was believed then
that people who remained indoors were more prone to tuberculosis, and since it was a disease Indians caught more
often than whites, they were sent outside, rain or shine.

That day they stood together under a shelter while it rained.
The girls pulled their black cardigans tight around their light
blue uniforms and shivered. Rena Graycloud discussed her
new beau. "Do you know what Bobby Duane says?" she
asked. "He says 'Ooh, la, la.' Now isn't that French?"

The schoolgirls giggled.

Some of the older boys whittled wood as they stood beneath the roof of the large porch. The curled shavings of
wood fell by their feet. Ben Graycloud, who was still at Watona Indian school, walked away from the whittlers and went
over to talk to Nola, but the matron saw him and went to
separate them. She knew the two of them would be up to no
good, holding hands or touching each other, and those
thoughts accounted for how Miss Gray, one of the school
matrons, missed Will Forrest standing in the rain by the fence
in his tweed cap. Will beckoned to Nola, and she walked out
into the rain and across the yard and joined him. At the fence,
even in the downpour, Nola and Will began to talk. Her wet
hair was plastered against her forehead and neck. She smiled
up at him. He opened his jacket, took out a white rose and
offered it to her.

"If it wilts," he said, "I'll buy you another one."

She laughed. "You're getting all wet."

"Me? What about you? Why don't we get in the car? It's
dry."

"I suppose it would be all right." Nola went through the
gate. That was when Miss Gray noticed the look on Ben
Graycloud's face. He looked so shocked, she turned and
caught sight of Nola and Will. The four strange protectors,

too, watched as Will opened the car door and Nola blushed, held her wet skirt, and got in, holding the rose.

Miss Gray dashed up to the fence, yelling, "Young lady, you get back out here, right now!"

Nola didn't look back at the drenched, angry matron standing at the edge of the schoolyard with her hands on her hips. Will turned on the wipers. He took off his expensive wet hat, threw it in the back, and drove Nola away in the rainstorm, imagining the taste of the rain on her skin.

Rena stood open-mouthed and jealous while Miss Gray corralled everyone back into the building. She yelled at them through the rain. Ben watched with stark terror on his face as the four Indian men vanished, and all the children knew they were following Will Forrest's new automobile down the road, and inwardly they cheered the men who were runners and could travel the long, wide distances to protect a girl of their blood. For the children, it was all refreshing and glorious pandemonium. And even the sky complied as the clouds twisted above them.

Will parked the car at a dry creekbed several miles from the school. He handed Nola five more roses. He looked into her eyes and smiled. The sky darkened and they didn't see the clouds begin to move quickly across it and gather into themselves. Rain began to pelt down and very suddenly, it seemed, the creekbed came to life. Nola held the roses against her cheek, smelling them. She was outlined by the dark gray sky through the car window behind her.

The rain crashed down, followed by hailstones so large they dented the automobile. The fragrance of roses was stronger than hail, but then the storm went silent and Nola knew a tornado was forming. She began to worry about her guardians. She didn't see them anywhere. But in the sky above the young couple, the storm clouds were shaping themselves into a whip-tail funnel.

Will kissed Nola on the cheek. "We'd better go." He started up the dented car and turned it around. They drove through the airlessness, the vacuum and silence that seemed to last forever until the air screamed and the storm broke. The trees bent and split, branches broke, but even so the two lovers were happy as they drove back to the school.

While the sky howled, Will parked the car and with his

arm around Nola, they went running toward the school. He opened the door, but the school was vacant. Everyone had gone to the storm cellar. ''Where's the shelter?'' he yelled at Nola. She pointed and they ran back outside to the entrance of the tornado cellar and beat on the door. Nola held her skirt down with one hand and protected her eyes from sand with the other, but when the door opened, the wind died down and Nola's skirt was suddenly still, hanging back down around her legs. The headmistress sent them away, saying that Nola was expelled from school for all time and that she didn't care if the wind blew them off the very face of the earth. Her cold eye backed up her words. The couple, fearing the stillness and silence, made a mad dash back to the car before the tornado reached them.

That same day, Leticia Graycloud refused to take cover in the tornado cellar. She locked the door of her room, and despite the family pounding on it with their fists, she did not open it. Lettie remained closed inside her own turbulent world. It was enough for her. As the storm beat against the house, and the lights went out, she held a match to a candle and sat calmly in the center of a braided rug with her hand on a Ouija board, asking for the initials of the killers. She thought the storm would heighten the energy of the spirits, but the uncooperative board, as always, spelled only ''Yes'' and ''No,'' and the tornado came so close to the Graycloud house that the vacuum of air sucked the fire from the candle and Lettie sat in the dark, her face pale and without expression, thinking this was still another undecipherable message.

   She did not hear Nola and Will drive up to the house, nor did she hear the trees uprooting at the next bend in the road, or the barns on the other side of town blowing over and flying a piece at a time over the churches. Or the screams of one cow hurled into another, leaving them looking like an interlocked puzzle down on the ground where they fell. And there were the squawks of Belle's germanium crystal radio down in the potato cellar where the rest of the family waited out the storm.

A few days later, when the yard was cleaned of the storm's debris, Belle decided there was too much darkness in her daughter's room. She forced open the door. Lettie sat in the same bed that had been infested with black, shining crickets. In the light of a single candle, her face was wax white. She held a spread of cards in her hand, and despite Belle's noisy footsteps, she was silent and deep in a trance.

Belle pulled open the curtains. "I've had enough of this," she said. Then she pulled the curtains down altogether, picked a deck of playing cards up from the floor, and blew out the candle. "You're going to start a fire in this old house." She folded the drapes. "And kill each and every one of us."

She shook Lettie's shoulders to wake her out of the trance while Louise and Nola watched from the door. Louise had never seen her younger sister look so vacant. She was worried, but she didn't enter the room.

Belle ran down the stairs and heated the coffeepot, poured the thick black liquid from the blue enamel pot, and returned to Le6tie's room. As she sipped at the coffee, some color began to return to Lettie's face. Belle confiscated the candles. "This is nonsense. Now get up out of that bed." Belle broke the French Ouija board over her knee. The crack of it startled Lettie. "No more of this," Belle huffed. She smoked the four corners of the room with sage and cedar while she prayed for any unwelcome spirits to return to their origins. With an eagle feather, she fanned the smoke over Lettie, and the room was gray and cloudy, and when Lettie began to cry it seemed like the sun came out.

"That's good," said Belle. "If you cry, you're doing better."

That evening, Lettie had dinner with the rest of the family. She ate two pieces of cornbread and everyone watching her thought she was almost normal.

Tornado Nola, as it came to be called, was a favorite topic in Indian Territory. The twister had touched down only in select locations. It destroyed the Catholic church, but it left the Baptist church untouched. The most devout of both faiths concluded it was God's will they attend the Baptist church. A good number of Indian Catholics converted at once, even though a few others pointed out how the saints and icons had landed unbroken in the forest; surely that was a miracle in its own right. Saint Francis came to rest perfectly upright in the crotch of an oak tree. A crucifix, unnailed from the church wall, stuck to the trunk of a nearby tree. Pale Mary stood in the shallow end of a pond with no scratches or damages besides a broken finger.

The priest, a soft young man named Father Dunne, set to work at once rebuilding the church in that place where Tornado Nola had set down the saints and the virgin. He announced to his flock that the message God meant to convey by this act of nature was that the church should be moved into the woods. His conviction about God's purpose was so strong it brought some of the Catholics back, and they went to the woods to worship, and still the women kept their heads covered with black shawls and scarves. And he heard confessions and for a time he divvied penance from behind the shade of a large tree.

And all this time, Will Forrest was taking fresh white roses to Nola Blanket, driving his car that was still dented from hailstones. He swore he'd never get it fixed, that the memory of Tornado Nola was sweet in his mind every time he looked at one of the dime-sized dents.

Belle Graycloud's vision was clear enough to see that Will Forrest, with his offerings of white roses, was not just keeping the florist in business, but was sincere about Nola Blanket. He was neither a fortune-seeker nor a schemer, she knew that, so it wasn't his courtship with a too-young girl that she objected to, but the presence of danger she felt inside the house. Even in love, or what they called love, Nola filled the rooms with a sense of impending doom. Her mournful eyes and tight lips still silenced everyone, until they felt compelled to speak in whispers, though it seemed this soulful quality was what had attracted Will to Nola. And though Nola took pills before she went to sleep in the blue-lighted hallway alcove, she woke up around three each morning with nightmares. When she cried out, Belle would tiptoe down the cold wooden hallway, pull the covers up to Nola's chin, and sit with the frightened girl until she fell asleep.

Nola's fear was an icy hand reaching into Belle, and the old woman felt forced to return to the thick-walled root cellar where no human pain or conflicts could penetrate her wise old flesh. Each evening, she came out for dinner and ate in silence with her family. They pretended that nothing was unusual. Moses did not ask Belle about her reason for exile in her holy cave. They'd been through this before. Instead, he spoke with Lou and Floyd about the casual goings-on of neighbors, cattle, and weather.

One Saturday night, after dinner, Will picked Nola up at the Graycloud's house. After he drove out to the country, he put a new fur coat around her shoulders and held her in the latest position Rudolph Valentino had used for seducing starlets on the screen at the Bijou. He was irresistible and he knew it. And she was like a soft animal. He adored her. But when he tried to put his hand inside the satin pocket of the mink coat, Nola pulled away from him. "What are you doing?" she asked. Will didn't answer. He was smiling. He brought out the purple velvet ring box and opened it in front of her. "If I could take you to Paris, I would. Here, give me your hand." He put the diamond ring on her finger.

She laughed. "Paris? Could I buy a new dress?"

"Anything you want. Dresses. Perfume. Satin shoes."

Nola beamed at him, embarrassed.

"You could have the Eiffel tower."

"Don't you love me?"

He nodded.

"Well then, be quiet about Paris and talk about me."

"You mean you're going to do it? You'll marry me?"

"Can we have white roses every day?"

"Twice a day."

She looked at the ring. It was too big for her finger and she said so. "Won't I lose it?"

"Don't worry. You'll grow into it."

Both of them laughed.

When Will returned Nola to the Graycloud house, light was spilling out the window on the dry winter grass. Will and Nola passed through that square of light and went to the door. They stood on the porch and kissed until Belle opened the door. As always, she'd been waiting and listening for their footsteps on the porch and now she stood in the open door with her hands on her hips. Will lost his composure, tipped his hat to the gray-haired woman before he walked back to the car, started it, and drove away. Nola was disappointed by his lack of courage and slipped inside quickly.

Ben had not yet gone to Haskell. He and Rena were home

from school for the weekend, and when Nola entered in her fur coat and held up her hand with the diamond ring on her finger, Ben was jealous. Rena squealed with delight over the ring. Ben lost his temper with her. "Stop sounding like a child." He turned around, pushed the dog Pippin out of the way, and ran down to the root cellar where Belle had erected a shrine and altar. He stayed there, fighting back tears. He could hear Rena's footsteps up above him in the house, rushing to Pippin's side. She was crying over the dog. He plugged his ears. Pippin, in the meantime unhurt, had rolled over on his back, wagging his tail. It thumped the floor, and Ben heard that too.

Nola paid no attention to the others. She sat down and looked at the diamond on her hand. It looked expensive. She wondered how Will earned his money.

"Don't sit by that window." Again Belle had to remind the girl that windows were unsafe places, were easily fired through by strange, passing gunmen.

Nola moved.

Lettie had followed the commotion to the living room. "What's wrong?" she asked. Nola sat with her arms crossed in front of her chest. Belle looked stern. Louise stared out the window and tapped her foot. Her face had reddened. Moses impassively sharpened a pocketknife with a whetstone and pretended not to listen. Rena was excited. She told Lettie about Nola's engagement. Lettie stared blankly.

"She's too young," Louise said, tapping her foot more quickly. "This is ridiculous."

Lettie spoke to Nola, "I know he's a good man," but the outraged Louise, her foot tapping faster, cut in. "You're kowtowing to her again! First she gets kicked out of school and now she's engaged. She's only thirteen, for Christ's sake."

But Nola silenced them all. It was the times, really, that backed up her argument. "It doesn't matter what I do," she told them. "My mother's money is in my name, my aunt's been killed, my uncle is in prison. I can't even sit by a window without being in danger, and every single one of you is looking over your own shoulder and watching every crooked shadow on the ground. Because I'm here."

They were silenced by the truth.

"I already thought it out," Nola said. "Even if he's crooked, I'm worth more to him alive."

She looked sad. It was true. It was the times, really, with headrights and claims to land multiplying with the birth of a child, and white men marrying Indian women to possess their wife's and children's allotments of land.

"I see," was all anyone could say when Nola was finished speaking. And they did see. Ben heard Nola's argument from the cellar. He felt sympathy for the girl. He went upstairs and put his arm around her. She leaned against him and held in her tears. Moses went out to the barn to check the last of his horses. He felt beaten, and he sat among the bales of hay for a while, escaping into the silence and rank odor of the barn. He was a man. A man was accustomed to taking care of things, and he could do nothing.

That night, the women began to plan, without joy, for a wedding. A wedding to a young man who hadn't enough courage to stay with his fiancée on the night she'd announced their plans. And that night Nola's nightmares stopped.

Later, in her room, Lettie moved aside the braid rug. Under it, she had painted a Ouija board on the wood floor, a board that wouldn't be broken over an old woman's knee. She asked, once again, for the initials of the killers. She'd been suspicious of Walter Bird's trips to the dentist. She was sure she'd seen him the night of Walker's murder and she had linked up the fortune-teller's words with his last name, but when she looked further, the story about the dentist in Tulsa had proven true. Her only option, she thought, was to find the woman who traveled with the carnival.

The next day, accompanied by Moses, Lettie went to see Benoit. Benoit was thinner and paler than before. He had placed dominoes on a board on his sagging cot and he stared out the barred window. It was his eye to the world. He stood up absently and greeted Moses and Lettie as if they were strangers. The vision of him was so frightful that the newly returned color drained again from Lettie's face, and it wasn't long until she wanted to leave.

Moses was alarmed, but as they left the cell, he said, "I've seen men go away like that before. When they are locked up.

It's a kind of freedom." He had seen it during the war, he told her, with prisoners, and he thought it was a good sign.

"You're lying," Lettie said, and when she arrived home she began to prepare her journey to find the fortune-teller.

That night, as she was packing, the sheriff paid a call on Lettie at home. He'd seen her at the jail and concluded that she was feeling better. He brought a blue satin box of Swiss chocolate. As a courtesy, Lettie bit into a piece of candy, but she felt sick and placed it back, uneaten, in the box. "Thank you," she told him. "It's very good." Sheriff Gold held his hat on his lap, watching her. He said very little.

"Well." He searched for words. "That big oil sale has sure made a change around here."

Lettie looked at him blankly.

"Business is good. New drillers are in. Even the royal family from England plans to visit. Will Rogers and that other trick roper, Fraser, are going to perform for them, and there's going to be an Indian show better than Buffalo Bill's group."

"I'm not really impressed." Lettie's eyes began to glare. Then she stood up. "I don't feel well." Without apology to the sheriff, she went to her room to finish packing. Jess Gold tried to hide his surprise, but his neck reddened with embarrassment. He looked at his watch and said it was late to visit anyway. "She doesn't look good," he said to Belle.

"No, she doesn't."

"I hope she feels better soon."

"Thank you, Jess. It's good of you."

She opened the door, and as he vanished like a shadow into the night, she glimpsed one of the protectors standing like a spirit at the edge of darkness, and she waved.

The next day, before she set out on her journey, Lettie stopped by the jail to see Benoit. He looked even thinner and more silent. She hardly recognized the fashionable, fiery young man she had loved, and though he'd been imprisoned in the narrow cell for several months, he still had not come to trial, and he was downhearted. "It's a waste of time," he said, when she told him that she was going to search for the fortune-teller, but he harbored a hope that the big-featured, heavy carnival woman might supply a key to the mystery of his troubles.

Before she left, Lettie said, "Benoit, I have to tell you something." She spoke quietly, so Bird wouldn't hear her. "Nola's getting married."

"What?"

"She's marrying a boy named Will Forrest. He's the son of your lawyer."

"Jesus!" Benoit said. He began to pace the cell. "Jesus Christ!"

Lettie was relieved that Benoit could still be angry. "No," she said. She put a finger to her lips. "It's the best thing for her. It'll save her. I know it."

"How do you know?"

"Intuition."

She left him with a stack of books to read, and a bag of fattening food. The bag contained a half dozen sweet rolls, cheese, chocolate, and fruitcake. At the bottom was a note that said "I love you." She stopped on her way out, in the sheriff's office, to retrieve her large fabric bag.

"Where are you going?" Jess Gold asked.

"I'm going to Claremore. To the hot springs. I'm feeling under the weather."

"I thought you looked a little tired." He sounded concerned. "How long will you be gone?"

"Just until I feel better." She lifted the strap over her shoulder.

At the train station, Lettie bought a ticket and sat on a bench, reading the board with its arrival and departure times. She worried about whether or not she should have told Benoit about Nola. By the time her train arrived, it was dark. She heard the moaning cattle being loaded in another car. She put her bag in the overhead. It was only an hour later when they passed through Claremore. She rode on past the Claremore station. She slept that night as the train went south, sitting with her head against the smoked-up window, leaning on the glass wall of night. Her hat was on her lap.

With the last oil sale, the town was full. All the hotel rooms were occupied. The most recently arrived slept out the cold nights on mats they laid outside the doors of businesses. Gamblers who heard about the oil boom had set up high-stakes poker games in tents in the woods. They dealt awkwardly with gloves on their hands. They wanted only to strike it rich and leave. Con men and drug dealers passed through town, stayed a while, then went on.

It was at this time when Hale convinced the pale girl, China, to marry John Stink. China was in love with Hale and she would have done anything for him, so after she thought about it, she consented. Next to Nola Blanket, Stink was one of the richest Indians in the territory, but few people knew it. And, if any of the crooked white people had thought he was dead and a ghost, they would have laid claim right-off to his money and his land, but the news had somehow managed to escape them. But Hale's plan was clever. He thought John Stink was crazy. Years before, Stink had given his father's Arabian thoroughbreds away, and now he refused to accept oil lease payments or live in a regular house. He liked nothing more than to pick up the golf balls white golfers lost and resell them, even though he was rich. He used the golf ball money to buy cookies for his mongrel dogs. That seemed even crazier. And Hale noticed that the other Indians in town never spoke with Stink anymore, or even looked at him.

China was both tough and innocent, a strange mix. She'd been seen around for some time. She was pretty, and Hale thought it was a cinch that John Stink would marry the girl, and he was sure Stink wouldn't be any trouble after the wedding, since the old man had no use for money, no concept of it even.

Stink was gleeful as a child with the attention China gave him. In her high heels and thin white legs, she carried cookies up to Mare Hill where Stink camped out. With him, she watched the golfers hit balls with clubs despite cold weather and freezing mud, and the golfers also watched her. The dogs liked her. That was a point in her favor.

Michael Horse knew Redshirt was out grazing the hillsides. He walked first in one direction, then another in search of the blood bay stallion. That's how he found the bat. It was twilight. The air had a chill to it. The red light was vanishing down the west side of the earth. Horse bent to look at the hoofprints of horses, and the bat was there. It was lying in a clump of dry grass near a stone. Horse bent over and looked at it. Its black wings were lined and webbed like a human palm. It had dark nipples down its furred gray belly, white sharp-looking teeth, and a lovely face. He could see why the older people respected the flying mammals. He gazed at the delicate wings and toes.

Horse had never actually seen one of the medicine bundles opened. Until recently, the bundles were buried with the body of the person who owned them, or maybe it would be more precise to say that the bundles owned the people. Now, with the grave robbers, the families of bat medicine practitioners did not want the bundles to fall into the wrong hands, so they kept them at home or buried them under their houses.

Horse held the bat in his hand. He needed medicine, and he knew it. Even though he'd had no sickness except toothaches in his life, and even though those were now covered with solid gold, he knew the world wasn't setting just right on its axis, and things had gotten all out of kilter. Every one of them needed medicine, needed protection.

He wondered what Sam Billy would have done to dry this bat. He studied it. He closed his eyes and concentrated on tapping into the bat realm, that nation of night people, those who sent a cry out to the world and through their own voices understood the placement of things. But suddenly the creature snapped to life, opened its eyes, twisted about, and the fangs seemed to grow longer, and it bit Horse's hand. He dropped it and then felt guilty for dropping it. And afraid. He remembered his cousin, infected with rabies, screaming inside the woodshed where his parents locked him, how he ate a hole into the wood before he died. They burned the place down to kill the rabies. Horse could still see the giant tongues of flame.

In this turmoil, he forgot about Redshirt. And the damage from the bat was already done, so Horse decided to keep it. He put it in the bag he carried. He would be silent in the presence of the bat and listen for it to tell him what course of action he might take for returning the world to its axis.

Along the way back to his tepee, he found another bat. This one also he thought he would take home. He put it in the bag, along with the first.

When he reached his tepee, he opened the bag and looked in. The two bats were locked together, mating. He took them out, put them in a little hole in the ground and covered them with dry leaves. They stayed together, mating, for four days, the male with his fangs exposed. By the last day, the female had found her way out of the leaves and flown away. The male was dead.

Horse left the male bat out to dry, for his own bundle of sacred things. The bat medicine Sam Billy had told him about must have already been working in his favor, for the rabies he expected to attack him never took hold. He knew he had a calling or something, a gift to offer the world, and that must have been why he was spared.

The year of 1922 was almost over by the time Nola and Will were united in marriage. In spite of the wedding, it was a year of separations. Not only were people turning away from one another, but there were other splittings, mind from heart, body from spirit. Some broke quickly, weeping openly and without shame in public places. In others, like Martha Billy, the changes were barely visible. Martha softened a little around the eyes, and began to wear moccasins on her pale feet. Belle, even though she was preoccupied with Lettie's travels, was the first person to notice the changes in the preacher's wife. She wondered if Martha was pregnant. Martha smelled like perfumed soap, and her blond hair was looser on her neck.

By year's end, the double lives of people grew more obvious on all counts. Martha wasn't the only one who changed. Her husband, the Reverend Billy, wore braids and moccasins to deliver his sermons and he finally wrote the main church offices that he was resigning from the ministry.

And most of the Indian people lost trust in the whites, so they stopped seeing Doctor Black for their illnesses and pains. The death of Walker didn't rest well with any of them. They believed the brandy-drinking Doc Black was involved, or at least had lied about the cause of death, and that he was in with those who conspired against them. They returned to the medicine people. They needed faith and hope more than they needed pills. And, in cases that the old medicine did not help, people went to the part-Indian veterinarian instead of Doctor Black. The animal doctor's reputation was cemented when he cured a man of a heart attack by giving him a concoction of horse liniment and hot water, and the man survived. Doctor Black didn't blame them. Who really could they trust? He began making plans to leave.

It seemed as though, toward the end of that year, people became the opposite of what they had previously been, as if the earth's polar axis had shifted. At the Indian school, two Creek girls were so fascinated with white heaven that they dyed their hair yellow like angels in pictures, and they wore white gowns they stitched together out of bedsheets. One of the school matrons, by contrast, began dying her hair black, and asked if she could attend the peyote church. She learned Indian songs, and she was so sincere that she was accepted as a bona fide honorary Indian. Then, to the disbelief of his friends, a man who preached peace and had protested the World War, whipped his grandson to death. And Father Dunne moved to the woods where the statue of Saint Francis had landed upright during Tornado Nola. He fed the birds and slept outside on the earth, even when it was snowing, like the night the bats dropped out of the sky all over town.

Lettie traveled for several weeks. The sheriff seemed genuinely forlorn. Belle began to think he was in love with her daughter.

But all Belle's thoughts about Lettie and the sheriff were interrupted by the wedding plans. Nola was spending her money in a way that shocked the Grayclouds, even Floyd, who was known for his own extravagant ways. She ordered Russian caviar for the reception, ordered thousands of white ornamental roses, and bought a bridal train nearly as long as the aisle of the church. She bought jars of rouge and bolts of pink silk. She brought home nail polish and chemical lotions that removed hair from legs.

"Why do you want to take the hair off your legs?" Rena asked. She propped herself up on Lettie's bed and watched Nola's reflection in the mirror.

"Because I'm getting married!" Nola was haughty and impatient with Rena's stupidity. Or at least she covered up her fears and misgivings in this way.

Benoit was too distraught to care that his niece was throwing money away on breadfruit and mangoes from the West Indies. He hadn't even kept track of how long Lettie was gone, but he did remember to remain silent when the gray-

haired attorney named Forrest paid him a second call, and
he remembered that Nola was marrying the man's son.

Forrest pleaded once again that Benoit tell him the details
of the night his home burned down, but Benoit didn't trust
him, so all he said was, "I'm innocent," and the lawyer,
frustrated, closed his briefcase and let himself out of the cell.

Lettie followed a trail of vague leads from Texas to Louisiana, searching for the woman who might know about the
murder of Sara. She went along the gulf and walked the many
miles of terrain not covered by train or bus. In Cajun country
she asked after the woman, but the men in their flowered
shirts only eyed her breasts and looked with interest at the
sweat that formed on her upper lip. They had no answers.
Likewise, the French-speaking women behaved as if they
had never heard English before. No one knew the woman
with unlined palms.

In desperation, Lettie went from door to door to each of
the little yellow wooden houses. The houses were set up on
pieces of wood and cinderblock so that water would not flood
their foundations, and in the heat and humidity, paint peeled
from the mildewed walls. At the last house down in Good
Earth Parish, a round woman invited her in. She looked Lettie over and said, "You better sleep here tonight. It's too
dangerous after dark. They found oil here and now we hide
at night."

The woman's name was Martine. Lettie told her that she
was looking for a fortune-teller. She'd learned the woman
who traveled with the carnival was from Terrebonne County,
she said, and a man's life might depend on finding her. Martine nodded in understanding, but she didn't know a woman
like that. There was a psychic and card reader over in Houma,
she told Lettie. An Indian, she said, as if it made a difference
to the young woman.

But Lettie, fatigued from the journey and her worries, began to fall asleep even while drinking the pink-colored craw-
fish soup from a white bowl. "You better sleep now," said
the woman, and Martine made a bed for Lettie by the door
so she could get up early the next morning, without waking
Martine, and head back to the train station in time for the
first train out. Lettie set her green hat on the floor beside her
and fell asleep, fully clothed, on top of the pallet. Martine

looked at the young woman and shook her head back and forth.

The next morning Lettie left a note wrapped around a silver ring, thanking the woman for her kind hospitality. She closed the door quietly and walked down the street, carrying her flowered bag. In the early morning, marsh herons cried out louder than the crowings of domestic roosters. Clothing, shirts, and dresses, hung still damp on lines. The morning was misty. Dried grasses rotted in the moisture and ghosts of fog rose up from water. Everything smelled of fish, earth, and decay. Lettie walked through it to the train station.

When the older woman received the letter from her sister, Martine, she knew its contents even before she opened it. She knew the man was sitting in a jail cell with a swollen-jawed fellow. She knew, also, that the events in Talbert, Oklahoma were like a dark wheel turning backward. She wanted to warn the young Indian woman who had paid her so generously, but she was afraid that her intrusion would have even more terrible consequences. Still, she was so nervous that the wrestler she lived with said, "Isabelle, you know I don't want you butting into these things anymore. You stay here now. With me, eh?"

Isabelle looked at him with her dark eyes. "Don't worry. I'll stay put. My feet are too worn-out for these travels." Somewhere inside she sensed she was lying, but she told him anyway, "Winter isn't the time for action anyhow. Even the earth slows down."

The wrestler looked at her. He knew she was already half-way back to Indian Territory.

Outside someone played a guitar and hummed. Isabelle listened. She saw, in her mind's eye, the man with the silver coins on his belt. There was nothing she could do to help him. And she had to look after her own life now, she thought. Billaye would leave her, he'd promised as much, if she went on the road again, so she tucked in her large red shirt, lifted her skirt up, pulled the shirttail down, put on her round glasses, and went out to tell a young woman's fortune, but even against her will she kept seeing the little town, the sign Talbert with the word marked over WATONA, and she saw the skeletal man in jail. He hadn't even had a trial. She was afraid she'd have to go against Billaye's wishes, but not now, she told herself, not yet. She told the young woman what she wanted to hear, that she would marry, have children, but not too many, and be happy in life.

The afternoon Lettie arrived home was Christmas Eve, just a few days before the wedding. Nola was in the living room sitting like a queen, barking out orders for the wedding to her young Indian girlfriends who were tickled to be part of the biggest event ever in Indian Territory.

News travels fast in Indian country, and Horse heard about the wedding from some of the Osages who passed by on their way fishing and hunting. He wanted to go. He hated to admit it, but he was a little lonely for human company. He walked to the closest road and hitched a ride over the land to Ona Neck's place. He knew she wouldn't be going to the wedding or any other to-do held inside a church. He asked her if she would come watch the fire while he was gone. "Where is your camp anyway?" she asked.

"Over at the Coffee."

"You want me to stay clear out there?" She stared at him, her lips tight. "Okay," she said before he responded. "Okay, I'll do it. You overpaid us for the bear grease last time anyway. It'll make things even."

Ona arranged for her son to take her to the river. They drove back and forth, trying to stay on the flattest land, but they still had to walk a good distance. When they arrived, at the tepee near the Coffee River, Ona looked at her dusty, laced-up shoes and said, "Lord, Horse, you've got to stop this nonsense."

Horse ignored her. "Keep an eye out for Redshirt, will you?"

"What if I see him? You expect me to catch that wild thing for you?" She laughed a gap-toothed laugh. "You just want his fire to rub off on you. You'll never catch him again."

Horse reached the Grayclouds late in the afternoon a day before the wedding. Belle was in a corner of the living room listening to the crystal radio set. The Dallas station had just come in. It was playing a program about President Harding's life. Belle hardly cared about the president, but she hadn't felt sociable ever since Ben turned sixteen and was put on notice that he had to leave for Haskell Indian School in Kansas. Belle was upset. He had to leave in January. He was young. She wanted him home. She already felt his absence. She closed out the world as she listened to the crystal set.

A Christmas tree was set up in the living room. The room was full of people, most of whom had arrived early, like Horse had, from the hills. Others were still arriving by train. Many of the Indians insisted on camping out above town, despite the freeze and the pellets of snow, but Belle planned to feed everyone.

That's what she'd said, anyway, and they all waited for a very long while before realizing she wasn't going to put down the earpiece to the radio. Finally, they began to cook the food themselves. To everyone's surprise and delight, Jim Josh brought fresh, out-of-season tomatoes. He wore new spats. Belle took off the headset for just a second, long enough to call out, "Hey there, Governor," which made him laugh. Everyone seemed relieved and stood up to go to the kitchen, expecting to eat. But Belle, who in the past had always been mindful of others, even to a fault, put the headphones right back over her ears as soon as she spoke to Josh. It was as if she wanted to shut out the world. Everyone supposed she was making a statement against the marriage of Nola and Will.

When Lettie came in, she was surprised to find the house full of people. She was weary and wanted to be left alone. Two older Indian women shook her hand in greeting. Lettie smiled weakly. She went to her mother. "I'm home," she said, tugging on the old woman's sleeve, but Belle did not look up, and as Lettie turned to go up the stairs, too tired to worry about her mother's indifference, Martha Billy arrived. Lettie stopped on the middle step and stared at Martha Billy. She was amazed at the sight of the woman. Martha had begun to look, in some peculiar way, like an Indian. She wore her long blond hair in a braid down her back. Her face seemed somehow stronger, more clearly defined. She raised her head and looked at Lettie. "Did you find out anything?"

Lettie shook her head sadly and started again up the stairs to her room. She carried her coat over her arm. But from the kitchen, Louise saw her sister and shouted with joy. "I was afraid you wouldn't make it home in time for the wedding.

Just wait till you hear the plans!'' She wiped her hands on her apron as she spoke, then she noticed the downcast expression on Lettie's face. "Nothing?"

Lettie shook her head.

Like Louise, no one knew how to feel in those days. Gain and loss, happiness and sadness were all mixed up together, and carried in the same bag.

Outside, Horse had again seen a horse trader talking business with Moses, and he went out. The trader, the man from Wichita Falls, offered cash, which was unheard of, for one horse. But McMann was a good-natured man and he'd traveled out of his way to talk to Graycloud. He was worried about the family. And rightly so, because the electric current had been shut off in Moses's house. They were lighting the place with cheap brown candles and kerosene lamps. Moses had relatives and guests to feed. He looked thin, and it was Christmas and the trader took pity on them. "I could use some saddles and rope, too, Moses," he said.

"Sure." Moses was slightly bent. He walked out to the barn, brought back a horse blanket and a hand-tooled leather saddle. The trader lifted them into the wagon and covered them with a heavy tarp.

"Why don't you stay for supper?" Moses asked.

"I didn't think you'd ever ask." McMann watered his horses, stomped the manure off his boots, and went inside with the older, darker man.

That night, Belle turned off the radio. She looked woeful, but her voice was angry. She said, "You've all been talking about me behind my back," and she ran off to the potato cellar for a while, then returned looking sheepish, and put on her apron and began to cook. By then, everyone had eaten, but they ate again, out of politeness, and said nothing.

After the second dinner, Moses blew out a candle. In the darkness, the stars and Milky Way lit up. No one noticed the electricity was turned off. The people all stood in front of the map of the universe, amazed by the lights on the wall. It was something, it really was, everyone thought. It was a fine, strong feeling, being there together with the stars lit up before them. Even if things were going wrong, the bad feelings disappeared in front of those stars. They wanted to touch each other that night and hold hands.

"They don't have a buffalo," Moses said as he studied the map. "No wonder we don't understand each other."

On the day before the wedding, Calvin Severance picked Rena up at the Graycloud house. He took her to the morgue where he'd been working as janitor and assistant to the mortician for over a month. Without the use of thumbs, he adapted ways to work, holding the broom with his palms and four fingers.

Shortly after Calvin began working there, a woman with extremely long hair was sent in. She had poisoned herself.

When the mortician unbraided her hair, it was longer than her body. He pulled it upward, above her head, measured it and cut off two and a half feet. He taped it at the end and stored it in one of the closets on a peg. He thought he could sell it one day as a wig. "Don't worry," he told Calvin, "no one will notice. Besides, it will grow back out." To prove this latter point, he opened another closet and showed Calvin the embalmed outlaw who'd been growing long whiskers and hair for over a year. The outlaw's mustache dropped down and his nails were claws. They curled under and were dangerous-looking.

"You mean they grow even after they are embalmed?"

"This one did."

The man's body could not be buried because of an identification problem, and the legalities of insurance claims. In the meantime, he was hooked on a peg, a bullet hole in his faded shirt, and growing a newly gray head of long hair. Occasionally a lawman or insurance agent came by to check evidence, asked why the hair was gray instead of black, and let the matter drop once again, as if they were certain that the dead man was someone else.

Calvin impressed Rena with the horror-filled world of death. She was already wide-eyed with his tales about the teachers at Carlisle Indian School where the founding father General Pratt's slogan was "Kill the Indian, and save the man." Cal's gone thumbs proved the cruel treatment of Indian boys. But he also told stories of ghosts rocking in chairs, and even though Rena wore Nola's rouge on her cheekbones that night, her face went pale.

Thinking she was scared, Cal offered her his hand. She took it. In this way, he courted her.

They sat on the velvet couch in the foyer and held hands a while, before Rena stood up and said she had to get home. "Everyone's there for the wedding. Nola ordered artichokes. Have you ever seen one? I haven't."

"Is it vegetable or animal?" Calvin smiled at her.

Rena liked his smile. "Will you be at the wedding?"

"Wouldn't miss it for the world. I've never seen an artichoke before."

He walked her down the steps. Just before she turned the corner on Main, the light from a building caught her golden hair and her mulatto yellow eyes. She turned back, once, to look at him. She waved.

At home, Ben was once again inconsolable. His unhappiness was compounded by his having to leave for Haskell. He had a broken heart and was hiding down in the cellar with potatoes and canned chicken. He'd started making use of Belle's cave, but just before three, he put on a false smile and went up to socialize with the wedding guests. They wanted to know about Tornado Nola and the murders that had taken place. They felt uncomfortable and nosey asking the adults but they asked him. His answers were vague. He kept glancing at Nola. She seemed unhappy. Whenever Belle asked a question about the details or arrangements, the thin girl snapped at her, "Whose wedding is this anyway?" Nola, they all assumed, had the jitters. She was sullen, also, when the guests asked her to tell them how she got kicked out of Indian school so that they could use her example to get their own children back.

The child bride had dark circles beneath her eyes. She had wept most nights, with a shawl pulled tight around her bony, still undeveloped shoulders. That night, Belle sat beside her, holding her small hand, and felt her heart go out to the girl.

But on the morning of the wedding, Nola had not a trace of misery in her face. She held ice to her eyes until the swelling disappeared, and her lips turned up in a rare smile. She was busy with the final details and still determined no one was going to help. She washed her hair in the kitchen sink, combing and drying it in the heat of the woodstove, and she talked with Moses.

"It's the biggest event of the year, isn't it?" she asked him, and her eyes were sparkling.

Moses was fixing a harness on the table. He looked up. He admired her strength. His smile showed it. She turned her suffering into a celebration. He was moved. "Yes, honey. It is. It's something you can be proud of." He went to her and tenderly he put his arms around the girl. For a moment, she was comforted by the sound of his old heart beating next to her ear and the scratchy feel of his shirt.

But then Nola went back to the wedding plans. She allowed Lettie to go to the church and check on the food. At the parsonage when Lettie saw what was for dinner, she was overwhelmed. There were over a hundred crystal glasses and a peacock carved of ice. Each tail feather was intricate with detail. Light shone through the ice like a cold fire, making rainbows in places on the walls. But even that was nothing compared to the inside of the church. The walls and pews were covered with thousands and thousands of white roses. The room smelled sweet and it looked like the inside of a cloud-filled heaven.

Ruth sat inside the church, alone, in the midst of the white flowers. Lettie looked at the back of her aunt's head, then saw Ruth turn in the pew to see who had entered.

"Hello," she said to Lettie, and half raised herself to stand.

Lettie went down the aisle and sat next to Ruth. It looked like she'd been crying. Love, Lettie thought, it hurts and gladdens us no matter what a woman's age.

Lettie, like everyone else, believed her photographer husband John Tate had only used Ruth first as a model and then a source of income. Ruth herself seemed to believe this and was embarrassed by her husband's presence behind the camera at every event.

They didn't speak. After a while Moses's twin said, "Moses isn't happy about this wedding."

Ruth and Moses often shared feelings and twin thoughts, Lettie knew.

The guests, particularly the Indians, sat dignified as royalty in the hard pews. Most of the older women wore traditional red broadcloth dresses and red leggings. They wore white feather crowns. Some of the men wore black, silk-lined suits while others wore otter fur hats and braids. Two men wore, over their clothing, the black Honor Blankets Mrs. Lookout had beaded with golden eagles. Stacey Red Hawk sat behind them. He looked around the church. Everyone was a suspect, the men in the back who wore trapper clothing, and even the local Englishwoman, Buckskin Liz, who lived the way she thought Indians ought to live, and wore a hand-sewn burlap dress with scissor-cut fringes. Stace eyed the group of Will's college friends. They wore the coonskin coats that were all the rage in the East. They looked like scrappers, with lips that curled up, and eyes that held know-it-all expressions.

Mr. Forrest sat in front of the boys. From his front row pew, he was calculating exactly how much money Nola had spent from her account on the wasteful flowers.

Reverend Billy, dressed in a man's traditional headdress, stood with his hands folded in a preacherly fashion, facing the dearly beloved who were gathered there together.

It was a spectacle the likes of which had never been seen, and the guests loved the large, extravagant wedding that had been planned by a thirteen-year-old child bride. They barely noticed John Tate taking pictures in the back of the church.

Rena stood not far from him, whispering to the brides-maids. As the maid of honor, she looked older than usual. She carried a white fur muff and wore too much of Nola's pink rouge. When the drummers stepped aside and the organ began, she walked down the flower-strewn aisle. She did not meet the eye of Calvin Severance, but she felt him watching her, and once she almost looked in his direction.

Rena was already at the front when John Stink walked in and sat down. Reverend Joe Billy was startled to see the ghost. He stared so long that many of the guests turned around to see what he was looking at. Even the ring bearer turned to the back of church and found himself staring straight into the ghostly face of John Stink. The boy quickly averted his eyes.

"Oh, no. A ghost at a wedding is bad luck," one of the guests whispered, and then hoped she wasn't overheard. All the Indians looked away from Stink, not wanting to meet his eye, but not before they noticed the girl who sat with him. She wore a white fake fur coat and had white hair and skin. She herself looked ghostly, like one of the spirit women who wandered the hills at night in search of their gone children. But, while the Indians turned away and didn't make eye contact with the ghost, the whites stared at the dark, scarred man who wore the red babushka and sat with a wisp of a girl who could have been anyone's nearly innocent young niece, dead or alive.

Finally, the people stood and turned to watch Nola enter and begin her journey down the aisle. Moses and Belle walked with her. They were dressed in traditional clothing. The white-gowned bride had a hand twined through the arm of each old person. They supported the girl, Moses in his otter hat and black, shined boots, Belle in the red and blue tear dress with a headband and a single eagle feather. As they walked down the aisle beside Nola Blanket with the roses in her black hair, Belle walked like she was dancing an old dance, each step a heartbeat, and Nola looked so much like an angel that the two dark girls with blond hair nearly swooned when they saw her.

Will looked on with tender eyes. As Nola reached the altar, he picked a rose from a bouquet and gave it to her.

She smiled at him.

"Who gives away the bride?" Joe Billy asked.

"I do," said Belle, and she looked around. Moses, on the other hand, looked restless and unhappy. It was because of John Stink's ghost, everyone thought.

But Ruth knew he was afraid and angry. She felt it in her own body. As the people watched through dreamy eyes, the young couple exchanged their vows, and then Will took the slight girl in his arms and kissed her and together they walked toward the white door of the rose-filled church.

Nola, to appease the traditional people, had woven the old ways in with the new, so immediately after the ceremony, she removed the long white dress, and changed into the long-tailed red military bridal coat that had been worn by Osage women ever since an Osage elder had visited the White House in Washington, D.C., admired the coat of a dignitary, and received it as a gift from the president. It was fine cloth with gold braids and epaulets. That elder had put it over his daugh-

ter's wedding clothing; it became a tradition. Since then all
the women wore the brass-buttoned coats at their weddings.

Belle helped Nola change from French satin shoes into her
moccasins and leggings, then she put the wedding crown
with tall plumes of red and white feathers on Nola's head.
Nola good-naturedly called it "the changing of the guard."
Belle laughed and embraced the high-spirited girl, but
couldn't help noticing how tiny the bride's legs were, how
thin her arms. And Nola's happiness made Belle believe the
girl loved Will Forrest and was not marrying him just to
ensure her safety. She hoped that Nola would not be hurt.
She felt a tender aching in her heart.

Will waited outside the church. He was patient. He stood
beside a wagon with two black horses. The horses would
drive the couple through town and country, showing off the
beautiful bride and the handsome groom. The horses were
also covered with blankets and ribbons. They wore beads
around their muscular necks, and headdresses of feathers.
They looked proud and they pranced with their heads
stretched high, while the snow fell quietly around them, en-
veloping the world.

The bride and groom rode up and down the roads. Will
held the reins, but Nola told him, secretly, how to use them.
Everyone who saw them believed she was silent and proud
and that he was the excellent horseman. They rode through
town and out along the dirt roads by the oil derricks that
looked like poorly built black towers reaching up toward gray
heaven.

After the promenade, the bride put on a giveaway, the
traditional kind. She gave away baskets of food, as well as
individual gifts. To Lettie Graycloud, she gave a hat with
ivory feathers and pearls sewn on in the shape of a bird. A
dove, Lettie guessed. She put the beautiful hat on her black
hair right away and the wedding guests admired it, but later,
after drinking champagne, Lettie started crying about the
bird, "Where do you think they got these feathers?" Nola
gave Ben a telescope for watching the night sky, but it was
small consolation. She gave Belle an eagle feather fan with
a beaded handle that had been made by Ona Neck, who was
out in the night watching over the fire of the Indian people
with a red stallion standing beside her. Nola gave Rena the

diamond ring she had once accused her of stealing. There was a fig tree for Jim Josh, blankets and saddles for other guests. She gave Michael Horse a watch and he was thankful even though he lived by the sun in those days. But the most wonderful gift of all was the red-coated horse she trotted out for Moses Graycloud. It was a mare and was equal in beauty to Redshirt. Michael Horse began at once to plot a way to bring the horses together. And while Moses stood beside the new horse for a picture, everyone rose up and remembered for a moment how life had been for Indians before the earth was broken open. Their hearts were full and it was more than just a few people who cried.

Later, Nola and Will danced together while a blanket was held open and carried around the room. The guests dropped coins and bills into the blanket. The women were so impressed by the generosity of the bride that they took off their rings and bracelets and dropped them in.

That night, the meteor shower was visible. While the stars fell across the sky, the Japanese fireworks exploded from down on the ground, gunpowder that wrote "Nola and Will" on the blackness of space. Standing outside in the thin layer of snow, the wedding guests cheered and hollered at the fireworks as they'd done when the oil lease sold for over a million dollars. Some of the men, a little crocked, threw their hats. Horses shied. Then it was dark and silent again with the odor of gunpowder still in the air. The revelers went back inside with their glasses of champagne. They complimented the ice peacock and the vegetables that had been carved into the shapes of lilies and birds, and the tall wedding cake with an Indian maiden, a cowboy, and a model of the Eiffel tower that looked more like an oil derrick than the real thing some of the younger men had seen in Paris during the most recent war.

Belle was tipsy and laughing. Horse hadn't seen her that way for so many years that he sat back and watched her. Lyle Billy, Old Sam's brother, wore a stovepipe hat. He made a long, drawn-out speech to Belle.

"Back in the old days it wasn't like this," Lyle told her. "My father had two wives. That's the way we thought it should be. Those women could cook a pork, you know. And work, they could work. Nowadays the women hire help and go out shopping, but those old-time women, they worked, and they didn't complain about a thing.'' He teetered a little. ''The men all had two wives. We thought that was the way we ought to live.'' He looked off, recollecting those better days. ''Then we found out my dad's wives each had two husbands and that was why only one of them was around at a time.'' He looked confused. ''So I can't tell you for sure that he was really my father or not, come to think of it.''

Belle was laughing. Rena cut Cal's meat. Then Nola cut the cake. The Indian maiden fell to the floor. It struck some people as odd and it set up a wave of silence, as if something had gone wrong, even though Nola and Will went out on the dance floor with their arms around each other, gliding across the room in time with the waltz.

The wedding put romance in everyone's minds. A few days after the ceremony, Belle and Moses took a tray of bread and meat to their room and remained until noon of the following day, holding one another in their older arms. Lettie visited Benoit at the jail and stared with longing into his eyes, not caring at all about what the sheriff thought. Calvin Severance asked Rena to the movies.

And late one afternoon, the pale girl, China, led John Stink into the county courthouse to purchase a marriage license. They had been drinking, and they were both smiling. China told the clerk they wanted to get married.

''Write your names on this paper.'' The clerk pushed a slip of note paper toward them. Stink nodded at the clerk and smiled like an old fool.

When China finished writing their names, the clerk took the paper, disappeared for a moment to check the records, and returned. ''I can't issue you a license,'' she told the girl. But before China could ask what was wrong, the clerk said, ''Say, aren't you the girl who took off her blouse and jumped off the balcony?''

China ignored the question. She put her elbows on the counter and fixed the woman with a pale-eyed gaze. ''Why not?'' she asked. ''The license, I mean.''

''Well, John Stink is dead.''

''Dead?''

"John Stink. He's dead." She showed the death certificate to the girl.

"He can't be dead. He's right here!"

"That's what our records show."

"But this is him. How can he be dead?"

The clerk looked over her glasses at the girl, said "Dead" one more time, then walked away from the two drunks, one of whom she believed was impersonating a dead man. The fortune-hunters were too much for her. She looked disgusted.

China looked into the square, scarred face of the old man, then turned and walked away. He reached for her. She shook loose of his grasp and left him behind. He looked sad. She walked out of the building and headed out of town and he followed. When she reached the town limit, she began running until she was out of John Stink's sight and far away from his whining, snuffling dogs.

It was beginning to turn dark. Beneath the lead-colored sky, she ran to the oil field, stumbling here and there over rocks. When she was close to the field, she saw a rush of activity. A group of men stood inside a derrick, pulling a chain back and forth. It was noisy. A gas burn-off hissed in the air. The men spun a pipe back up from the earth and added another section to it. Behind them the vast horizon was obliterated by the dark numbers of skeletal derricks and the gray shacks that contained diesel pumps. The men were muddy and fatigued. It was past quitting time and they were overworked and anxious to leave when suddenly the ground began to rumble and shake. China felt it move up through her shoes. She watched with horror as the pipe the men held flew up like a bullet, shooting up from the ground, rising up the derrick into the sky. It flew out with the great hot pressure of inner earth. The men ran away, looking back over their shoulders at the flying pipe which began to crash back down, landing partly inside the breaking derrick where the men had stood, tearing apart the wood and metal as if the framework were nothing more than a toy.

China watched the explosion that came from inside the earth. It burned and roared like God's wrath against Baptists. She remained standing at the edge of the woods as the fireball rose up and lit the sky like a new sun. It melted the hard earth, melted the metal derrick until it was nothing but golden flux on the ground. She shielded her eyes from the fiery glare.

From where she stood, she saw Hale run toward the men, yelling. He jumped into a truck with four laborers, and they drove to a mound at one side of the oil field and they began, frantically, with a giant bit, to open up the earth. Despite the roaring fire, China thought she could make out Hale's words. "It's burning out all the oil in the goddamned earth," he screamed. "Plug it! We've got to plug it!" And they did. The sweating men worked in the intense heat with steam rising from their reddened, flushed bodies. They dug a hole and plugged one side, and even as they worked, the snow beside China melted off the ground. It steamed upward, and the vision of it changed her. It was like watching hell rise up. She knew then, she knew that the earth had a mind of its own. She knew the wills and whims of men were empty desires, were nothing pitted up against the desires of earth.

In town, the land rumbled like an earthquake. Lettie was in the cell with Benoit. She had given up caring what the sheriff thought, or even if Walter Bird eavesdropped on her words. Her sorrow had turned to careless rage. It was as if the fiery land took the caution from deep inside the murmurings of her own skin. Sheriff Gold, who already knew about the love between Lettie and Benoit, wondered at her sudden imprudence in the way she sat close to Benoit on the cot and held his hand without having spoken so much as a how do you do to Jess Gold. It was Nola's wedding, he figured, that fired her up. Or at least partway.

Lettie that day told Benoit she wished they were the ones who had gotten married, that all her life she'd wanted nothing more than to marry him and be a couple like other couples.

"You mean legally? Under white law?" he asked.

He didn't say he thought his time was running out.

She took off her hat and stared at his eyes. She didn't say that she thought he would never again go free.

"We could do it," he said. "Why don't we?"

Lettie turned away for a moment. She considered how the sheriff had courted her, how she led him on, then sat down that day with Benoit in front of Jess Gold's eyes. How would she explain this turn of affections? She wondered whether or not he'd permit a wedding in the jail. But she knew that visiting with a prisoner often enough to have loving feelings was something that happened all the time. It was one of the funny things about women, and many of them came to love men behind bars, men who were taken out of the daily work of their lives.

"All these years," she said, "I never thought our lives would end up like this. I never thought the world would fall apart around us and break up piece by piece." She looked at him.

"Neither did I."

"How do we know if you'll ever get out?"

He put his skinny yellow hand beneath her chin. "Because I'm innocent. Even if the world's falling apart."

He held her face inside his hands and smiled at her. She let herself feel reassured.

And so, Lettie, when she left the cell, went outside and walked around, then went back into the office and sat down across the desk from the sheriff. It was dark. She was nervous and hesitated a moment, then looking at the floor, she told him, "I've been coming here so often that, I hate to tell you, but I think I've fallen in love with Benoit."

The young sheriff's pale and flat-boned face went blank. Lettie thought he was heartbroken. The burn-out was still rattling the cups and windows and locks. He was quiet. He looked at the maps of Oklahoma territory on his walls. He stood up and said, "Of course, why didn't I see it?" He offered her a cup of coffee, then took one of her warm hands inside both his own cool palms and wished her well. After a while, Lettie went out in the dark and saw the fire in the sky above the edge of town.

China still watched inner earth's fire. Near where she stood, the heat was so intense that some trees burned from the root upward, grew dark and fell over, and the stones grew hot, and she heard the hissing sound of the fire moving outward to places where the snow was still unmelted.

After the exhausted men put out the fire and went home, China walked into the office. Her face was smeared with the flying ash. Her coat was singed and discolored by smoke.

She sat across from spider-legged Hale. He was weary and had purple burns on his face.

She told him the bad news about John Stink being dead.

"What do you mean, dead?"

"He's dead. That man ain't even Stink. Stink died."

"What do you mean it's not Stink? Of course it's Stink."

"The clerk said John Stink is dead." She repeated "Dead" to Hale in the same way the clerk had spoken the final word to young China.

"When did he die?"

"Well, how the hell would I know? You're the one that paid me to marry him. To marry a goddamned corpse!"

Hale sat down. "Calm down," he said. He was tired from fighting the fire. He brushed back his hair. He tried to think. "You went there with him, right?"

"Yeah, that's who you said it was."

Hale ran his hands over his face, then looked up at her. "Jesus." He shook his head. "Let's talk about it later. Have you eaten?"

Before he got up from his seat, she was already combing her moon-white hair and putting the heat-melted lipstick on her mouth. She turned toward the thin oilman and smiled. But her heart wasn't in it. She was thinking of the gas fire still burning underground.

That night, out in the copse of trees, Father Dunne was asleep on the frozen ground when it began to thaw. He sat up and opened his eyes. "What's going on?" he said to no one. In the darkness, he saw firelight behind the trees and remembered the story of the burning bush and the words that came out of it. He was sure that he heard words behind the bush. It was the sound of earth speaking. It was the deep and dreaming voice of land. It was as if he had wakened for the first time, as if his eyes were at last opened. He put aside the Bible and the rosary he kept wrapped about his newly callused fingers. The real words of God were in the bush. He should have known it. He took the crucifix down from the oak and gently filled the wounds of the tree with soft mud that formed as the earth melted and murmured, and he decided to pack up his things and go, on foot, to find Michael

Horse. He was sure the old man would know the meaning of this sacred event.

Father Dunne thought he and Horse were both listening to a voice inside themselves, and that voice was God's earth.

Horse had been back up in the bluffs since the wedding. Unlike the priest, who was excited by the burning bush, he knew the words the land spoke were words of breaking, moans of pain. He didn't mistake them for the voice of creation. He knew in his dreaming, that Will Forrest had given Nola a sharp-toothed monkey for a wedding gift. A monkey. It seemed to bode ill. He knew also that Leticia Graycloud, whose toughness was hidden by her dreamy face, was going to marry Benoit at long last. He knew, even though it was winter, that the season had already turned. It would soon be spring and there were at least two wild mares up in the hills, carrying the seed of Redshirt.

When the priest reached Michael Horse, he wanted to know what Horse had seen, and he asked, "May I see the ledger books you've been writing in?"

"I'm sorry," said Horse. "I've seen nothing. No, I'm sorry, the books are private."

"What about the fire?"

"Which one?"

But Horse told him it wasn't the voice of God. "It's the rage of mother earth."

That night the priest didn't quite believe the old man. Still, after that, he visited regularly. He'd started blessing chickens, he said at the next visit, and when Jim Josh bought a new pig late that winter, he took it to the priest and had it sprinkled with holy water. The Indians began to call him the hog priest. And they said it was the year when the priest went sane.

But the priest, who visited with people in town, was useful to Michael Horse. He kept him up with the goings-on in town. He told him how Will and Nola had moved into a new large place on the other side of town from Grace's, but how Nola nevertheless had decorated the house with items nearly identical to what her mother had bought. There were crystal chandeliers, and the painted rooms were white and pale blue, so there was a similar, icy feel to the place. Unlike her mother, however, she had Catholic leanings and placed

anemic-looking statues of saints, Jesus, and the blond virgin
Mary throughout the rooms. She burned candles at the feet
of the statues. And her monkey wore a rhinestone collar. It
adored her. It laughed when she laughed. It held a cup of tea
exactly as she held a cup of tea. It imitated her in every way,
the priest said.

One afternoon, Will Forrest walked up the stone stairs to the
courthouse and went inside. He sat at a table with John Hale,
his father, and two other businessmen. Mr. Forrest nodded
at his young son, though he hardly seemed to see him. Then
he announced that he wanted to outbid both Skelly and Phillips oil companies at an upcoming oil lease auction, and that
if Cosden Oil put in a bid, he wanted to get them out of the
way, too.

"The *Wall Street Journal*'s picking all this up in New
York," he said. "Every little man after a buck is coming out
here on the Tulsa trains. Those small companies are shooting
up like Johnson grass. We've got to put them out of business
or we won't make a go of it ourselves. They're tapping into
our pools and draining them. We can't afford to let them take
out any leases."

It was true. Even a woman had arrived, dug her own well,
and struck oil. She made so much money she filled a mattress
with it just to protect it while she slept.

Mr. Forrest looked across the table at Hale.

"It's crazy here," he went on. "Our best bet is to be part
of the craziness." He looked Hale in the eye. "Otherwise
we're going to lose our shirts. On the next auction day you
be out there under the tree at one sharp when the bidding
starts! I'll back up every bid you make."

Hale nodded, but he was silent. They were already in trouble and every man's muscles were tight. Even their hands
were held in fists. Then the men all rose to leave. Except
Will, who remained behind, fidgeting and nervous for reasons of his own.

Forrest turned to his son. "What did you find out about
grazing leases?"

"Not much."

"What do you mean, not much?"

"Well, I haven't really looked into it." His voice sounded hesitant. "I have to ask you some questions."

"Good. That's the sign of a good business mind. Go ahead. Shoot. What can I tell you?"

Will was uncomfortable. He twisted a piece of paper in his hand. "Nola's statement came and I looked it over. I noticed some of her money's gone."

"Yes, I invested it."

"What did you invest it in?"

Mr. Forrest stood up. He placed his hat upon his white hair. "Hale's company." He was disappointed at his son's prying question.

"But you lost some of your own money in his company, didn't you?"

"That doesn't mean anything. It's still a good business." Mr. Forrest cut his son off. "What's the point of this questioning? I'm the attorney here. It's up to me to decide about Nola's estate. I believe in Hale's company." Forrest was angry, but more than that, he was afraid, although he didn't say it. "We're in trouble here, Will. I've got to risk it." He was worried, and he was fighting a battle also for the inmate Benoit, for a trial of inquiry. Benoit was being held without arraignment. Because of his citizenship in an Indian nation they had not yet brought him to trial. Federal court did not want to try the case, though they claimed that Indian country was federal jurisdiction. County court couldn't try Benoit even though they held the young man in county jail. And the tribal court wanted him released for lack of evidence. It was argued from place to place who had jurisdiction and who didn't. Forrest believed Benoit was innocent, but Benoit would tell him nothing.

But Will saw only his father's cool silence and as he looked at the older man's professional veneer, he felt his childhood drop away. He saw an older version of his own face, hardened a bit, turned sharp and tired. He didn't trust him. Will gathered his strength and said firmly to his father, "You should ask before using Nola's money."

"Why would I ask?"

"She's my wife."

"Yes, Will, she is. She's your paycheck. Now she is the one who pays for your good suits and hats." He turned away

and went out the door. He looked strained, but he spoke
back over his shoulder. "Fill me in on the grazing leases
tomorrow, will you?"

Outside, on the courthouse steps, Will watched the heavy
snow fall, and he felt helpless. It was nearly evening and it
was quiet. The busy motions of the town were absorbed by
winter's whiteness. Will himself had thought it an embarrassment to have no livelihood of his own, which was why
he had taken an interest in helping to manage Nola's royalties
and holdings. But now, dismissed by his father, he felt
ashamed of his own lack of legitimate work, and he mis-
trusted his own father, even though there was nothing his
father had done that was clearly illegal.

Will buttoned his coat and started down the steps. At the
bottom of the hill, a lone car drove by on the quiet street,
braked, and honked. Will recognized his friends. They
opened the door for him.

"You still living with that . . ." Squaw, his friend almost
said, and Will knew it. But his friend finished by saying,
"that woman?" He passed Will a jar of whiskey. And although Will became defensive and corrected the boy, he took
a drink. "Her name is Nola."

"Hey, we'll take you home."

They drove out toward Will's house, but when it came into
view, the driver stepped on the gas and sped past the snow-
covered flowerbeds Will had planned but not yet tilled.

"That's the place." Will pointed. "I live there."

"I know," said the driver. "But you're looking pale these
days. We're taking you to the city. I said we'd take you home,
didn't I?" He reached behind him for the whiskey. "You
need a good night out. You look terrible."

Will looked at the faces of his friends. A few months before, they were the closest friends he had. Now he disliked
their smirking grins and bloodshot eyes, and the smell of
whiskey turned his stomach, but he knew them well enough
to know that he couldn't convince them to turn the car around,
so he took a drink from the whiskey jar and watched the
white fields blur past the car window.

"Hey," said one in a raccoon coat, "I hear you're in the
artifact business."

"No, it's not a business. I just collect them."

"He doesn't need a business. He's got an Indian wife."

Will grew silent. By the time they reached Tulsa, it was dark and cold, and his face was set in a nervous smile. They went into a speakeasy where people were already dancing, their movements outlined in yellow light and cigar smoke. Will sat at the bar and ordered a beer while his friends scanned the tables for women they could invite to dance. The driver already held a small, dark girl close and he shut his eyes while they two-stepped, locked tight together in one another's arms.

While they danced and bought drinks at other tables, Will sat alone. He had asked several people, without success, if they were driving toward Talbert, and he had given up on returning home at a decent hour. While he sat there with his head propped up on his hand, a young woman walked up to him and said hello.

She was as out of place in this speakeasy as he was, her blond fine hair all in place, her clothing tasteful and expensive. Despite his longing to be home, Will was taken with her fresh good looks and her inviting, open smile. "Your friends are all over the place." She smiled up at him. "Mind if I sit with you?"

He moved aside to make room. He looked away, but she kept his face fixed in her eyes until she caught his attention again. "You're quiet," she said "I like that. Would you buy me a beer?"

"Oh, sure." Will ordered a beer for her.

"What's your name?"

He told her.

"You don't look like an Oklahoma boy."

Her name was Vinita. He answered her questions politely, but he was nervous and wanted to be home. Later, riding home that night, he sat in the back seat while the driver spoke over his shoulder. "You know what you ought to do, Forrest, my boy?" said the driver. The car skidded on ice. "You ought to donate some land to the city. The Will Forrest Memorial Hospital or something. In your own name. You'd be famous. They'd all forget where your money came from."

"Goddamn. Watch where you're going," Will said. He pulled the collar of his coat up around his ears as if to protect himself from the drunk and leering faces of his friends. It seemed like forever before the car drove up the road toward his house.

From upstairs Nola saw the car lights. She'd been up keeping her monkey warm in her arms and pacing the floor. When she saw the lights, she put the monkey in its cage and ran downstairs. She opened the door for Will. He stood on the other side, fatigued and wrinkled. He smelled of alcohol, and he was apologetic. "I was kidnapped," he told her.

She thought he was lying. She felt heavy all of a sudden, dull.

Outside, it was still snowing. Nola closed the door and latched it. The four watchers were silent, standing at the edge of the trees as if the cold could not touch them.

Later that winter things appeared to return to normal. Moses began to train the new red horse that Nola had given him at the wedding party. He called the horse Redcoat, and he brushed it daily until its fur was sleek and shiny. On cold days he covered it with a woolen blanket.

Ruth spent more time at the Graycloud house, and she would watch Moses work with the horse.

Indoors, Ben's telescope was set up permanently in a window. At night, the family gazed through it at the turning stars. "Doesn't it make our problems seem small," Belle said, "to look up there at the universe and know earth is just a small light in the tail of a galaxy?" Even in the dismal face of graft and land theft, they were all "just motes of dust," she said. And Ben tried to study the constellations of the white world. He thought it was a key to their thinking. He studied Libra, the unbalanced scale of justice.

In town, normal business went on. After the burn-out, the oil fields had been reworked. And despite Will's late night out, Nola forgave him. With the monkey wrapped around her neck, she continued to furnish the house with glass and crystal. It was her desire to put everything in its place. She wanted things in order and permanent, yet she felt desolate; every glass-filled room looked fragile and breakable no matter what she added, no matter how solid and dark the furniture.

The difference between Will and Nola became more apparent as time went on. She purchased silks and tried to convince her more practical partner that her love of crystal was not "a terrible sin." But Nola began to think that even their marriage was like glass and that it would take little to fracture it. She liked European imports while he liked stone and clay artifacts. Looters sold him arrowheads they found near graveyards and small pots painted with spirals and birds. He did not ask where they came from and Nola tried to ignore their growing presence in the house, but she was superstitious, as Will might have said, and she didn't want anything around that belonged to the dead. Will purchased a trumpet made of human thighbone from Tibet. It frightened Nola. "All your things," she said when they argued, "come from the other side of life." She began to think that she herself, as an Indian woman, represented something old and gone to him, something from another time.

One morning Joe Billy picked up Doctor Black's bags and took him to the train station. Along the way, they both remained silent. Finally, Joe Billy asked, "What about the new doctor? Are we going to like him?"

"No. He doesn't use horse liniment."

At this Joe Billy laughed. "I'm going to miss you, Benjamin. Who will I talk with?"

When they reached the depot, Benjamin Black looked at the streets, the people. "Maybe I'll be back someday," he said, as if it would make his departure easier. Then he stepped into the noisy train. Joe Billy waited a moment amid the smell of smoke, oil, and metal, then he turned away.

Joe Billy waited to hear about his own replacement at the Indian Baptist Church. For the time being, he refused to perform any more weddings or funerals. He wanted to be relieved of his duties. Knowing this, Belle sent word to Horse that Lettie and Benoit were going to get married and would he return to Watona in order to perform the ceremony? Horse had been speaking with some of the Indians in the hills and he asked one of the runners, a woman, to watch over the people's fire for him. She readily agreed and she watched as he packed his red blanket with sage and prayer sticks. She laughed as Horse miraculously and awkwardly managed to corral Redshirt against his will, and probably for the last time, to ride to Watona. It was just luck that the old man caught the horse. He knew it, too. He slipped the bridle over

Redshirt's head. Redshirt shied. Horse stood on a stone and mounted the tall red stallion. The horse chomped at the bit and pulled away and the whole way to town it was a struggle between man and horse. By the time they arrived Michael Horse was stiff and he wondered aloud why the hell he'd traded his car for a horse that was so nearly impossible to handle.

Horse walked into the jail office just when Belle and Lettie arrived with two bolts of Nola's fine silver silk. They were going to use it to cover the discolored walls of the jail. They wanted to disguise the U.S. Geological Survey maps and hide the faces of wanted men, but just before the two bolts of cloth were unrolled, the sheriff announced a change of plans. Due to the overcrowding of the state prisons, he said, the county jail was going to be used to hold the overflow of prisoners. "The jail's going to be busy all day," he told them. "There's not enough room for a wedding." Instead, he said, the wedding would be held at the Stanley Hotel. He had already reserved the ballroom for them, and had even made reservations for Lettie and Benoit for the night.

Lettie was delighted, but in the presence of Jess Gold, she did not show it. She looked at him with gratitude. Then, she and Belle carried out the bolts of cloth and took them to the hotel.

"Say, will you give me a boost onto Redshirt's back?" Horse asked the sheriff. Gold laughed at the old man on the wild horse as he watched them fight with each other down the street of town.

At the hotel lobby, Benoit was under guard but he walked about with more freedom than he'd had in half a year. He looked good. The color had returned to his cheeks.

Lettie held Benoit's hand. Just before the ceremony, Joe Billy arrived to wish the couple well, and just then, the hog priest came in from the wilderness. He was a sight, his hair had grown wild, and his beard was long and scraggly. His wool pants were dirty and worn stiff. He looked nothing like his former pale, narrow-boned self. He'd come to town for a tank of fresh water, heard there was a wedding, and decided to attend.

Lettie, the bride, wore the ivory hat on her rich dark hair and a high-collared satin dress.

Michael Horse had already lit the sage and smoked the couple when the priest cut in and spoke about the wedding of all things, including man and earth, sky and water. Horse stood back and let him finish having his say, then Horse pronounced the man and woman married, and they kissed each other tenderly. Then he took hold of their hands and prayed in Osage and waved one of the prayer feathers over them.

Ruth Tate, Moses's sister, looked unhappy during the wedding. Her square face sagged and her dark eyes were weary. Her husband fidgeted next to her. He ran his hands back and forth along the rim of his hat nervously. He was uncomfortable without his camera. Ruth had insisted he leave it home.

Will put his hand on Nola's arm as they sat there, as if to remind Ben that she belonged to him, and Nola looked so lighthearted that Horse and the others nearly forgot about the four men who followed her everywhere, until they saw one of them standing at the hotel door, his face strong and alert, his muscles lean from years of running, and he was poised as if ready to leap to action.

Jim Josh was impressed with the hotel's long windows. "Wouldn't this southern exposure make it a good place to grow cucumbers indoors?"

Belle nodded. "How's your fig tree?"

"Good. Real good."

Ruth put her hand on Lettie's arm and kissed her and said, "In the spring sunlight, everything will look different. Maybe we'll all be smiling and laughing. And Benoit will be home."

Lettie embraced her aunt, but her voice would say nothing.

That day Moses put his arm around Benoit. The two men stood together, looking down at the polished floor beneath their shined shoes. There was nothing either of them could think to say.

Then it was time for the couple to leave and they went up the stairs, shyly, and all the people watched them rise up until Lettie's white dress was no longer visible ascending the steps, and under the watch of an armed guard, Benoit lifted and carried Lettie through the threshold of the door.

He was gentle. He laid her down on the bed and they kissed. He unbuttoned her blouse and folded it carefully on the chair beside the bed while she kept her eyes closed. He took the hat off her head. He unpinned her hair and loosened it down around her shoulders and he looked at her. She opened her eyes and looked at him, and he saw the smile turning up at the soft corners of her lips. He held her close and caressed one of her shoulders. He wanted to cherish her presence. He felt her arm touch his own, her skin against his.

They had all night and for this they felt fortunate. They were slow. When Lettie was wearing only her skirt, she unbuttoned Benoit's shirt and laid it beside her own clothing and pressed herself, naked, against his chest.

All night they were tender and when they weren't making love they looked at one another's hands, turned them over and looked at their palms. They admired their naked feet. Benoit touched the soft rims of Lettie's ears and the downy hair on her face.

After midnight, Lettie began to cry. She covered her face with the blanket. Benoit said to her. "Don't cry. We don't have time for tears tonight."

"I can't help it," she said.

He pulled back the blanket and smiled at her face. She put her arms back around his thin body. He felt small, smaller than she did, and yet he had lifted her.

It was still dark in the morning when the guards knocked on the door to return Benoit to his cell. He kissed Lettie good-bye and left her in the hotel room where she cried and held the pillow he'd slept on. Then he was taken handcuffed, down the stairs, and the guards placed a black coat over his shoulders. They drove him to the jail. Lettie forced herself to stand at the window and watch them leave. Then she stared at the bed, absent of Benoit, and remembered his bony form beside hers.

That morning the jail was full of men. There were roughnecks and drunks, forgers and cattle thieves. None of them was dressed in fine clothing like Benoit and they stared at his pin-striped pants that he himself had altered to fit his narrow hips, his belt of hammered silver conchos and coins, and his starched shirt.

Jess Gold unlocked Benoit's handcuffs. "Morning, Benoit. You've got company," was all he said. "Lots of it."

Benoit's nails had been buffed and he ran them nervously through his black, thick hair. Suddenly he felt a wave of anger or anxiety. His muscles stiffened. His face went pale. Before Gold left, he grabbed both arms of the sheriff and looked into the blond man's eyes. "I can't stay here," he said. "I didn't do it, Jess. I need to get out of here."

Jess Gold looked around the cell at the other men. They were watching. "Benoit," said the sheriff, trying to quiet the man. "Benoit, you're safe here. Your trial's going to be soon. I guarantee it. We're working on it."

"But I was set up. You know that, Jess. You know me." He stepped back from Jess Gold. "I don't trust anyone, not even you, and goddamn it, I want a new lawyer and I want out of here. That goddamn Forrest is probably in on all this!"

"Benoit, I'm doing what I can." He shook his head. He looked sympathetic but he walked away.

As Benoit heard the keys disappear down the hall, an irrational fear overtook him. He lay back on his cot and drew his knees up. He tried to calm himself by thinking about the wedding and Lettie's face in the lamplight. He tried to ignore the sound of the men shuffling about in the cell, the sound of a key in the latch.

As Jim Josh walked toward the jail that morning, he thought happily about his fig tree and how next year it would bear sweet, seed-filled fruits. It was still a little dark that morning when he arrived at the outside window of Benoit's cell. He had come to offer fresh tomatoes to the new groom. He had planned in advance how he was going to surprise Benoit. He'd looked over the window and noted that it had a double sill. It was designed so that thin-handed prisoners could not reach through to the glass and use it as a clear, jagged weapon. The bars were close in. But there was a space between the bars and the glass. It took a key, Jim Josh noticed, to open the windows. But he did not want to bother the deputy, so instead he used his knife like a lever inside the crack, jimmied the latch, and opened the window without making too much noise. He smiled at his own craftiness. He placed the brilliant red tomatoes on the ledge one at a time. He whispered, "Benoit!" but there was no reply. Jim Josh looked around. He searched the ground for something to stand on, saw a stone, and rolled it into place beneath the window. He climbed up and peered over the tomatoes into the silent cell. He was smiling.

At first the cell looked empty, but then he saw the shining black shoes of Benoit. They were suspended in air. They were floating. Josh's eyes rose up. Above the shoes were the creased pin-striped wedding pants Benoit had worn. Josh squinted into the gray light of the cell. With a shock he recognized the white shirt with its ghostly sleeves and the leather belt gleaming with silver conchos tight around Benoit's elegant neck, holding his body in thin air where it hung limp and lifeless.

Josh stared with disbelief at the hanging figure. It looked like nothing more than a scarecrow. He blinked his eyes again, then covered his mouth and fell down from the stone. He left the fiery tomatoes on the cold ledge, left the window glass leaning against the building, turned, and ran. He breathed hard and fast. He ran down the dirt road to his home, clambered up the porch and went inside. He was sweating and cold and out of breath. His hands shook. He fumbled with the wooden box full of coins and keys until he found the silver key to his car.

The car was filled with red and blooming tomatoes. Josh pushed them aside, knocking over some of the boxes, and he turned the key in the ignition. The engine turned over on the third shaky try. With great effort, the old man shifted the gears, went backward, then went forward, then drove the car full of tomatoes along the dirt road to the Grayclouds' house. He was barely visible in the car. He was overwrought and reckless and he couldn't see the road for the tomato vines that filled the windows of the car. He hit the mailbox as he drove into the Graycloud yard, but he didn't stop. He parked the car, then ran toward the house, weeping, his new spat shoes slipping in the snow. He fell once, then got up and ran.

Moses sat at the table across from Lettie. She still wore the wedding hat with its beautiful bird, and Belle was heating up the coffee when Josh threw open the door and stood before them. He looked stunned and could not catch his breath.

Belle looked at him with curiosity and put down the kettle. "Come in, Josh."

He had tears in his eyes and he told them the sad news. "It's Benoit. I saw him. He was hanging from his own belt." He covered his eyes with his hands.

Lettie stared at him, then pulled back, her heart thudding. "I don't believe you." She jumped up from the table. "You're wrong." She looked at him, as if waiting for him to tell her it wasn't true. "I'm going to go see for myself," she said, angry at Jim Josh as if he were lying. And before anyone could stop her, she left the table. She started Josh's car and drove to town surrounded by the leaves of tomato plants.

Later, Josh would try to remember if Benoit's hands were tied—he swore that they were—or if they were free, but all he remembered clearly were the white shirtsleeves, the pants, and polished shoes the young French-Indian man wore, and the belt with its silver conchos, although when Benoit was taken down from his death, all that remained of his beautiful belt was the leather.

Belle sat down. She did not lift her eyes. In the moment between the time Jim Josh walked in the door and the time Lettie dashed out to the car without a coat, Belle grew older. Her face grew new lines and her body seemed to shrink until she looked like a small old woman. From outside they heard the sound of an airplane. They knew it was Roscoe Turner, a stunt man, who'd been flying around advertising oil with a lion cub. The house went dead quiet. They could hear the falling snow brush against the outside walls of the house and the windows, the soft howl of wind. Rena came downstairs and sat still, and she also looked older than her years, as if time had finally caught her. She kept her hand over her mouth, maybe to keep herself from speaking or crying, and her eyes were full of pain.

They sat in silence that way most of the day, drinking coffee and smoking, occasionally breaking out in tears in the hot kitchen, until the fire went out of the stove and the air grew cold. Then Belle got up and put in some wood, struck a large wooden match against the wall, and put her hands above the cold stove as if warmth were already escaping.

It was nearly dark when Lettie walked in the door. She

looked like a ghost in her white wedding dress. She never said where she'd been, but her shoes were muddy with clay,. her dress was wet, and snow had frozen in her hair.

She was limp. Belle took one look at her and said, "Moses, come over here. Let's get her up to her room."

Moses held the young woman up and they all went upstairs, helping her. In the bedroom, Moses removed Lettie's muddy shoes. He was gentle. Jim Josh stood at the door watching. Belle covered Lettie with the blanket, then settled herself by the window. Rena wrapped Lettie's wet hair with a towel.

Everyone remained in the bedroom. Louise and Floyd stood by the window. They were worried. They looked at the floor, then at Lettie, then again at the floor. Ben brought in another blanket to cover his shivering aunt. Moses held his daughter's hand. They were praying. None of them spoke. No one had to. The silence was stronger than words. After a while Belle went over and laid down against the back of her daughter and put her arm around her and held her.

The day of Benoit's funeral, the earth was frozen. A black hearse drove up, followed by limousines and other slow, dark cars. Behind the windows, the Indian and mixed-blood passengers sat straight in the back seats. They all stared ahead as the cars passed by the stands of barren oaks. A white minister had come to perform the service. He wore a cross and his face was solemn when he shook hands with all the people.

Joe Billy was there, wrapped in a blanket. He greeted Belle and Moses who were walking hand-in-hand across the white snowfield from the car. Ruth sat beside Lettie on a cold black iron bench, and the snow behind them covered the stone mounds where the traditional people were buried, covered the crosses and smaller statues, and even the small houses Indians had built over the graves of loved ones.

It was not far from where John Stink had been buried, but in the falling snow, no one noticed his disturbed grave.

China, who had wooed the dead old man, was standing at the edge of the crowd in a heavy black winter coat. It was new. She watched the Indians with interest. The majority of them, even women who wore makeup and had permanently waved hair, wore blankets. China eyed the younger women with an outsider's curiosity. Nola, who looked close to her own age, wore pearl earrings. And farther back were the four silent watchers in coats made from woolen blankets and long hair, good-looking men with serious dark faces.

Stace Red Hawk stood far behind them all, watching.

A few deer passed silently behind the mourners. They were delicate, walking across the snow. Lettie turned and watched them while the men unloaded the heavy casket she had selected. It was decorated with white iron. They carried it to the hole in the earth and only when they put it down beside the hole did Lettie's gaze leave the deer.

The coffin lid was opened and the mourners passed by, placing items inside for Benoit's long journey from one world to another. He wore his wedding clothes. The people spoke as they placed their gifts in the satin folds that held him. Their words were quiet prayers and good-byes and pleas for salvation from the forces that had turned against them. Moses placed a pistol inside the coffin. Belle offered blue-beaded moccasins with bells tied to them. She wanted to hear Benoit's feet dancing from the world of spirits. The moccasins, like all burial shoes, were fully beaded on the soles. John Tate, to Ruth's dismay and embarrassment, photographed the body.

The white-haired China eyed each item placed inside the box with the once-handsome young Indian man; there was tobacco, small blankets, and pieces of silver. Then, as if she'd known him, she felt moved to remove her new coat and put it inside with Benoit. The Indian girls watched her. They wondered who she was. She wore a flimsy blouse and it was cold and she pulled her arms across herself, her shoulders high and bony and tight.

Then Lettie placed strands of beads around Benoit's broken neck. She opened his stiff fingers and put a handkerchief full of food and meal inside them. When the casket was lowered, the old people covered their heads with blankets and wailed out loud while the younger ones hid their faces behind their hands. As the clods of frozen earth were dropped on the last worldly home of Benoit, Lettie was still. And then the hole was filled in, a small mound of stones placed over the filled grave.

There was the sound of a hunter's rifle in the distance.

Ruth Tate took Lettie's arm to lead her to the car, but Lettie pulled away. "I want to walk."

"It's too cold," Ruth argued, but weakly.

Ben, noticing there was trouble, asked Ruth, "What's wrong?"

"She wants to walk," Ruth told him. Out of the corner of her eye, she saw John Tate photograph the three of them. She turned away.

"But it's miles," Ben said to Lettie, but she'd already started walking away from the gravesite.

Ben followed a short distance in order to convince his aunt to ride in a car, but when Lettie stopped and looked at him, he saw by the set of her jaw that she was determined to walk home. "All right then," he said. "I'll join you."

"So will I," said Ruth. Like Ben, she sounded resolute.

And with the two women wrapped in blankets, Ben walked toward town. He watched the landmarks and winter trees. The funeral cars passed them by in silence. One old woman raised her hand to them and then was gone, and they were alone walking in the deep snow off to the side of the road as if they didn't want to travel the easier trail that had been broken by machines and automobiles.

When their footprints were visible a long way behind them, a car passed on the road. A deer was tied across its roof. Ben watched the car, and when they entered the town, he paid careful attention to his surroundings. He noticed, with a wave of suffocating fear, that there were no Indians on the streets of Watona. He saw two Chinese men who worked for the railroad, and there were many of the newly arrived Italians parking their cars. There was an abundance of white men and roughnecks from the oil fields, but there were no Indians. This seemed strange to him. He looked from person to person, searching for a familiar face. He felt a wave of fear in the pit of his stomach. He was leaving for Haskell in Kansas the next day and he knew he was leaving his own people in a circle of danger. He could hardly bear the thought of going. But he said nothing to the two women who walked beside him, and after a while he stared straight ahead as if he did not notice how the two Indian women in blankets were being watched by the people in town, but he kept his hand on the knife inside his pocket.

Nor did he see Stace Red Hawk standing at the window of the Stanley Hotel watching them, his presence half-hidden behind the heavy curtain.

It was getting dark. Red Hawk took his dark coat off the hanger.

"Where are you going?" Levee sat on the edge of the bed. He watched Stace put on his coat.

"Out," said Stace, buttoning his top button. "I just want to go out."

"Want me along?"

Stace went out the door without answering. He walked quickly down the dark staircase, his hand sliding down the top of the banister. He could feel the fear in the town. As he walked, he glanced up at the dark windows of the other buildings, wondering if someone else was looking down.

In the middle of black winter trees, Stace sat down on a stone, and he prayed to the old ones and to the little spotted eagle. "I want peace," he said out loud. He offered his pipe to the south. He began to feel strengthened in his mission to help the people. He offered the pipe to the west. The people he was up against here in Indian Territory were the ones who did not love the earth and her creatures. Much of what these people believed to be good, was not good. What they believed was evil, was not.

"I have prepared a pipe for you," Stace said to the deep winter air. He held the pipe up toward the north. He could see his own breath.

He was praying. He was asking for help. He was asking for the people, the Indian people. He was asking for the eagle people as well, those who had been taken out of the sky. Their absence had left the people downhearted.

As a boy, Stace knew the constellations of the older people. In the sky he saw the planets and stars take the form of eagle, wolf, and buffalo. Stace had known the man called

Black Elk, who'd said that the Indians were now living in a broken circle. And he looked now toward the elk and the horses in the sky.

He offered the pipe to the east.

PART TWO

SPRING 1923

In spring, when the barren season passed away, there was a feeling of hope in the air. Rain billowed down in thick sheets and flooded the fields. Roads were washed out by the runoff. The rivers were swollen into streaming rapids. The small creeks carried the rushing red water downhill, out of the bluffs and into the area around Watona, or Talbert as it was sometimes called.

It was the spring of umbrellas, as if heaven and sky itself could be kept at bay by the thin circles of silk.

But the rain brought life, and it was welcome. When the heaviest rains subsided and the grass rose up out of the land and the frogs were singing, people turned their minds to planting. A few of the older people, including Belle Gray-cloud, conditioned their fields with words and songs, first sprinkling sacred cornmeal that was ground from the previous year's corn, to foster the new life. The old corn would tell the new corn how to grow.

Belle dressed a scarecrow in old black pants and a thin white shirt with a frayed collar, and placed it in the field. She worked in the fields daily and without fatigue. When she was not with the corn, she was cutting wild asparagus from along the roadways and taking watercress home for dinner.

Some of the younger people made fun of her. They were embarrassed by the old ways and believed the old people were superstitious. They were forward-thinking young people and those of them who still planted corn replaced the

209

corn ceremony with chemical fertilizer. But after a few
weeks, Belle's corn began to germinate and push upward
while their fields remained bare, except for an occasional
weed. Those few younger Indians who still planted corn stood
by silently looking at their empty fields until finally they
swallowed their pride and asked Belle if she'd come by and
bless the crops. It wasn't beneath them, they decided, to ask
for such help since Jim Josh's nephew had told them about
the launching ceremony of the Titanic, a funny little ceremony in which a bottle was broken and a ribbon cut. "Yes,
but it sank," said one man's sister before the man left to go
talk to Belle Graycloud.

When Belle went out to his cornfield to bless the ground
and the corn, Lettie went with her. Lettie carried the large
basket with the meal and tobacco and sat down on the bare
earth while Belle walked up and down the furrows.

It was a new season of life. Lettie wanted to give up her
sorrow. She had looked at herself in the mirror and said, "It
is time." But it was as if her reflection belonged to another
person. The face in the glass did not take on a sunny smile
at the young woman's will. As she sat there, in the spring
grass, smelling the turned soil, she studied her hands. Her
skin was dry and thin. She thought of the history of her
hands. They were like her grandmother's hands, were made
up of them. Belle's mother. Her grandmother who had come
to Oklahoma over the Trail of Tears. Soldiers had forced the
line of people west, out from their Mississippi homeland.
They were beaten and lost, forced to give up everything that
had been their lives until they thought of nothing more than
how to go on, to preserve their wounded race, their broken
tribe. Along that trail, when women would fall and weep
over a child who had been killed by the soldiers, the others
lifted her up, took her along with them, saying "We have to
continue. Step on. Walk farther along with us, sister." And
so Lettie looked at her hands and they were their hands. She
thought of her sorrow, and how even the corn had its season
of death and loneliness, its season of desire. She felt a breeze
of air, or maybe it was the touch of Benoit, she thought,
across the backs of her hands all the way from the world of
souls. We have to continue, she was thinking.

After helping the young men with their planting, Belle

went home and swept out the chicken coops. All the while she raked fresh gold straw, she spoke to her chickens in the same affectionate tone as she used when speaking to her girls and to the corn. She nailed a calendar with pictures of winged angels to the wall of the chicken house, and put in a statue of Saint Francis, and began to keep track of the number of eggs each chicken produced. Pippin, her fat dog, still occasionally followed Belle about, but he had become antsy and fearful, growling at thin air and cowering with his tail between his legs. "He sees ghosts," was all Belle said about the spotted dog's behavior. He'd barked once at the ghost of John Stink, who was now going around with an ear horn, trying to listen in on the world of the living, the world in which people tried to overcome the pain of their winter losses on early spring nights, when the streets were full of staggering men, noisy women, and firecrackers. Ben still noticed how few Indians were visible on the streets of town, a couple of dark men, perhaps, sitting on the running board of a car. He said nothing about this to anyone else, but he knew the Indians were going home. They were going back into the heart of their lives, back into the hills and back to older ways. They'd become peyote men with long hair and some of these were still the richest people in the world. They'd entered a house of fear and closed the door, become invisible once again. But out in the country, their homes and barns were strung with lights in hopes that no secrets would hide in the darkness. In other circumstances, the lights in night's black country would have been beautiful. But these were lights of terror, and farther out, the fires could be seen scattered around the dark hills while people went to the roundhouse and the peyote lodge and sang and drummed, and the drumming joined the early rains, and it was felt in the topsoil and subsoil of earth. It filled up the hollow dark nights when the moon was swallowed by earth's hazardous shadow.

"It's a good year for planting," Josh said that spring. "I can feel it through my spats."

Belle agreed, absently, but she was worried that the floodlights were interfering with the corn's rest and sleep, and it was true that the plants grew spindly from leaning toward the electric bulbs.

Joe Billy returned to his people a little at a time. He'd

resigned from his post at the Baptist Church and now his
closest proximity to white religions was an occasional visit
with the hog priest who'd lived throughout the winter in a
copse of trees.

Joe Billy awaited the return of the sleeping bats. He had
been going up into the hills to visit some of the small caves
on the opposite side of town from the bluffs and Sorrow
Cave. In them, the bats slept in the cool weather and were
lethargic even if disturbed. Joe Billy made his way over the
stone outcroppings to sit in the cold caves and keep watch
on the flying mammals as they hung quietly from the ceiling.
He felt their presence and smelled the musky earth, and the
living odor of stones. He was waiting for a message of some
sort, a vision or a revelation. He was on to something, he
felt it. It could not yet be named or spoken but inside the
caves he was returned to a life inside himself. Martha felt it
too. She understood her husband's new ways. One day she
joined him, sitting beside her straight tall man on the cold
stone floor of a little cave. She unpinned her hair, let it fall
down around her shoulders, and she never put it up again.

One day a truck parked not far from the Grayclouds' house.
It stopped on the little corner of land where Belle's allotment
joined with that of Moses. Belle was territorial, and she
walked quickly toward the truck. The driver jumped out of
the pickup, went to the back, and took out a post-hole digger
and sledgehammer.

Belle recognized him as the man they called "Montana,"
and he'd just hired on as a hand for Hale. "What are you
doing here?" she asked.

"We're putting in a fence." Luke was his Christian name.
He remembered his manners and tipped his hat. "A buffalo
fence," he said, as if the matter-of-fact information would
explain his presence. "A stockade. Hale leased this land
from the Indian agent."

"It's my land," said Belle. "No one spoke with me about
it. I think you should leave now."

"I'm sorry ma'am." He took off his hat and squinted
toward her, as if the sun were too bright. "This land was
leased out at the agency." He went back to digging the post
holes, and before the day was over, the fence was in and
Belle went raging at the new Indian agent from D.C. who'd

leased part of her land as grazing pasture for a payment of only twenty-five cents a year.

"You didn't improve it," he said as he sat with his light gray eyes on her face. He'd seen fit to strike up a deal with Hale. "It's best not to leave the land lying idle," he said.

And only a day later, a cattle truck roared up the road, turned around, let down a chute, and delivered a herd of the large, dark wooly buffalo. The ragged animals were docile and slow and they walked without resistance through the gate into the fenced pasture on Belle's land. It was as if they, too, had given up.

Early in April, a black convertible from South Dakota arrived in town and headed out toward Crow Hill to Ona Neck's house. The car was driven by a young white man. Sitting beside him was an older Indian man named Lionel Tall. He was straight and silent. He was glad to be in Indian Territory and wanted to see Stace Red Hawk. Behind Tall sat two young Indian men, the spring air brushing their faces and tangling their hair as they rode forward. Lionel Tall had met Jim Neck, Ona's boy, at a Brahma bull sale in Alliance, Nebraska. Now he and his helpers were coming to help out the Indian people in the territory. He'd heard, from his network of traditionalists, that the Oklahoma Indians were in deeper trouble than even Neck had indicated. The older man took an occasional sip from a bottle of Coca-Cola. He carried sacred stones and a small leather suitcase of ceremonial items. He was going to set up an altar and perform a sing, a ceremony for healing everyone, even the injured earth that had been wounded and bruised by the oil boom. He knew he could not stay long or he, too, would lose his inner core of harmony. This was the problem with places in the world that had been broken.

Ona Neck sent word to Lettie that there was to be a ceremony and that sometimes the spirits, even the voices of the dead, gave information to select individuals. She knew Lettie was preparing another journey in search of clues to the deaths of Sara and Benoit. In any case, even if she learned nothing, it was a curative meeting and would be good for her to attend.

Lettie mistakenly thought it was a seance. She wanted to hear from Benoit. She knew he was trying to contact her from the other side of life. She felt his presence in the wind, in the rain, and the first heat of April sun.

That evening, carrying a tin of biscuits and cash to give the men from South Dakota, to help them with gas, she caught a ride to where the roads forked and walked the rest of the way to Ona's. It was spring dusk, with soft evening light. The air was alive with pollen and the fragrant blossoms of fruit trees. Lettie walked by the place where Michael Horse had kept the people's fire. The circle of earth that had been the floor of his tepee was still without grass, though some of it was starting to return. Walking by his absence, she felt like crying.

The black convertible sat outside Ona Neck's house. There were other cars as well. A crowd of people had gathered to attend the ceremony. Lettie walked past the cars and knocked on Ona's front door. By then it was nearly dark. The windows of Ona Neck's house held no lights and Lettie was nervous to be knocking on the door of such a dark house, and even more afraid when a young white man unlatched the screen and silently let her in. Had she not heard Ona's voice, she would have turned away and gone back home.

Inside, the young men were covering the windows with wool blankets and tacking them up to the walls so that no light, not even from passing cars, could enter. In the dim glow of a single lantern from the small kitchen, Ona's house looked as it usually did. It was a warm place, with doilies, photographs of her sons, and the smell of venison stew. In the kitchen, the older man sat across from Ona, bent over the table and bent that way, his chest seemed caved in, but when he straightened up, his body could have been mistaken for that of a younger man. He measured three teaspoons of sugar into his cup and stirred. He didn't speak with anyone and Lettie could tell by looking at him that he was already part way to the other world, the one where earth spoke stories into his ears.

Ona made tobacco ties to offer the spirits. A bowl of tobacco sat before her and she pinched it out a little at a time and placed it on a small square of red cloth. She prayed for her son. That he would find a woman. He was fifty and still single. He was well-respected and traveled about with elders, but when a woman was present he acted like a child. He stared at the floor or he smiled too much or worse yet, if he were especially attracted to a woman, he turned away as if he were made of ice even though it was actually a blush that he hid, out of fear. But it wasn't only her son that she prayed for. She tied each bundle round with string, seeking help for all the people there in Watona. Her string of prayers was longer than a rosary, and filled with more hope than a necklace of mustard seeds. Cal Severance counted her bundles of tobacco. There were fifty of them. They were all red. "That's good, Mrs. Neck," he said. She smiled up at him. He put a big hand on her shoulder, and she put her hand over his bad thumb.

More people arrived. Deputy Sheriff Willis had heard about the sing, and he wanted to be there. He was returning to the older ways, he said, and wanted to move out of town to the country near the Blue River.

Stace Red Hawk stepped up the wooden steps of Ona's porch. Lettie heard his boots on the wood and opened the door for the man. He was calm. He caught her eye. "Thank you," he said. Then Red Hawk nodded at Lionel Tall, the man who had written him back in Washington, D.C. The old man nodded back. Stace knew the man was along the invisible road, hearing the first voices of eagles and bear. Stace left him alone and sat down next to Lettie. He glanced at her. She looked raw, he thought, from the hanging death of Benoit.

Ona's son sat down on the other side of Lettie, and as soon as he was near the young woman, he began to gulp air and his face began to sweat. Lettie didn't seem to notice, but Ona rolled her eyes toward heaven and let out a sigh.

Michael Horse was the next person through the door. He was accompanied by Floyd. Floyd was quiet and inconspicuous. He went in and sat in the circle. Horse had come on foot a long way from where he'd set up his new camp. He looked exhausted. He carried the metal box that was lined with moss. Inside the box were the coals that were the eternal fire of the people. He touched Lettie's hand, then he sat down and placed the box on a worn old blanket in front of him. "There's no one to watch the fire," he explained, and he took from his pocket some sticks of hardwood he'd brought along to feed the coals. He put the little sticks on the fire and blew on the coals. They smoked only a little.

"Don't look at me," said Ona Neck. When everyone laughed, she looked at the old man from South Dakota and explained, "He's always bamboozling me into watching the fire."

The man understood. They had firekeepers, too, in South Dakota. And bamboozlers.

When Lionel Tall placed sacred stones on the floor, the people began to feel at peace, even Jim Neck, who'd been swallowing hard and sweating next to the beautiful Leticia Graycloud. The stones came from a long tradition, from the movements of earth. One of them was the stone Crazy Horse had worn under his arm, and the people could feel the presence of something, of spirits, maybe of Crazy Horse himself, that warrior who'd loved his people. The sharp smell of burning sage added to their comfort. The smoke wafted across the room. The people were silent. They were small in the world and they knew it. Their human woes were small. Their time was short. They didn't want to live their lives eaten up with grief. They had come for a healing.

When it was all dark the singing began. The men, including the white man who had driven the black convertible, sang a rich song. It moved through cloth and skin and touched the spirit. It was a wind, caressing the world. Above the people, from near the ceiling, flint stones began to strike together of their own accord, and sparks of light flew out from them, jagged across the blackness. No human there was tall enough to clash the stones together. The people took faith, took heart, in the sounds and the sparks, and the occasional cool brush of air that entered the room like a hand, touching every person on the shoulder or the head or on the skin of a hand.

Lettie felt it. At first, the voice was only a harsh whisper at Lettie's right ear. She didn't know if it was real. It told her to go search a cornfield. It said, "Dig deep in the center of the field of corn," and then the voice grew louder. A few others heard it say there was something to be found in the midst of a cornfield. Something was hidden there.

Then it was quiet. Michael Horse, who was accustomed to talking with spirits, and did not reserve a reverent tone of voice for them, said, "As long as you are locating things,

can you tell me where Redshirt has gone?'' Almost as soon
as he asked it, he saw an image inside his mind. He recognized the place. It was near Sorrow Cave. Redshirt was
standing with a muscular mare and a small red colt. A bat
flew out above them from inside the cave. Horse wondered
why he hadn't thought of looking there before.

Later, while they ate Ona's stew, Mr. Tall advised Lettie
to go out and dig in the ground in a field of corn. She would
find something important, he said, and when no one else was
listening, he gave her some of the landmarks that had been
revealed to him. There was a broken statue, he said, a mailbox, and a mattress in a cottonwood tree. The place that
matched the description was out on South Fremont where
Benoit's house had stood before the explosion.

"What's out there?'' she asked.

Lionel Tall felt bad for her. He could see how much she'd
been suffering. He gently touched her hand. "I don't rightly
know,'' he said. He broke open a roll.

After the ceremony the younger men from South Dakota
went home to stay with Cal Severance, but they kept their
distance from him and remained silent. They didn't like his
drinking. They couldn't and didn't blame him, but they were
traditional, and they felt uncomfortable with the other men
their own age who had gone to school and returned with lives
full of holes. Cal took out two blankets, using only his palms
and four fingers, and he unfolded them for his guests. "What
happened to your hands?'' asked one of them.

Cal looked at his hands. "It's my thumbs,'' he said. "They
broke them at school.''

The quiet men understood. They helped him with the blankets.

When they began to breathe evenly, Cal got back up,
looked at the two sleepers, drank some whiskey, and said,
"You and your old people can go to hell!'' and he staggered
out the door looking for better company.

The next day, spring thunder arrived. The sky was yellow.
The white man who'd driven Lionel Tall to Oklahoma was
driving alone when he saw China. She was walking away
from the train station carrying a large cardboard box. He
pulled up and braked the car. "That looks heavy,'' he said.

She smiled at him. "It is.''

"Let me give you a lift." She handed him the box, shook out her pale hair, and climbed into the car. For a change she was quiet. She looked at him, then out at the land.

His voice was soft. "Where are you from?" he asked.

"Arkansas." She shrugged, as if he would know the hills where she'd lived, the little frame house, the red-faced papa she'd run away from, and how her life here could not be explained, let alone understood. Her face grew rosy with embarrassment, and even with sorrow.

"What are you doing here?"

"Oh, I work here and there. I keep books out at the Willard oil field. Saturday nights when they need extras, I wait tables at the Regis Café."

He nodded. She was single. He was sure of it. A married woman wouldn't work two jobs. He drove past the Stanley Hotel and glanced up at the rooms. Lionel Tall was in one, staying with Red Hawk.

Inside the hotel, Tall caught Stace Red Hawk up with his family. "Your younger sister, Imogene, the one who looks like you, goes out a lot at night."

"She's too young." Stace shook his head.

"They are like that these days. It's not good. She goes to all the rodeos, though."

"What about my mother?"

"She still has her chickens." He thought a moment. "She seems lonely. Even with her new boyfriend. He's John Hand, the tribal judge. He works all the time. He moves fast. He talks fast. He walks fast. That's bad for a woman."

"It is," Stace agreed. He nodded, but he was drifting off a little from exhaustion.

"You'd think he was from New York," Tall went on. "A woman needs a slower man. I ask her out, but she doesn't go."

"Hmmm," said Stace. But Tall was thinking of the murders in Oklahoma. Even though he barely read English, he looked through the stack of notes in Stace's table. He changed the subject.

"Every other tribe in the country wants to know what's going on down here. We know the papers don't get the story right. They want it straight from the horse's mouth." He shuffled through the papers on Stace's desk. One of them read, "Talbert Funeral Home. Undertaker." Lionel Tall looked from the paper to Stace. "So what's going on?"

"I can't say for sure yet. No one will talk. There's a wall of fear."

"What about this? What does it say?"

"It says 'undertaker.' "

Tall changed the subject again. "You've been in Washington long enough. Why don't you come back home with me?"

"I'll be back." Stace picked up one of the notes. He tapped his fingers on the desk.

The older man sipped from his coffee cup, then sat down on the bed. "Why can't you pin anything on your suspects?"

From the window, Stace looked down on the town. "Because not one of the murders took place on Indian land. We can only move on federal land. Whoever's guilty is smart as a whip. Sometimes I think they, or he, works for the government."

"Maybe they do. I've heard stranger things."

Evening was falling. Stace was quiet, thinking what it would mean if the government was in on it. It might even include Ballard who'd told them their only job was to observe and listen. Then there was a jangle of keys at the door, and it opened a crack and the clerk peered in, saw both men and said, "Uh, hello." He sounded uncomfortable. "Sorry to bother you." His face was red and embarrassed. "Mr. Stanley says that we charged you for only one person. We have to charge you for two if he's going to stay here." He glanced toward Lionel Tall. "Is he?"

"Yeah. How much is it?" Stace asked, digging in his pockets.

"Five dollars a night." He looked nervous. He'd never seen the young Lakota Sioux man without his hat. He was surprised to see Stace's long hair.

Stace reached into his pocket and handed the clerk a five-dollar bill, plus some change. He gave him a warning, "Next time you knock."

The young clerk closed the door behind himself. Lionel Tall said, "They're reading your notes."

"I know. Those notes are all lies. I wanted to mislead

them.'' He made a bed for himself on the floor so that the older man could sleep more comfortably on the bed.

Lionel looked at Stace. "The undertaker?"

Stace nodded. "A lie. I hope."

"I don't know about this, Stace. It's too dangerous."

Stace took off his pants and climbed under the sheet on the floor. Lionel Tall pulled a blanket up over himself, leaving his naked brown chest exposed. He was thinking.

Lionel Tall never slept well in beds other than his own. He lay back and stared into the darkness. He was remembering the past. Tall had been a young man when the Ghost Dance took place. A new messiah, a mixed-blood Indian, had gone north and west out of Nevada and preached a new faith. Wevokah, he was called; Jack Wilson was his Christian name. He was an Indian who was thought to be Christ, and he preached that if the people danced and believed, the buffalo would return, life would return to what it had been before settlers and hunters, and the ancestors would return. The ghost dancers wore muslin shirts and fringed garments, white buckskin with the images of life painted on them. They were painted with yellow stars and the moon, with blue turtles and birds, painted with the world and the sky. They would not be injured. Bullets would not penetrate these garments, the messiah said, and how they had wanted to believe it, had to believe it to have the slightest ray of hope to continue. It was a faith of survival, of the desire for life. It was water for the thirsty, food for the hungry. It was survival.

Lionel was thirty that year. He was young and taken up with the hope. He believed the prophet Wevokah. He went away from his home in order to spread the new religion in Canada, up where the Cree people lived. He rode a white horse and covered its back with white muslin and with painted red hands and blue horses. He could see it as he looked back now, could smell the horse and see its breath in the cold air. He remembered the sound of his horse's hooves traveling over the borderland between countries and peoples. And then the snow. It was deep and hard on the surface and the horse's legs were cut by the crust of ice. They bled from the cuts and left a red trail behind them. But when Tall reached Canada, along that red broken trail, the Cree rejected all his attempts at conversion. Tall remembered what the Cree leaders told him, that survival was their religion, and that was enough to occupy them, just finding food. It was a hard winter and Lionel thought about staying among the Cree and he would have, but he had a young child at home and he was anxious to return.

It was on Christmas Day when Lionel left Canada and began the trek homeward. And it was on Christmas Day that the Sioux people were murdered by the cavalry all riding uniform gray horses.

When he rode in from the Badlands, he found his people gone, the bodies of children frozen in the snow. The frozen women lay in broken clusters where they'd tried to escape. When Tall saw his wife, the young son in her arms, he sat on the ice beside them. He tried to put the frozen organs back into the boy; they spilled out onto the snow. He prayed to bring them back to life. He sat there in the blue-white light of evening until his hands were frostbitten and his clothing had frozen to earth. He didn't feel the cold. And finally a white nurse who had worked among the Sioux chipped him from the ice, took the man's arm and led him away. She was crying. Tears had frozen on her skin.

Lying in bed that night in Oklahoma, Tall still grieved. He remembered the body of a small girl whose cap had been embroidered and beaded with the American flag. She lay there, one of her blue hands stretched out, as if asking for help. Uncle Sam was a cold uncle with a mean soul and a cruel spirit. And the world was full of many visions gone awry, which was the reason he wanted Red Hawk to go home, and why he no longer placed stock in any belief except for the laws of nature and wilderness. He thought about Stace and about faith, and how vulnerable human men were. They were soft and hopeful as children, and their lives easily dispensed with. That was the history of the world. But he never spoke these words to Stace. He remained silent. He wasn't one to sit in judgment on any other man, but he was thinking that Stace believed too deeply in the people who paid his wages. He thought that even a prophet, even a warrior, could not survive the ways of the Americans, especially the government with rules and words that kept human life at a distance and made it live by their regulations and books. The older man was restless. He turned over, then turned again.

Stace propped himself up on his elbow. "What's on your mind?"

"I can't sleep."

That night, while Stace grew more and more homesick and lonely, and while Lionel Tall was disturbed about the young men's new ways, Hale drove into town with a truckful of cattle. He was going to cross-breed them with the buffalo and start a new herd. He'd turn the "Hale" grass into pure gold in his pocket. The cattle were crowded together and they moaned.

Belle woke that next morning to a loud droning sound. Something was gone wrong in her beehives. She put on her robe and went outside to look, and what she saw there was the herd of buffalo and the new collection of cattle. Their presence disturbed her bees. They were too close to the hives, and it was a well-known fact among beekeepers that bees hated buffalo, cattle, and mules, and true to that belief, the bees put up an angry roar from inside their hives. They were so distraught that morning that they attacked Belle's chickens, and as she stepped outside she saw one of her laying hens covered with bees. It writhed in pain, bees buried among its golden feathers. Then, as Belle watched, the hen went limp and died of a poison that had its beginning in flowers and sweetness.

Still wearing her robe, Belle dug in the ground and buried her hen. Then she set about moving her temperamental bees to a new location. Down at the creek was a fresh water spring. It would be a perfect place to take the bees, she thought. There were wildflowers, and later in the season there would be fields of sweet clover.

She hitched one of the workhorses to the wagon, then went indoors and put on her white beekeeper's clothing. The veil hung loose about her face and shoulders. She taped the sleeves of her shirt and put on her gauntlets before she went back outside, covered the three hives with white canvas and lifted them into the wagon. The hives were still light; they were still empty of honey. As they rode away toward the creek, the bees hummed loudly. They were agitated. The workhorse that remained behind called out to its partner. It was jealous that the other horse was able to work, but nervous about the nature of its job. The call was answered by the horse Belle drove. Then there was just the clip clop of hooves and the woman dressed in white sitting tall, holding the reins like a bride or queen from another country.

When they reached the fresh spring and its little pool, Belle lifted down the boxes, but she left the bees covered until they settled down. Then she uncovered the hives and sat on the new grass in front of them, watching the mysterious, intelligent worlds contained in the white boxes. Then she turned the horse and the empty wagon back toward home.

"Damn it." Ballard slammed the flat of his hand on the table. His face darkened. "My job's at stake here, and now you want me to call Washington and tell them you're taking time off?" He glared at Stace, then took a deep breath and a sip of his Coca-Cola and said more calmly, "What is it exactly you want to do?"

"I'm going up to the hills and rest. I'm looking for something and I need quiet to find it." Stace looked at his colleagues. He stood in front of the window. The sunlight from Ballard's hotel room window was behind his head. He could see them clearly, but they couldn't catch his own peculiar expression. He felt a sudden dislike for them, particularly Ballard. He needed distance. "I want to go up to the hills and see if I can find some old-timers. People down here are close-mouthed. They're afraid. Everyone we've talked to up to now has either refused to talk or changed their story." He tried to sound confident that he could collect information pertinent to the case. But it wasn't information he was seeking. He had a feeling that he should go up beyond the roads, up to the bluffs and ridges. He knew that the facts weren't always all they needed. He didn't know what he wanted; he just had a feeling.

"If you're looking for something, you turn things over. Right, Levee?" Ballard wanted encouragement. "You lift them up like a rock covering a scorpion and you look underneath. You're not supposed to go sit in some hills and dream and talk to people who haven't even been civilized."

"I need time."

Ballard turned to face Levee. "He needs time. Do I hear him right? I'm going to get fired and he wants to go think."

Levee shrugged. Stace was his friend and he trusted his judgment, but he wasn't taking sides.

"Look," Stace confronted him. "You're the one who's been dragging your heels."

Levee softened. "Well, there's nothing we can do right now anyway, is there?"

Ballard turned away from the younger men. "Remind me not to hire another Indian. They want time off for family. They want time off for feasts and ceremonies. Now he wants time off to think." Ballard was fuming. He picked up the phone.

"You can't call Washington from here. The operator, remember?" Levee pointed to his ear.

Ballard slammed the phone back down. "Okay," he said. He looked at Stace. "But be back on Tuesday. No later!"

Stace didn't move.

"Well, go on before I change my mind!"

"There's one more thing."

"What's that?"

"I need my pay. You have my paycheck. I'm going to buy a horse."

Ballard glared at Stace. "Add to my list of reasons for not hiring Indians that they buy horses." He opened a drawer, shuffled through some papers, and handed Stace his paycheck. "What do you need with a horse?"

Stace didn't answer. He remained standing in position with an expectant look on his face. Levee turned away to hide his smile.

"Now what?" Ballard said.

"I need it cashed."

Ballard reddened, but he unlocked the small gray cashbox he carried whenever he was on assignment, especially for Stace, since no bank trusted his dark skin.

On his way out the door, Stace looked back. "We're barking up the wrong tree, you know." He closed the door, then remembered something and opened it again. Both men looked in his direction. Ballard's eyes darkened.

"By the way," Stace said. "Does this sheriff know that we are investigating crimes in his municipality?"

Levee nodded.

"Is he cooperating?"

"Yeah. Why?"

"You trust him?"

Ballard's face turned purple. "I thought you were leaving. Of course I trust him. What else? Now get out of here."

Stace went down the stairs, noisily, and out the hotel door. Lately he felt uncomfortable with the other men. He thought it must have been those nights spent with Lionel Tall. Tall felt like home to Stace, the color of his skin, the tone of his voice, felt like the comfort of South Dakota and other Indian people. Tall reminded him of the great differences between him and his co-workers.

And then, Ballard's impatience bothered Stace. Ballard was so anxious to get on with this case and close it down that Stace thought they'd arrest anyone and say it was done. And they still couldn't even move on it until something happened on Indian land.

Stace put his hands in his pockets and walked up the road to the stables where he'd seen a sleek black mare, a talkative and energetic horse that had been sold off by one of the Creek Indians who'd had to move to the outskirts of Tulsa and had no way to feed or care for a horse in the tar paper village they'd gone to inhabit.

She was a head-shy horse. After he paid for her, Stace stood carefully at her side and slipped the bridle over her ears without touching so much as a hair, then he mounted her. It felt good to be astride a horse again. He rode up toward the bluffs.

One morning, when the corn was only six inches high, the clothing was stolen off Belle's scarecrow. At the same time, three large holes mysteriously appeared in the cornfield. It worried her. A cornfield was the very heart of life and Belle nursed her corn. She knew it needed more than water, light, and food; it needed the care of a woman. So she was filling the holes back in with a small hand shovel when Will Forrest's car drove slowly up the road, accompanied by the runners.

Belle stood up slowly, her hand on the ache in her back. She watched as Will opened the car door. Nola stepped down out of the car. She was dressed all in white. She carried a white parasol. The breeze ruffled it. Even dressed this way, she looked so much like her grandmother, Lila, with her widow's peak, that Belle almost called her by that name. And Belle knew instantly that the girl was pregnant. Her eyes could almost see the other life inside the beautiful young girl. Nola's narrow hips had shifted a bit, and widened. Her skin was softer. She looked like a new fruit tree blooming in spring before it has leaves, a tree preparing already for the sweet fruits of survival.

Will looked back at his wife, waved, and drove away. It was plain for anyone to see that he was in love. His eyes were filled with adoration for the young, dark girl. Still holding the small shovel, Belle walked toward Nola. She could smell the blooming lilacs. "Shoot, girl, as far as he's concerned," she told her, "no flies could ever land on you."

Nola looked at the older woman. She didn't seem to believe what Belle's sharp eyes had just seen on the face of Will.

There was something different about Nola, something changed and older. It wasn't just the widow's peak or that she so closely resembled Lila Blanket, but the way in which she looked at things. She wore one of Lila's vigilant expressions as she took in the sober sight of the empty barnyard. Then she looked at the pasture. The land was bare. In only a few days, the buffalo had pulled the tall grass up by its roots and eaten the land down to nothing, and now they were standing on the desolate-looking earth and their own manure with vacant eyes, eyes that had seen too much. They were on their way down in the world, were themselves fallen people, and they knew it and so did all others who looked sadly on.

Nola said nothing, but Belle knew in the way she looked, the way she turned her head, that the girl understood. Nola touched her stomach as if assuring herself that, yes, life would continue, that she was not as barren as the fields were becoming, the burned forests, the overgrazed land, the core drillings, as empty as the dark, tragic eyes of the buffalo. Belle saw this gesture and knew her first impression was true, that the turning over of life was at work again. "It smells like a feed lot, doesn't it?" Belle said. But Nola only looked out toward the fruit trees. "Where are your bees?"

"I had to move them." Belle sounded shaky. "The buffalo

disturbed them. They're down by the spring. You'll see them down there.''

Just then Rena opened the screen door and waved. She had a big smile on her face. ''Hurry up!'' But even after Nola went inside and picked up the lunch basket, and as they walked to the spring on Belle's land, Nola was already calculating how to give some of her money to the Grayclouds without embarrassing them. She thought she would have Will check on her trust and let her know how much she could spare and then ask Mr. Forrest to help her find a way to get the money to the proud people who had been so good to her in this world, loving her like one of their own.

That afternoon, the watchers followed the girls down to the spring and creek. Other than that, Rena had planned on it being a carefree day. She packed food enough for the men, and each of the girls carried a large willow basket down through the green meadow, into the brush, and past the humming beehives.

Before they ate, they waded in the water. They were cautious on the mossy underwater stones. At first they tucked their skirts inside the legs of their underwear, but they gave up and wore only their bloomers, hanging their damp skirts over the bushes to dry in the sun. In her cotton bloomers, Rena felt embarrassed. She knew the watchers were hidden in the shade of the woods, looking in their direction. It disturbed her. She thought they should leave Nola alone now, that enough time had passed to smooth out the crashing currents their lives had been. She looked toward the trees. ''Do they bother you?''

''No, they watch over me. I feel safe with them here.'' She spoke softly.

Nola lay back and listened to the drone of the bees. She was glad they were bringing in their gatherings of pollen, working to care for the queen and her new life. She closed her eyes, listening to the water, the bees, the breeze in the grasses. Rena looked at her friend's closed lids until they were still. Then she gazed out at the woodlands on the other side of the creek. Her golden skin was flushed with the sun's heat.

The creek came from a spring that existed on Belle's land. It was called The Place Where Earth Has No Bottom, and was the watering place of the old ones, the quenching water for the air and sky. It was a place of peace.

After a while Nola woke. The sun was full in the sky. The girls fed the watchers and went to sit beneath a shade tree on the bank of water. Nola opened the basket. Rena watched the small lives in the water, the water walkers, minnows, and the tadpoles. "Don't you ever wish you'd wake up one day like them, and be able to live in two worlds?"

Nola looked gravely at Rena. There was deep meaning behind these words. "Yes, I do." Her eyes were troubled. "I do." And after she said these words, her face looked grieved. She stood up abruptly as if in pain, but she masked her feelings by laughing like a child and she went splashing down into the water.

Rena watched her friend with affection. She was thinking of how they'd been children together for so many years, then suddenly Nola cried out and lost her balance. Stunned, Rena watched as Nola fell into the creek, face down, landing on her stomach. "Nola!" Rena jumped up in horror, running toward the wet, narrow form of the girl, the white blouse soaked and sticking to her flesh. All she could think about was the baby. But when she reached Nola, for some reason, the girl could not rise up and she cried out in pain, "My foot! It's stuck."

And it was. It was wedged between stones. Hurriedly, Rena tried to dislodge one of the stones, but they were too large for her to move, and they were slick with moss, and when the watchers came to help, their hands also slipped off the rounded river stones. They were afraid that they would injure the girl if they moved a stone and it slipped back, so quickly they rigged up a lever out of a branch, to protect Nola's fragile leg, and when the stone was moved out of place the water filled up with a surge of darkness. At first it looked like blood. Then they thought it was silty clay seeping up from the bottom of water, but then they smelled the oil.

One of the men said something to the others. He sounded anxious. Rena didn't understand his language. Nola responded. What she said was something about the Gray-clouds. She sounded panicked, but Rena smiled with pleasure and excitement. "Oh my God," she said. "It's oil." She was, they were, going to be rich. Her grandmother would have a new stove. They would buy back their cattle and horses. They would no longer talk of selling the Buick. But the men began immediately moving stones over the place, trying to cover up the source of the oil seep. Rena didn't understand. They did not want such good fortune. It made no sense to her. Her skirt was blackened around the hem from being in the water and it stuck to her legs as she ran toward home, happy that they could replace their cows. And when she turned around to see if the others were coming, they were not there. The watchers had taken Nola away. They didn't want to be around the broken earth's black blood and its pain.

Rena cried herself to sleep that night, her small body wracked with sobs. Her happiness over the oil turned to fear that they would be killed. Floyd and Moses had spent the day at the water covering the seeping oil as best they could, their faces grim and set against everything, praying that no one else would see any oil the water might have carried downstream as swirling rainbows on its surface. And that evening they strung up more lights on the house and barn. The house looked exposed and naked in the white light, and even that didn't offer them security from things that take place in the dark and they feared the lights would attract the devil people like it attracted the June bugs. The lights made it appear to be daylight, and a rooster was fooled into crowing. Moses's tired face looked hard in the square of light that lay across the bedroom. He put a gun beside the bed. ''I can't sleep,'' he said.

''Maybe if we put a blanket over the window,'' Belle offered.

Moses got up and opened the blanket chest. ''Where are the tacks?''

''How long have you lived here?''

''Why?''

''You still don't know where the tacks are.'' Belle got out of bed and took out the tacks and helped him hold the wool blanket up to the wall above the window. The light came in only around the corners.

''Are you afraid?'' Belle curled up to Moses.

''Yes.'' He held her hand. Such comfort in the flesh. Then he turned toward her, grateful for her presence, and held her, and because the desire for life goes on under all circumstances, they made love.

The next day as he rode on toward the bluffs, Stace Red Hawk felt a renewal of faith, the kind of feeling that comes to a man in silence, when he takes notice that a tree is older than himself, and that it will remain when he is gone. He was going to seek a vision, to find a cure deep in the heart of earth.

The black mare had a smooth gait. She rode like a Cadillac. He'd thought so from the way she stood, her hipbones higher than other horses, a different stance about her legs.

Stace rode past a dump yard. It was filled with old rusted car parts and tires. Here and there broken bottles reflected day's light, and the hills were red, as if light came from inside them.

He rode past one of the new, conical peyote churches made of wood. He was following his heart and instinct, so he closed his eyes and gave the mare her head, settled down in the saddle, relaxed the reins, and she walked onward, then turned off the road and headed toward the place that held the caves.

Once in a while, Stace would open his eyes to see where she was taking him. Then he'd close his eyes again. It was still warm and the earth smelled fertile and damp.

For a while, the mare continued her uphill path. When she stopped, Stace heard a man's voice. He opened his eyes and pulled back on the reins.

"Whoa!" yelled the voice. It sounded a little shaky. Stace watched the old man named Horse. He was a short, slight man and he carried a bucket of oats in one hand, and a rope in the other. He was walking toward a glistening red stallion with a tail and mane so long and beautiful that even Stace, who knew horses, wanted to see it up close, wanted to touch its lean red muscles. He'd never seen a horse like it before. No wonder his new mare had taken that route.

He watched Michael Horse walk toward Redshirt. Off to the side a ways, watching, by some stony outcroppings of rock, stood a red mare and a lithe rust-colored colt.

The old man put down the bucket of oats and tried to sneak up slowly to the horse. He walked a little sideways, hoping to catch the wild horse off guard and fool him into a halter.

But the horse was on to him and while Redshirt moved sideways and escaped the rope, the red mare stepped out and ate from the bucket of oats Michael Horse had carried.

Stace almost laughed at the ridiculous sight. The man was outsmarted by the horse. That red stallion, he could tell, had an instinct to be wild. But the older man wasn't giving up. He called out to the red stallion, "Over here. Over here," and Stace broke out into a wider smile, but he stayed back and watched the nervous stallion clamp its lips together, then set its ears high, turn, and kick at the older man, who ran off like a rodeo clown.

The red stallion knew Stace and the mare were there, behind the bushes and trees. He whinnied nervously in their direction. Stace pulled back a little, out of sight, while the old man approached his horse still another time. This time he succeeded in getting the rope lasso around the red horse's neck, but as soon as it was on, the horse bucked and the older man ran off again, while the horse went to stand with his mare and offspring, the rope dangling from its neck.

Stace knew that horse. Already. It was a crazy horse and it needed a crazy human to catch it. The old man wasn't crazy enough to slow the stallion down.

Michael Horse was frustrated, but he decided to try again. Only this time the stallion moved to the side, then back, and charged at the man, chasing him, running at high speed. The man turned and ran, a look of surprise and fear on his face. "You're going to give me a heart attack!" he yelled back over his shoulder. Then the man sat down and put his hands over his face, waiting to be trampled and have it over with.

Stace laughed out loud. Horse turned toward the bushes, and his presence discovered, Stace said, "What are you doing?"

"I'm meditating. I'm trying to think like a horse."

"You'll never think like that one." Stace cast a sidelong look at the red stallion. It looked like a biter. And Stace knew, also, that he didn't dare step out from the trees. Horses like that one had what was called "splitting." That is, they would see a man move away from a shadow and think a tree had doubled itself and split. It terrified them when reality changed that way, so Stace remained standing and talked to Michael Horse from the shadows until the red horse turned

its back on him. Then he dismounted and walked over toward
Michael Horse.

"He knows he's got the better of you."

Horse was defensive. "Not necessarily. I was trying to
teach him how to charge at people." He looked at Redshirt
and said, "Sic'em." Redshirt pranced. "See, he won't do
it. Yet. But we're getting close." A big smile broke out on
his face, showing off his gold teeth.

Stace and the dark mare stepped out of the shadows.
"Here, maybe I can help you."

Redshirt got a faraway look in his eye. One of his ears
turned in the direction of Stace's voice. He was listening to
his words. He set his horsey jaws. He readied himself for a
larger struggle. Stace saw this and shook his head and whistled through his teeth. "That's one hellion you've got there."

Horse noticed immediately that Stace knew more about
horses than he did. "Can it be cured?"

"I don't know." He turned his mare toward the other
horses. "I'll go around this way," he pointed. "You move
over there, by that bush. We'll try to get them cornered by
the rocks over there."

But Redshirt understood English and he turned and
neighed at the black mare Stace rode, and she balked just
long enough for the red horse to stride off. "Look at that,
will you? I'll be damned. He intimidated her." Stace stared
off in the direction of Redshirt. "If he gets away this time,
he'll be so cocky you'll never catch him. I've seen it before.
They get in it for the fun." He reined in his horse. She
refused to follow, but he pulled even harder and she turned.
He didn't want her to get the idea that she had won. Then
Stace dismounted, tied her, and walked up toward the cave
with Michael Horse.

The old man said, "Say, aren't you the fellow from South
Dakota?"

"Yeah."

"You better stay here and eat."

Stace looked around. There was no house or dwelling
place. "This is where you live?"

"Well, I used to live over at the Coffee River. Right now,
though, I live here in Sorrow."

"I'm sorry. I'm real sorry." Stace spoke sincerely and took off his hat.

"Why? I like it here." Then he realized he'd confused the younger man. Horse laughed. "Sorrow's the name of a cave."

Stace looked relieved. He smiled and replaced his hat, "Oh, you live in a cave." He followed Horse on up the rocky footpath. A little distance from the cave entrance, there was a fire burning. It was hot and strong. Beside it was another one.

The older man cut up a brown squirrel and put it on sticks over the fire. He went inside the cave and returned with some lard. "What are you doing here, anyway?" he asked Stace as he stirred the fire.

Stace removed his hat again and pushed back his hair. "I was just looking for peace and quiet."

Horse understood. "Time to think. I used to be like that. Still am." He looked up at the sky and thought for a moment. "You better stay with me here tonight. You can wander off tomorrow. But tonight it's going to storm."

Stace looked up at the cloudless sky, but he didn't argue.

"Besides, that foolish horse might find you on the ground and break your bones."

After the two men ate, Horse buried the little bones of the squirrel in a small hole he dug in the ground. "Used to be a fellow named Stink who kept a herd of dogs. We didn't waste any bones around them."

The name rang a bell. Stace wanted to hear more. "Where did Stink go?"

"He died. But his ghost's still around." He stood up. "Say, you look tired. Let me show you your accommodations."

Stace liked the man. He knew they were going to be friends. He followed him.

Horse looked at Stace a little closer. "Woman troubles?"

Stace shook his head "no," and followed the older man into the cave.

Michael Horse lit a lantern. It filled the gray womblike opening with golden light. The walls flickered with shadows. At one upper edge of the cave, Stace saw a few swallows' nests like clay pots built from mud and water. On the floor beside the light was a cedar trunk and next to that was a small typewriter with a sheet of paper wound into it.

Stace glanced at the paper, to get a hint of what it said. Across the top it read "The Gospel According to Horse." The rest of the page was blank. Stace pretended not to have seen it.

"Here," said Horse. "Here's your bed." He laid down a smooth little pile of blankets on the cave floor.

Stace noticed that the floor of the cave was smooth and had been swept clean with a broom. On one stone wall was a picture of a guardian angel. "How long have you been here?"

"Not long," said Horse. He took the paper out of the typewriter and opened the chest. Inside was a large stack of typed pages.

"Are you writing a book?"

"No, I just keep track of everything."

"What do you write?" Stace was curious.

"About the people here. Our troubles." He was shy about his writing.

That night Stace crawled into his bed. He was silent. He heard Horse blow out the light and climb into his own stack of blankets. The cave had a cool, hollow sound to it.

Horse's breathing grew even, and then there were a few snores. Stace felt comforted, embraced by the stone walls. He thought this man might have answers to some of his questions, and soon he, too, fell asleep inside the musty-smelling earth.

When daylight finally entered the cave, it was late in the morning. Stace sat up. A mouse scurried away from him. He smelled the fresh odor of rain outside, but then he noticed that there was not just one, but two men besides himself asleep in the cave. The stranger was by the door. He was covered with a dirty, ragged brown blanket.

When Horse heard Stace rising, he woke up. And when he saw the other man in the cave, he crept over to get a closer look at the intruder. He pulled the blanket away from the sleeping man's face. "Just as I thought. It's the hog priest."

His words woke up the scrawny man. The man looked startled and embarrassed. "Excuse me. I didn't know you were living here now." He got up to leave. He held his blanket up to his chin as if he were naked. "I just came in from the rain."

"Sit back down," Horse commanded. He sounded gruff, and the priest laid back down on the cave floor and blushed. "We're Indians. You aren't allowed to leave here until we make you eat breakfast. You wouldn't want to seem ungrateful."

The priest was intimidated. He put his head back down on the roll of cloth he'd brought inside the shelter with him, and said, "Sorry."

"That's no excuse to stay in bed all day, though."

Stace watched with amusement.

Horse went out and made the coals burn hotter, then he broke quail eggs into a pan and scrambled them. He was boiling coffee grounds when the priest went outside. "You don't happen to have an extra cup, do you?" asked Horse.

The priest opened his pack a little shakily and took out a metal mug. Horse poured coffee into it and handed it to Father Dunne. The priest sipped the scalding coffee. It burned his lips but he didn't show his pain. He looked from one man to the other, nervously.

It was a warm day. Spring was blossoming on the sweet locust trees.

When the sun was at its brightest, Stace decided to go look for Redshirt. He knew the horses would all be standing still, swishing botflies away with their tails. But that night while they slept, Stace's mare had disappeared. All he found was her halter hanging empty on the branch, attached to the lead rope. Redshirt had unbuckled it. There was even a toothmark in the leather. When he found Redshirt's narrow tracks, they went in circles and lines and crossed over one another as if the horse had deliberately tried to outwit the men. But Stace could feel the horse watching. He knew he was there, like an outlaw, just outside his own line of vision.

When he went back to the cave, Stace tried to hide his discouragement from the two men, but Michael Horse took one look at the younger Indian's face and knew immediately that the stallion had outsmarted him, that even the young horseman who, if Horse's judgment was correct, might be a rodeo man, had never dealt with this kind of a horse. He felt satisfied and a little proud of Redshirt, too, of his rebellious nature and big green teeth. He saw, also, that Stace was going to do all he could to bring in the wild horse.

Michael Horse looked at Stace. "He's got a harem. He's like old Sam Billy used to be," and in spite of himself, Stace laughed, for even he, in the short time he'd been there, had heard some of the stories about Sam Billy.

Horse saw that the Sioux man had something on his mind. He looked preoccupied. Horse watched him a minute and then said, "I think you better stay here a while. Maybe you'd read some of my writing."

The priest felt left out. It had been a long time, anyway, since he'd been around people, and he felt tense, his face reddening at times. When Horse opened his cedar box, the shy priest said he was going outside to do his prayers. "Why don't you come back tonight?" Horse asked. "It's lonely in this cave."

The priest smiled awkwardly. He'd forgotten how to be with other people. His softness touched the other men. "Very well," he stammered.

After he left, Horse took out one of his journals. "This was from a year ago." He removed a page and showed it to Stace. It was written in beautiful calligraphy, in the hand he used before he'd been given Grace Blanket's typewriter. "I'll tell you what it says. There was an explosion at the house of a man called Benoit. You know about him?" He handed the page to Stace, looking intense, as if he believed Stace could help in some way.

"Yes, I've heard about him," said the younger man. He looked at the paper. "Who else did you show this to?"

"Just you."

"Why me?"

"I don't know. I just wanted to. Maybe it's not good for an old man to keep too many secrets in his head."

Stace read a little. "What about Sara?"

"She was next in line to receive the money."

"And Benoit?"

"After she was gone, it was his. And Nola's. Nola was Grace's girl. But she's still a minor, so she can't inherit the money directly yet." Horse took out a page that had lines and boxes filled in with names. "They assigned her a guardian." He looked toward the darkest, innermost section of cave. "He was Benoit's attorney, too. Oddly enough, Nola's married his son."

Stace gazed at the page, "And Benoit married Lettie Graycloud?"

"Yes. But it's not a legal marriage, not by the white laws, that is. But I don't know that they realize it. Anyway, I think most of the money is tied up in lawsuits. And the property's been taken away. Except that horse out there. He's Benoit's stallion."

"That's a neat little circle, isn't it?" Stace looked at the older man's face. "Why are you telling me all this?"

"I don't know. Just a feeling." Michael Horse looked away then looked back at him. "Maybe you can help us."

The hog priest returned to find both of the Indian men quiet. Father Dunne thought they didn't want him there. From time to time, he'd look at one or the other of them. But the men were just thinking. After a while Stace broke the silence by saying, "Where's Nola?"

"I think she's safe for now. She has guardians. Plus, the young man really cares for her. Everyone sees that."

When the priest realized the men were talking about the murders, he grew nervous and he went to the door of the cave and began to pace back and forth outside. He couldn't tell them he'd heard a confession and that he had an answer, or part of an answer. Horse, sensing Father Dunne's tension, scrutinized the priest's back, but then the priest stepped out for a walk in the sunlight.

That evening when Father Dunne returned, Horse took the two men down to a creek. He was teaching them how to shoot fish. "It's like this, see," he said as he leaned over the silvery surface of water. "You have to anticipate it, which way your fish will move." He looked at the trout. It was resting in a little pool of rocks, down in the deepest part of the creek. He pulled back the arrow, then let it go. It entered the water. Horse grabbed the arrow and pulled the shining, twisting fish up with it.

The priest said last rites for the trout. Then he turned his attention to Stace. "By the way, how did you escape being a Catholic?"

"My family hid me."

That night, after they cooked and ate the fish, the men

stayed together in the cave. Horse told the others to be silent and they would see something wonderful. He left the lantern very dim, so it would not be discernible from the outside, and the men retreated back into a small corner of the cave and waited. They heard only their own breathing.

At the first opening of darkness, the deer came inside the cave.

There were seven of them, three beautiful does, a buck, and three young and spotted fawns. The men watched the graceful animals who had come to lick the salty minerals off the cave walls, but when the deer turned to leave, suddenly the air itself cracked open with gunfire. The bullet hit the inner walls of the cave and ricocheted and the small herd of deer broke from each other and panicked, not knowing which way to run. Two ran out the entrance. The buck moved farther back inside the cave until it sensed the men there. Then, in a clatter of hooves, it bolted. The young deer were still. They sat down on the floor, the way instinct told them, and didn't move an ear. There was another shot from outside, and then it was silent. After a while, a doe returned and made soft noises at the fawns. They rose up on bent, trembling legs and followed her out the door.

The men remained standing against the back wall. Horse was the first one to move, after he was certain that the poacher was gone. He seemed to be smelling the air. He looked for the bullet, picked it up, and put it aside.

That night they left the lantern dim and spoke only in low voices among themselves. The priest, happy to be in their company, told them how he had become a priest and how he now realized that the life spirit lived in hogs and chickens as well as inside churches and cathedrals.

The other men nodded at his words.

When they were quiet, thinking of the souls of hogs, a piece of rock gave way in the back of the cave. Its sound startled the men. But the cracking noise was followed by a little squeal and Horse took the lantern back in there in time to see a bat emerging from a little break in the stone. He was excited. He couldn't hide his pleasure.

"What's so great about a bat?" the priest asked. He looked confused.

"Its soul, just like the pig's." Horse tried to climb up the

little chink in stone. "There must be another room in there."
He wanted to peer into the darkness. "There must be another
entryway."

Another bat began to squeeze out the hole, saw the men,
then turned and vanished back into the stone.

The other men seemed uninterested in Horse's quest for
the bats. Stace was plotting out how to catch the horses. He'd
paid good money for the mare, and didn't want to lose her.
The priest was thinking about the intelligence of pigs and
about the last one he'd christened for one of the elderly men
in town, Jim Josh, and he was thinking about how he'd been
taught, wrongly, that animals don't have souls. So Michael
Horse gave up talking about the possibility of other rooms
behind the cave and sat quietly, thinking of bats and old Sam
Billy and all the strange things that happened in this world.
He tapped his fingers nervously on his knee. He was anxious
for the other men to leave so that he could investigate the
cave and search around for another entrance.

Later that night he heard an owl. It was eating the same
mouse who'd shared their cave the night before. Horse
thought, but didn't say, "The owl is asking the same question
I'm asking. Who?" Then he went out and tried to imitate
the owl. The other men listened. They could not tell one
voice from another. After a while, Horse returned to the
cave. He said, "I am the wisest of men but sometimes a little
stupid. For the life of me I can't understand the owl. Yet he
understands me."

That night, while it was dark and the other men slept, the
priest left the cave. He had decided to tell as much as he
could of what he'd learned in the confessional. He wrote what
he knew in sand at the entrance to the cave, and he did not
mention any names. Then he made his way down to the
creek.

When Michael Horse went out the next morning to stir up
the fire, he didn't see the writing. It was only when he saw
Stace peering at it that he went over to read what the earth
was saying. It said: "One man was not in jail the night another man was killed." For Stace it was the first solid lead
he had. He sat alone, thinking about what the information
might mean, that perhaps a man had escaped from jail and
committed a crime.

Michael Horse walked around the stony walls outside the cave. He scoured the flesh-colored rocks for the entrance he was certain existed.

When Horse returned, Stace was gone. His footprints led down the hill and disappeared. Horse was glad to be alone. He set about searching for bats. He pulled his trunkful of papers over to the corner of the cave and stood on it. He began to hit the inside wall with stone. A piece at a time, he broke into the cavern behind Sorrow Cave. He could smell the dank odor, the moist mildew scent of bat guano. He heard the startled bats inside, a flutter of wings, a high-pitched sound, a scratching on the ceiling of the cavern. His breathing was heavy with exhaustion when he broke enough stone away that he could almost put his head through the opening and look inside the next cavern.

He stepped down off the chest, opened it and took out a candle. When he lighted it, he held it up to the opening. There was a flurry and flutter of wings. The bat sounds, like rushing water, told him where the opening was. He put out the candle, peered inside the dark room and waited for his eyes to adjust. Sure enough, he saw a little crease of light. He went outside and around the hill, and began to search in the vicinity the light had come from.

He was hot and tired when he found the entryway. It was disguised and he saw how easily he could have missed it if he hadn't followed the light. It was covered with a plank of wood over a small doorway, and in front of the wood was a pile of stones. There was a small break in the wood that allowed just enough room for bats to come and go. Someone had kept this place secret and hidden.

One at a time, Michael Horse rolled away the stones. He was sweating. He stopped to rest. Then he pried the wood plank out from the cracked stone wall, and when at last it heaved and gave, the entryway was flooded with bats. They flew out, away, to escape the intruder and his lantern. They rose out of their home, the darkness, and took to the light.

Carrying his lantern, Horse explored the room. It might have been the first of several chambers. What he found, to his astonishment, was a painted and quilled medicine bag that he knew had belonged to old Sam Billy. He recognized it instantly; it had an American flag beaded on one side of it.

Inside the humid cave, the medicine bag lay beside a bowl of blue corn kernels that Billy had been famous for growing.

Horse picked up the bundle. It was moving. It bulged and struggled. He opened a corner of it to see what was moving inside the bag when a bat flew out. Horse was so startled that he fell backward against the stone wall and scraped his shoulder. But even with an aching in his back, even with his skin scratched and beginning to bleed, he stirred a finger in the kernels of corn, and when he dared to open the bag one more time, he saw that it was empty. But Sam Billy was there in spirit, Horse knew that. And the bats had come out of the medicine. The medicines were coming alive.

That spring, nearly all of the full-blood Indians were deemed incompetent by the court's competency commission. Mixed-bloods, who were considered to be competent, were already disqualified from receiving full payments because of their white blood.

And that spring, Moses Graycloud received notice that his hearing was to take place in mid-May. Uncertain which of the attorneys could be trusted, he prepared his own case, but in spite of his intelligent arguments, he was assigned two legal guardians, and any further lease money that might have been earned by his grazing leases would have to go through the attorneys. By the time they deducted their legal fees, for services rendered to him, he owed them large sums of money. Michael Horse's car, in Moses's possession, was impounded and sold. The last of the cattle were taken away, his bull bought and paid for by Hale. Ben's telescope was sold to the attorneys. And Belle, afraid they'd take her prize possession, wore Star-Looking's meteorite inside her clothing so that no one would see it.

But at least the discovery of oil on Belle's land had not been revealed. As it was, they felt helpless and depressed. Moses slept with a rifle beside the bed. Belle argued with Moses to leave the territory. "Listen to reason," she told him. "We're in danger here." But he pointed out that even leaving was dangerous. "Look how many of us have been followed and killed on the roads," he reminded her. And it was true. The ring of murders ranged all the way to Europe. Three Osages had been found dead in England. One Osage woman had been murdered by her husband in Colorado Springs. No place was safe and they had to bide their time however they could, making themselves silent and invisible until things turned around once again. But they were afraid. Each time Belle rounded a corner, she stopped first and listened. She walked past every window with hesitation and felt fear rise in her chest each time she passed a stand of trees. She hated the money-hungry world and how her land had involved her in it, and she hated without limit the man named Hale. By then he'd fenced in yet another part of the Graycloud land holdings. They were almost surrounded by the leased-out land. And already the land around them was shorn and bare from the grazing of cattle and buffalo. In places it had only the slimmest chance of recovery. Where the fires had burned, however, the charred land was again sending forth new shoots of life and for this small gift, Belle was thankful.

"Do not be too afraid," Michael Horse had once told her, in such a gentle, calming voice that she listened and remembered. At night, with her eyes closed and her hands clasped together, she would repeat that phrase to herself. "Do not be too afraid." But everything that took place grieved her. Especially the digging that went on at night.

One night Belle again heard the sounds of shoveling. It was out in the darkness. It sounded close to her cornfield. The next morning she woke to find three large holes near the naked scarecrow in the middle of her field. She was puzzled. A day later, there were two more holes. The new plants were cast aside and the soft earth overturned. One night, as she watched like a ghost from her bedroom window, she saw the exiled Angus bull from across the way unlock his gate and walk down the road to stand at the fence where he cried and watched his cow women that were locked in with the buffalo bull Hale was trying to mate them with.

Other nights, Belle heard Lettie moving about her room, sleepless, or crying softly into the blankets, and Belle knew Lettie's wounds of sorrow were not healing.

Around two one morning, Lettie, remembering the words of Lionel Tall, got up from bed and dressed herself in the moonlight from the window. It was like daylight outside, the moon was so full. She stole across the ground to the barn. As Lettie picked up her shovel, the last two lonely work-horses whinnied at her. The air smelled rich and acid with manure, and moist. She started out down the road. It was white in the moonlight. She shifted the shovel from hand to hand as she walked the distance to Benoit's, thinking of what Tall had told her. When her arms both ached, she tried to hold the shovel across her arms, like she would carry a child. It was heavier than she expected and the handle was starting to splinter.

On Fremont Road, Lettie saw a glove. It was lying in a dark thicket like a ghostly hand trying to touch the earth. It was stiff and dusty. It was one of Sara's.

In the cornfield, too, parts of Sara's and Benoit's lives were strewn about. An unbroken jar of hair pomade sat beside the road. Lettie picked it up and twisted open the rusting lid. It smelled like Benoit and she remembered him leaning against the window of the car on the night of the explosion, and how his head had left a trace of the sweet-smelling oil on the glass. She laid her shovel down, sat in the field, and cried. The field smelled like spring, yet nothing grew there except de-vil's claws and other choking weeds, and at that time of night, the weeds looked black around her. Still, it contained the dead, dry stalks of plants from another year.

Then she estimated the field's center, put her foot to the shovel, and set to work pushing it into the earth. It was good ground, easy to shovel. There were few rocks, only the ob-stinate roots of hungry weeds. She dug a knee-deep hole.

That first morning Lettie thought her labor was fruitless. She found little things, little nothings, that had belonged to the household. There was a package of razor blades, a key, and a deep blue bottle that contained rosewater. The pink rose was still visible on the partly burned label. But fruitless or not as her work might have been, she put these things in her pocket, as if their closeness would whisper secrets through the pores of her skin. She wanted them beside her, to read with her hands as she walked.

She walked back home slowly. Though she was tired, the physical labor comforted her and she felt stronger. The sun was beginning to rise, and the dawn made promises it wouldn't keep. Spring was rich and heavy in the air. All the plants were turning over, beginning another journey upward toward the sun.

It was almost daylight when she returned the shovel to the barn. Then she went down to the creek and spring to think. But when she neared the creek, she saw John Stink's ghost. It was crying and heaving and wiping its eyes. She didn't know that it was crying because an enormous fish had caught and dragged its dog down beneath the smooth, leaden surface of water. She left before it saw her, returned to the house, turned back her sheets, and laid down in bed. The spirit's unhappiness reminded her of her own, but she was tired from her labor and she slept.

One sleepless morning a few days later, Belle pulled the blankets aside from the window and peered out. She saw the figure of Lettie coming up the road, carrying a shovel. It was the second time Belle had seen her. She watched her grow nearer, then listened in the hallway as Lettie made her way up the stairs and tried to steal quietly into her own bedroom. Then Belle slipped outside and examined her cornfield. The plants were nearly a foot high by then, but the holes were numerous and spreading outward. Belle was worried about her field and now she was certain that Lettie was the one destroying it. Angry, she marched back up the stairs to Lettie's room, knocked loudly on the door, and without waiting for a response, flung it open and went inside.

Lettie could hardly hold her head up. She smiled at her mother.

"Show me your hands," Belle demanded.

The smile vanished from her face. "What's going on, Mama? What is it?"

Belle examined her daughter's hands. As she thought, there was dirt beneath the fingernails and new calluses on the palms. "All right, Lettie," she looked sharply at her. "Why have you been digging in my cornfield?"

"I haven't."

"Look at your hands."

"It isn't me."

"Don't lie to me. I saw you with the shovel."

Lettie pulled herself up from the bed. "I'm not digging here. I'm digging over at Sara's cornfield."

Belle's hands were on her hips. "Why are you digging at all?"

"To look for clues. Mr. Tall told me to."

Belle thought it over. She looked at her daughter. She wished she could tell her to forget the past, to forget clues or solving things, but she herself was overwhelmed with the situation and she softened. "Did you find anything?"

"Nothing, just a key and some razor blades." She pointed to the dresser. Beside the key and blades was the dirty glove and a blue bottle of rosewater.

Belle went over, picked up the items, and examined them. "This looks like the key to our car."

"That's what I thought. Yes, it's a Buick key."

"But it looks like ours." The thought horrified Belle.

Lettie blinked.

"What would it be doing out there?"

They were both silent. "Mama, what if it's Floyd?"

The thought struck them both with terror. "No. No, it couldn't be," Belle said. But later that night she went out to try the key in the car. It fit. She was unsettled, thinking of Floyd and how he knew about the oil that was trying desperately to seep up in the water on her land.

A few nights later, there was another ceremony at Ona Neck's house. Lionel Tall was still in town. His reputation had grown and so many people appeared for the ceremony that they had to split it into two separate gatherings. One crowd of people waited outside while Mr. Tall set up his altar. Stace, whom people believed to be a younger medicine man, assisted Lionel Tall. It gave Red Hawk credibility in the eyes of the local Indian community.

Many people came down from the hills on horseback. Others came from town and parked their cars along the dusty road. Two men came on bicycles, squinting through the road dust. The white girl, China, was there. She had been spending her time with the driver of Lionel Tall's car ever since the last ceremony. Like Martha Billy, and the driver of the car, China was beginning to reject her own people. And Floyd

Graycloud, who had already adopted the Indian ways, sat at the farthest edge of the crowded room.

When all the windows were covered over with wool blankets, and the singing almost ready to begin, the door opened a crack and Michael Horse, breathing heavily, squeezed in. He'd walked all the way down from the settlement. In the little opening of light, he saw Stace, went over and squeezed in next to him. The others made room for him.

"What about the fire?" Ona Neck wanted to know. She sat down a ways from him. She looked stern.

"I left it in the hands of the hog priest," Horse told her.

"What? You left our people's fire with a Catholic?"

"Yes. He's a good man." Father Dunne had been forced out of his regular camp by army ants and scorpions and had moved in with Horse. They were becoming friends, of a sort.

Ona eyed Horse. Her lips became thin and tight.

Accompanied by the gourd rattle and the drum, the singing began. It was dark and peaceful. The people were silent, with prayers just starting to form in their minds. Some of them had already begun to soften and cry when suddenly there was an angry buzzing outside, a loud drone of an airplane flying over Crow Hill. It landed on the road. The bushes along the road were tattered by its propeller. And then there was a loud knock on the door, a voice announcing "Police." And the door was flung open. A bright floodlight shocked the people. They sat motionless, blinking in surprise, seeing only the light. The man who held it was invisible behind it. They were like shocked deer in a poacher's field. One of the singers rose to turn on the light. "Don't move," said a menacing voice from the blackness behind the light.

They were looking for moonshine and gin, those men who interrupted the holy. They were tax men. Flying revenuers. They were looking for other spirits. Their sacred eagle was on paper and coins. Ironically, Stace knew, it cost more to pay them than they would ever haul back into the government's coffers.

When his eyes adjusted, Stace stood up to talk with one of the men. "Halt!" one of them yelled at him, dropping his body, bending his knees to shoot. Stace saw the man's fear and sat back down and said nothing.

As the Indians and the few white people in the room sat

stiff and afraid beneath the barrel of the sawed-off shotgun, the revenuers searched the house. They found a thirty-year-old bottle of sherry. They took this as evidence and in the harsh light Ona seemed to crumple and she began to cry. The sweet wine had been her husband's. "It's old," she told the man. "I don't drink it." It reminded her of Isom Neck's body as it lay in his cask in the earth. It was all she had of him, of his dark, strong hands and their touch. But they took the bottle.

That night after the raid, Floyd Graycloud went home and began to empty all the bottles of illegal rum he'd stored around the house. Louise followed him. She was upset. She yelled at him. "How do you think we'll make any money? What are we going to eat?"

"We'll do something. We'll dance marathons. It's not worth it to sell this stuff. I saw what happened. They half tore down Miss Neck's."

"Damn you!" She turned and ran into the house. She smelled the rum. It would take weeks, she thought, to get rid of the smell.

The next day, when Lionel Tall left town, China sat between him and his driver, her white hair wrapped up in a blue filmy scarf. Unlike Lot's wife she didn't look back at the destruction that was behind her. In fact, she asked herself how she could ever have been in a town like Talbert, involved with a man like Hale. He was smooth on the outside, but that only covered a frame of knife-sharp bones. It chilled her just to think of him.

After Lionel Tall left, Stace walked all the way back up to the hills with Michael Horse. He wanted to retrieve his own mare and help the older man out with the wild red stallion. This time, he didn't ask Ballard for permission to leave.

He stayed in the cave once again with Horse and Father Dunne. The two men tried to pry information out of the father. He denied that he was the one who wrote in the sand.

After two days of looking around the hills, following a few hoof tracks here and there, Stace always wound up back in the same place, full circle back to the beginning. The horses were too smart for him. They outwitted him. Stace began to think his only choice was to count his black mare as one of his losses. Finally, he gave up and went farther up into the hills, to be alone and to think.

He walked from morning till night. It was good. He felt the spirit of the land. Out there, it was strong as the Paha Sapa, the sacred black hills. He walked along the Blue River, not far from the Hill settlement. He felt the beauty and power of the river. He was becoming clearheaded. He was certain he'd made an error of judgment by taking a job with the government. It took his real life from him. He knew good men worked there. But even those had a sense of duty that overruled what they sometimes knew to be right. Like General George Crook who was asked if the Indian wars bothered him. Yes, they do, Crook said. It bothered him that the Indians were in the right. Yet he carried out his work, trying to negotiate between the tribes and the government. Sometimes Stace thought that the people were doomed, but at other times he knew the future was an open land, and he had to find a new way through it. He fell asleep beside the river.

After several days, Stace returned to his hotel to nurse his blistered feet and feed his empty stomach. He was dusty and his hair had blown loose around his face. He carried four round river stones along with him. One of them was black. He was just placing it on the west-side floor of his room when there was a knock on the door. Levee called out, "Are you in there?"

Stace unlatched the door and opened it.

"What are you doing?" was all Levee said. "They're ready to fire you."

Stace remained silent. His face was set in a smooth, distant expression. He moved slowly, with a full sense of his body.

Levee looked bewildered. "Where have you been? Ballard's fit to be tied."

"I'm on to something."

Levee became quiet. Red Hawk had a reputation for being right. "What did you learn?"

"I don't know yet. I need more time." He carried a round yellow stone to the east side of his room and set it down on the floorboard against the wall.

Levee watched. "Stace? What are you doing?"

Stace picked up the red stone and carried it to the south.

"I just had a feeling to do this." He straightened up and looked at the young doctor. Levee's face looked drawn and tired. He'd been sticking up for Red Hawk. He took note of the Indian man's face. It was placid and strong. "Hmm, I diagnose a very bad case of Indian spirituality."

Stace grinned at him.

"Ballard's trying to get you off this case, you know."

"It doesn't matter." Stace walked around the room, moving the stones an inch here and there. "If this murder sweepstakes isn't solved pretty soon, this won't be a safe place for any of us." He looked directly at Levee. "That includes me and you."

Levee looked worried again. "Why does it include us?"

"It's a feeling I have." He motioned for Levee to sit down, then he pulled back a chair and sat across from him. "This isn't the business of just a few murderers. It's larger, too large for us to see."

"It can't be, Red Hawk."

"No? Well look at how many lawyers are swindling their Indian clients."

Levee shook his head. "It's money," he said. "They just want the money. They wouldn't harm anyone. It was that way in New York. It's that way in Wyoming. They're greedy."

"It doesn't matter what they want. It's too big. It isn't just that fellow Hale, even though he has a lien on just about everything Indians own around here, including their horses."

But then Levee noticed the leather strap Stace wore. It went around his neck and under his left armpit, like a shoulder holster, but it wasn't. "What's that around your neck?"

"It's leather." Stace didn't explain to him that, like Crazy Horse, he was wearing a sacred stone in his armpit, close to his heart. It was directing his thoughts. It spoke to him, to his body.

Then Levee noticed Stace's limp. "What's wrong with your foot?"

Stace looked as if Levee had violated his privacy, then relaxed and said, "I keep forgetting you're a real doctor. I've got blisters."

"You better let me look at them."

"No, it's nothing." Stace looked hesitant, but then he

gave in, nodded, and removed his shoes and socks. "This is humiliating, you know."

"These are horrible blisters. How did you get them?"

"I've been walking."

"Walking? What happened to your horse?"

He paused only a second, just long enough to give away the truth, then he lied. "I loaned her to an older man up in the hills."

"That was generous. Does that mean it ran off? Here, let me make you a plaster." He went down the hall to his room, came back, and while he moved about, pouring water on the powder and mixing it up, he caught Red Hawk up with the news. "We had a bad case of rabies day before yesterday. A girl." He leaned down and put Stace's right foot on a chair. "Horrible. I've never seen a case of rabies before."

"What happened?"

"All the family knew was that she drank from a dish of water that a mad dog drooled in." He looked up. "Her mother shot her. To kill her. I knew it. But I pretended I didn't. After I heard how sick she was, I would have done it myself." He shook his head. "Can you imagine having to do that? After I was there, they burned down the house, with the child's body in it, they were so afraid of catching it. I had to sign the papers. I said she died in the fire." He stood up. "Keep off your feet. In the morning, wash them with peroxide." He opened the door. "You hear me?"

Levee left Stace's room and went down the stairs and down the street to his office. He removed the stitches of a man who'd been sliced up a few weeks earlier in a knife fight. He was absentminded, though, trying to understand what Stace was up to. Stace was a good agent and an honest man. He'd never acted strange before he was around these particular Indians. Even in South Dakota he'd behaved in a manner suitable to a federal agent. Maybe, like Ballard said, he had too much heart invested here in this case, or maybe it was that man, Lionel Tall, whose presence had reminded Stace of his own, older ways.

By the time her corn was two feet high, the holes in Belle's cornfield had grown wider and deeper. One night she decided to hide outside and see if she could catch the culprit.

She lay down in the furrows and waited. Perhaps it was an oil wildcatter, an independent digger, working by hand there in the night, and maybe someone knew about the secret river of oil beneath the land.

Belle tried to make herself comfortable. She could hear the breeze in the long leaves of corn. And finally, just as she drifted off, she heard the noise, the shovel cutting into the field. She stood up slowly, bent, hoping not to be seen behind the plants.

There, wearing the naked scarecrow's clothing, was Cal Severance. He was drunk. He teetered as he tried to shovel in the center of the green corn. He looked around, as if to dig elsewhere, then carried his shovel not far from where Belle was concealed. She stood taller and looked at him. Her presence in the row of corn startled him. He jumped back. "You scared me," he said. "What are you doing here?"

"It's my cornfield," Belle said.

"Oh." He held the shovel handle by only his eight fingers clamped down across the palm, and began to dig once again as if she were no concern to him. His eyes were bloodshot. He looked pitiful and bad.

"What are you digging for?"

"I don't know." He continued to dig. "I just heard that there was hidden treasure in a cornfield."

Three turkey vultures circled in the sky over the Graycloud land. They had spotted the dead buffalo bull. It lay on its side like a brushy mountain growing out from the barren, grazed land. Luke, the Montana cowboy, and another one of Hale's ranch hands tied it with ropes in an effort to heave its massive body up from the ground, but they couldn't do it. The bull was too large. They stood silently and stared at its blank dark eye as if the answer to the dilemma would come to them. In its eye, they saw their own reflection. The buffalo cows watched from down the road where they were fenced in with an Angus bull. Hale stood by the door of his car, next to the sheriff. Belle kept her eye on all of them. She knew the cause of death was a mystery, even to the veterinarian who knew so much about domestic cattle and horses, but she knew the bull had died of sorrow. He died longing for his life on the land, for his freedom, for his buffalo women. And the other Indians agreed with her.

A number of people stood on the road and watched as Luke finally dragged the enormous dark bull behind his truck over the road to a pit that had been dug in the barren field. He and his helper poured kerosene over the bull and then lit a fire to burn it. As it caught, they jumped back, and the smoke began to rise, black and odorous.

It was from behind this smoke that Ben Graycloud walked past the Graycloud home and headed directly for town. He did not want to see his family. At the Blue Store he asked for Cal Severance. An oil roustabout, out of work, overheard the boy. "Excuse me," he said. "I know where Calvin is. He's at Tar Town up the river. I just came from there."

"Tar Town?" Ben looked blank. He'd never heard of that settlement of the dispossessed.

But the man just said, "Ask people. They'll tell you where it's at."

Ben thanked him, then he went outside and sat on a bench in the sun. He tried to smooth out his wrinkled shirt. He could hear the sound of music in the speakeasy and he thought he'd go in after a drink, but not just yet; for now he wanted only to feel the sun on his face, on his arms and shoulders. He felt a weakness and his head began to ache. He was restless and tense. His hands were curled tight into fists. He wanted a drink, to erase his pain, and with a deep wave of sorrow and fear, he stood up, walked down the street, and entered the smoky speakeasy.

He blinked while his eyes adjusted to the darkness. Then he looked around. There were couples dancing, leaning on each other, inside a roped-off area. The wicks of lamps were turned down low. Ben could see people sleeping at tables and the coats draped over chairs. The air was stale. The dancers were at the edge of endurance. Then he heard the radio announcer talk about the couples in the marathon, and his voice egged them on a little further. But they were alert for only a few moments before their faces went listless once again. They were dancing for a car. It was inside, inside the ropes. It was a baby blue Ford. Ben went over to examine the car, and as he looked at the leather upholstery, he heard his name called out.

"Ben!"

He turned toward the car. It sounded familiar. On the other end of it, he saw his mother. She was inside the rope, dancing with his father, who looked numb and absent. He hardly recognized them. Louise reached toward him with an outstretched arm, but he took a step back. She appeared ghoulish, as if she reached up from the underworld. She was barely breathing. Her muscles, other than the arm, were limp.

His father held her hand, loosely. Ben was shocked at the way they looked, both of them white-faced, their eyes glazed and distant. They looked wasted down to nothing, and they smelled like the stale room, he was sure of it.

"Ben." She smiled again, like a demon. He turned away. He could see the hurt in his mother's eyes. He could also see himself reflected back, his own dirty, wrinkled clothing, his drawn face, his own foul breath and hungover expression of pain. He downed a whiskey, turned away even more, and went out the door.

In the broad daylight of the street, he asked the first person he met to tell him the way to Tar Town, and he started up toward the hills. When he was partway there, he lay down in a gulley and fell asleep.

His dreams, as always, returned him to what had happened. He dreamed of the stone walls of Haskell where he had gone crazy and removed his clothing and run away naked.

And while Ben dreamed, his parents removed their shoes. Louise elevated her feet, weeping in her chair, crying for her son, or what she thought was her son, that apparition of the boy, and wept that she and Floyd had sunk down to the dirty floorboards on the dance floor and collapsed and lost their chance at the soft and shiny blue car. Her hair was damp and pulled straight back away from her face. Doctor Levee bandaged her feet while she cried.

A different kind of peace prevailed at the old settlement of the Hill People. A silence lived there, one that went deep down into the fiery bones of earth.

At night the owls roosted nearby and flew down, hooting, from tree to tree. It was a dry place. Dust was a shadowy haze in the first red light of day when people began to move about the mill quietly down to the Blue River to wash themselves before they offered their prayers back to life and carried water up to the cookfires. They washed their hair and were refreshed before they spoke with one another. Time had not stopped for the people of the hills; there were new kettles, combs the women used to hold their hair away from their faces, mirrors and other gadgets, but the people did not in any way reflect the stresses and strains of civilization. Their bodies moved easily.

Out of the morning's dusty haze, the runners became visible. It was a way, running, and as the people ran, they greeted the day's sun, breathed earth's rich odor inside themselves, then out again. It wasn't only Nola's four guardians down in Watona who ran so fluidly across the land. There were others, each with a task of living, each one a living prayer, a flute the wind played. They were lithe, beautiful, long-muscled men and women.

One runner, a woman, was the teller of history. She kept the people informed about what was happening down in Watona. Her name Na-pa-cria had been shortened simply to "Cry." She went into the flat town, down streets between the red sandstone buildings, and returned with the news on her tongue. One day Cry ran up to the bluffs and tried to describe a marathon to her people. "The dancers never stop. They dance until they are dead on their feet. They eat standing up. They hold each other like one tree leaning on another."

Oh, said the people, that's good, an offering. Is that for the corn crop? And in town, too; who would have thought it of people who didn't seem to love the land.

"No," said the young woman. "They do it for money." She looked grave and shook her head.

The people looked off in the distances and thought for a while before they turned their thoughts back to things more practical and returned to their work of soaking beans or feeding sticks to a fire.

Floyd and Louise Graycloud were among the marathoners the newscrier had seen. The white man and Indian woman left the dance floor weeping that morning, looking like skeletons with hardly any skin and with eye sockets black from fatigue.

"They don't love their bodies down there," said the runner.

The people nodded again and went back to their chores.

"Another thing," she said.

They looked up again.

"A white-haired girl named China taught the men a new dance called the tango and then she rode away to South Dakota with Lionel Tall's driver."

Two older women ground corn and thought about the white-haired girl. One said, "Why in the world would anyone want to go to South Dakota?"

"Especially a blonde," said the other woman. "I could see it if she was an Indian."

Michael Horse wanted to move to the settlement. He was becoming lonely. He was given a little house with two rooms, one behind the other, for his night typing, so that it would not disturb the others when they wanted to sleep. The other room was for his sleeping, eating, and resting. But he still remained outside by the fire for the better part of every day and on good days he took the typewriter with him.

The fire he had carried with him was in the center of the little village. It sat side by side with the fire that belonged to the Hill People. Michael Horse sat before the fire. The hot flames of the different fires met one another in midair above them and in that burning they joined, one with the other. And the fire taught him. Anyone who ministers to a fire, he knew, would learn very quickly that the world lives in a fire. And he wrote these thoughts down at night.

Horse watched the glowing coals at the bottom of the fires. Some days he would see an eye in the wood, looking back at him. Or he would learn wind from the way smoke blew toward him. He learned the space of air that lies between one drop of rain and another falling on the fire, and those were just three of the elements. The other one he knew from birth.

When the oil-rig trucks passed noisily down Main Street, buildings shook and coffee cups rattled on tables and shelves. Lights hanging from the ceilings rocked to and fro. The rattling disturbed Martha Billy. Her hands began to shake whenever she heard the first rumble approach from the far end of town. She wanted to move away and she had taken it up with her husband several times, but he'd said nothing about leaving town.

"I'll never get pregnant in such a place," she told him tearfully one day, and those were the last words needed to convince him. The next time she said, "I want to live in the bluffs," he nodded at her and said, "It's only a little longer now."

Martha Billy took fast to the Indian ways. She was like a convert to another faith, and she dropped so fully into this world, that she gave not even a single glance backward at her past.

It was a shame, Joe Billy thought, that she felt this way about her own kind and wouldn't even look for the good that lived in so many of the townspeople.

But Martha had become a dreamer. One morning, with tears in her eyes she told Joe that she'd dreamed of sleeping beneath a treeful of bats.

Joe Billy had never said a word to Martha about the bat medicine, so he looked very serious and he asked her, "What happened then?"

"They dropped a small shining circle, a globe, down to me and while it rested on my lap they spread a shawl around my shoulders. It was as thin and light as their wings."

"It must be a sign," he said, and he got up immediately and set about packing his belongings. "It's what we've been waiting for."

"What are you doing?" She looked puzzled. "I don't understand."

"The bats protected you." He packed a knife. "They offered you a living world." He packed a blanket and a cooking pan. "Bring just what you think you'll need."

She opened a drawer and went through it.

"What's all this about bats?" she wanted to know.

"I'll tell you later." He took a bowl, a shovel, a coil of rope, and a little bag bulging full of shining seeds of corn that had been given him by the gardener, Jim Josh. "I think you are right about the baby. A child is a small glowing world. That must be the meaning of your dream."

There was more to the dream, she told him.

"What is it?" he asked her. He stopped packing and listened.

"After that I took the light with me and I walked on a red pathway past seven faces carved in red wood."

"Cedar," he said, then stopped his bustling around and looked at her again. "Was I there? In the dream, I mean."

"Yes. You were in front of me on the path." She finished packing a small bag of personal items. She took along a hair net and a bottle of rosewater. "I don't suppose I will need fingernail polish, will I?"

Joe Billy laughed. "No. Toss it away."

On their way out of town Joe and Martha passed through a section of town called Rag Row where the oil roustabouts lived. The oil workers were dancing to the music of their Victrolas. They were laid off for a while and poor, but they were certain they'd be back on the job before long, and so they relaxed and played as if they were on a holiday. They stopped to watch the Indian man who carried a pack full of goods and the white woman who carried several pots tied to her back by ropes all beneath an umbrella opened above her to protect her pale skin from the sun. The roustabouts thought the two were ragpickers going about to sharpen knives and sell blue and purple skeins of thread. If they'd had any cash, they would have stopped them to make a purchase.

The bluffs would not have been much more than a full day's hike for other walkers, but Martha and Joe Billy were burdened by their belongings. They carried their lives on their backs like snails. It slowed them down, so they rested often. Before dark that night, they put down their packs. Martha covered a bolt of flowered cloth to protect it from the rain, and set the cooking pans down beside it. They stopped for the night. Their camp was not very far from Sorrow Cave and they could hear the screech of bats above them.

"That's just how it sounded in the dream," she said.

"You know," Joe Billy said, stirring the fire, "One of the best things about bats is that they are a race of people that stand in two worlds like we do."

Martha lay back and watched the sky. A single cloud moved across the first pale light of the moon.

He went on, "And they live in earth's ancient places."

"I love them," said Martha.

In the firelight, she looked like a yellow-haired angel of religious paintings, the angel who helped children across the bridge. She fell asleep.

"Are you dreaming?" Joe Billy asked, leaning toward her.

Her eyes fluttered as she watched the world that lived inside her eyelids. Joe Billy looked on, but he felt left out. He wondered if he would feel the same way when she carried a child within her.

The next morning, Joe Billy walked away from the camp and went down to the creek to pray. He offered tobacco, and he offered a voice, as it is said when a prayer rises from a person's lips. While he stood tall in the sun, speaking, remembering to pray for the afflicted and the hungry, the lonely and the sad people without helpmates, he saw a brilliant red movement between trees and heard a clopping of horse's hooves, then saw a glimpse of the unmistakable lean-muscled horse, Redshirt, running, its tail flying out behind it. And before he even returned, stumbling, to Martha, he was already crying out, "Look. It's the horse!"

But Redshirt vanished into thin air. "It's still giving Horse the runaround, I know."

That morning, along their way, they came across Sorrow Cave. It was cool inside. It was a wild place, as if no human had ever been inside. The ceiling was full of scratches made by bats who once lived there. It looked like an alphabet, a mysterious writing that wanted to be deciphered. There were no signs of either the crazy man who'd hurt children, or of Horse who'd stayed on there before moving to the Hill settlement.

At evening of that next day, the journeyers saw the red bluffs. The bluffs fit into the spreading darkness as if it had moved aside for them, had let them nestle against it for a while. There were no fires, no signs of the people who inhabited the settlement. The Hill People had learned the secrets of invisibility. But Joe Billy knew that he and Martha were being observed. From the bushes, eyes were open and watching as they neared the hills and found the path.

Martha had never been to the old settlement. The footpath had been worn smooth by the passing feet of Hill Indians.

Along the sides of the path there were large red stones, carved
into faces and animals. She looked about her at the beautiful
stones and carvings. A red turtle with its round, smooth shell
sat before a clump of rabbit bushes. "What kind of people,"
she wanted to know, "live at the end of such a road?"

"They don't live at the end of it," Joe said. "They live
along it. That's the kind of people they are."

The footpath was red in color. In the evening light it was
deep crimson, and it looked something like the road she had
dreamed. She saw a large circular stone, with a hole and
spiral cut into it.

There were also wooden ornaments carved in red cedar.
A stalk of corn was carved in one, a star in another. But in
spite of the carvings and structures along the way, the path
was barely visible before a person happened upon it.

When they reached the settlement, the men and women
came to greet them. They fed the tired travelers bowls of
cornmeal mush in silence, and gave them a bed in which to
sleep. They would learn the purpose of their visit in the
morning when it was appropriate to ask.

The next morning, Martha woke to the sound of tapping.
"What's that?"

Joe Billy shook his head. "I don't know."

It sounded like a telegraph machine clicking out an important, coded message. "Do they have a Western Union
depot clear up here?"

But it was Michael Horse and he was typing. He had taken
his typewriter outside and sat bent over it on the ground. The
people would come by now and then and wonder why it was
that old man Horse would work with such a machine. There
was nothing to eat there. It was odd too, they thought, that
it had belonged to their Grace Blanket. What would she have
wanted with it? And it was worse yet, that while the gold-
toothed man typed, the red horse he wanted so desperately
trotted by several times a day and the man never once looked
up and saw it. The people knew he had a desire to possess
this horse, so they took satisfaction in the events. They liked
the red stallion free, so they never mentioned its appearance
to Horse. Some of the children even began to make minor
disturbances in the other direction from where the horse
passed, in order to turn away the man's attention. Horse was

bewildered. It wasn't the way Hill children behaved at all
and he thought they were becoming as bad as the children in
town. But the bewilderment became the better part of the
joke the Hill Indians played on Michael Horse and the fathers
and mothers would hide their faces from the old man and
laugh. Occasionally a man would say to Horse, "They've
been like that ever since the invention of razor blades."

Joe Billy went to investigate the tapping sound and he
found Michael Horse. "What in the world are you doing?"

Horse straightened up from his typing and said, "Oh
hello," but he was lost between the words and the page and
he drifted back away from the conversation.

In addition to his writing, Horse was learning the languages of owls and bats. It didn't come easy for him. He was
poor at languages, he thought, even though he'd learned Chinese during the Boxer Rebellion and some Spanish from horse
dealers in the older days, but he thought if he could learn the
few difficult words of Creek that he knew, he could learn
anything, so at night he'd go out with some of the Hill men
and listen to the darkness.

On the third night, after the owl men returned, there was
a full moon. While Michael Horse was opening and closing
his eyes like an owl, Joe Billy brought out his offering for the
people. He sat before the fire and opened his little leather
bag. He held the tiny kernels of corn in his palm. "We should
plant these seeds tonight," he said. "In the light of the
moon."

"But isn't it a little late?" asked one of the Hill men who
had been out owling. He spoke quietly, careful not to shame
Joe Billy for suggesting they plant at such a bad time of the
year.

"The corn in Watona is already five feet tall," said Na-
pa-cria, the running woman.

"They'll grow here," Joe assured them. "These will
grow."

Before she put her hoe to the ground, one of the older
women questioned him once more, "Even this late? Is something wrong with them?" She was afraid the corn might have
forgotten its lifeways, the way some people had, but Joe Billy
convinced them to try the kernels.

The old women, according to the custom, planted the corn

by the moon. They sang as they planted. It was a new song made for the new corn, and it was so sweet and fascinating and delicate, it sounded like a river running.

It was such a gift, the corn. In only a few days the first rising blades broke through the ground. It grew and grew.

One of the older women was standing just inside the arched gate of the settlement when she saw Father Marshall Dunne, the hog priest, approaching. The priest was thin and bony, but he had a softness about him that was new. He hummed as he walked, and he carried a walking stick.

"Hello, my sister," said the priest. He could hear Horse's typewriter clacking. The woman smiled and took his hand. Joe Billy also shook the thin hand.

That night, around the fire, the priest said with great and wise authority that he had something very important to tell the people, so they sat near him to listen.

"Two days ago," he began, "in the heat of the afternoon, I accidentally came across a rattlesnake." He paused to let them take in the full danger of such an event. "It was a diamond-backed rattler," he added.

"Yes?" said one of the women.

"It was coiled up."

The people listened expectantly.

"It struck out and bit me."

They nodded. They waited for the rest of the story.

"Well, to make a long story short, I discovered that I was afraid of dying." He looked to see how they reacted to this confession.

The people knew that humans were most always afraid to die. "Oh yes," said one of the men. "We are like that too." He nodded for the father to go on.

"Well, that was in spite of my promises to other people that they would enter the golden world of heaven when their days on earth are ended. I felt like a hypocrite, don't you see?"

Joe Billy translated for the people, explaining that a hypocrite was a man whose words had broken away from his heart. They knew people like that.

"I wished I had the faith of a mustard seed or a crow that

could move mountains a grain at a time, but I didn't have such faith. Me being a man of the cloth, too.''

They listened more politely now. They understood the persistence of crows.

''I did not expect to live, but then I tried to think like a snake and see things from its point of view, and in that effort I merged with the snake.''

Joe Billy translated. ''He was one with the snake.''

They nodded, go on.

''I felt my own snaking spine and double tongue, my own searching for warmth and food, my slabs of muscle and shedding of old skin turned inside out and abandoned. I knew this: that the snake is my sister. And when I knew that, the sting and burn of venom went away from my leg.'' He showed them his bony white leg. There were the two fang marks on it and a little blue spot where the poison had moved through the tissue. ''And I didn't die.''

They looked from his leg to his face.

''The snake is our sister,'' he said. ''That is what I came to tell you. It is wisdom to know this.'' He hoped they understood that from his story. They still watched him, waiting to hear the important new thing he had to say. But he was so silent after those words that they thought he'd changed his mind about whatever it was he wanted to tell them.

''The snake is our sister,'' he repeated.

They waited. ''Yes, so what new thing did you learn?'' asked one of the children.

''Don't be rude,'' said his mother.

One morning that season Nola woke with morning sickness. Lying in bed, eating soda crackers to quell her nausea, she looked around in her bedroom. It was beginning to look foreign to her. The wallpaper with its white roses was glued to alien walls. It reminded her of her mother's beautiful rose garden. The furniture was heavy and cumbersome, the way her body felt. She looked at Will, asleep on the bed beside her. He appeared weak that morning, and while she looked large with all the life growing inside her, he looked small and diminished. For that, when she laid back down, she turned her back to him. And for other things, too, she seldom spoke to the young man any longer, and when he came to her in the night, she turned away.

The truth was, Nola had become afraid of Will Forrest. After the discovery of oil on Belle Graycloud's land, Nola had asked Will to look at her finances. She wanted to see what she could spare for her friends so that they would not be forced to lease more of their land. But the news he brought back was that his father had squandered much of her money investing in companies that were now going broke. And her old fears returned to her and she again suspected her young husband. She believed he would murder her one day. Not while she was pregnant. The child was her safeguard, but later, or maybe he would wait for another child, as others had done.

It didn't matter to Nola that everyone, even the worst of the town gossips, who looked in on the marriage could see that Will was in love with the beautiful Nola. But the gossips saw, also, the tension between the two young people and it was so great that they all held their breaths in fear of what would happen next.

Will himself was torn between his wife and his father. He would make it up to Nola, he knew, but there was a split between Will and Mr. Forrest, like a log wedged clean apart in icy winter.

The gossips were wise enough and old enough to know that men and women were not like one another at all, so they knew that the acts and offerings of love Will made did not seem like such to Nola. The diamond ring sat on the chest of drawers, too small for Nola's swollen fingers, and even at that, she believed it was an offering made out of the crystal stones of guilt.

Her face was set. Day by day, a piece of her retreated. She was leaving him a little bit at a time and he did not even know it.

The agents met in a secret little cove away from town where no one could see them. A single dim lantern sat on the ground in a patch of grass. The men talked beneath the cover of night. Luke, "Montana," was there, and so was one of the new men, an insurance underwriter with a too-tight collar. Stace didn't know him. "The only consistent name that

comes up with every death is still Hale's," said Ballard. He
chewed on his unlighted cigar. "We know it's him. But there's
nothing to pin on him. In every case he's clean and legal.
With witnesses." He drank from his bottle of Coca-Cola.

"It was the letters," Levee said. "We got Walker's letter
before his death. John Thomas's letter came a month or so
before his death."

"Walker and Thomas sent letters?" Stace sounded surprised.

"You didn't see them?" Levee looked closely at his friend,
as if he doubted his word.

"Why didn't you tell me?" This information opened another door of suspicion in Stace's mind.

"I thought you knew," Levee said. "Everyone else saw
them."

In that margin of doubt, Stace thought there might have
been other details he hadn't been told.

Ballard interrupted. "We don't have time to go over this
right now. All we know is that most of the people who wrote
letters have been killed." He put the cigar in his pocket.
"And Michael Horse was one of them. We haven't got a clue
about what's happened to him. He's disappeared into thin air
without leaving a trace for us to follow. We've got to assume
he's dead."

Stace kept silent about Horse's whereabouts. "What about
Moses Graycloud?" he asked. "What's been done to protect
him? Have you sent him a warning?"

"No," Ballard said. "We think he's been safe because his
land isn't productive. But we're posting a guard there tomorrow."

"Why? What's changed?"

"It doesn't matter anymore if there's oil under it; if it's
land, someone wants it."

Stace got up and paced a restless distance back and forth.
Then returned to the knot of men. They spoke in quiet tones
even as they had watched him, but suddenly Ballard turned
and lit into the Indian man, "Stace, you're too involved in
this case." Ballard glared at Red Hawk a moment, then he
turned back to the other men.

"We have a leak somewhere. Maybe at the post office."
Ballard was quiet a moment, then he said, "We should

send a letter.'' He looked at the Montana cowboy. ''You should do it. We'll protect you. Some more of our men are coming in by train tomorrow.'' Ballard's face showed that he was stumped, and there was a look of embarrassment about him. He knew what a simplistic plan this was, but he said to Luke, ''Write a letter stating that you have information on the murder deaths in Indian Territory. Then we'll follow you to see what they do. First, you'll have to quit your job with Hale.''

Levee was concerned. ''I don't like it. What if they find him somewhere else?''

''We'll look out for him.''

Stace interrupted. ''How do you know it won't take a month for them to go after this bait?'' He pointed at Luke.

''They're getting desperate,'' Ballard replied. ''Look around you. The ranchland is overgrazed. Rag Row is full of unemployed oil roughnecks. Tar Town is full of evicted Indians. Even the woods have been burned.''

After the meeting, Stace and Levee walked together back to town. The night air smelled good and fertile. They were both silent. It seemed too easy. Stace doubted that it would work. He doubted first of all that Luke would survive when the criminals were smarter than the best agents. But even more than that, he doubted the bureau. ''It's a stupid idea.''

Levee tried to change the subject. ''Have you found your black horse?''

''It's still running wild.'' But he wasn't concerned about the horse. It was better off than he was. Stace stood alone and outside the circle of the other agents in too many respects. He had fallen through the gap between their worlds. Whichever side he happened to be on, it was the wrong one. He didn't say anything more to Levee. In his mind, he began to sing one of the old songs from home, a lonesome kind of song.

But Levee broke the silence. ''They're going to get rid of you, Stace.''

''I know.'' He stopped his inner singing. His eyes filled with tears. ''But I might quit first.''

Levee glanced at his friend. Though he said nothing, Stace knew that the white man could not help but think tears were a sign of weakness, so he held back his feelings. But his heroes were men who would weep. Men like Crazy Horse who had spent and lost his life in the work of helping his people survive. He'd lamented and cried for a vision from the stone people, the shadow people, the daylight people, from all the spirit helpers on earth.

When the tears passed, Stace said to Levee, "You know, many of us have a sickness that makes us cry. Your kind of people don't get this disease or the deep sorrow that comes with it." Black Elk also wept. All the good, strong men cried.

They walked in silence. As they entered the hotel, Levee said, "Good night," squeezed Stace's hand awkwardly, and closed the door of his room. For Stace it was not so easy. He opened his door cautiously. He felt afraid, but once he was in his room, he glanced around, grabbed a jacket, and went back out through the dark corridor and into the street.

His first thought was to warn Moses Graycloud that he might be in danger. But a little ways down the street, Stace stopped abruptly as if he'd just remembered something. He turned back toward the hotel.

In his room again, he took out pen and paper and wrote a letter to his sister: "Dear Imogene, I am leaving here and coming home. Please read this to our mother. Tell her I am on my way at this very moment. I miss you."

He remained sitting at the desk. He wondered if the letters had been withheld from him intentionally. Then he wrote a note to Moses Graycloud saying that his life was in danger because of the letter he'd written to Washington. He folded that note and put it in his pocket, but he sealed the other envelope and addressed it to Imogene Red Hawk, General Delivery, Manderson, South Dakota, put a stamp on it, and dropped it into the mail slot in the hotel lobby. Then he went back outside in the clear fresh air and headed to Moses Graycloud's house. He thought he was being followed, but he walked in the open without even the camouflage of trees. In the hills he could see the lights burning. When he came to the sweet-smelling lilac bushes blooming by the mailbox, he made a turn. In the moon's light, and the string of electric lights around the barn, he walked to the Grayclouds' front door and slid the note beneath it, out of reach of anyone who might have followed him. Then he breezed away, into the dark shadows of trees. At the creek, he tied his jacket around his head and waded into the cool water where he knew he could not be traced or followed. One part of him said he was being overly cautious, but another part was held tight in fear. He went with the creek toward the Blue River and Sorrow Cave that was up in the hills above it like an open mouth.

It was still dark when Stace stepped out of the water. He felt defeated, but at the same time, he felt free. Still wet, he walked across the land. He saw the eyes of a raccoon, out foraging for eggs. He remembered reading that Zebulon Pike had reported shooting in these hills, forests, and prairies 770 wildcats, 300 female bears, and 3,000 deer. Pike had written to invite people to come to the place where game was in abundance. And they arrived, on trains, on foot, on horseback. Like a flood, the people came.

Stace circled round his own trail once, to see if anyone had caught up with him. When he was sure it was safe, he headed up to where Michael Horse had been dwelling in the cave of sadness.

He was still thinking of Crazy Horse as he walked, Crazy Horse who'd had eight horses shot out from under him but was never wounded. Crazy Horse, the man who wept. When Stace took the job of tribal policeman, his mother had said that Lakota policemen had helped to kill Crazy Horse after promising him safety, immunity they called it. They persuaded him to go speak with the men who represented the government of the United States, but it was a trap and once there Crazy Horse was held by his own friend, Little Big Man, so that the government officers could kill him. Other men, younger and jealous, ones who had taken solace in the spirits that live in bottles, shot Crazy Horse as he was dying.

"The people will never trust you if you are with the police," his mother had told Stace quietly, and he could see her now, her long hair hanging down the back of her nightgown.

When he was dead, Crazy Horse had been cut in half to fit in a box. As if he'd not been divided enough in life. His parents took him away. No one else followed. They grieved too deeply to say good-bye to his severed body. The Lakota still mourned for that good, strong man who had loved and looked after his people, the man strong enough to cry.

Stace looked up at the sky. "Grandfather," he said and his own words stopped him in his tracks. He looked up and wept. He sat in the long grass. The night was the only thing he could trust. He stayed there the rest of that night, and when the first gray of morning began to rise up in the east, Stace stood up and sang a morning song, then he continued his journey toward the cave.

Long after he watched Stace Red Hawk slip the note beneath the Grayclouds' front door and disappear into the night, Floyd remained hidden behind the magnolia tree. He was waiting for his boy Ben to return home.

Just before dawn, Ben and Cal staggered in on the road. They sat outside the house, tipped a bottle and began, one at a time, to shoot out the floodlights, laughing between shots.

Floyd was afraid to move, for fear they would shoot him. No lights went on inside the house.

Indoors, the Grayclouds moved away from the windows and waited quietly for the shootings to end.

Floyd no longer knew his son, nor did he trust him. He waited in silence. After a while, Cal fell asleep on the ground and Ben staggered inside, mumbling to himself. Floyd followed behind him. He picked up the note on his way in and before he reached Ben, he read the note, went pale, and sat numbly down in a chair, forgetting his drunken son.

The rooster began to crow as he sat there, and when Moses came down the stairs, smelling of Wildroot Hair Oil, Floyd showed his father-in-law the note and together they decided that they needed extra protection at the house. Then Floyd went up the stairs to the bed in the hallway where Ben was fast asleep, and sat on the edge of the bed. He shook his son gently. "Ben?"

Ben turned away. By then, the morning light was in the hallway.

"Ben?"

Ben blinked his eyes a few times and his muscles tightened. "Leave me alone," he said to his father.

"Ben. I want to talk to you."

But Ben sat up in the twisted sheets, then grabbed his knife from beneath the cloth.

Floyd moved back. "What are you doing?" His eyes were wide with surprise.

His own flesh was going to knife him, he thought, but then Ben held the knife to his own arm and cut the skin. A deep fear ran through Floyd's veins. "What are you doing?"

Ben screamed, "Get out of here. Leave me alone!"

Ben buttoned only one button on his shirt and dashed toward the stairs. Floyd tried to block him, and they struggled together a moment until Ben hit his father on the chin, ran down the stairs and out the door toward Tar Town.

Floyd sat down on Ben's unmade bed and touched his bruised chin, then put his elbows on his knees and his face in his hands.

That morning the sheriff arrived to investigate the report of gunshots the previous night. "It was a family dispute," Belle said. But as an afterthought, she said, "It sure took long enough for you to get here." But she knew how much fear all the lawkeepers felt in those days, and she didn't blame him. And she thought that if he had been there that night, he might have shot Ben and Calvin.

The sheriff invited himself into the kitchen and removed his hat. He was a calm, even-tempered man. They welcomed him.

That morning, when Lettie came down the stairs, he seemed happy to see her.

"Ben's not himself, not since he went away to school," Lettie said.

"Like Tom Longboat," the sheriff said.

Lettie's brows lifted into a question. "Who's that?"

"Longboat. He was a runner, you know," the sheriff said. "He went to the Carlisle school. He was so good a runner that no one even enjoyed the races he was in. They always knew he would win. There wasn't enough challenge."

Belle tried to listen but she was tired from being awake so much of the night.

Floyd mentioned the letter to the sheriff. He took it off the table and unfolded it. "What do you make of it, Jess?"

Belle scanned the outside area around the house even as

she baked biscuits and when she put them on the table in front of Jess Gold. She watched him eat. Finally, she asked, "Could you spare someone to watch over us?"

He looked closely at her. "I don't know. I don't know if you really have cause for concern." He looked from Belle to Floyd. "Well, I can send someone over now and then, if it will make you feel more comfortable." He stood up. "Will do," he said. He smiled into Lettie's eyes before he left.

A few hours later, they saw one of the deputies drive by on the road, turn his car around, and drive past again, but Belle still wasn't happy with the situation. She prepared herself to leave early the next morning. She wanted to go into the hills to see if anyone there could help them.

When Stace Red Hawk arrived at the cave the next day, it had a different sound than before, and the wind played it like a flute. It smelled dank and moist as if it had changed dimensions. Back in the far corner he saw the hole where the gunshot had chipped away at the stone. A bit of light shone through and Stace could hear, and feel, that there were other caverns connected together behind the one where Michael Horse had lived. There wasn't a trace of him. Stace worried about the old man. He sat at the mouth of the cave and thought about how to find him. Finally, he decided to look for the red stallion. The old man would not be far from Redshirt.

He walked around a patch of trees and an outcropping of stone and soon he saw hoofprints and knew he was traveling in the right direction, and by early evening Stace found himself on the red road to the settlement. It was a fine and beautiful road, one with carvings of the animal people lining the direction. It reminded him of home as he walked past the red sandstone carving of a hawk, like the ones that perched on fence posts in South Dakota. He passed a carved snake coiled in a spiral. Surely the red horse would be in such a place as this.

It was nearly night when he arrived at the settlement, and it had grown chilly. A woman came to meet him. She could have been any age. She looked timeless. Her face was smooth. She offered Stace a soft hand. When they reached the settlement, Stace was surprised at the community of people and the earth-colored huts they lived in. "I never knew you people were here."

"You can't see us from down below."

"I'm looking for Michael Horse," he asked her.

She gestured toward the fire. "Over there."

Michael Horse sat at the fire, feeding it with small, split pieces of wood. The gold fire smoldered in the first blue fireline of evening. Horse watched the glowing coals at the bottom of the fire. That was all he saw, not Stace, and not Joe Billy who was nearby kneading dough for oven bread.

The fire smoked toward Horse. He coughed and moved aside. He stirred it with a stick, then he blew on the coals to make them hot again.

The Hill Indians were like Iowans that evening. Stace smiled at his own thought. They were watching the corn grow. They were elated with the new corn and the speed with which it grew. But they were not yet sure if a corn that rose up as fast as this corn could bear sweet juicy kernels.

Stace sat down beside Michael Horse and was silent. Horse didn't look up. With his rod, Horse caressed the stones. Then he took some egg-shaped stones from along the edge of the fire and held one of the warm stones against the top of his shoulder. "It's such hard work," he explained. "To sit and watch a fire. It makes my back ache." He flashed a smile at Stace and the firelight caught on his gold teeth.

Just then the priest passed by with a smoking censer. Stace watched him pass, then he asked Horse, "Why is he up here?"

"Everyone is coming up here. The people are beginning to worry. I have a feeling Ona Neck herself will come up here one of these days. But the father, he was driven out of his own place by the army ants. He happened along the path by accident."

The priest stopped when he heard Horse mention the ants. "They were terrible," he said, after he greeted Red Hawk. Then he turned to Horse. "I wonder why you don't have ants here?"

"We do. We feed them. That way they stay away from our food."

"That never occurred to me." The father wagged his head, looking incredulous at his own ignorance.

"We also feed the crows," Horse said to the priest. "That's why the corn is still alive and no blackbirds are eating it."

Then Stace saw Martha Billy out in the cornfield, moving among the green bladelike stalks and leaves.

"She looks darker every day," Horse said. "You'd swear she was Indian."

Most of the Hill People stayed away from Stace, Horse, and the priest. They were taught to be wary of those who came from the town. And despite the fact that they knew Belle Graycloud as one of the mothers of Nola Blanket, they remained silent when she arrived the next day and asked to meet with the council of elders.

Finally though, when enough time had passed, they gave in to her request to meet with the elders. That night, she sat before them and let them look at her for a while, as was the custom. Then a woman said, "What do you need?"

"I need help. When Nola was in trouble, you sent the runners down to watch over her."

They nodded.

"Now we are the ones that need help."

"Hmmm," said the oldest woman. Her hair was white. She listened as Belle spoke. Then she said, "So he wrote a letter to the United States? And now he's in danger. That is why we don't talk to their government." She continued to eye Belle.

"Another thing," Belle said. "My grandson. He came back from the Haskell school and he was sick. He stole a horse. He cursed his father." She let her words trail off. She was struggling with tears.

"Yes," said the woman. "They come back with a quick fist. They hit their own mothers and fathers." She was quiet only a moment. "You have been good to us, Belle. You've loved and cared for our children. You've traded with us, always honest. We will spare you two of our runners. One will go to watch over your home. The other will stay with Ben. And our new runners speak English now, so that should be of help."

Belle felt much gratitude. She nodded thanks and sat with her head slightly bowed.

The old woman turned her head and spoke to a young man. He left but returned dressed in town clothes. Then she spoke to a girl. Immediately the girl stood up, and the old woman turned to Belle. "She is going to guard your house."

"But a girl?"

"Okeena's no ordinary one. You'll see."

The girl, dressed in soft white buckskin, was already gone.

"Now you have to eat," the old woman said and she motioned Belle over to the fire where the other people sat.

Belle was surprised to see Stace. "Why is that Sioux medicine man here?" she asked, but before anyone answered, Belle saw Horse and she addressed him point blank. "What are you doing here?" But then she saw the priest, and before she could say a word about the whole of Watona being up at the settlement, Horse told her, "I am writing a new chapter of the Bible."

The priest looked startled by Horse's words. He interrupted, "You can't do that."

"And," Horse added, "I am looking for my red horse." Then he turned toward the priest. "I thought maybe you would know how I could get this chapter added to the whole book."

"So. You still haven't found Benoit's horse?" Belle looked at him.

Michael shook his head. His brows wrinkled a bit. "That is one wild horse."

The priest was irritated. He interrupted again. "You can't write a chapter of the Bible. That is the word of God."

"Well it has men's names in it. Like the Gospel of John, for instance. Why not the Gospel of Horse?" He continued the discussion without looking at Father Dunne. Belle Graycloud went to sit across the fire with the other women.

But the priest didn't give up the argument. "They copied down what God told them to say. That was different."

"That's what I am doing." Horse glanced at the father. "I just want to know how to get it copyrighted, is all. I thought you would know about that."

The priest's face was rigid.

"Well, son," Horse said to the priest, "I think the Bible is full of mistakes. I thought I would correct them. For instance, where does it say that all living things are equal?"

The priest shook his head. "It doesn't say that. It says man has dominion over the creatures of the earth."

"Well, that's where it needs to be fixed. That's part of the trouble, don't you see?"

That night, Jim Josh hobbled up the path. He smiled at the elders. They didn't smile back and he felt at first like a foolish old man. It was nothing personal, but he didn't know how much it added to their worries that one more man had found them, and they exchanged glances with one another when he said to them, "I heard about the corn."

"What about it?" asked one man.

"I wanted to see it."

"It's over there," one woman pointed.

Even Josh was amazed at the healthy green sheaves growing in their field.

Early the following morning, Belle left. She was accompanied by a runner. The man wore a western shirt and a pair of jeans, much like the cowboy ranchers wore. He was lean and wiry. His name was Silver.

Belle and the man were going to Tar Town, in order to look for Ben. They walked in silence for most of the morning. Belle could see that his eyes missed nothing, not so much as a pink-eared jackrabbit. She felt safe with him. They walked over a bridge that crossed the Blue River. Belle looked at the placid blue water and the river's rust-red banks. It was a beautiful sight flowing out of Kansas, over the flatlands near Tulsa and on past the bluffs near the Hill settlement.

"It's beautiful, but Hell has four such rivers," Belle said to him. "And I know one of them is the Great Blue." The devastation of the surrounding land made the river even more jewellike in its clarity. In places the banks were black from oil seepages like the one in Belle's spring, and there were rusted oil drums stuck in stagnant pools along the area, and swampy, polluted places where insects thrived.

Toward evening they saw a coyote pawing at earth. They passed trees that had been killed by bagworms. Many of the fields had been burned black, and those that were not burned had been overgrazed by hungry cattle the world-eaters raised. It was a desolate sight.

Then they saw the beginning of the shantytown called Tar Town. The camp was an extension of the black and destroyed land, a scramble of structures stretched out a long distance behind the mesquite hills. The shacks and shelters had been put together in any way possible in order to provide cover from the rain, and most of them were covered with black tar paper.

Seeing the once-beautiful people living there in poverty and misery, Silver became very quiet. Belle thought how many ruined great people lived in that tar-paper village, broken men and destroyed women who had once been singers and kind mothers. The scrawny brown children did not look full of a future. Both Belle and Silver were silently afraid that the sickness of despair, as devastating as smallpox, might be contagious.

They prepared themselves for their journey through such a miserable underworld as they undertook to find Ben.

As they approached the encampment, they could hear the murmur of voices and smell the human smells of living, of cooking smoke and burning things, of human bodies that had gone to decay. Dogs chased around in the dust beneath clotheslines. Old men elevated their swollen, sore feet, and there were wracking coughs that sounded like tuberculosis.

All the while he walked, Silver prayed for the wounded people. He remained silent. He vowed he would eat or drink nothing that was offered in this broken world, hell's tinderbox.

Belle looked at the people. Pain had a way of changing the body. Human skin became something else, a wall, a membrane between the worlds of creation and destruction. She remembered this, it was the first thing she had learned from Sam Billy who'd been the helper of people for so many years.

It was bad enough what had already happened to the people, but this, this other misery, fell through her in a sinking hopelessness.

They asked a man if he knew where Ben Graycloud was. The man's dark eyes were sad as he shook his head and looked away.

When finally they found Ben, he looked gray and emaciated there in that wasted place. Behind him was a dump yard of broken and discarded vehicles that had once held the proud Indian men and women as they drove over the curved earth.

Ben stood at a makeshift table. He stood with his legs apart the way he thought a man should stand. Across from him was Cal. Cal was wearing the clothing he'd stolen from the scarecrow in Belle's cornfield. They were working at something in front of them, but when Ben saw Belle approach, he covered the object before him with an old red oil-stained cloth.

"Ben, I'm so glad to find you," Belle said. Then she looked at the table. "What are you doing?" Belle asked the young man.

"Nothing." Ben avoided her gaze. With shaky hands, he pushed his hair back away from his face.

Belle noticed the blood on his hands. She stepped forward and lifted the stained cloth. In front of her, under the filthy cloth, was a golden eagle. Its head was turned to the side on a limp neck. Its golden brown wings stretched out in death. One of them with its pattern of smooth feathers was partially severed. It was a poor job of cutting. The bloody knife the boys had used was dull and the wing had been partially torn away from its body. There was a gunshot wound at the soft-feathered chest.

Belle was frightened.

Ben looked at her sorrowfully. "Grandmother," he said. His eyes pleaded with her to understand.

"What have you done?" Her voice was quiet.

"We wanted to pray," he said. "We only wanted to pray." He began to cry and he did not even bother to wipe the tears from his face.

"You killed an eagle for its feathers?" She spoke in disbelief. "You took a life in order to pray?"

Ben hung his head.

Belle turned and began walking away. She held back her tears. As she left Tar Town, people who had known her called after her. "Bring us some coffee," said one. A woman, large with child, asked for bananas and shoes.

A few long-tailed rats scurried away as Belle walked. A cloud passed over. She did not speak. Nor did Silver. Both of them walked in silence, with only the sound of their shoes on the hot dusty earth.

When it began to rain, Belle thought, "Even the sky is crying."

The raindrops left spots where they hit the dust.

They picked their way through broken glass and old, torn clothes. They walked through the night. They passed piles of garbage and refuse until they came to a place that had no oil drums littering the land, none of the rats and other scavengers that had learned how to survive near people. There they stopped and rested for the night, but neither of them slept.

When they found a clean place, one that seemed untouched by the destroyers, they laid down on the green grass and gazed up at the night sky. The grass smelled new and fresh as spring.

"You know, Europeans have different constellations than we do." Belle was thinking of the sky, how where she saw a man and a woman standing together, the ones called sky and earth, they saw twin boys. And how where she saw two people holding one another, they saw a man and a weapon. And how, at least, they did see a god who had learned his healing powers from a snake, but then she thought, Bats! They don't have bats. She fingered the meteorite around her neck.

The next day, as Belle and Silver neared the region of Sorrow Cave, they heard the excited, high-pitched sound of young men talking. A shot was fired. It was followed with cheers.

Belle turned in the direction of the noise and walked far enough to see a number of men clustered together around the dark mouth of Sorrow.

Unknown to the Indians around Watona, a war had been declared on bats after the case of rabies that killed the young girl. They mistakenly believed bats carried the disease. There was a one-dollar bounty per "flying rat," as the newspaper called them. And now a good number of well-dressed young men and their fathers stood outside the cave and shot into it, knocking the frightened bats to the ground, then shooting randomly while the animals screamed with terror, unable to escape the man-blocked entrance to the cave.

"Be careful of the bullets, boys. They might ricochet," said one of the fathers.

Belle recognized another group of men as unemployed oil workers. They were smoking cigarettes and waiting for the younger men to finish up so that the older men could go in and gas the cave. The sheriff was among them, as was the mixed-blood Deputy Willis.

As she approached the cave, Belle heard the tumult of the animals inside, and she saw the guns in the smooth hands of the boys. They were excited. Their hands shook as they fired. One of them ground his teeth.

The sun was overhead. Belle stood in the shadow of a tree and watched, then she said to Silver, "Go get some of the people to help us. Tell them what is going on. Tell them these boys are shooting bats."

Belle calmed herself. She held her emotions in check and tried to empty herself of anger, for it was dangerous to have strong human feelings feed a situation such as this. She felt the warm wind blow out of the west. Then she went up the hill toward the cave, picking her way around the stones.

The sheriff greeted Belle, but she didn't speak. She walked to the entrance of the cave, took out her pistol and pointed it in the direction of the boys. "Stand back," she said calmly.

They looked at her. One of them whispered, "She's crazy. I think she means it. Get back." The boys stepped away from the cave's mouth.

Belle looked inside Sorrow for just a moment. In the shadowy cave, she saw some of the dead and bleeding animals. And some of them were trying to escape through the hole in the back. The place was alive with their fear.

She looked down at the men. "No one enters this cave." She pointed a pistol at the men and fixed her face to show that she meant business. Behind her she still heard the crying of the bats.

A couple of young men snickered and scuffed their feet. "Ah hell, she's just an old woman."

They made a move toward the entrance, thinking she would give up easily. But Sheriff Gold, standing behind the men, knew better. "Get back, boys," he said. The boys turned toward Gold's authoritative voice and walked away.

"Jesus, Belle, this is serious," the sheriff said. "Violence never solved anything."

"You're wrong about that. Around here violence solves everything."

"You can't go losing your head over every bird and

snake.'' He sounded tired. ''C'mon, get out of the way, Belle.''

She lifted the gun. ''Don't come up here.''

He cleared his throat. ''We have a rabies problem here, Belle.''

She aimed at him. ''It probably comes from your biting people.'' She didn't move. ''I'm staying. And I want all you men to leave.''

Silver walked up the hill a ways before he disappeared from her sight. None of the men or boys had seen him; their attention, all of it, was fixed on Belle.

The men and boys milled here and there, talking among themselves. ''What are you going to do?'' one of them asked the sheriff.

''I don't know yet,'' he said. The sun was in his eyes as he kept watch on Belle. She looked like a mountain. A raven flew in front of her and cawed. Gold called out, ''Belle. Come on down now. Don't be so backward.''

But Belle pretended to hear nothing as she remained there protecting the double world of bats with their whistling songs and their lives in the cool and deep darkness, the bats who were husbands to trees, the beautiful creatures who were hated by those who lived in what they called the light.

One of the boys spit on the ground. ''Shit, she's crazy. She doesn't even make sense. Why don't you just shoot her?''

Belle decided to keep silent. She wasn't going to strike up any bargains with the law. She didn't want to offer them even so much as her voice, so when the sheriff called up to her, ''Bats are pests. They aren't good for us,'' she kept still.

The afternoon light took on a gold cast. Belle stayed just inside the shade of the cave. She could feel the cool air on her back. Behind her, the dark animals made soft yelping sounds now and then, and shifted their positions. Some of them, sheltered by the old woman, were busy dying, those animals whose voices were their guide like a prayer opening the way, showing them the passage through life. Others settled back into silence, opening and folding their wings, some hanging from stones and looking toward the doorway with their glittering eyes.

''Go get Moses Graycloud,'' Jess Gold said to the Indian deputy, Willis.

A few of the boys sat down on the ground.

It was almost evening by the time Willis returned with Moses. Along with them walked Okeena. She was silent and guarded. The sheriff was relieved to see Moses. "Come talk some sense into your wife's hard head."

"What's going on?" Moses asked, as if the deputy had not already told him.

"Bats. She won't let us exterminate them." The sheriff handed him a megaphone. He looked at Okeena. "Who's she?"

"A family friend." Moses took the megaphone, held it at his mouth, and looked up toward the cave. "Belle!" he called. But there was no answer. "Belle," he cried out again. "Can you hear me? I'm coming up." He didn't bother to wait for her answer. He began to climb up the hill toward the stony entrance.

"Be careful. She's really dangerous this time," Jess said as he stood aside to let Moses pass.

It wasn't long until they heard Belle and Moses talking from inside the cave. They listened for the descent of the old couple, but suddenly a gunshot cracked open the air. The men hit the dirt and Jess blurted out, "She shot him!" But then, the voice of Moses spoke out through the megaphone. "I'm staying here," he said. "If anyone comes up here, I'll shoot."

"They're all going crazy," said Jess. He looked toward where Okeena had been. She was gone.

Only a moment later, a throng of Hill Indians loomed up out of the land itself.

"Where did they come from?" asked Jess Gold. "I've never seen any of them before."

His deputy pointed up toward the red hills.

Gold seemed bewildered. "You mean they come from Kansas?" Then he saw Joe Billy and Martha among them. He hardly recognized Martha. And the hog priest was there. The Red Hawk fellow from South Dakota. And Horse. He didn't see Jim Josh who had taken off his shoes and was massaging his pale feet.

He watched them go toward the cave.

Belle was prepared to resist arrest. She stood at attention

while the lawkeepers looked around the land in search of another way to enter the cave.

Finally, Jess Gold sent one of the boys down to town to call in reinforcements from the state police.

One man laughed, "We're going to call out the militia for a fight over bats?"

"Tell them it's a potentially dangerous situation." Jess Gold turned to where he'd last seen the deputy. "Willis!" he called sharply. "Where's Willis?" he asked one of the boys, his eyes scanning every face.

The boy pointed up to the cave.

Dr. Levee had heard about the standoff and reached Sorrow Cave at the same time as the state police. By then it was almost dark.

With the arrival of the reinforcements, even the air had seemed to relax. The men felt more comfortable. They squatted and lighted cigarettes and talked about work and money and the valuable bats.

Belle looked proud and arrogant as she sat at the mouth of the cave in the graying light, a gun in her hand.

Levee glimpsed Michael Horse. The old man was standing at the entrance to the cave, talking to Belle. Levee was confused. He'd thought Horse was dead.

The sheriff talked to the officer from the state, then called up to the cave, "Belle. We're going to do as you ask and leave."

"Leave?" asked one of them. "Leave? You ought to have your head examined." But the sheriff ignored the protests, even when the men began to move about and talk to one another about what a bad decision it was to leave the Indians in the cave. "You're setting a precedent here," said one of them. "Now they'll resist everything."

"Yeah," said another one. "We're within the law here."

Jess Gold formed a megaphone with his hands and yelled up the hill, "We'll leave. But we're coming back. We want you out of there by tomorrow."

Up at the cave, the people heard the men depart. "Did we win?" asked one of them.

But others weren't so sure. "He's lying," Belle said. She could feel them there, but nevertheless, that night inside the cave, after the old women tried to help the bats that were injured and the men placed the bodies of dead bats outside the cave, the people laughed and talked. They were light-spirited. They drank from gourds of water the Hill People had carried along with them. Up in the sky was a full moon. "It looks like a gold coin," someone said.

"Don't say that. It will probably get stolen."

But they were relieved at the way things had turned out. The deputy, Willis, had defected, if only for a little while. He sat with them, happy to be with so many of his own people again. He smiled contentedly.

The priest was happy that night in so much company. The people had grown to love him and his face was a little rosy. Now and then he would talk to someone in his philosophical manner. He turned once to James Josh and said, "I think, I think we are the earth. Do you know that?"

Josh smiled at the man. "Yes, we are," he said. He looked into the priest's eyes.

"Who is watching the fire?" Belle asked Horse.

"Do you remember I told you that Ona Neck would be up there someday? Well, she is."

"Is she grumbling about it?"

"She is." Horse was proud of Belle, but he said nothing more. That night, for the first time, Okeena noticed the black meteorite that hung from a leather thong around Belle's neck. "Oh, look," she said. "Star-Looking's meteorite."

Several people went over for a closer look.

"Usually I keep it hidden. But tonight I thought the stars would like to see it." Belle sat back. She tried, but failed to get comfortable on the stone floor. "You know, I wouldn't give up this night for a featherbed." She squirmed. She felt the ghosts of children in the cave, but she didn't say it. She said, "I don't know when I've felt better."

That night children slept on the hard stone floor while the adults talked happily.

By the next morning, except for the dead and injured, the bats were gone. Their disappearance confirmed Horse's be-lief that the cave extended even farther back, deeper than he already knew, into the ground. He thought the bats must have left through the hole in the wall. He began to feel the walls of the cave. "There are other rooms behind here, I'm sure of it. I've already found another entrance.'' He pulled at the stone by the hole. A piece of rock crumbled off and clattered to rest near his feet.

Then he saw a line of army ants in the cave. They were disappearing at the floor of the back wall. Horse grew excited. ''See? This is it. This is the way to the rest of the cave.'' He further explored the wall with his fingers, then knelt down and pulled at the stone by the floor.

''Could it go back much farther?'' Joe Billy wondered aloud as he knelt beside Horse and put the blade of his knife between two stones.

''Yes, anything is possible,'' said Father Dunne, and he, too, bent to help them.

After prying around, they found a small opening, with its stones perfectly disguised in a rough corner of the dry cave. The opening was narrow, barely big enough to allow a man to crawl through, and on the other side, there was another spot of light than the one Horse had already seen, just enough to give him hope.

The men bent and squeezed in through the opening. The ceiling was low. Belle watched the soles of Joe Billy's shoes vanish through the corner. Stace Red Hawk went next, and the older men followed, and then one by one all the people entered the back of the cave and were gone except for Belle and Moses who remained behind in order to stand guard.

Behind the wall was a network of caverns, but only a few were accessible. Joe Billy and Stace discovered the first of the larger chambers. Inside it were the mummified remains of a human being. Joe Billy leaned over the mummy. It smelled dusty and its teeth were exposed. His father had told him the stories of the old ones, here before their own time, but Joe had always thought Sam Billy meant they were spirit people from myth or legend.

Jim Josh followed the younger men into the chamber. He carried his shoes in his hands, but he worried about stepping on a scorpion.

Joe Billy touched and examined several little pots that had been placed around the body. They were perfect vessels, red clay, round, and open. Each of them had been painted with a spiral design. In one of the pots were kernels of an ancient corn and when Josh saw the seeds, he lost all interest in scorpions and reached out toward the pot. "Let me see those," he said. He picked up one of the kernels. He reached into his pocket and took out the jeweler's glass he carried there, looked through the curved glass, and studied the pale yellow kernels carefully, then without being seen, he slipped a kernel into his pocket.

From behind him, the priest spoke, "Sorrow runs deeper than we ever knew or could have guessed." But just then Joe Billy found a ceremonial room and found inside it a large item wrapped in buckskin. He pulled the buckskin aside just enough to see the familiar brown fur of one of the bears who had, in earlier times, populated the region. He pressed the leather back into place.

On the wall there were paintings of bats. Red bats. In a hallway there were blue fish, and more bats with red, opened wings, and the paintings of black buffalo. It was a sacred world they entered and everyone became silent and heard a distant dripping of water in the caveways, the echoing sounds, the breathing of earth.

"Don't touch," said one of the mothers to her children.

In the caves, they were intruders. Invading an older world, the silent places of the ancient ones, all of them knew that they would not be back, that they would seal this world away forever when they left, so they looked around and let the vision of it come to rest inside them and then they followed Stace Red Hawk on through the passageway until they squinted at the sunlight, blinked, and saw the great expanse of land in the distance, the Blue River running right beneath them, with steam rising off the water in the growing warmth of day.

Belle yelled through the opening. "They are coming back. Fix the hole. I hear them talking."

They knew they weren't safe from the law. Horse leaned over to pick up a stone. "Can you hold them off?" he asked Belle.

She whispered loudly, "You can get out?"

"Yes, over by the river. I found another opening. We have to climb down, but I think we can make it."

Horse and some of the younger men piled rocks back over the entrance. From their side, Belle and Moses smoothed out the stones, spread soft dust across them. Belle was worried. "If you look close, you can see it. It's not so good."

Horse filled the bullet hole with a small stone from the other side.

At that moment, the sheriff yelled into the mouth of the cave. "Your last chance!" but neither Belle nor Moses replied and both were hastily smoothing out the wall when the sheriff threw in a tear gas bomb.

A visible wall of oily smoke went up in the cave. Belle and Moses both began to cough. They put their hands up to their weeping eyes, and walked out of Sorrow Cave, wheezing and coughing and rubbing their eyes.

"Where are the others?" asked the sheriff.

"What others?" Belle's face was burning and red. "We are alone here." She bent over and wiped her swollen eyes on the hem of her skirt. It only made things worse.

The lawmen and their new posse looked inside the cave. They shone a light, but the gas was thick and they did not enter far enough to see the narrow opening. They saw only that no one else was there.

"They got past us," said the state officer.

When the gas cleared up, the boys went inside the cave to look for the remaining bats. "They scared them away. They lost us all our money," said one, but he stopped to pick up the carcasses just outside the entrance.

While they were writing up the reports, Jim Josh walked up from behind the sheriff. "Morning," he said. He looked sly.

Jess Gold looked at him sharply. "How'd you get out of that cave?"

Josh's face went blank. "Cave?"

Jess glared in the old man's eyes. "So that's the way it's going to be." He looked from Josh to Belle to Moses, and spoke over his shoulder to a deputy. "Take the Grayclouds in and book them, will you?"

The deputy nodded. Belle and Moses got into the police car without a fuss. They were still wiping their eyes and lips when Stace strolled up. From the car, Belle saw him stop to talk with Levee. Then the deputy drove them to jail.

"Where the hell did you come from?" asked Levee.

"I've been in the hills." He pointed to the barren-looking place above them.

"Ballard said you went home to South Dakota."

Stace stopped short. "What?" Then he said to Levee, "He read my letter."

Levee eyed his friend. "What letter?"

"How else would Ballard know where I'd gone? I sent a letter to my sister."

Levee took this in for a few seconds.

"He's in on this, Levee. I know it." Stace's voice began to rise.

"Ballard wouldn't read your letter." Then he reconsidered. "Maybe. Maybe he would. He probably doesn't trust you either."

"No. I'm sure of it. Ballard knows something he isn't telling."

"No wonder everyone thinks you've cracked up."

The Hill People had followed Stace and Josh out from the other opening to the cave. No one saw them walking up the hill. As they walked, the heat waves shimmered up above the land, wavered for a little while, then settled back down, and the people were gone.

Later that morning, at the jail, Belle heard Willis, the half-breed deputy, talking with the sheriff.

"Where were you?" Jess Gold asked.

Willis sounded nervous. "I tried to get in the cave last night," he lied. "They caught me though. They wouldn't let me leave."

Belle laughed to herself. She covered her mouth with her hand as if she might be caught grinning.

"You mean they held you against your will? Two old people?"

Belle listened for his answer and heard only a faint "Yes." She was afraid the young man would lose his job.

The sheriff looked at Willis. "How did you get away?"

"I snuck out this morning."

"How many people were there?"

Willis looked stumped. He thought for a moment, then he remembered that Belle and Moses were probably the only ones there when the law arrived. "Just the Grayclouds," he said.

"You mean two old folks held you prisoner?"

"She had a gun."

Jess Gold shook his head back and forth. He was thinking that he was sick of Indians and there was not a one of them in the whole bunch that wasn't rotten in some way or other. Even Willis, half white, was lying.

Later that day, Louise Graycloud came to bail out her parents. She said to her father, "I can understand Mama being here, but you?"

And when the sheriff returned with Belle, from the women's cells, Louise said, "Why can't you act normal?"

"This is normal," said Belle. But something on the wall caught her attention and she had a strange look in her eyes. She didn't turn toward the sheriff for fear he would read her mind. She knew the blood had drained away from her face. But she saw it. On the new yellow geologists map was an oil pool blacked in on her land, beside the spring where the seepage had materialized. She thought fast, turned toward Louise. "Where did you get the money to pay our fines?"

"I borrowed it from Josh." Then she looked haughtily at her mother. "You're speaking to me now?"

That silenced Belle. Then she put her arms around Louise and kissed her and held her tight. Her eyes welled with tears.

"Mama, I am proud of you," Louise said. She buried her face in her mother's soft chest and heard the woman's heart beating beneath the heavy meteorite that had fallen all the way, burning, from the stars.

Deputy Willis had noticed the strange expression on Belle Graycloud's face and after she left the jail, he stood staring at the same map. "God, she's got oil out there on her allotment land."

Gold went to stand in front of the map beside Willis. "That map is just conjecture. An oilman had it drawn up. It's a speculation of what might be in the area. I'm glad you mentioned it. We should take it down in case someone gets ideas about Belle's land." He took it off the wall and put it in his desk.

Willis thought out loud, "I've been thinking about all these crimes. We're all sure, us Indians, I mean, that Hale is the killer.''

"Who knows? He's always been real good to people here. Still, it could be anyone. Your guess is as good as mine.''

Later that day, Jess Gold walked across town to the Blue Store. He was stiff-looking, Palmer thought when he saw him, and his jaw was tight. Palmer smiled at the man. "What can I do for you?'' he asked.

"Well, we've got a problem,'' Gold said as his eyes took in the store.

"Oh? What's that?''

"Just today I heard my deputy talking on the phone.'' But he interrupted himself and changed the subject. "Where do you keep your safe?''

Palmer looked worried. "In back,'' he said. He gestured toward the door at the far end of the store. "Why?''

"Well, it's Willis. He's in trouble. Gambling or something. I overheard him tell someone he was going to rob you tonight.''

"Rob me?'' Palmer grew anxious.

"Yeah, I'm sorry to say it. He's been a good one. One of my best, up to now.''

He went on. "But there's more to it than that. I want to stay here with you tonight and catch him red-handed.''

"Sure, whatever I can do to help out.''

"Maybe you could stay here, just sit with me, maybe back me up. We probably won't need it, but I'd feel better. He's armed.''

"I see.''

"Why don't you stay out here near the register and I'll hide in back. We can catch him by surprise.''

Palmer was nervous. With his sleeve, he wiped some dust from the counter. "You want me to stay out here?''

"I think that would work best. You keep a gun?''

Palmer swallowed and nodded. "Two. I keep one back there for when I'm in the office. One out here. But I've never used them.''

"You probably won't have to use them tonight either.'' Gold sounded reassuring. He went into the office, scouted around the back room, looking things over. He opened a drawer and located the pistol. "I'll be back over later." He smiled at Palmer. "And Palmer, thanks. I think this will uncover the crime ring hereabouts."

Palmer watched Jess Gold leave. He didn't like the feel of this.

That night, from Palmer's office, Jess Gold called the deputy on the phone. He said, "Go over to the Blue Store, Willis. I got a tipoff Palmer's getting robbed. Keep your gun out and ready. It's probably a gang, so be careful and watch yourself. I'm on my way, but you should go now and catch them in the act. Keep your gun drawn." Then Gold sat back and sipped his coffee. He took Palmer's pistol, a big .45, in his hand and waited for Willis to arrive.

From outside the store, Willis peered in. He saw nothing, only Palmer standing at the register. He opened the door cautiously, looking in first through a crack, then, feeling safer, he opened the door and said, "Palmer." But when Palmer saw him, the gun in the deputy's hand, he jumped aside from where he was standing. "Jess!" he yelled, and Gold, before anyone could think, jumped into the doorway and screamed out, "Don't move," and fired two shots at the deputy. Willis fell back. Both wounds were in the chest. He died right away. "Oh my God," said Palmer. "He didn't even look like he was going to shoot!"

But Jess was in action. He ran over to Willis's body as if to help the dead man, but then, quickly, he took the deputy's gun from the floor, turned, and shot Palmer. Once. In the head. Then he waited a few minutes to see if the shots attracted attention, and he made a phone call to Ballard, the federal agent.

Later that night, after Ballard had looked around Palmer's store, he and the sheriff went through Palmer's account books.

"He was overcharging Indians, wasn't he?" Gold asked Ballard.

"It looks like it." Ballard was tired. He rubbed his face. "How well did you know Willis?"

"I thought I knew him pretty well."

"Well, this was a piss-poor burglary attempt, especially for a person familiar with the law. Maybe they were working together. You know, taking money from customers. Running a swindle.''

"I don't know. I thought Willis was a good man.''

The crying ghost of the buffalo walked across the closed-in field. The bellowing kept Belle awake. She was filled with a longing kind of sorrow. Every so often the sky would light up with heat lightning and the distance would rumble, and she would try to sleep again, only to toss and turn. But in the morning she put on a thin, dark dress and tied back her silver hair. With her arms held up that way, pinning her hair, Moses remembered the girl she had been. He walked up behind her and held her in his arms, then kissed her lightly on the shoulder. She turned toward him and they pressed together and held each other.

It was the Fourth of July. The two of them walked to the picnic grounds and pavilion. It was humid and the flies were busy and they walked slowly, as if they had all the time in the world. Cars and horses passed them, but they stayed at the side of the road and refused to be hurried.

Trees rose up on each side of them as they walked. In the background they could see the burned forests and a horizon of black derricks.

As they neared the grounds, they heard children chasing each other and lighting little firecrackers. They heard the sound of running mules pound the earth, and they heard Jim Josh arguing with their son-in-law, Floyd.

"You can't bet that saddle,'' Floyd was saying.

Josh argued with the young white man who had adopted the Graycloud name. "But it's hand-tooled.'' He held the saddle in front of him. He was bent under its weight.

"It don't matter what it is, it isn't yours.''

"They don't know that,'' Josh said. He could smell the rich odor of its leather. "Besides, I am not going to lose it. This saddle is just going to make me some money.'' He shifted its weight. "Here, hold it for me a minute, will you?''

Floyd was red-faced, trying to talk sense into Josh's head but he said nothing more. He took the saddle and set it down on a bench beside Lettie.

All around them, wagers were taking place in a great circle of commotion. Bets were placed. Indian people loved to

gamble and they never minded losing. They waited in lines
to place bets. They leaned on sticks and smoked cigarettes
and bet on the mule races. One man bet on a dark mule that
urinated, arguing that it would run better now that it had
relieved itself. The stakes were high. They bet silver and
horses and cows. They bet orange and purple woolen blankets that had been in the families for years. Old women put
up their dance shawls and the baskets that had belonged to
their grandmothers. And staggering young men bet their unfortunate medicine boxes and bundles, willing to lose even
the sacred to dollars. It broke the hearts of many people to
see that they put everything up against money and odds.

The gossips sniffed the odor of a hog roasting, and watched
the young men back from schools try to borrow money in
order to place bets. The boys were convinced they would win
and pay back the cash. "I saw an eagle today," they would
say, as if that guaranteed them good luck.

Even before the race, the mules were nervous and skittish.
Ben and Cal were in the crowd. "You see that mule," one
old man said to Ben, after Ben had asked him for a loan. He
pointed at one of the red racing mules. It wore blinders.
"You know what that is, don't you?" He didn't wait for Ben
to answer. He looked sharply into the young man's eyes. "It's
a cross between a thoroughbred horse and a donkey. That's
what your families are like these days. You're turning into
jackasses. And I'll be damned if I give money to a jackass.
Now get out of here." He waved him away.

A pistol was fired into the air and the next race began, the
mules kicking up dust and breathing hard, the little jockeys
bouncing on top of them. The dark sides of the mules foamed
with sweat and the whites of their fearful eyes rolled inside
the blinders. The young boys screamed out, "Come on Saw-
dust! Come on George!"

Moses stood with a cluster of Indian men. Most of them
were dressed in short-sleeved white shirts, even a pair of
suspenders among them, but they still held red wool blankets
over an arm, their dark faces hard-lined with unspoken sadness. They tried not to look at the young broken men, but
they saw them anyway, out of the corners of their eyes.

Belle sat down on a bench with a few other elderly Indian
women. Silver stood in the background behind them. The

women watched people. They were full-chested summer
gossips holding their hands over their mouths as their eyes
glanced about. Ruth sat beside Belle. She looked sadder than
ever. Belle thought how much she loved Ruth, Moses's twin
sister, how close the connection between the two, how they
had grown together in the same body. And Belle was more
accepting of Tate than Moses was, because she had seen with
a woman's eyes the loneliness of Ruth, the need she had to
not be alone in her life. Moses believed Ruth could not see
Tate, his smallness and drive toward money and influence.

"Look at poor Nola Blanket, so big already with her
baby," Ruth said to Belle. Another woman said, "I remember when I was that big and my back and legs hurt so bad.
With that gambling son of mine inside me too. The one that
never visits. Do you remember him at all?"

"No," said a woman in a blue dotted dress and thin black
braids. "I've even forgotten his name."

They talked. Ona Neck said to Belle, "Did you dye your
hair? It looks darker," but the women mostly looked at Nola
Blanket and Rena, who sat beside her watching the day's
activities with interested golden eyes. Nola kept her own eyes
lowered. Her face looked thin and bony. "Do you think Nola
is eating well?" Ruth asked.

"Yes, she is eating liver," said Belle. "I know that for a
fact. Will makes her eat it."

No one could guess by looking at Nola that her feet were
hot and swollen, her breasts grown uncomfortably heavy,
and her back ached. Turmoil and fear lived inside of her, and
in her mind, constantly, she talked to her baby. She talked to
the baby day in and day out. "You aren't even born yet,"
she would say, "and look at this world. Look out from my
eyes. You see the way the very sky is on fire? You are so
young and already you know a hard world. It's in your blood,
baby. It's in your bones."

The sounds of the fireworks were nervewracking, but there
was a circle of silence around Nola, as if she and her child
were somehow protected, and by something more than just
her guardians.

Now and then, Rena spoke to Nola and Nola nodded absently. She picked at a mosquito welt on her skin as if she
were peeling her own dark flesh away. "I don't know," she

was saying to the life that was inside her own life. "I don't know about any of these people."

Rena leaned toward Nola. "Where's Will?"

Nola looked dreamily at her. "He had a meeting with his dad." But she was saying to the new life, "Oh, poor child, you don't even know if you can trust your own daddy."

It was noon and it was hot. The people who were already gathered at the park for the picnic and fireworks were wiping their foreheads with napkins and handkerchiefs. Mothers left their rashy babies naked, and young boys played as if they had forever in their bodies, lighting fireworks and running away like wildfire from the explosions. The day was still young, but the small paper flags held by little Indian girls were already torn, and there was already a tension in the air. The adults looked more somber than in the past. They were in a trap, a circle of fear, and they could not leave. Money held them. It became a living force. One way or another, if they had it or if they didn't, it held them like the caged parrots a vendor was selling. The parrots were green and red. They were crowded in cages. They all faced south toward the deep, wet jungle, their homeland.

The Indians and whites sat apart from each other.

Young women wore black skirts and white blouses with wide-brimmed summer hats, and their eyes looked desperate for love and worried about the world. Only Lettie was hatless.

"See how it is," said Nola to the infant inside her. "Lettie has lost her pride." Nola remembered the beautiful hats in Lettie's blue bedroom.

Lettie fanned herself with a newspaper, but she still looked hot. Jim Josh sat beside her, the heavy, hand-tooled saddle on the bench beside him. He held the bag of racing money he'd won. Now he could take the saddle back to the farmhouse where he'd found it and no one would be the wiser. "You should have seen that mule," he said to Lettie. "It was a fast one. Did it ever run!"

"Where'd you get that saddle?" She fingered the gun in her pocket. It felt heavy against her body.

"I just picked it up today. It's a heavy one, I'll tell you that."

"You borrowed it Indian style, huh?"

Out in the distance she saw Dr. Levee. He leaned against a tree like he was holding it up, and he watched the older Indian people line up to talk to Stace Red Hawk. With his hands still in his pockets, Levee walked toward Stace and the people. He overheard a woman's medical complaint. "It's real bad when I walk," she said, but when she saw Levee, she turned away and her face showed how little trust she had for any science of healing that came from a tradition other than her own.

The sheriff walked toward Lettie and Josh. He tipped his hat and said to Lettie, "Nice to see you." Lettie nodded but he didn't stop. She was baffled by his silence and his lack of interest. His look had been cold. She watched him walk away.

Josh said, "What if the sheriff is in on it? The murders, I mean."

Lettie stared at him. "The sheriff? Why do you say that?" but she gave up the idea as soon as Josh said it. Anyone was suspect—Floyd, Jess Gold, the undertaker, Dr. Levee—just by the white color of their skin. Everyone.

"Oh, I was just thinking," said Josh. He leaned over and hooked his spats tighter. He was sorry to have said anything.

Lettie was silent the rest of the day. Josh's words opened a door in her mind. Through it, she heard the Cajun woman's words about the jail. She cast a glance toward Nola. Nola was watching Ben. He staggered around with a dirty face and asked people for money. Nola's eyes were filled with tears as she watched him.

But Lettie's mind was working. It would make sense, Lettie began to think, that if Benoit was killed in jail the law might have been involved and not the other inmates as she had previously thought. But she didn't want to think it. Benoit and Jess Gold had been friends. Jess was liked by most everybody who was law-abiding. Lettie eyed Jess Gold from the boots up. No, not him. Still, too many of the missing pieces of the broken puzzle could fall into place if Gold were involved.

Josh was sorry to have made such a careless remark. But just then a cheering went up and they turned toward the sound. An impromptu footrace was taking place, with five men running in dressy, black shoes and good white shirts. Two were Indian men, two were white, and one was Chinese.

At the lead, an Indian named Jimmy was neck-to-neck with one of the white men.

From the bench where the older women sat, Belle stood up. "C'mon, Jimmy!" she yelled. She waved her arms and screamed. "Get moving! Go!" She turned to the others. "He's like a grandson to me." She sounded proud.

The boy's face was red. His shoes barely touched down.

Except for Ruth, the other old women followed suit and began to cheer and yell. One even slapped her thighs and whistled.

Then the whites hollered for the white runners, and the older Indian men, who were usually more reserved than the women, got carried away, too. Jim Josh yelled for Sam Lee. "Come on, Lee. Catch 'em." He turned to Lettie and explained in a quiet voice, "He's my friend, you know." Then he yelled some more. His face grew red.

Jimmy won. He looked at Moses and the other Indian men, pleased with himself. The Indians sat back with happy expressions on their faces, but when they noticed that the white people were silent, their faces lost joy.

"Sore losers," said Ona Neck.

In Kittredge, one of the small neighboring towns, Michael Horse sat outside the dentist's office surrounded by several Hill Indians who wanted to see what dentists did. Horse was in pain. His jaw throbbed with a toothache. It had kept him awake all night and grown worse during the day. As he sat out there, waiting for the dentist to arrive, he could hear the distant sounds from the picnic, the crack of the pistol that fired at the beginning of the mule race. The dentist, reluctant to work on the Fourth, even for emergencies, kept him waiting.

It was nearly night when the dentist finally arrived and called Horse inside. By that time Horse was pale and sallow from the pain. He had been drinking Bromo Seltzer. He stood up weakly and went inside the office. The Hill People followed him and they leaned over the nervous dentist's shoulder to peer into Horse's mouth as they watched the operation. It made the dentist nervous. Once in a while, one of them would smile and point and say something that neither Horse nor the dentist understood, but the others would nod and

respond. "The whites have a lot to offer us," said one of
them. "Dentistry, aspirin, Bromo Seltzer, and Burma
Shave." In spite of himself and his pain, Horse smiled on
hearing this mention of commercial products.

Toward night, at the picnic, a few women looked like they
wanted to dance. They tapped their feet and looked toward
the men who seemed to need at least another hour of talking
among themselves, playing cards, and drinking another glass
or two of liquid courage. It was getting dark and the lanterns
were lighted. The band was a combo of Indian men and
women called Tulaluska. They had traveled the United States
and a few countries in Europe singing popular dance songs,
blues, and even some jazz. And they sang songs, too, that
only Indian people knew and when all of them joined in to
sing about lovers and fights and broken-down cars, it was a
shared world, between all tribes, all nations.

The Tulaluska's last job had been in Sioux City, South
Dakota. China had met the band there and she traveled back
to Oklahoma's Indian Territory with them. And now she was
at the picnic, even though the look on her face was remote,
and in the darkened evening, her face looked gray beneath
the shocking lightness of her hair.

Hale watched her from where he sat in the borderland
between night and the artificial light of the lanterns. He was
just out of her sight. She had a shyness, a way of lifting her
shoulders a little high as if they would protect her tender
years and soft heart. But he watched her with a cold eye and
while he watched, he saw John Stink, who was reportedly
dead, put his ear trumpet in his pocket and walk up to China
and try to grasp her hand. Stink's dogs were wagging their
tails at the edge of the pavilion. Floyd went over now and
fed them a bit of meat scraps from the tables.

China tried to pull away from Stink, but he was persistent
and he smiled at the white-haired girl. He believed she liked
him.

The Indians pretended not to see the ghost chasing the
woman, but the white people stared, anticipating trouble.
Belle thought, "They are all watching her. They think she's
crazy, talking to herself." She lowered her own eyes, so as
not to catch sight of the eyes of the ghost.

"Someone ought to have another ceremony for that poor old man's ghost," she said out loud to the other women.

"It's been tried so often."

"It's the most real-looking ghost we've had around here. It's even got the hots for a blonde, just like you'd expect."

They glanced at Stink and looked away again.

That night, a flame swallower passed through the crowd, blowing gusts of fire. The people let him pass. His hot breath sounded like a dragon's and the children followed behind him from light into a darkness broken only by the man's fiery breathing. And when the band was on break, the trick roper, Fraser, tied a lariat and spun a burning circle of rope in the center of the empty dance pavilion. It lit up the eyes of people who watched, and it danced shadows across their faces and the dirty plates that sat on the tables.

When the band returned from their break, the atmosphere loosened up. Sam Lee, the Chinese runner, danced with an Indian woman who hardly moved at all. An Indian man did the Charleston with a scrawny black woman in a pea-green hat. A white woman danced with an Indian man and looked into his eyes as though he were the tree of knowledge itself, holding up the noisy night sky above them. Babies cried. Nola and Will got up to dance as close as her belly would permit, Nola looking silent but talking all the while to her baby, "I don't know if he's a good man, your father. It's a sad life you are coming to but I will love you."

Nola's protectors watched her. They kept their eyes on the movements of the other people around her.

Away from the benches and tables, Floyd and Louise argued with each other, over Ben. Louise's voice traveled. Rena pretended not to hear her mother say, "He's drinking too much. You've got to get him out of here. He's shameful."

"He's sick. He can't help it."

"You tell me that. You of all people. Selling liquor half your life to drunks. And now he steals money out of my bag."

The veteran named Keto, who was a member of the Native American peyote church, wore his uniform and talked to Martha Billy, but all the while he was looking at a group of young women. "Do you think I should ask her to dance?" He finally asked Martha. "That one." He looked at the girl.

Martha followed his glance. "Yes, she'd probably be happy to dance with you, Keto. Her name is Jewell. She's a Billy girl. I think she's one of Joe's half-sisters."

Rena sat alone, watching Nola and Will, and when the music ended, Will went over to shoot craps with his friends. Nola sat back down with Rena in front of a citron candle and their faces were bright with the flame.

Nola stretched her back. It ached.

From where she sat, Rena saw the sheriff approach Lettie.

"What are you drinking?" he asked.

"Soda pop."

"Do you want another?"

She looked at him. She felt confused by his earlier distance. "No. I'm fine."

He sat down a minute. "I know how hard its been," he said. He sounded sympathetic.

By then, Josh was tipsy. He'd been dancing with Ona Neck who was stiff and ached. He returned from dancing, sat down, and drank some more beer. After a minute he said to the sheriff, "Say, I had a thought." He sounded drunk.

"What's that?"

"What if your deputy was mixed up with the killers?"

"What do you mean?"

"Well, wouldn't that explain about how Benoit got killed? Because I saw his body hanging there in an empty cell when so many people had been arrested the night before."

"I hadn't thought of that before," said Jess Gold. He looked closely at Josh's face. "You have a good point, though. And Willis was a thief, it turned out."

"Well it had to be somebody in there."

And when the children lit sparklers, their faces were blue in the light. From behind Nola, Rena saw Will. He was approaching them when a woman materialized out of the trees. She was a different kind of woman than they knew. She wore clothes like a city woman, and her hair was blond and bobbed. She smiled at Will. He stopped to talk to her. Rena could tell that they knew each other. He leaned toward her as she spoke. She put her hand on his arm. Will gestured toward Nola, but the woman wanted to talk some more and by then Nola had read the expression on Rena's face and she turned sharply around just in time to see Will glance at his watch, nod, and turn away. The woman walked toward the cars. At a glance it looked like he planned to meet her later. She watched Will return to the table.

He sat down beside Nola. He leaned toward her in the same way he had just leaned toward Vinita. "I won a hundred twenty-eight dollars," he said, but Nola only stared at him.

"Who was that woman?" she asked.

He wasn't concerned.

Nola searched his face for signs that he was lying, but he was nonchalant.

"I'm going to buy you a parrot," he said. He smiled happily at her, jiggled his money in his pocket, and walked away. Nola stared after him.

The woman, she'd been able to see, was everything she was not. She wondered if Will loved her. She was more like him than Nola was. She was city and blond and slender. She wasn't awkward with a baby.

The fireworks began and the band played the national anthem. All the veterans rose up and the Indian women, who were less patriotic, grudgingly put their hands on their chests. "I'm no American," said one of the women to Belle. "I don't even like them." But she nevertheless held her hand over her big heart.

Still Nola looked at Will. She felt cold and afraid and she swore to the baby inside her that they, mother and child, would go away, away from Will and from Watona, away from danger. She watched Will return, carrying one of the green and red birds in a fool's-gold cage. Her heart felt swollen and hurt. He put the parrot beside her. It started when the sky filled with the explosions and the smell of gunpowder. There were flashes of red, then of gold. The sky was illuminated, then it was filled with trails of smoke. In one flash, Lettie thought she saw the prisoner Walter Bird. In another flash of light she saw Nola and Rena sitting alone, a caged, nervous parrot on the table before them. She saw the resigned face of Belle in another spark of light. By then, she knew it was Walter Bird out by the cars. It went dark.

Lettie jumped up from her seat. Another flare of light showed Keto and Jewell out by the parked cars, smiling at each other. They didn't see Bird. Lettie began running. She took the small pistol from her pocket and went toward the cars. Keto and Jewell passed the parking lot and began to walk down the dirt road. A car drove toward them. Lettie ran. The car lights exposed the couple, vulnerable and blinking, and they looked back. Then the car lights went out and the sky darkened and in jumps and starts, Lettie saw two men leap from the car. She ran toward them. "No," she cried. But her voice wasn't heard.

It was dark. Then it was light. There was a struggle. The men grabbed Keto. He fought free of their grasp. Jewell started to fight also, but was pushed back out of the way, screaming and unheard in the scream of the fireworks. Lettie drew closer, pistol in hand, outlined by the moment's new light. The men carried Keto to the car. Lettie shot into the air, but it made no sound in the loud popping sky. Keto put his arms straight out to avoid being pushed into the car. A man hit one of Keto's arms with a rifle butt. Jewell screamed again, but the crowd cheered at the lights.

In the next light, the car was gone, and so was Keto, and Lettie ran to Jewell and held her and they wept.

It was three in the morning when Floyd took Lettie Graycloud to the doctor's office on Main Street. Floyd was afraid for her. Her terror and her crying would not stop and he thought she should be sedated. She was sobbing uncontrollably and had bitten her own hand with her teeth and left bloody lacerations on the skin. She felt numb and faint. Dr. Levee looked at her and took out a needle, but when he tried to give her a shot, she fought him and cried, "You want to kill me!" She struggled away from him.

Tenderly, Floyd gathered her into his arms, but she continued to fight. "You murderer! You white man. I found your key!" And when the needle penetrated her skin, she screamed even louder, then gave up and let her knees collapse to the floor while she sobbed.

"Okay," said Levee, and the men lifted her to the cot.

Lettie's voice became quiet, her face lost its grief, and she fell into a deep untroubled sleep.

Stace Red Hawk watched. He understood her fear. There were enemies, and they both came from deceived people.

Even he felt the fear, felt himself casting cautious glances around the street when he was walking.

On the wall in the back room of the doctor's office was a chart of a human body. It showed what was beneath the surface of skin and beneath the side-curving slabs of muscle. It laid the body open all the way down to the heart and its arteries, the lungs, and liver. Stace Red Hawk looked at the chart as he poured warm water into a wash basin. Without speaking he soaked a cloth in the water, wrung it out, and handed it to Lettie.

She was grateful. She washed her face slowly with the warm cloth. She looked at him. She remembered him from the ceremony at Ona Neck's. "Thank you," she said quietly.

Stace said nothing. He gave her a cup of tea. She sipped it. It was hot. Her eyes were swollen. "I'm sorry," she said, meaning about the scene she'd caused.

He sat down across from her. "Have you ever noticed that when a person acts out of their heart, they are always sorry?"

She shook her head.

"What happened last night?" he asked her.

She peered at him closely. She wanted to trust him. If not him, she thought, whom would she ever be able to trust? He had wise eyes, but she looked at him warily, for she had been told that the medicine man and the doctor had been seen meeting with other men in the woods.

She told him about Bird and Keto. "Bird. He's supposed to be in jail, but I know I saw him there."

Stace asked her more questions. "What can you tell me about the explosion?"

She looked reluctant. She said, "We don't know who to trust."

He nodded. "I don't know whom you can trust either."

But she told him about the blast and fire and how Benoit was not ever tried in court. Then she washed her face again with the cold, damp cloth.

Stace gazed at the chart absently. He did not mention his suspicions about the sheriff, nor did Lettie repeat what Jim Josh had said the night before.

Stace thought about Bird. It made sense. Bird had a tight alibi because he was in jail. But if the sheriff were involved, and if Bird were the killer, it would stand to reason that Bird could have been released from jail in order to commit the crimes.

Stace opened the door. Floyd had waited for Lettie and was asleep in the waiting room. Stace gently shook his shoulder. "She can go home now."

When Floyd and Lettie left, Levee closed the door behind them.

"What's happened since I've been gone?" Stace asked.

Levee shook his head. "Not much. Nothing."

Stace was tired. He made for the door.

"Where are you going?" Levee asked.

But Stace didn't answer. He turned once to look back at the man he'd worked with—and trusted—for several years, then closed the door, as if he were closing a world behind him.

By the time the sun rose over the horizon, the circle of elders had already met and decided it was time to hide the path to their settlement. They feared the madness of people who lived in the town as if they were carriers of a contagion. They wanted to make certain that the insanity would not form itself like a turn wind in the air and travel up the red clay pathway to their own world.

Stace traveled on foot. He carried only a blanket, some food, and a pistol. It was hot and as he walked toward the bluffs, he was soaked with sweat. The air was humid and he had a slight headache. He paused in the shade to rest. The sky was hazy with dust and pollen and at first Stace thought the mist obscured the old settlement and the path toward it. He rested beneath a large oak that had been twisted and gnarled by years of strong winds.

As he squinted into the distance, Stace Red Hawk thought of how he would never be able to explain things to Levee. He no longer lived in Levee's world, and Levee had lost substance in Stace's new dwelling place.

It was getting late in the afternoon when he went past the dark mouth of Sorrow Cave, and had it not been for Stace's good, strong memory, he would have thought he'd had a heatstroke, for the path to the settlement was nowhere to be found. He skirted around the entire region until it was nearly dark, then gave up and circled back to Sorrow Cave in order to rest.

That night, it rained heavily. The inside of the cave, usually dry, was damp and smelled moist. Far back, in the other chambers he knew were there, he could hear the water dripping down from the ceiling. The bats, he was certain, had found refuge from the bounty-hunting boys in the deeper reaches of the underground network of caverns, and he was glad.

The next morning, Stace searched again for the path. Still not finding it, he gave up and decided to go climb down the rocky hills and follow the Blue River up to the settlement.

But by evening he'd reached Tar Town instead, and the red banks of the river smelled rotten, and he did not know how he had passed by the Hill settlement without hearing a sound or seeing a single person. The wind was howling at the shantytown. Stace went closer, as if he were a spy, and he looked closely at the people. Gravel and sand blew in the wind, and the people sheltered their eyes with arms held across their faces, and small, torn squares of cloth held up over their eyes.

It was almost dark, but Stace turned around and walked back along the river in the deepening blue dusk. Again he neared the cave and wondered how he'd passed the settlement a second time without seeing so much as a fire. He wondered if he had, as Levee suggested, gone crazy. Or was it possible a whole people could vanish into blue air?

The next morning he was sitting in front of Sorrow Cave when Michael Horse stepped out of the first light. The brush around him was silvery gray. Stace waved at the older man, but Horse did not look in his direction. Horse walked quickly. He carried a rope in his hands. Then Stace saw that Horse was chasing Redshirt. "Whoa." The old man tried to coax the shiny horse, but it only kicked up its heels as Horse neared him.

Standing under some trees, two young red colts and three mares—one was black—watched the stallion evade the man's grasp. But Stace thought that Horse only halfheartedly went after Redshirt. In reality, he admired its spirit. It had an incurable wildness in its veins, and Horse was secretly glad for this, so his attempts at catching the horse were weak ones, but still the horse kept up his part of the show, bolting about as if the old man were dangerous and could possibly catch and tame him.

By the time Horse neared Stace, he was breathing hard and looking happy to see the younger man. He shook his head. "A hell of a year that stallion had. Look at those colts. He's bad as Sam Billy." He shook his head in admiration. "You know, he's got to be related to Man O' War who ran away from Aqueduct a few years ago." He caught his breath, looked back toward the stallion, and wiped his forehead with his arm. "It's going to be a hot one." He faced Stace directly. "What are you doing here?"

"I was looking for the Hill settlement. I couldn't find it."

"They had to hide it. Too many people coming up. I'll take you on up. I know you're welcome there."

Horse led Stace toward the bluffs, and soon they were on the road. It was clearly marked. Stace wondered how he could have missed it with its carvings and cairns and markers. The older man said, "You know, this path has two names. To those at the settlement the path leads down to town and for this reason it is called the terrible road. From town it is called the good, red road."

Up in the hills, they were drumming.

The debt collector knocked on the Grayclouds' door and presented Belle with a statement. He told her he was there to collect the money for the calf she had butchered. She stared at him with disbelief. "I don't know what you mean," she said, but the collector had experienced all kinds of debtors, and he knew the kind who tried to deny their debts. He nodded crisply and provided her with a written account of the balance she owed Hale. Hale claimed that Belle was the thief of one of his young Angus calves pasturing by the creek.

"There's no pasture down there," Belle said.

The man looked her in the eye. He was unyielding. "Would you pay in full at this time, or will you prefer to pay by the month?"

Belle was angry as it occurred to her that again they'd expanded the pasture, without her consent. "I prefer not to pay at all." She began to close the door against him.

But Moses had heard the noise and he joined Belle at the

door to see what the ruckus was all about. The collector, a
thin man, the kind who had no calluses on his hands, looked
at the dark Indian man, turned away, and walked stiffly back
down the path to his car.

The older couple watched nervously as he closed his car
door, started the engine, and disappeared down the road.
Then she and Moses left for the creek to see what had taken
place there. "When was the last time you were at the creek?"
she asked.

"It's been a week or so."

"He said cows were pastured down there."

When they reached the creek, the boundary lines Hale had
erected earlier had been expanded and moved. One wire even
stretched across the creek, and Belle heard the loud angry
hum of bees. She was afraid their honey would turn to black
treacle.

Moses examined the barbed wire fence. Inside its limits,
with access to the spring water, were several of the new cattle
Hale had been trying to breed.

A short time later, they arrived at the Indian Agency and
demanded an explanation from the administrator of the bureau. "Yes," he said. "We leased out some more of your
land." He got up, turned his back, and put some papers in
a stack. Then he glanced toward them, swallowed, and said
quietly, "So sorry, Belle, Moses. It's not me doing it. It's
not even the leasers. It's what is legal."

Belle sat down. "Why is it that so many crimes are backed
up by your laws?"

The man returned to his desk. He met her eyes. "I don't
know."

A few days later, Ben and Cal staggered in. They were coming to ask Belle for help. Cal had fallen into a barbed wire
fence and torn out his right eye. It hung out of the socket.
Not knowing what else to do, Ben had taken hold of the
eyeball and replaced it in the horrid, gaping hole. It was red
and sore. Alcohol didn't deaden the pain, so the young men
decided to go to Belle for help.

She could smell the stale liquor on the disheveled boys.

"Yes, I will help you," she told them. But she knew they
needed help of another kind. Her mouth formed into a hard

and determined line. "I will help, but you must stay here until you dry out." They looked at each other, sadly, it seemed to Belle, and they began to walk away from her kitchen.

She moved to stop them. "If you leave now his eye will get worse. The infection will go into the brain. It's already so close. It is the worst way in the world to die. I've seen it happen. It's worse than rabies."

In their moment of hesitation, while they stopped and remembered the girl who had died from rabies, Belle opened the cellar door, grabbed Ben's collar, and pushed him through the door. He caught the handrail to keep himself from falling down the steps, and while he scrambled to get his balance and force his way back out, Belle sent Cal flying down into the cellar behind him.

"Shit," said Cal. "I don't believe that old lady."

Belle locked the door. It was dark in her holy cave, and it smelled of cool plaster, lye soap, and dill.

"Open the door." Ben knocked. He knocked harder. "Open it!"

Belle didn't answer. She leaned back and tried to catch her breath. She locked the door from the kitchen side.

Later that night, Cal began to cry, wiping his tears away with his fingers, his eye aching from the salt. Ben also cried. But they could not see each other. Cal was afraid of the sickness that came when he did not swallow alcohol. He was afraid of the dark that surrounded him with nothing but himself and his friend. But the tears soothed and comforted his injured eye and he sat down on the bottom step and put his head down on his knees and cried for even his broken hands.

Later, Ben again went up the steps and knocked on the door. "Hey what do we do if we have to go to the bathroom?"

"Go in that pot down there!"

He squinted around the blackness. "But I can't even see." Grumbling, he began to feel with his hands.

After a while, the young men became desperate, and Ben, searching for liquor, opened a jar of pickles and tried to drink the vinegar and salt brine, and he was not yet even at the bottom of his desire for drunkenness. And though Belle ached with the thought of their horrible pain, she loved them too much to be kind.

Louise sat at the table and wept when she heard her son calling for help. He sounded like a child again, calling "Mother, help me. Mama." It broke her heart. She could not eat her meals in the kitchen, thinking of her Ben locked down in the dank, black cellar with the boxes of blue potatoes.

After four days, Ben began to cry more softly and it was then that Belle decided it was time to open the door. She prepared a meal of cornbread, parched corn, meat, and black tea. She opened the door. "Come up," she said down the stairway. "Come and eat." They stepped up one stair at a time, weakly, and squinted in the light. They stopped at the threshold a moment, blinking in the light, and then came out. Their clothes were wet and rumpled.

"You went away. You thought you were in heaven, but you were in hell. Now you're back from hell and it's morning for you." Belle ladled flour gravy over their meat. "Eat," she said. Her voice softened. She smiled at Ben. "And welcome."

In spite of what his son thought, Mr. Forrest was a gentleman. He had a straight, long body and he knew about the devils who took advantage of their wards, and he knew Will thought he was one of those. But he was a man who tried to deal honestly with people.

That afternoon, Forrest hung up the telephone, let out a long, hard breath, gathered some papers into his satchel, and left the house. His walk was brisk. He took along the raincoat that he carried by habit, but seldom needed.

At the railroad depot, he checked the arrivals and departures aboard, then went inside and bought his ticket from an old, slow-moving man at the window.

He was preoccupied and hardly noticed when the train started with a jerk. From his seat, he saw into a house where a family was having an early dinner, the way farm families do. Their tablecloth was clean and white. But then the world began to blur past him and he became very still inside. He'd been unduly nervous, he thought, and tried to keep himself calm. But he kept hearing the desperate voice of Jim Josh over the telephone. Josh had asked to talk to him, insisted really, about papers he'd been forced to sign. He sounded afraid. He said that someone had tried to kill him.

Forrest believed him.

The rhythm of the Oklahoma City–bound train relaxed Forrest a bit. He put his head back against the seat and thought about the old man who grew tomatoes in his car. Forrest was not blind to the fact that there were dangers in this journey between towns. More and more, he felt fear in the air, its presence as distinct as a storm of dust. And the noise of the train, its whistles and porters walking back and forth, asking to see tickets, made Forrest anxious. He thought of his son, Will. They had become split from one another, blood divided from blood, each of them accusing the other of taking advantage of Nola's money.

It was nearly dark when he disembarked in Oklahoma City and took a taxi to the hospital. At the hospital, he tipped the driver and put his wallet back in his pocket.

The hospital smelled stale. The corridor was made of black and white tiles. He followed them to Josh's room, but when he turned to go in, a nurse started to say, "You can't see him now," but Forrest was an attractive man and she only blushed and smiled and went about her business.

James Josh's shoes were on a table beside the bed. They were placed neatly side by side. Josh looked small and weak. He tried to raise himself up from the bed to greet Forrest, but his wrists were tied with white cloth to the bedrails.

Forrest hardly recognized him. His thin, aged skin was bruised and there was the shape of a hand on his arm, on flesh that looked like too-ripe fruit.

Forrest looked at the straps of cloth that held the old man down. "I'll be back," he said, and went out to get the nurse. "Could you please untie him?" he asked the nurse.

The nurse looked at Forrest. "We can't. He's delirious." Her voice was filled with regret. "He believes he's in danger. It's alcohol poisoning. They always think someone is out to kill them." She went back into the room, followed by Forrest, and placed the black and white spats on the floor beneath the bed. "We get a lot of his kind." Indian, she meant, but she didn't say it.

For a moment Forrest entertained the thought that Josh

might really have the d.t.'s. He listened as the sound of the nurse's white shoes walked out the door and down the hall. As soon as she left, he untied Josh's hands. His wrists were purple from the straps.

"They don't believe me," Josh said. He rubbed his wrists. His dark eyes were intense and piercing. "This is my death-bed."

Forrest ignored his statement. "Why don't you tell me what happened?"

"It was Walter Bird," Josh said. He opened and closed his sore hands. "And Hale."

"Hale?" Forrest wondered why they would attempt to murder the old man. Josh was no longer receiving payments and his property had little worth.

As if reading Forrest's mind, the old man said, "I think I know their motive. On the Fourth I talked to the sheriff. I'd had a few, you see, and asked him what if he, or even Willis had been in on these deaths and wouldn't that explain a few things. I was just talking. But as soon as the words were out of my mouth, I knew, in my body, that the sheriff knew something."

Forrest liked the sheriff. He didn't want to believe Josh. "But why Hale?"

"Hale's boys. They made me sign the papers. They held a knife to my neck."

"But if they benefitted from your death wouldn't they be suspects anyway?"

"That's just it, you see. I signed it only yesterday. But the paper was dated over a year ago."

Forrest fell silent. He needed to clear his head. He went over to open the window. It opened only a few inches, not enough to let much of a breeze into the room. He leaned down to it and smelled the outside air. Down on the streets, cars were coming and going.

Forrest was puzzled. "But why would they try to kill you and then take you to the hospital?"

Josh looked at the man and he took stock of the situation. How could Forrest understand that the word of an Indian wouldn't hold water in any court of law? It would be assumed that he was a drunk. But he said, "If they poisoned me and I didn't die, and they brought me here for help, they wouldn't look like murderers, would they? They'd look like they were trying to help me.''

Forrest wrinkled his brow.

''I'm just telling you what I know.''

Forrest rubbed his chin. It was dark outside and he could see the lights of cars like stars moving on the dark ground. ''I'll be back.'' He put on his jacket. ''I need to check around.''

Josh looked vulnerable and small, every bit like he was waiting for black-robed death to claim him. The nurse returned to tie his hands back to the rails. ''I thought you might do that,'' she said to Forrest in a half-scolding tone. She pulled the cloth tight. ''It's for his own safety.'' She bound Josh like an animal. He tried once to struggle against the ropes, but then he gave it up and waited.

''You'll be out of here in no time,'' she told him.

''Yes, I will, but not in the way you mean it.''

On the train, Forrest tried to think about this new chain of events. He rented a Pullman so he could rest before he returned to town. Outside, the railroad tracks were like silver ribbons twisting through the night. Forrest opened the Pullman door and looked out beyond the curtain, then pulled it closed again. He undressed, carefully folding his clothes, and laying them down on the Pullman bed. It was dark, and he was tired but the rocking motion failed to comfort him. He was thinking. The train picked up speed again and it lulled him, just for a moment, to sleep. And in that moment, the door flew open.

''This is it. Indian land. It's our baby, our territory,'' said Ballard. He looked down the hill at Forrest's body. Forrest lay dead and bloody and broken down the hill from the railroad tracks. His body had been stopped grotesquely against a tree trunk. He wore only his long underwear. No one had yet found the briefcase or raincoat he always carried with him.

Ballard put a peppermint in his mouth.

His excitement bothered Levee, but Levee understood it too. Forrest was their key. He was the casebreaker. He was white, educated, affluent, and his body was found on Indian land, which gave them federal jurisdiction.

Ballard half slipped down the hill to the tree. Small rocks were dislodged and fell before them. "Okay, let's go to work."

Levee followed him. As he watched Ballard examine the beaten body, he said, "I thought sure Forrest was in on it."

"Maybe. Maybe he was a swindler, but I didn't have him figured for a killer." He looked at the body.

"How do you know he didn't kill Josh before he was killed?"

"Just a hunch."

"A hunch isn't good enough."

From behind them on the hill, they heard the sound of boots. A few rocks rolled downhill. Ballard and Levee looked up. The sun was behind the sheriff as he approached them. He looked taller than usual.

"You're a little out of your jurisdiction, Jess," Ballard said. He walked toward the sheriff, to keep him away from Forrest.

The sheriff nodded at Levee. "Hello, Doc." Then to Ballard, he said, "I just wondered if I could be of help."

"Sooner or later I'm bound to need you." Ballard began to walk the sheriff back toward his car. He spoke to him close to his face. "Yeah, I'm going to need you. This is confusing as hell to me." He opened the car door for Gold, and Gold, hardly realizing it, was silently coerced back into his car. Ballard closed the door, leaned over, and said into the window, "Keep an eye on things in town for me, will you? I'll be by to see you when I'm done with Dr. Levee here."

The sheriff watched Ballard in the mirror.

Ballard saw him watching. He waved, but he said, "He just doesn't smell right to me, if you know what I mean."

"None of them do," Levee said. "That's the problem. The whole thing stinks."

"What about the dentist? Did you ever check on him?"

"Yeah, he says Bird was there on the Fourth. With a tooth-ache. But Lettie Graycloud saw Bird on the road that night, she swears to it. I think the dentist is their cover. Or partly, anyway."

"She could be lying."

Levee was bothered by the suggestion. "I don't think so."

Beekeepers have a saying that honey begins with a drop of sugar, and misery starts with a mote of dust. It was late afternoon. Belle was dressed in her white muslin beekeeper's clothes. The veil of the wide-brimmed hat wrapped about her shoulders. She went through the gate, thinking about beekeeper's misery as she walked down to the hives at the spring-fed creek. The sun slanted west in the sky. There was a loneliness dwelling in this place, the placed called "Where Earth Has No Bottom," where the waters rose up from deep inside the planet.

She was tired. She touched the pistol in her pocket. It weighed heavily against her thigh, but between the gun and the clothes that made her invulnerable to the stings of disturbed bees, she felt safe.

The trees were dead-still that afternoon, with no breeze and not even the movement of a single leaf. Only the hum of the bees could be heard.

Star-Looking's black meteorite hung from the leather thong around her neck. The stone was heavy on her chest. It had its own feel of life, and Belle loved it.

Dressed in white like a bride, wearing the veil, Belle walked slowly, feeling one with the land as if old Osage Star-Looking himself, the man who had seen the black stone fall burning from the sky, walked with her, heard through her ears the sound of water, saw through her eyes the green hills in the background. Her face looked older, more lined, her gray eyes darker.

With the air hot and muggy, it was the busy season for honeybees. The wildflowers were yielding their rich golden harvest of pollen. Bees were like Indians, Belle thought to herself, with a circular dance, working together for the survival of the next generations.

Belle could hear the enraged hum of the hives as she approached. But before she took their anger to heart and attempted to soothe and tend them, she checked the creek to see that no more oil had seeped out. It hadn't, although there was an oily film on the surface of the water. She was relieved, but she was in danger and she knew it. It dogged her heels, that danger, and it was so heavy in the air that it almost drowned out the vicious sound of the bees as they railed and raged against the poor cattle inside Hale's illegal fence that crossed the water. The bees were honest, at least, hollering out their anger, and for that, she respected them.

She checked the hives for treacle, the bitter fluid that took the place of sweet honey. The bees had been disturbed so much that they were bad-tempered and vulnerable to disease.

She straightened up and that was when she noticed John Stink's ghost. It was sitting by the creek. Its presence bothered her. It was just one more annoyance to the bees. As much as they hated mules and buffalo, they hated ghosts more.

The ghost sat by the water with three dogs. It was crying and it held an ear trumpet, trying to listen to the water. After she watched it a few moments, Belle felt empathy for the poor thing. She wished she could comfort it. But as she watched Stink, Belle did not know that she was being sighted, that she was scoped in the dead center of a rifle's cross hairs and when the impact of the bullet hit her it was like a great wall of force. She heard the loud crack of a bullet and then another and she saw leaves fly off the bush beside her, but she saw no one. She sank to the ground, both hands held over her chest, the breath knocked out of her, and she lay there and her last thoughts were about death and how to give herself up to it, yet it was suffocating this way, being shot, and nothing at all like any death she'd ever planned. There were tears in the corners of her eyes, though, a deep sorrow at leaving. The last thing she heard as she surrendered to death was the horribly raised drone of bees swarming toward the trees from where the shots had originated, and then the noise grew fainter, and she fell into something like sleep, only darker, deeper.

When she opened her eyes again it was only moments later, and Belle saw the red stain of blood on her chest, over her heart, and to her surprise, Stink's ghost had hold of her wrist. He was bewildered and his eyes were wild and she knew he had come to welcome her into the society of the dead. With his other hand he removed the veil hat from her head and looked into her face. His solidity surprised and confused her, but she was afraid, and the ghost world was pulling her away, and all she wanted was to pull free from its grasp.

"It's not my time!" She protested loudly. The ghost did not hear her complaints, though she quaked so badly that he let go of her cold hand for just a moment, long enough for her to strike out and push him away. Her voice took on a higher pitch. "Get away from me. Get away."

Stink looked sad and confused.

Lettie had heard the gunshot and was racing down the path when she saw her mother being dragged away by the ghost of John Stink. "Mama!" she cried. She caught up with them, and she too began to hit the poor spirit, all the while yelling back to her father, "The ghost has Mama! Hurry! He's trying to take her away!"

But poor old John Stink, all he wanted was for Belle to see what had happened to his pitiful dog that had been dragged down like the others by the water monster, and when he saw Belle collapse, from a heart attack, he thought she had entered his world of death's limbo and he forgot his dogs and he ran to her, feeling ashamed that he was so happy to have her company. He would no longer be living alone on middle ground between the worlds. But he was baffled that she had pulled away and become hysterical with fear and horror, and when Moses caught up with them, Stink stood back, but Lettie grabbed him and stared with amazement. "My God. He's solid, Papa! Feel him!" Then she let go and buried her head against the old woman's heart.

But the killer was still out there. And Moses tried to pull Belle to cover and then through the trees, toward the house. Stink followed, with his dogs behind him. And by the time they reached the house, all of them were breathing hard and Belle had lost her color, and Lettie had looked behind her and seen John Stink.

"Get a doctor!" Lettie yelled out as they neared the house. "Floyd! Get the doctor!"

When he thought they were safe enough, Moses opened Belle's dress and touched her wound. "Wait!" he said. Lettie turned toward him, anxiously. The bleeding appeared to have stopped and Belle was breathing.

Moses exhaled a sigh of relief. "She's all right. It's only a surface wound." He looked at the bloodstained tear on her dress. "It must have hit her from the side," he said. But Belle's face was still without color and he was afraid the shock had been too much for her. He pointed to the kitchen, remembering Louise's cure for shock. "Get some coffee."

Moses touched Belle's lips and pushed back her hair with a gentle hand. He gathered her into his arms, rocking, as if she were a child. It was a sorrowful thing, to live in a dangerous world. He was afraid for all of them.

John Stink watched while Lettie gently poured coffee into Belle's mouth and broke ammonia ampules under her nose, then Moses said, "Go get the Sioux medicine man. Red Hawk. He's in town at the hotel. We need him."

Lettie obeyed her father. She went out and started up the Buick. Her hands were still trembling. She noticed the car was nearly out of gas. As she pulled out onto the road, another car was in front of her. She beeped the horn impatiently. The other driver pulled over. She shifted gears and passed around it.

At the hotel desk, Lettie asked after the medicine man, Stace Red Hawk. The bellman made a call to one of the rooms. After a few moments, while Lettie fidgeted, Stace Red Hawk came down the stairs, carrying his bag. The bellman watched as the young man walked out the door with Lettie Graycloud.

By the time they arrived back at the Grayclouds', Belle was sitting up on her own looking at her torn dress. "Good Lord," she rasped. "I'm not dead." She looked from Moses to Lettie to Stace. From the corner of her eyes she saw John Stink's ghost like an angel of death waiting to take her away at her first sign of weakness. So she set her jaws and looked powerful, and avoided his eyes. "I knew I wouldn't die like that." She tried to sound convincing. "I was sure of it."

"You've still suffered a shock," Stace told her. "And you should go to bed and rest for several days."

"You can't keep this old woman down," Belle said, glancing toward Stink. She wasn't letting him see even a hint of her weakness.

Moses followed her eyes. He went over to touch the ghost and smile at it, and Belle's eyes widened. "Get away from it. It's here to take me away."

"It's all right," Moses reassured her. He went over to the

desk and took out a pad of paper, took Stink's hand, and placed a pencil in it. Stink wrote, "I am dead." Then he pushed the pencil and paper away and looked toward the wall.

"See?" That proved her point.

Moses was relieved that Stink had remembered some of the words he'd taught him to write years ago. Moses tapped his shoulder and shook his head while looking in Stink's eyes. He wrote on the paper, "No. You are not dead."

Stink was baffled. He looked at Moses with puzzled eyes. He wrote, "I am a ghost."

Again, in an exaggerated manner, Moses shook his head.

Stink looked confused. Then he wrote, "Is that why my body is missing? I am wearing it?" A grin began to break through the shadows of his face.

Suddenly, behind them, Belle cried out, "My meteorite!" She felt around her empty chest and looked at her floor. She began to panic. "It's gone!"

"Maybe the bullet broke it," said Stace.

"That's it. That's exactly what must have happened. Star-Looking saved me. I knew it was a holy stone. We have to find it." It concerned her, even with her bruised heart, that the sacred gift from the sky might have been broken. But in spite of her concerns about the stone, and her fear of John Stink, after her unraveling outburst of words she fell back into a deep dark sleep. She remained in bed for three more days. While she slept, Ben and Cal stayed at the house. So did Stace Red Hawk and he looked in on her from time to time. On the second day of her sleep, Belle's hair turned white, the white of old, old age. It was from the shock, Stace told them. He'd seen it before, how fear could change a person's hair overnight. He sang for her. Unlike their southern songs, Stace's was from the north, and he sang high up on the scale. It was an eerie and strange register to the southern Indians but they were glad he was with them.

Stace went back to his hotel room, in order to think, but that same night, a note was slipped under his door. From Levee, he supposed, who might have heard him walking down the hall. The note was important. He returned to the Graycloud house, taking it with him.

When he knocked on the door, Moses let him in. Stace sat at the table across from Moses. "There's a warrant out for Belle's arrest," he told Moses. "She's being charged with involuntary manslaughter."

"What?"

"For the keeping of vicious bees," Stace explained, showing him the note.

According to witnesses, the sheriff, covered with an outlaw swarm, had gone racing out of the trees and onto the road. The bees were a dark shadow over the sheriff's skin. A motorist who stopped to help the unrecognizable man also suffered stings. But Gold had endured multiple stings and before they reached town he was swollen up with venom and was having difficulty breathing. It was a pitiful sight. By the time they reached the doctor's office, he was wracked with convulsions. He died shortly thereafter.

"It was the sheriff," Moses said with disbelief. "It was Jess who shot Belle."

They talked about what to do. Stace hadn't wanted to tell Levee about the shooting of Belle Graycloud. He thought it best to have her lay low, but with a warrant out for her arrest, there was nothing he could do. His best move, he decided, was to have Belle taken up into the hills. It seemed her life was in more jeopardy now, as was the rest of the family, not just from the oil money she was keeping silent about, but from the law as well.

The sheriff, they were certain, had tried to kill her. Benoit had died under suspicious circumstances in jail and Stace couldn't be sure that the deputies weren't in on it. Or anyone else, including Ballard, and none of them were sure Belle— or anyone else—was going to be safe.

Levee arrived at the farmhouse with the investigators, in order to make a record of the bees' location. He was surprised to see Stace there. "Where's Belle?" he asked his friend.

"Come with me," said Stace, and he walked with Levee down toward the creek.

"Belle's dead. The evidence points to the sheriff, but we need to look at who else was involved."

Levee shook his head as he looked over the meadow. "That would clear some things up a little, wouldn't it?"

"It could. Mrs. Graycloud was with her bees at the time they attacked the sheriff. That's where we found her."

"Where is her body? I need to see it. I need to check some details."

"You can't see it."

Levee was surprised. "You know we have to see the body. I have to make a report."

"It is not their custom."

"C'mon Stace, you know it is against the law to bury her without being embalmed." He looked at his partner. "On top of that, what about our investigation?"

"Does her death help convict anyone?" He paused. He saw the confusion on Levee's face. He leaned over and spoke more closely, "Think about this, Levee. These people here aren't part of the rules. Look at them. They're old-timers. You know what I mean. They don't have any regard for what's legal. But I know one thing; the old woman was something like a saint to the people hereabouts. Everyone loved her. They want to bury her in private. Hell, you'd have fights coming out your ears if you tried to embalm her. This is an explosive situation out here. To them, you're just a doctor from a city."

Levee knew Stace spoke the truth. He remembered the looks that passed over the faces of the old people who had gone to Red Hawk for help on the Fourth of July. He argued anyway, "You'll destroy the evidence."

"Like I said, there's no need for evidence. There's enough bodies around here for any court docket. This one won't change things. And what's making this situation worse is how much money Indian bodies are getting on the black market from museums and roadside zoos. We couldn't afford to have another one stolen, not Mrs. Graycloud, anyway. Go out there and look at the cemetery. There are at least fifty holes dug out there and those are just the ones no one's bothered to fill back up." His voice sounded deep with authority.

Levee was surprised at the formality of Stace's voice. He cast a glance around. He was surrounded by big men, dark men. Moses had arrived and stood with his thick brown hands on his belt, watching them. Ben Graycloud had grown a mustache and it made his face look hard and angular. But it was the look on Stace's face that finally changed Levee's mind. In that look he knew Stace was not with him, not in any way.

That afternoon, Moses drove into town. He had no money

left. All he had to his name were the two workhorses, the wagon, Redcoat, his prized possession, and the Buick. The farmhouse was about to be foreclosed. He hitched the workhorses to the wagon, and went to the funeral home and struck up a bargain with the overfriendly mortician. "I'll trade you my Buick for that wicker casket over there." He pointed at it.

He offered the mortician the key and the man took it from his hand. "It's yours," said Moses. "Pick it up at noon, would you?" Moses started for the door, and looked back. "And thank you."

"Wait," said the man.

Moses turned a little toward the mortician, enough to see that the man barely hid a smile. "That car. That car of yours. It's got some miles on it. It's worth less than the casket. Throw in some cash to boot."

"By all means. If you'll help load that casket on my wagon."

"Sure thing." He moved quickly for a heavy man.

Late that afternoon, while they filled the casket with a hundred pounds of sandbags wrapped in a large, colorful blanket, Belle worried about nothing except the meteorite. At the creek Louise had searched the ground thoroughly and brought back as many pieces of the meteorite as she could find from beneath the empty hives. Belle studied the fragments. "How will I ever be safe again if this is broken? Look how it saved my life." She rubbed the bruise over her heart.

But Moses worried about their scheme. "Maybe we should just tell the truth. I hate to put people through another funeral."

"It's too dangerous," said Stace. "The land's in her name and there's a warrant."

So, late that night, Belle Graycloud was wrapped in a blanket and taken out to the wagon. Stace and Moses drove her over the sad, dark land in the moonlight and up toward the encampment. Ben and Cal went with them.

It was becoming harder and harder to find the path, even for those who lived there, and it was nearly daylight when they finally arrived. They approached on foot, for the path had become too narrow for the horses, and when the people saw Belle's white hair and heard what had happened to her, they lit bundles of cedar and waved the smoke toward her while they drummed and sang out their gratitude that death had only visited and gone on without her, thanks to Star-Looking. Then they smoked Moses and Stace and the men returned to town.

The next morning when the sun rose, the funeral began. Numerous cars parked around the Graycloud house, and the yellow dust from the early morning travelers filled the air. The Graycloud draft horses were yoked to the wagon. They whinnied at horses that carried people in from the countryside.

The casket was closed and there was the sound of a low wail inside the house as the grieving people sang the beautiful and woeful mourning song.

Several old women held handkerchiefs up to their faces. Moses felt terrible to see them go through so much sorrow. Even to protect Belle, he hated the fact that this had added another number to the account of human pain.

Ruth was there, with Tate. She hadn't told him that Belle was still alive. He had been caught up in the flurry of buying and selling that had fallen across the town, and she no longer trusted him, with his brocade bag of money and the deer heads mounted on the walls of her mother's house.

Reverend Billy wore a black blanket. He stood beside the closed casket, and although he had been told that Belle was alive in the hills, he felt weighed down by tragedy and his eyes were moist and Martha held his hand. The room was filled with the fragrant and musting odor of gray cedar smoke and sage.

Young men stood leaning against the wall and doorway in the back of the small room. Then several of the men went outside, and as was the old custom, Moses opened the window of the living room. Cedar smoke drifted outside. Several of the men then picked up the casket. The sound of the wicker creaked as they carried it to the window and began to lift it out, and the arms of the men outside reached up to take the casket.

Stace was moved by the funeral. He regretted that he had inflicted this pain on the mourners, but at the same moment, he looked from face to face, tracing the lines of money, the headrights. It wouldn't have been Moses, he was almost certain, since their marriage would not be considered legal by white law. It could be one of the daughters, but it was likely the money would go to Floyd, as a white man married into the family.

As far as Stace was concerned, Floyd was suspect. He'd said so to Moses, but Moses had argued against such an idea. Floyd was a member of their family; he had fought for them in the past. Still, Stace had seen a flicker of doubt cross Moses's face. And what about Nola? With her guardian dead, she would have another appointed. Maybe not so honest as Forrest. Something still needed to be done about the girl and her money, but with her at least, there was time. She was saved by her pregnancy, by the fact that she was now worth two headrights, two royalty payments, two allotments of land. All Stace knew was that whoever was behind all this, whatever happened, he was staying close by.

The procession moved slowly toward the burial grounds. Louise walked beside the wagon. Her face had taken on an expression of strength and resolve. There was no more question for her about who she was or which people she was bound to. Almost overnight she'd given up the white world. She wore her traditional clothing, leggings and blue-beaded moccasins. She carried a fan of eagle feathers and her daughter Rena walked with her, and even in the midst of all the miserable events, Rena had turned into a woman, serious and strong. Lettie walked on the other side of the wagon, straight and tall.

Ruth and Nola rode in one of the long cars. Tate drove. He just barely peered over the steering wheel and out the window. Nola was too large to walk the long distance to the cemetery, even if it was the traditional way to pay respects to a lost one. She cried bitterly inside the car. Nola felt a terrifying loneliness, knowing her husband could benefit from her death. "He might have killed his own father," she said to the unborn child. She never spoke these words to others, though if she had it might have relieved her to hear them say how much they knew the young man loved her.

Ruth sat beside Nola in the back seat. She was overwhelmed with grief even though she knew there was no body. She felt the weight of fear that Moses felt for Belle's life, for his own, so deeply connected the two were, at the heart and core of one another.

The horse-drawn wagon with the casket was outlined by the early fire of morning light. It was followed by cars, then by horse-driven buggies, and finally by solitary Indians riding on horses. As the red sky lightened and the land beneath it turned gold, the procession passed by the hole-filled cemetery and went on past it to the traditional burial grounds. But the cemetery was an incredible sight looming like a mighty otherworld beyond the travelers. The white angels with their stone wings stood tall and serene beside white lambs. And no one saw Levee in their midst. He looked like one of the statues. But he watched the procession.

When the casket was buried a few feet in the ground, the white and ochre-colored stones were piled over it by the people. Many of them moved awkwardly because they were concealing guns. The weight of pistols in their clothing felt strange to them, and they were afraid; if Belle had been killed, any of them could be next.

There was the sound of rock on rock. An older man straightened and wiped his forehead with a white handkerchief. He gazed up at the sky. "Look." He pointed. The others looked up. Seven eagles circled overhead. They soared above them into the blue sky, up, and then they disappeared into the top of sky, and there was only the slowed sound of a drum.

From the hills, the doings of town seemed distant and hazy to Belle. She fell into a new rhythm, more like the rhythm of earth, the cycles of night and day. But she limped, and with the same leg that limped the day she'd fought the eagle hunters.

One of the elders of the Hill People asked to examine her. Belle agreed and she was taken to the elder's lodge. The person was so old Belle could not tell if it was a woman or a man. The door was closed and no one else was allowed to enter. Belle felt strangely afraid and childlike. The old one sat in front of her without speaking.

"Which leg?" asked the wizened old person. Belle pointed. The elder helped Belle to lie on her back, then held a piece of wood over her bad leg. The eyelids of the person closed. Belle stared at the face. It was filled with lines and beautiful. Light seemed to come from the skin. The old one sang a while, then sang louder and faster, in a voice that resembled neither a man's nor a woman's, then suddenly the elder broke the wood. It split with a snap. Startled, Belle sat up quickly.

"Every time the sacred is killed," said the old one, "you limp. So you have to put what's sacred back in its place. Go away from us. Go stay by yourself until it is returned to you. You are not as strong now as you think you are."

Belle looked at the ancient one with a creeping fear. She ached, but she didn't want to be alone. She knew the advice was good, but what if someone found her? She was in danger. She was supposed to be dead.

One of the runners returned from town that day and said that a court of inquiry was going to be held.

Belle looked closely at the young woman. "Exactly what is that?"

"They will decide whether or not there is evidence enough to press charges against Hale."

"All right," Belle said to herself finally. "I will go. But first I will wait to see what happens." She stood up and limped to her room.

Across the land, oil derricks numbered as many and as far as the eye could see. Hidden in clouds of dust, cars passed back and forth across the rolling land, making the land itself seem busy.

Stace Red Hawk sat at the window in his room watching the dust rise up in lines and settle back down on the roads and hills. He watched the train turn away from the town. Jazz music rose up from the bowels of the hotel.

It was the night before the trial in Talbert, Oklahoma. Down on the streets, the town was lively. Women had arrived made up to look like porcelain dolls with hairstyles bobbed or waved flat against their heads, with white skin and red lipstick, and even when they danced their hair did not come undone or fall out of place.

Even before it began, the trial had turned into a kind of celebration for onlookers who gathered as if it were a holiday. It was a business opportunity as well for merchants,

who were already making their profits by selling miniature
stick derricks and hand-painted statuettes of Indians.

Stace thought back to his part in this spectacle; he'd had a
hand in creating this crime sensation with its web of murders,
weddings, and schemes. He was the one who had contacted
the journalists back in Washington. Even though making the
murders public had been his only choice at the time, now he
regretted it. Journalists had shown up from papers as far
away as Belgium in order to write the sensational story of
murdered Indians who had driven enameled hearses slowly
along the red, dusty roads while pointing out, one by one,
their oil wells.

And so, that night, when horns blew and voices passed
beneath his window, Red Hawk had trouble sleeping. He laid
back, shirtless, on the bed and smoked a cigarette, watching
the smoke curl upward. As night fell darker, he grew more
and more restless. The noise on the street bothered him, as
did the insects that craked noisily against the windowscreen,
stopped by what they couldn't see in their relentless flying
toward light.

He pulled himself heavily up from the bed, walked across
the wooden floor, and closed the window, but as soon as he
did, the room was too hot. He opened the window again and
looked out. Then he sank into the chair and sat up, listening,
and sometime during that noisy night, still sitting, he slept.

The next morning, Stace was in a dark mood as he left for
the courthouse. The sun was not yet up, and it was misty and
humid. A light fog rested over the hills and the red town.
But already he could see clusters of people standing on the
steps of the courthouse beneath the thin layer of fog, eerie as
shadows, but talking excitedly about the trial. He could see
their breaths as they talked, the words vanishing like steam.

The newsmen were rude and pushy. Stace disliked them,
even if he'd been the one who had tipped them off. As he
approached the steps up to the courthouse, he set a cold eye
upon them. Despite the fact that he'd officially resigned from
his position with the bureau, that he believed the bureau
might in fact be involved with some of the crime, he walked
through the crowd with some posture of authority. They all
grew silent, watching him, as if an unspoken stretch of time
and space lay between their kind and his, and the voices died

down, and they parted to let him pass. Stace went inside the building to await the opening of the wooden doors to the large courtroom, and as he entered, he heard the voices outside start up again.

Just before the doors opened, the crowd outside grew larger. Moses Graycloud was there, and Michael Horse with his notebooks and pencil, and the cigar-smoking ghost of Stink stood back a ways from the others.

Many of the Hill People had come down for the trial, and when finally the double doors were opened, they went inside and took their places standing in the back of the room, against the wall, their arms folded across their chests. They were dressed in traditional clothing. Some of the men carried small red blankets over an arm or a shoulder. One, like Stace, wore a red scarf about his neck. The women wore skirts and loose-hanging blouses and had quiet, watchful eyes. They did not look at the other people who were seating themselves on benches and chairs in the flat, artificial light. They stood ready to listen. They eyed the neat stacks of paper on the tables where the lawyers were busy arranging themselves or loosening collars of stiff shirts.

"Can I sit here with you?" Moses Graycloud asked Stace as he stood beside him.

Stace smiled slightly, met his eyes, and nodded. He moved over a little to make more room for Graycloud's wide shoulders, and looked at him as he sat down, then felt his arm against him, his bodily warmth and movement as Moses adjusted himself on the bench in the hollow-sounding room.

After a while, Hale came into the courtroom with his lawyers. He was all friendly business. He smiled and shook hands with several of his friends and business associates before he sat down. He wore a gray suit, and he looked calm and collected. Hale had no remorse; or at least if he did, it didn't show on his countenance. He looked, in an odd way, handsome and untouched by the weight of events. Because of this, Stace thought the audience and jury would favor him. Many of the Hill men in the back of the room, despite themselves, exchanged glances with one another. They composed their faces into rigid, emotionless masks and stood straighter and taller, but Stace knew these people; they were like his own, and the more impassive they appeared, the stronger the feelings inside the heart.

The judge sat before them in his formal black robes. He wore thick glasses, but his face was young and smooth.

Hale pleaded "not guilty" to charges of first-degree murder. As Stace looked at Hale, a cold, hard knot formed in the pit of his stomach. He'd seen criminals of all kinds, but none of them gave him that fist of ice. Hale sat tall, almost self-righteous; his circle of stolen money and power had built him far beyond human feeling and, it seemed, far above the law. He leaned over to whisper to his attorney. His every movement and expression seemed calculated to his advantage, as if he were playing a game of chess, thinking of which pieces and plays supported his holdings.

One of the first witnesses to take the stand for the prosecution was a man from the notorious, bank-robbing Al Spencer gang. He had been transported down from Leavenworth, where he was incarcerated, to testify as a witness in the trial. When asked his occupation, he replied, "I am a thief," and some of the people in the room looked like they might smile and shifted their bodies. When questioned, the thief told how Hale had approached Al Spencer through the trick roper, Fraser, about killing some oil-rich Indians. The Leavenworth fellow was strangely articulate. He related how Al Spencer had been insulted by the offer. "Spencer was outraged," said the thin-haired thief to the prosecuting attorney, "that these men would stoop to commit such horrible crimes. Spencer himself would never have murdered so many innocent people so cold-bloodedly in that way."

Stace thought he sounded respectful of the gang leader, and that this would take away his credibility, and while the convict spoke, Hale kept his eyes on the witness as if listening for a flaw, a wavering tone, another sign of weakness he could enter and pry apart. Hale occasionally shook his head, only slightly, in disagreement, as if secure in the knowledge that his own attorney could later throw doubt over the testimony because it came from a convicted thief who had been a member of a notorious band of criminals.

That first morning there was another witness for The People versus Hale, Mardy Green, who nodded his head as he spoke, and as the people listened, the story unfolded a few words at a time. He told a tale of misery and of crime against the Indian people. As he talked, he began to blend in with the room, his voice, hesitating now and then, becoming one with the walls, a part of the wood, a part of the stone, a part of history. He simplified the war against the dark-skinned people: they were in the way of progress. Everyone needed the land, the oil, the beef-fattening grass, and the water, and all was fair, he told them. "We have to go on, as a race, I mean." He looked earnestly at the eyes of the others. "It's like clearing the land for your farm, or hunting the food you eat. They shoot deer, don't they? Well, maybe you would call that a plot," he said, "or call it murder, but here it's just survival."

"He believes it," whispered Moses.

J. M. Springer, the attorney for the defense, interrupted. "This is irrelevant to the case at hand, your honor. I object."

The judge looked down and scribbled something on a piece of paper, then looked back at Mardy Green and said, "Mr. Green will please state only the facts."

As if he had not heard, the prosecuting attorney asked, "Were you aware that the Osage Indian people here had bought their own reservation land?"

Springer was becoming agitated. "Your honor, this is immaterial."

But in spite of the objections, the story continued to come to light, a small ray at a time. According to Mardy Green, the man named Bird had been released from jail in order to commit the murder of Walker. The sheriff had been involved, but the idea was Hale's, he said. "You see, Hale had taken out the life insurance policy on Walker for twenty five thousand dollars. Walker owed him money. After payments were cut, the Indians couldn't pay off their debts. It's common practice here," he told them, insisting that Hale had no ulterior motives, that Walker was going to commit suicide and that would declare the policy null and void. "It was on the up and up."

"Just answer questions. No personal opinion."

Mardy looked sincere when he said again, "The insurance wouldn't have been valid otherwise, if Walker'd killed himself."

"He gave you a car and a thousand dollars." It was a statement and not a question.

"Yes."

"And the car was the Buick?"

"Yes. It was."

"The stolen Buick?"

"Yes, it was stolen."

"But you didn't turn him in?"

"No, he said he'd get me off. He has friends in high places, so I knew he could do it."

"But didn't you plead guilty to the theft of that Buick?"

"Yes, I did, in order to protect Hale."

Then the prosecution asked, "Wasn't that car involved with the murder of other Indian people?"

"Yes, I believe it was. That's why I realized I had to come forward with this story."

The defense raised a hand. "Objection. This information isn't pertinent to this trial."

But the attorney for the prosecution continued. "Would you say there was a plot against oil-rich Indians here?"

"Objection, your honor. The prosecution is asking the witness to speculate."

There were a few tense, whispered conversations taking place throughout the room.

"Sustained." The judge waved his hand.

When it was Springer's time to ask questions, he asked Mardy, "Did it not turn you against Hale that he gave you a car that was stolen?"

"No. I don't believe he knew it. He's an honest man. It was an honest mistake."

The Hill People in the back of the room listened quietly. Then two of them turned to leave. They walked silently toward the door. The reporters and curiosity-seekers stared at them as they walked, straight-backed and without speaking, their eyes fixed far into the distance.

When the lunch recess was finally announced, the jury members were taken away first from the room so that they could hear no comments. As he watched them file out of the room, Stace took a deep breath, and when he turned to speak to Moses Graycloud, he saw that the seat beside him was empty.

Outside Stace made his tired way through the crowd. When he reached the bottom step, Levee, who'd been standing with Ballard, walked toward him, stopped, smiled slightly at Stace, and said, "They could get rich charging admission here."

Stace looked at Levee but he remained silent. Out of the side of his vision, he saw Ballard turn and walk away.

Levee went on. "Hale's so damned self-righteous looking, you'd think God himself had commanded him to act. And what do you make of his lawyer? A cocky fellow, isn't he?" He straightened his collar and spoke more quietly, looking directly at the Indian man, "So how are you, Stace?"

Stace did not know whether he should trust Levee. In spite of their differences, they'd had a solid friendship, but now he didn't know what held, what spilled over from the past. He looked at Levee warily, nodded, and said reluctantly, "Good. Pretty good." His voice sounded tense.

"Buy you some lunch?" asked Levee.

Stace followed him. They went through the restaurant door, just ahead of the crowd, and found a table. The waitress tossed the silverware carelessly down on the table and took their orders.

Like Stace, Levee was frustrated. "They're saying people more prominent than Hale are involved."

"Like who?" Stace wanted to know. He looked sarcastic, Levee thought, unlike himself, but just then Stace saw something through the dirty window in the café, and he half stood up to look. On the road, passing, was a caravan of cars and trucks. Some of them pulled painted trailers behind them, filled with garden tools and black chests and overstuffed maroon chairs. Some had tied small wooden trunks to the car roofs with rope and baling wire. One carried a cage with chickens, a leather saddle tied on top of it, one of the clattering stirrups hanging over the already frightened chickens.

The drivers and occupants of the cars were Indians. As if memorizing the trees and the hills, they drove slowly, looking at the town, looking at the land, the oil derricks pumping and clattering rhythmically in the background.

Stace went over to stand in the doorway, barely aware that he blocked the path of people who wanted to enter and leave the café. They stepped back from him. Anxiously, Levee followed behind him. "What the hell's going on?" Stace asked. His face went pale.

"You don't know?" Levee looked at his friend.

"What?" Stace turned to stare at Levee.

"There were rumors. That the Indians here were going to be relocated. God, Stace, I thought you'd know." He searched Stace's eyes.

Stace looked anxious. "What are you talking about?"

Levee waited to continue. "I know it's unbelievable that it could happen." He measured the effect of his words on Red Hawk. "They were told the army was coming in to move them." He turned toward the caravan, saw an Indian woman in a pink hat. His voice drifted slightly. "They sold their land." He did not want to be the person to tell this to Stace.

"Who told them?" Stace sounded more calm than he looked.

"We think it was someone in the federal employ."

Stace stared at Levee. "Why didn't someone tell them it wasn't true?" He felt weak and shaky.

Levee looked down. "They did. But by then they didn't know who to believe, Stace." He looked toward the passing cars, the dust on their windshields. He placed his hand on the frame of the door, as if to support himself. "They thought they were cutting their losses. They sold the land. They signed papers. It was legal."

Stace was dumbfounded. Beneath his jacket, his shirt was wet with perspiration.

Levee stopped talking. He could hear Stace breathing, and saw a moment of confusion on his face, but then Stace Red Hawk became larger, expanded with his anger, and the buildings around them grew smaller and reflected a dusty red light like the sun was falling at dusk. Large this way, Stace stepped through the door, leaving Levee, leaving the curious diners, and with long strides he went out to the street and stopped in the dead center of it. Holding out his arms, he stopped the traffic. He stood before a gray car that was being driven by a young mild-faced Indian man. Beside the man, a woman held a crying child. She bounced it on her knee, speaking softly, trying to silence the child. Stace went to the window and spoke with the man. The woman tried to hear what Stace and her young husband were saying to one another.

"Where are you going?" Stace asked.

The man didn't answer. He only shook his head back and forth.

"Don't go. Don't let them make you leave."

Still shaking his head at Stace, the young man said, "No. It's not safe here. We have to go." He lifted a hand in a gesture of surrender, looked ahead and began once again to drive slowly away from the dusty town while the woman strained her neck to look back at the Sioux man who had stopped the next car and was speaking to the driver. The sound of the engine went quiet a minute, and Levee heard a few words the driver said, about danger and giving up. Then that car also passed and drove away from Stace Red Hawk, and Stace, looking toward the next driver, yelled, "Stop. Don't leave. It's your town," and the veins stood out rigid on his forehead, but that car also went around him and left him standing in the street and in the midst of the movement, he looked alone. For a moment, Stace looked at the road ahead, then at the cars still coming, and the air went out of him. His shoulders dropped. He took a step backward, then turned slowly and walked back toward the courthouse, past Palmer's store where a group of reporters were standing, past the red sandstone buildings, past the Baptist church. The traffic moved steadily now. All the people watched him. They had temporarily lost interest in lunch. Levee stood rooted to the spot, his hand fallen away from the doorframe, hanging limp at his side.

When he reached the courthouse, Stace went up the steps, slowly, then he stopped to catch his breath. He stood for a moment. His skin felt clammy and he felt the world reeling beneath his feet and his heart beating quickly and he touched himself, as if checking to see if he were still there in his body. Then he gathered himself together and in spite of the staring people, he walked away, alone, down the street, and he kept walking in the other direction from the leaving cars, until he was only a small figure moving.

The next day Stace Red Hawk entered the courtroom as if nothing had happened. His hair was still damp and neat, his face freshly shaved. He was square-shouldered and he wore a white shirt beneath his jacket. After a few moments of watching him with curiosity, the people in the room began to talk with one another, forgetting that they had seen his look of desperation as he had signaled cars to stop the day before, had seen him vanish, walking in a held-back way in a straight line out past the town.

Stace sat down and leaned forward a bit to listen.

People filed into the dusty room, the stale odor of smoke and breakfast bacon clinging to their clothes.

Stace sat not far from Nola Blanket. He was close enough to study her face. Sitting between two of her dark guardians, she looked brittle as old paper, and she sat straight, motionless, and very alone even between the two men who were dressed now in more modern clothes—one wore a blue plaid shirt—and looked less like saving angels than they once had.

Nola was a beautiful child, frayed at the edges, but still delicate. Her face looked flat and tired, but her eyes were intense with an inner fire, with an anger pointed at Hale.

Stace tried, but failed, to concentrate on what the first witnesses said that day, and even when one of the key witnesses called did not appear, it did not surprise him, though it caused a general stir in the courtroom. It was already clear to Stace that the trial was going to be beset with numerous problems, missing witnesses being only the smallest of the difficulties. His mind, trained in the legal language, already predicted that the charges would not hold because of insufficient evidence or because Hale had an alibi for every night a murder, or any other crime for that matter, had been committed. On the night Walker was murdered, he was at a stock show in Walnut Springs. There were two witnesses who testified that he had bought and paid for several head of cattle that night of Walker's death. So the crime, really, could only be murder by proxy, and as Stace listened that afternoon, he knew that any charges would be hard to prove by the circumstantial evidence of liens, insurance policies, and other legally sound contracts and agreements whose outcomes benefitted the narrow, gray-suited man.

It was hot and stuffy in the courtroom and the information was an impossible maze for even the most attentive listeners, and after the afternoon recess, word got around that the trick roper Fraser, whose testimony was important to the case, had been found dead in a car accident. Between that new information, the fact that witnesses did not appear, and the disturbing exodus of many of the Osage people the previous day, many of the Indian people gave up on justice and went home. They dissolved into the town, absorbed by shadows and streets and the leaves and trunks of trees. They might never had been solid, never have been really there.

Stace also left the courtroom. He bought a newspaper from a skinny boy on the desolate street, went back to his room, and unlocked his door. He was uneasy and raw, his nerve worn down. He looked around the room, by habit, checking the windows to see if they had been tampered with, opening drawers, looking to see if any of his papers had been touched or moved. The last of the afternoon light was on the floor. The room was quiet.

A picture of the world was forming in his mind. One eye opened, one eye closed, that was the world, only half of a scale of justice. He opened the newspaper and the indelible image of Mr. Skelley, one of the oil barons, filled the front page. Skelley was shaking hands with a full-blooded Indian outside the door of the courthouse. For the picture, they each wore a feathered headdress. Stace closed the paper and pushed it away from himself as if the words and images themselves were unclean.

That night Stace remained in his room. His throat felt tight and closed. As he tried to piece together the bits of information he had learned, he could still see little more than the vision of the leaving Indians, with furniture piled on the cars and solemn children's faces through the windows and with this vision, he fell into a restless sleep. He woke again later and it was raining a summer rain, warm and heady, and there were fireflies blinking off and on in the darkness.

Something inside Stace was falling, falling as into a grave, down a well, into earth.

And when it rose back up, it was light outside and there were voices in the hallway, the sounds of people walking, the smell of bread.

Each day, fewer of the Hill People and town Indians went to the courtroom. They grew tired of staring at the face of the defendant. Out of the one hundred and forty witnesses subpoenaed, more than half failed to appear. Their absence grew monotonous and predictable. Finally, on one day, one of the jurors was found to be missing from his room, and on that day, also, one of the disappeared witnesses was arrested as he was leaving town with two thousand dollars in his pocket, and he confessed that he was on his way to Mexico and that the defense attorney, Springer, had paid him to leave.

The man was indicted, as were fourteen others later, and J. M. Springer was charged with contempt for attempting to influence, threaten, and bribe witnesses, and with jury tampering. That was enough reason to declare the trial a mistrial, but in addition, Stace learned that the original indictment, for reasons never made public, was found to be faulty. And it seemed as if there were only a few minutes of talking and confusion before the energy went out of the room, like smoke spreading and vanishing.

Soon after, the town went dead and quiet, with only the voices of people at the depot waiting for their departures. Only a few quiet people stayed on to see what would happen next. They did not know yet, they had not heard, that the Osage tribe had given $20,000 to the federal agents to conduct an investigation of their own, and almost as soon as the trial was over, the federal officers issued a new warrant for the arrest of Hale. For the murder of Forrest, on federal land. The trial date was set for two weeks later in federal court, in Guthrie, Oklahoma.

The town was quiet, as if a door had been closed and locked. Stace Red Hawk looked out the window at the hot sun, dressed himself slowly, and counted his money. He neatly folded his clothing and placed it in his suitcase, then he placed manila folders with his notes in between his shirts and pants, pulled on his scuffed boots, and went out the door into the hallway. He carried his dark bag full of medicines and sacred pipe in one hand, and the bag of clothing and documents in the other. He walked down the long empty hallway, uncertain about where he was going, and just as he reached the top of the stairs, he heard the hall floor creak beneath footsteps. He looked back and saw Levee standing at the door to his room. Levee knocked on the door. Stace slipped away, down the stairs, hoping that Levee had not seen him. At the desk, he felt like he'd left something behind and patted his pockets. He gave his key to the clerk, who asked without interest, "Everything all right?"

Stace nodded as the young man handed him his receipt, then without glancing back, he went out the door and down into the sunny street.

Stace did not know where he was going, but he carried his bags as he walked through town until they began to feel heavy. He was thinking about the two Graycloud sisters who lived with their parents and were so unlike each other, and Red Hawk's feet, as if they knew his mind, turned up the red clay road toward the Grayclouds' house.

It seemed farther than it was, and when he reached the silent farmhouse, Stace stopped in the road and put down his bags. He was sweating. A car sped by, honked, and swerved around him, but he was unshaken as he stood there and looked at the house. He didn't know why he had come here, and he was tired and slow.

The grass surrounding the Graycloud house was a rich, deep blue, and in the background, the forest of burned black-jacks was sprouting up in a new cover of green, but the Graycloud field that had held the buffalo and cattle was dry and bare, and the lots where Moses had once kept his own fat cattle and shiny horses were empty except for the two workhorses that nibbled on dry little clumps of grass. The house itself looked worn. It was much in need of paint and care. The shades were drawn, making it appear strangely abandoned and dark, as if no people's lives were held inside its walls.

Stace bent and picked his bags up from the road and carried them up the path toward the door. He was not in a hurry. He stood before the weathered wood listening to a mead-owlark a while before he knocked. Then it was still a moment before Lettie Graycloud opened the door. She was taller than he remembered. She shielded her eyes from the sun and looked at him, without speaking. Still quiet, she let him in. It was dark inside. He followed behind her to the kitchen. Her hair was pulled up in a thick knot and he noticed that wisps of it escaped into the neck of her dress. She looked back once, to see if he was coming.

In the kitchen, when Stace's eyes adjusted, he made out the shape of the old man sitting at the table, straining in the

poor light to read a newspaper. Moses did not get up when
Stace entered at first, but then, remembering his manners,
he nodded, and after a while he said to the younger man,
"We're all quiet in this house." But he put aside the newspaper he was reading and turned his attention, in part, to the
young man who was still standing. Moses noticed that Stace
carried his bags. "Put those down," he said. "Sit here." He
pointed to a chair across from him.

Stace put his bags against the wall and sat down, but said
nothing. Louise wiped down the kitchen table with a gray
rag, but she left the spot around Stace. He felt the cool air
around her. He put his hands on the table, folded before him.
"I've been wondering how you are doing out here," Stace
said, offering a reason for his presence.

"We're not going to leave, if that's what you mean," Moses said.

Stace had not seen or heard Floyd enter the room. In moccasins, his feet were silent, but Floyd sat down and looked
steadfastly at Stace. His long, blond hair was thinning. He
spoke directly to Stace, "Why didn't you tell us you were
with the government?" Floyd's glance wavered and Stace at
once understood the silence and distance; they were angry
with him, they were betrayed. He began to defend himself,
saying, "I couldn't," but then he gave himself up to the
surrounding silence. He couldn't tell them his history, how
his younger mind once believed he could help the people by
going to work in Washington. He could barely even form the
words that explained his growing distance from the bureau
and from the friend he once trusted, or how he'd begun to
feel that everything was hopeless, so he swallowed their anger and distrust without a murmur.

Lettie crossed the floor behind them. She busied herself
taking a biscuit off the tin and sliding it on a plate. She ladled
white gravy over it and took it to Stace. "Let me feed you,"
she said as she placed the food in front of him. "Then you
should leave here. It's not good if you are here."

Stace nodded as if he understood. He watched her pour a
cup of tea and set it down before him. He felt paralyzed.
They glanced sideways at each other.

But in his silence, the Grayclouds' trust for him renewed
itself, if only a little, for only a moment. He had not rushed

to explain himself. They thought it meant his reasons were deep ones. Both men looked at Stace.

"What will you do now?" asked Floyd.

"I don't know. I'm going to wait for the next trial."

They all fell quiet and after a while he sensed it was time for him to leave. Stace finished his tea and pushed himself back away from the table. "I think I am going up to the hills."

Moses nodded. "That's a good idea."

"Here," said Lettie. "You can leave your bags upstairs." She again led Stace Red Hawk through the darkened house, this time up the narrow staircase to her bedroom. It was the only room with opened windows and it was bright, with colorful hats hanging on hooks on the walls. A large cracked mirror hung above a chest of drawers. A window was taped together. The bed sagged in the middle but was covered with a clean blue and white quilt. Through the window, Stace heard the fresh sound of birds.

"Put your bags here," Lettie told him. She pointed to a corner, and Stace set down the larger bag. He paused a moment, considering whether he should take his folders of notes along with him.

"What about that one?" Lettie gestured toward the smaller bag he still held, the one that carried his pipe. "Do you want to leave it?"

He was conscious of her standing before him, her face with a question on it looking at his. "No. I want to carry it with me," he answered.

"I understand," she said and she was already inside the hallway, and she went back down the stairs. He looked around a final time and followed.

It was after noon when Stace left the Grayclouds. As he walked, he thought of them. The house was too silent and the rooms were filled with the musty, hopeless odor of a sickroom. Even the outside air felt close about him after he'd been in that darkened house. He speeded up his pace, walked past the dry ponds and white patches of alkali, out past the oak forests and beyond the cemetery filled with the spread and delicate-looking stone wings of angels.

He walked briskly and it was still light when Stace Red Hawk reached the entrance of Sorrow Cave.

Inside Sorrow, the floor was cool and dry. Stace remembered the other entrance to the place of inner earth and the magical chambers behind Sorrow, and he planned to go around the hill the next morning and enter into the holy recess of this land.

As he sat at the door of the cave watching the sun prepare to go down the horizon, from a distance, from the direction of town, he saw a small person walking toward him. It was a woman. He watched her make her way across the drying land. She was the gold and warm color of the earth, and she looked like a mirage wavering in the still rising heat. After a few moments, she came into focus. It was the woman, Napa-cria, the teller of events, the woman who carried the weight of history on her back, and as she drew nearer, he thought she looked like it had started to bend her, just slightly, around the shoulders and neck.

Cry, they called her, he remembered. She waved her arm in greeting, and soon she was there and sat down beside him on the ground.

"What are you doing?" she asked. She wore a light blue summer dress. It was soft against her dark skin.

"I don't know what I'm doing," he told her. His face looked darker, as if he were confessing. "I'm trying to understand something."

At this she laughed. He felt foolish, but she quickly grew serious. "We are all trying to understand." She looked at him with warmth. "Why don't you come home with me? We will take care of you." She stood up. "Come on now, before it gets dark." She looked straight at him.

Something in her tone led him to stand. He felt his feet sink a little in the soft sand. He brushed himself off, picked up his bag, and together they walked through the red and gold light of the lowering sun. And soon they were on the obscure footpath up to the settlement. The evening insects were a low hum around them. They walked past the piled cairns of red stones, past the carved eagle on the path and then, rounding a small hill, Stace saw the flickering light of the fires up at the settlement.

Two old women were standing on the narrow path, as if expecting them. They were small, older women. One of them took the hand of Cry. Stace recognized her from before. She had wise, smiling eyes. She said to Stace, apologizing, "We are taking Cry to be cleansed. You should go over there." She looked toward the small fire where Belle Graycloud was sitting beneath an umbrella as if the sun had not just gone down and the sky turned a deepening blue. The umbrella was rooted in the ground.

Belle held her arms across her breasts. She did not see Stace Red Hawk approach her, nor did she see the women lead Cry away. She was humming to herself and watching the far horizon. Stace sat down on the grass beside her, and still without looking at him, she stopped humming. Still gazing at the sky, she said, "So here you are. Have you seen my family? Tell me how they are."

"They miss you," was all he said. He looked out to the point of sky that she'd been watching. He did not tell her about the dark, quiet house. He turned his head slightly, saw the backs of the women leading Cry through the softly rounded door of a small hut.

"They cleanse her when she returns," Belle said, as if reading his mind. "They give her a stone cup full of the black drink. It takes out of her what the world puts in."

Stace had heard of the black water before. When swallowed it made a person vomit. It was an old custom. It purged the body and it made the mind clear.

"They will smoke her and remove all things from her, take her clothing away and launder it. They will wash her and dress her hair." For the first time, Belle glanced at him. "Then they will gather around her and listen as she empties herself even of words." Still looking at him, she said, "Tell me about Lettie. She's too soft. I worry about her."

Stace said nothing, but he thought he felt Belle inside himself, reading his inner words, and he felt embarrassed. He could not empty himself of the picture of Lettie's cream-colored neck with the black wisps of hair, her soft hand offering him a cup of tea.

Belle studied his face. "She is a good woman," she said to him.

After dark, the women returned with Cry. She wore a white dress. In the firelight her face looked clean and her eyes were clear, dark orbs. Her hair was damp. She passed by Stace and Belle Graycloud, and she smelled fresh, like

the spring rain. She sat down before the fire and others joined
her. One of the women put a bucket down beside her, then
ladled a stone cup full of cool water and handed it to Cry.
The others sat down while Cry drank the water. One woman
smoked a pipe and watched the smoke flowing up from it.
Another pulled her knees to her chest, and soon Cry began
to tell them of the trials that had gone on down in Watona.
As she told them, the people were silent. Then the first
woman again ladled water into the stone cup and handed it
to Cry. "Here, drink."

Belle remained beneath her umbrella with Stace beside her
while Cry spoke. Cry neglected to repeat many of the most
painful spoken things, such as when a witness would say of
a victim, "He was just another Indian," but in spite of these
omissions, word by word, something like an evil found its
way through her story and into the settlement. The people
began to understand the town people and why they fought
among themselves and drank. They began to see white people as wisps of smoke stealing by and around their own more
solid world, and so did Stace. He knew he would not go back
into that world even though its pull had been so great on him.

And in the old language Cry spoke some words and all
the old ones turned to look at Stace. "Ah," they said as they
studied his face and nodded. He knew what she had said,
that he'd been one of the unfortunate ones who'd worked for
the government and no longer knew what to make of things.

Cry continued to talk. She told about the tragic figure of
Nola who sat at times in the courtroom with her thin brown
hands over her face and was heard to speak to the child growing within her, saying, "Little one, I hear you crying already
and your hands and feet not even touching this air. But I will
love you, so don't cry now, I will help you."

Through the words of Cry, the others saw Nola sitting on
the hard wood bench, held in by the fresh paint on courtroom
walls, her long fingers touching the skin of her face. "Good,"
said the old woman with the pipe. "She is talking to the
future. That's good."

Then it was silent a moment while people looked at the
distant stars. The clouds, alive with moonlight, arched in
the dark sky above them. They sat with folded arms, like
they were protecting their hearts.

Stace heard the sound of water in the pail as someone gave Cry another cup of the cool water.

"Hmmm," said one of the men thoughtfully, "and what about Horse? Tell us about him." He looked out toward where he'd seen Redshirt just the previous day, flying past, kicking up his heels like it was young spring with buds tender on the trees.

The more Michael Horse wrote down, the more his thoughts had become clear. One night with a full moon, he wrote, "It was a fatal ignorance we had of our place; we did not know the ends to which the others would go to destroy us. We didn't know how much they were moved by the presence of money."

He felt tired and dry. During the course of the trials, his body appeared to shrink in size. On some days he could hardly lift his feet as he went up and down the courthouse steps with the others. But he had listened tirelessly to what was being said in the courtroom. And each day he wrote with shaking hands such entries as: "Right or wrong. For us, it is such a simple thing, only a matter of whether a wrong has been done, or someone harmed. But they have books filled with words, with rules about how the story can and cannot be spoken. There is not room enough, nor time, to search for the real story that lies beneath the rest."

He had listened daily in court, and listening was an act that held no mercy, for time after time, Hale was described as a good citizen, an upstanding and honest man. And each time it was said, Horse felt an even more urgent need to write, as if he could write away the appearances of things and take them all the way back down to bare truth. Those who sat near him in court grew used to the scribbling sound of his words on the paper. It became part of the trial. He was writing for those who would come later, for the next generations and the next, as if the act of writing was itself part of divination and prophecy, an act of deliverance.

He wrote: "The land is ravaged and covered with scars and so are the broken people. Those of us who still have an ounce of strength have been losing it during these testimonies in the courthouse."

And he wrote about the exodus of the people, the people

who were bent under their losses, no longer a part of their
land, no longer in their own lives. "They left like a lost and
hungry trail of ants. They were going to where another world
would bloom in the spring, to where the stars would turn
another way in the sky, to where deep summer would be another green. They were leaving one place and entering another that would be full with other kinds of loss.

"I saw them leaving, the men in their cotton summer shirts
and straw hats, the women with clean brushed hair, the
brown-faced children in white smocks with their dolls of
cloth and cornhusks. I saw them leave, carrying their dishes
and black skillets. Some had wagons with new, clean calves
that were headed for another pasture. Some of them had blue
peacocks that screamed up at the sky they were moving beneath. They took their shining racing mules in trailers behind
them, or tied alongside their slow carts. They stared ahead,
into another future.

"I am an old man. I have seen too much. I saw the people
leave and the streets and pathways go silent. I saw the grandmothers sitting in rocking chairs in wagons, the breezes stirring their hair as they watched the land pass by, their soft,
moist eyes looking over the fields that moved back and away
from them. They were driven out, or maybe it was that they
escaped, that they survive by leaving this land and its waters
and rich black earth, the rain that sets in like a wall holding
up the sky.

"I knew those people, knew their lives and bodies. I saw
the grandmother leave who had lost her ring and hired me to
find it, saw the people leave whose land I had searched for
underground water, saw the frightened men carrying their
loaded guns in full view."

One morning, Stace Red Hawk woke to the sounds of birds
and the heat of sun. He stood and stretched, then went down
to the water and washed his face. He splashed water on his
temples and his hair and smoothed it back with his hands. It
comforted him. The sun was beginning to rise. He greeted
it, clean and ready. A peace was in him, a clarity, as he knelt
beside the water. He was going home. He had decided. He
was going to be there to offer strength to his people. He
would sing around the drum with his uncles. He would hold

children on his knee. After the trials. He braided red cloth into his hair, stood up and walked back to the settlement.

Belle Graycloud was waiting for him. She looked fuller than he remembered. She stood short, with a rounded stomach, her snow-colored hair loose down her back, soft and white in the sunlight. "Come with me," she said and walked toward the little room where she stayed while in the hills. She still limped.

He bent to pass through the doorway of her room, then straightened and looked around him. The room seemed made of clean, white-washed walls and blue morning light. It smelled of moist clay, and on the floor was a pile of corn. Belle's skirt brushed against the drying stalks and leaves of the corn plants. It whispered.

"Come here," she said, and the young man stepped a little deeper into her room. She opened a wooden box and took out a dark blue feather, red on one side, and handed it to Stace. The quill was beaded with tiny red and blue beads. "It is almost time for you to go to the trial in Guthrie. Take this to Lettie. She always wanted this feather. She is going to the trial with you. Tell her I am coming soon." She placed the feather in his hand. "Now go. Don't stay any longer to eat this food. Go without any of the peace you have found here. It is the only way toward change. Go with a confused and angry mind."

She took up her walking stick and walked with him to the beginning of the path before she stopped and turned away from him.

As Stace walked, he felt as if time hadn't passed. But in the weeks he'd been in the settlement, the land had gone dry and the insects had become more shrill and desperate sounding. He carried his pipe bag and the macaw feather. He was hatless. He felt the heat of sun on his forehead and on his back.

Belle watched him leave. When he was out of sight, she went back to her room, took out her umbrella, and limped down the path toward Sorrow Cave in the terrible direction. She passed by the carved cedar eagle. Its eyes appeared to watch her, and so did those of the stone faces, the red sandstone figures of the ancient ones. Though her steps were unsteady as she walked, she felt strong within herself.

The river was clear that first day, and she heard its murmuring voice.

Up through the back way, above the Blue River, Belle made her way toward the caves that were on the other side of Sorrow. She walked until the terrible path ended, and then she walked on, beyond it.

Time slipped by quickly and soon the shadows of trees grew longer, the shadows of stones grew deeper and sharper. She heard the animals hidden behind bushes, the occasional scuff of hoof or paw, an occasional cracking of twigs. The world around her was alive and moving. Even the plants that closed their flowers at night and opened them again in daylight.

There was nothing to do. The world had turned under and over, and now they were left, left to go on, to survive.

She stopped a moment, standing in the open mouth of the cave, and looked down over the river. Below her, the world stretched on, curved around the horizon. And then it was night, and the smell of the land was rich and fertile with the dank odor of grasses and herbs.

Then she went inside the cave that was behind Sorrow. There were four chambers there, like a heart. Some of the bats still lived there, and for this Belle was grateful. They would always be there, she knew, living in the borderland between worlds.

She sat in the open mouth of the cave and thought of the fallen world, the fallen houses and the fallen people.

That night, the moonlight was an entrance into still another land. She went out from the cave and stood before it, in the light of earth's reflected face. She raised her head and looked up at the sky. It was beautiful and enormous, the world that lived far beyond theirs, beyond the stars, and beyond even the constellations of buffalo and deer.

She slept on the ground of the cave that night, feeling the land, feeling it move up through her. She saw her own self lying there, a white-haired woman, a strong woman, part of earth's terrain. In the cave she remembered how there was hope in the land, hope and tomorrow living in the veins and stones of earth.

She remembered that the river was going to the sea, had

been rain clouds and lakes. It had been snow. Now it was on its journey back to the great first waters of life.

As he neared town, Stace thought he saw, from the corner of his eye, the figure of Cry slipping down between the trees and red bluffs, but each time he looked for her, no one was there.

When, later that day, he reached Graycloud's sagging house, he noticed that the wooden porch seemed even more dry than before. His boots sounded hollow against it.

He knocked on the door. As if she was expecting him, Lettie came out, hatless and carrying a pink flowered bag. Stace could tell it was silent inside the house, and cool. "We don't have time to stop or to eat," Lettie told him. "But I have food in my bag and we will eat it once we are on the train." She did not so much as glance at him. She walked quickly on the dusty clay road, her dark hair braided in a single rope that was pulled forward over her shoulder and fell across her breast. She wore flat leather boots and they showed beneath her billowing skirt and ground at the soil. She was pale from being inside too much. Together they passed trees. Stace took the flowered bag from her hand and he walked alongside her, thinking not only of the trials, but wondering, in spite of himself, what they looked like walking together, him with the red cloth braided into his hair, her with the blue glass pin holding together the place where a button was missing from her neckline.

"Hurry," she urged him. She sounded impatient, and Stace, aware that he'd given his own will up to these women, followed. He was in their world. It was an honest one. He trusted it.

They reached the train just as it began to move, and Stace leapt up the step. For a brief moment he lost his bearings, but Lettie reached up to him and seeing her hand steadied him and he clasped it and pulled her onto the platform. The air was charged with the moving train's electricity.

The train was nearly full. Lettie asked if a child couldn't move out of a seat he occupied alone and he went back and joined his dark, tired grandmother. Lettie sat down and looked out the blue and dusty light of window as the train moved forward, past the grasses growing in the fields.

Stace noticed for the first time that her dress was darned, her face sad.

They passed by oil derricks and diesel shacks, horses and cattle, and then the land picked up speed and started to blur past. They both fell silent, but there was something between them, an unspoken kinship, and she knew it, too. They remained quiet, and they forgot to eat.

The rain was coming in. They could see it from the distance as the metal road curved ahead of the train. It was a lead-colored shaft of darkness moving across the land.

In Guthrie, the air was motionless with the coming rain. Stace and Lettie walked together from the depot into the flat gray of the town. They were watched by curious onlookers. A woman, outside sweeping, saw them walk toward her on the street, grew uneasy, and went inside her house and closed the door, leaving the broom leaning against the rough stones of the building.

The rain was catching up with the town. There was the rumble of thunder in the distance and the streets turned dark blue. When they entered the inn, the light was gray. The innkeeper came in from a back room. "We would like two rooms," Stace said to the man. He reached into his pocket for his money, but the man at the desk did not speak with him. He looked at Lettie instead and said, "Only one room. For the woman." He took a key off a nail and handed it to Lettie, saying to her, "The rest are full." Then he formed his lips into the shape of a whistle and looked away, but Stace and Lettie understood; Stace Red Hawk was too dark. He wasn't welcome in this cold place. Lettie glanced at Stace, then began to address the clerk, but Stace interrupted and said. "Come on, I'll carry your bag to the room," and moved away from the desk.

The clerk watched them walk down the hallway, suspicious, to make sure that Stace left the room in a short amount of time.

The fresh smell of the coming rain did not enter the room. It was cramped and had a tired-looking bed, a worn chair, and smelled of mildew.

"We should eat," Stace said, as he set down the cloth bag on the bed. "We should eat at a restaurant, a hot meal."

Lettie brushed her hair. He watched her. She brushed it slowly and carefully.

Outside the color was completely gone from the world. It was evening and the buildings were nearly black. A light came on in a window, then another. They walked to the restaurant four doors down. It was filled with men hunched over tables, and when they entered, the others became silent, straightened, and watched them. Then, one of the men told a loud story about rabbit hunting and the others nodded in such a way that Stace knew they'd heard the story for years on end and still not grown tired of how the rabbit screamed like a woman.

They ordered ham and eggs. As the two of them ate, the rain began to billow down. They watched through the window as people ran to cover and the streets became wet and silver. "Where will you go tonight?" Lettie asked him.

He smiled at her. He felt protective of her in this room of tired men. "I'll sleep outside. It'll be good for me."

"But what about the rain?" she said, and the rain began falling harder and thicker and it covered her words.

They drank coffee and looked through the steamy windows as they waited for the rain to subside. There was an air of excitement in the room, as if the falling water brought energy to the bent men who sat a little straighter and talked a little faster.

Stace looked at Lettie. "You know, when we came here, to Oklahoma, I thought we were doing something right. I thought there would be witnesses, honest people, and I thought the picture would come clear, the killings stop."

She studied his face.

"I worked hard to get them to come here. I didn't know it would be like this."

Outside it was moist, and night smelled like the beginnings of life, of spring, of brine ocean.

Stace walked Lettie to her room and at the door, he awkwardly took her hand in his own a moment, then he said good night, stepped back, and closed the door. But he felt her presence, felt her remain just on the other side of the wooden door. He turned and walked away.

He took nothing with him except his pipe bag and a clean shirt. Guthrie was not far from the Cimarron River, but he walked east across the grassland plains. It was normally dry country with a wide sky, but that night it was close with the heavy moisture of air and wet herbs. His boots grew wet as he walked through the grass. But it smelled fresh, the field, and the earth felt good beneath his feet.

Stace reached a little mound of stones and two old, silent trees, and decided to remain there through the night. He sat down with his back against one of the stones and looked back at the field he'd just passed through, wishing he could see that clearly everywhere he had traveled, everything he'd been. He knew from the stories he grew up with that there were times when a person could do nothing but wait and be silent, that an answer would sometimes come out of nothing, that there were times when a man couldn't meddle with the workings of the world. But a man by his nature wanted to act, wanted to stir things and direct them into their movement, and Stace felt damned, having to sit, small and helpless.

His bag. He put it on his lap and when he opened the dark leather, he thought he'd packed loneliness in it, for that was what escaped. He saw the feather he'd forgotten to give to Lettie. He took out the pipe, carefully, and he filled the clay bowl with tobacco and poked the center with a twig, stood up, and lit the pipe. He stood tall and with his legs slightly apart and he held the pipe up to the air and offered it to the sky. He prayed. He prayed for justice, for change, for a world grown kinder to her little ones.

He stood alone on that stretch of the planet and he heard a night hawk flapping its wings up the sky and a coyote in the distance began to talk.

Before working in the city, Stace often slept outside, did so from choice, from wanting to feel the skin of earth against his back and shoulder blades, but that night when he laid back on the damp land, without the fire and soft earth of the Hill settlement, his shoulders began to ache. And just before daylight, his only recourse was to walk off the pain, so he left early, walking farther away from Guthrie in his wet boots. When he came across the oiled road, for a moment he thought he might keep going, but then he thought of Lettie and the trial and while it was still dark he turned back, and soon cars whizzed by him, and in between cars there was only the hollow sound of his boots on the oiled gravel and a first bird waking up the others, happy about the rain's clear new morning.

In Guthrie a clock struck.

Stace walked slowly toward the courthouse, as if he didn't want to arrive at the gray building that looked so much like all the others with marble walls and steps that were cut from the quarries of earth.

There was a small group of Hill Indians who had shown up to witness the trial. Nola stood within them, heavily, the child grown large within her. The watchers beside her were strong and lean-muscled, but even in their street clothes they did not fit in with the crowd and the clothing was not cut for their bodies.

Stace joined the cluster of Hill People. They knew him. Two of the men leaned toward him, shook his hand, and looked back away. Stace could see that Nola was held tight in the clasp of the trials. For her, the outcome meant survival, and survival for her child as well. She had to know what had happened and who among the many were guilty. She walked with great difficulty up the steps. They went inside the courtroom and sat down. Lettie Graycloud joined them. "Did you sleep?" she asked Stace.

That day, again, while court was in session, it rained heavily and the walls of water hit against the building with force. And then, in the middle of that rain, while the land was turning wet and muddy, things took an abrupt turn in the courtroom. Mardy, who had signed a confession and a statement about his dealings with Hale, retracted both, claiming that the government men had forced and tricked him into signing the confession. In addition, it was found that the man named Bird had said the same thing. There was a stir in the courthouse. The possibility was more than considered; the two had been sequestered and had no dealings with one another.

Mardy was on the stand. He did not look like a man who had made up such a story. His face wore a serious expression.

"Do you know the consequences if you were to perjure yourself?" the judge asked Mardy.

"I do," he said, and his eyes shone with honesty.

Stace looked from Mardy toward Levee who had come in and seated himself near the back of the room. Levee had gone pale and his mouth dropped open, but he stared dumbly at the witness who told about the attempts of federal agents to force him to sign a confession.

Ballard was the key agent, Mardy said, nodding at the heavy man. "When I refused to sign the confession," Mardy said, "they put a leather hat on my head and hooked me up to wires and what they called electrodes, and gave me a shock. I turned my head while they were talking to me. I saw the shadow of a gun pointed in my direction, held by another man. I saw it through the ground glass door. Then they held a gun on me and said if I looked back again they would beat me and if I didn't sign they would give me the hot chair. Those were their words."

The prosecution handed him the confession.

He looked at it. "Yes, this is it. They told me they were after Hale and if I would sign this, they would leave me alone. They said they'd even drop the charges on the stolen car."

That afternoon the judge called a private meeting with Ballard and the other agents in his chamber.

"You too," the judge said to Stace Red Hawk. "You're one of them, aren't you?"

"I was. My official duties are ended."

"I want to see all of you."

Stace began to walk away, then stopped and let the silence grow. Without turning his head, he heard Ballard approach and then he turned his head and looked back at the man. Ballard's hands were behind his back. He looked like a crow, Stace thought, come to pick meat off the bones of the dead.

They walked together into the judge's chamber.

That afternoon the agents were read a reprimand. It was from the governor and it addressed problems of conduct and harassment of citizens.

Ballard staunchly denied any wrongdoing as far as confessions were concerned. "We did nothing of the kind. And," he said, "I resent your intrusion into these federal matters." He emphasized "federal." He went on, "And what about the governor? He pardoned the investigator he sent in to find out what was going on in Indian Territory. The investigator, I remind you, was sentenced to twenty-five years in jail and the governor pardoned him."

The judge was attentive to the crow words of Ballard but he looked as if he wanted to hear no more, and when court resumed, the judge firmly stated that no agents, to his knowledge, had ever lied in court, and that the case continue.

But something about the whole transaction eluded Stace Red Hawk and he believed Ballard might have been guilty of forcing the confession.

He did not go back to court that day. When he left the courthouse he wanted only to cleanse himself. He walked all the way to the water of the Cimarron River, and sat quietly for a while, then offered tobacco and prayed. He washed in the muddy water. He didn't know the truth. He doubted he would ever know it.

The next day, in spite of still maintaining that his confession had been forced, Mardy Green shed light on many of the events that had taken place. His long testimony unraveled much of the complicated plot involving Hale and the sheriff: Hale could not kill both Benoit and Sara because the money had to go through Benoit. They were certain the sheriff would later find a way to marry Lettie. Then they could claim the money through her. The sheriff intended to win Lettie over after the death of Benoit. He had already paved the way. The night of Benoit's death, the sheriff paid people to stay in jail overnight, and he had let them go early. They were not prisoners taken in for infractions of the law.

Everyone avoided looking at Lettie. She felt ashamed, as if she herself were guilty of wrongdoing by the fact of the sheriff's murderous courtship. She knew that she might actually have married the sheriff. He was kind. She had liked him.

The room was silent as Mardy continued. Palmer had kept store records and was nearly always a witness when a lien was filed against an Indian's property, so he too was implicated, but he'd been another citizen the Indians knew well and liked.

But the plans went awry, the man said. First there was the information that under white law Lettie was not legally married to Benoit. Then the sheriff thought they should murder Belle, and that was when the unforeseen took place, when Belle's bees attacked Jess Gold, resulting in his death.

At the mention of Belle's name, the Indian people who

remained in the courtroom looked down. Then they looked up again and listened as Mardy told about the killing of Willis. This had been the sheriff's most brilliant move, and he had boasted about it. Willis had known about Belle's land, Mardy told them. The sheriff had seen him looking at the geologist's map. Jess Gold knew that Willis was more Indian than he looked. Because of this, Gold feared that Willis would try to warn or help the old woman.

It seemed as if everyone was involved, Palmer and his books, the banker, the dead cowboy and roper Fraser who knew too much, and a large number of the attorneys who were guardians for oil-rich Indians.

That day also, China was called to take the stand. She took up for the Indians, as did Benjamin Black when he was asked to speak. "Yes, I loved him," she said of Hale. "Everyone did, you have heard that." She looked around the room. Her white-blond hair was pulled back off to the side, almost as white as the hair of Belle Graycloud's ghost.

The defense wanted to know if her testimony was revenge for unrequited love.

"No. I was the one who left him."

Then she told about John Stink and how Hale had coerced her to marry the old man. The Indians looked at Stink's ghost sideways. "When Hale discovered that he was dead, well he was dead on paper, I mean, he went to the courthouse and filed a lien on Stink's money." She paused a moment. "I was lucky," she said, "not to have married Stink. I would have been the next victim in line." Some of the listeners knew, however, this was not true; white women marrying Indian men could not receive their headrights, not being the dominant marriage partner. Only white men. And that was just one more complication that confused and worked against the tribal people, but they couldn't help but think it had also worked against the killers who could hardly keep it all of a piece themselves.

Outside a gust of wind was blowing. Almost as soon as he heard it, Moses's leg began to ache, worse even than it had ached the year before. It was a turn wind and the way his leg hurt, he knew another rain was coming in with it. With difficulty he stood up and limped out of the courtroom. He stopped for a moment outside in the sun and watched the skinny street dogs beg for crumbs while thin cats disappeared around corners.

He saw the clouds roll in.

Moses sat for a while, squinting on the sun-warmed steps. The wind picked up. It was cool and smelled fresh of the new rain.

As if she had just wakened, Nola stood, ill at ease and surrounded by the looming, polished furniture in her own living room. It was evening. In her hand she held a dish of cut fruit for her monkey. She looked around her like she'd been fast asleep in a foreign world. The house unsettled her. The walls were cold. The wallpaper, with its ivory roses, looked artificial in the light. The wood was polished to a shine and on every shelf were meaningless objects. The wind set up an inner current and as the house breathed in and out, the chandeliers moved slightly.

The despair of it touched her whole body with exhaustion. It wasn't Nola's world. Something, a force or deep current, was carrying her away. It was still distant. She closed her eyes a moment, then she looked again, turned out the light and let darkness fill the room with another life. The house creaked as if it would collapse.

Out in the distance, the wind slammed a door.

The restless sound of the wind and an occasional gust of sand hitting against the windows made the monkey nervous that night, and in spite of her fatigue, Nola went in and took the fuzzy-headed creature from the cage and held him tenderly in her arms. It closed its eyes and leaned against her heart, and when she returned it to the cage, it whined like a child.

Nola was careful not to disturb Will, but she looked at him for a long time, at the sleeping man, her husband. He was not her world either, but part of the shadowy white world that was losing its focus. She was afraid of him. She was afraid he would kill her. Within her, the child quickened and turned. It already knew. Already it had wisdom. Tears fell from Nola's eyes. "Baby," she said to herself, "I'm sure of it. Even your father is a bad man." She touched her own cheek softly, the way a dreamer might caress her waking self,

touched herself as she would touch the child when it was
born.

Just before Nola turned her back to the sleeping man, she
thought she heard the voice of water, a voice like a river. It
called to her. She stopped breathing to listen. She lifted her
head from the pillow. It was only the wind, but it struck a
familiar chord in her, in some deep way she did not know or
remember. She laid her head back on the pillow.

The next morning when Nola woke, Will was already gone
to Walnut Springs to sell artifacts he'd found. Nola got up
from bed and dressed in her traditional clothing. She dressed
slowly and with great care. She let out the Osage skirt and
made room for it to circle around her wide belly. She looked
at herself in the mirror, her dark eyes, then she bent uncomfortably to tie the leggings behind her thin knees, put on her
moccasins, and walked outside to greet the early morning
sun. She looked to the east. Her black hair was loose and fell
like a mane over her shoulders and down her back. The turn
wind had let up for a while, but a slight breeze caught at
Nola's hair and lifted it.

The watchers exchanged quick glances with one another.
Nola looked calm as she faced the dawning light, but they
saw deeper than that, and beneath the surface, Nola was
wandering about like a crazy woman, desperate and running
through the forests of burned blackjacks, slipping in the mud
of creeks. She was as intent on living as the hard-shelled
turtles migrating on the dangerous, hot roads. She was trying
to survive.

The watchers came to attention.

All that day, Nola looked at the world around her. The
house was not her house. In the morning light, she saw the
plaster ceiling bordered all around by elegant, carved flowers
she'd never seen before. She sat down weakly. She knew the
house. She had known it as well as her own palm. But now
even her palm was a mystery to her.

In the uncompromising light of noon, the furniture was
large and heavy. Thick velvet curtains touched the floor like
women's dusty skirts. The glass figurines were of no use at
all. It was another Nola, not this one, who had gone from
store to store looking for a slender glass swan, another Nola

who had turned pages in a catalog searching for fragile items to place inside the walls of her life.

The day continued to turn, and when it was dark Will came home. His day had been successful. He'd turned a big profit selling his artifacts to a collector from the East, but he was tired and the death of his father had depressed him. Thinking Nola in bed, he turned on the light, but he was startled at the strange vacant figure sitting on the chair; she was dressed in her traditional clothes like a relic from another, past world. He looked at her a moment too long, and he leaned down to kiss her. With his hand, he raised her face toward him. But her face felt cold. She only barely saw him; he was as strange to her as the furniture. He was puzzled and afraid. "Nola. What's wrong?"

But Nola didn't hear him. She looked straight ahead, like someone who'd seen a ghost.

Will didn't know that Nola was busy talking to the future. If he had known, he might have understood her better. Or if she'd voiced her fears, he might have dispelled them. But Nola was speaking only to the future, and that future, though it lived only inside her, was another land, a distant continent emerging. "You come from an old people," Nola said to the child. She did not see Will's look of fear. "An old, old people, one of those who belong to the sweet earth and the shadows flying across the moon."

Will's voice came from afar. "Nola?" He led her up the stairs. He undressed her. She was stiff. She lifted an arm as he pulled at the sleeve. He looked at her round belly. The veins showed through the dark, stretched skin. She was beautiful and full. He put a white gown on her, then bent over and lifted her legs up and onto the bed. She was limp and baleful, her breathing shallow. She did not turn toward him. He covered her. He had a sense of dread.

The heat lightning went from place to place across the dark horizon, lighting a little cove of cloudy sky here, a group of burned trees there. Will had difficulty sleeping, but he dozed once, then jerked awake to find Nola gone from the bed. He went down the stairs to look for her. From the last step, he saw her sitting in a trance on a cane-seated chair, her feet planted flat on the floor and a little moonlight on her bones.

Gently, he guided her back up the stairs to bed.

By the next morning, she had again found her way down-stairs. When Will found her, she was shaking her head back and forth as if something, some invisible force strangled her. Her eyes were fixed on the parrot in the gilt cage. "Poor thing," she moaned. "Poor, poor thing." Nola felt a terrible pity for the bright-colored bird. The bird regarded her care-fully, its eyes searching her face.

Always, the parrot strained its neck south toward its home-land, pulled by its blood. Always it had the rain forest in its dreams. No, in its eyes, Nola thought to herself. Yes, she could see it there, the wide green, feathery leaves, the vines and blue waters. She slumped over. She held her hand over her heart, as if that were the organ that tormented her.

Overwhelmed with her grief that way, she did not see Will go to the next room and sit down at the table. He lifted the telephone receiver. He tried to speak calmly. "Operator? Please put in a call to Dr. Levee in town."

Nola did not hear his quiet words. She was thinking of the monkey. It was another life taken out of the jungle world, torn away from its own kind. She had loved them both as if they were something they were not, as children, as friends. But her love had imprisoned them. She bolted up the stairs, unlocked the cage that held her monkey, lifted him out from the bars, and let him move about freely. It followed behind her as she went down the stairs. It eyed her, cautious, know-ing that something was not right.

As Will waited for the call to go through, he heard the first crash and tinkle of breaking glass. The sound gave him a terrible feeling, a forewarning, that something dangerous had happened or was about to happen. He feared for Nola. He whispered a hoarse and desperate "Hurry, hurry" into the phone. The operator heard him, and heard the second crash of breaking glass. She too became afraid and willed an an-swer to the phone. And then there was the voice on the other end, the "Hello" of Dr. Levee and then his promise to start out for the Forrests' home right away.

Even when he hung up the phone, Will did not move to stop the monkey's rampage through the house. Because he saw from the doorway that it was Nola who was broken, something inside of her shattered. She still wore her sleeping gown and she sat weeping, her hands over her tragic face.

Then he saw her rise, go over to the golden cage that held the parrot, open the cage door, and take out the bird. She carried it to the window.

On the other side of the window, it had grown foggy. Nola pulled the glass up. Will moved quickly to stop her. In her white sleeping dress, she held the green and red bird with both hands outside in the hazy air. One of the bird's emerald green wings found its way free of her hand and it flapped helplessly. A cloud of mist came in the open window and when Will saw it, with the beautiful girl standing in front of it, almost inside the gray sky, the bright red and green bird in her hands, the sight horrified him. The bird had taken on brilliant, monstrous life.

Outside, the watchers heard the breaking of glass. They were alert. They watched the black-haired girl as she opened the window, the bird held like a bouquet by its stemlike legs. And they heard Will's voice behind her crying out, "What are you doing?"

"I am setting it free."

Will tried to reason with her. "This isn't its world. It won't live here. Are you trying to kill it?"

Nola's voice was shrill. "It's not mine either. It's not my world." The words she repeated hit her desolate heart. They were true, though she hadn't known it until she heard herself say them. A rage welled up inside her.

The parrot grew still.

"Nola!" Will tried to struggle with her. "Wait, just wait. I called the doctor."

But she screamed and cried even louder at the mention of the doctor. Now she was sure they were going to kill her. And it wasn't just her. It was the new life, also, they would kill. They would say she died of natural causes, she knew it, and she had gone too far now and when she felt the baby kick her from inside, she thought she heard it saying, "Help me. Help me."

Nola tossed the bird away. It settled, confused, on a branch in the foggy world. Inside, Nola's face was twisted with pain, and her heart had broken like a window, and her anger and fear were flooding out. She would not listen to him, she would never believe him again. She knew he was a killer and she screamed this at him. He jumped back, shaking his head, "No, no," but she went on: She knew he had used up all her money, she said. And she knew that he was seeing the blond-haired woman and that he was going to kill her and the child. Will tried to get hold of her, but she rushed over to the drawer and took out the pistol she had placed there. Will's face was strained, his arms strong. He tried to take the gun away from her. But it was her life, her child's life she was trying to save and the urgency pressed her on, the instinct for survival driving her to a strength greater than his, and when the watchers heard the gunshot, and the large window exploded outward, they ran inside.

Nola was doubled over, weeping beside her dying husband. Her black hair hung over him like a shroud. His face showed astonishment and betrayal. He stared at Nola as she sobbed over and over, "I loved you. I loved you." She cried like a child. "Why? Why did you do this?"

The watchers spoke quickly to one another in the old language. They moved with great speed. One of them pulled Nola away from her husband's body.

There was mist and the drowning fog moved over the land. The watchers carried away the young girl, her black mane of hair falling down her back. The men half lifted her by the underarms, held her, her head dropping to the side, her feet lifeless and dragging over the ground. And then they entered the fog as if it were a door that closed behind them somewhere at the hazy fringes of the world, and they were gone.

When Levee arrived at the house, the fog had socked in everything, and it was silent. Too silent. The air felt burdensome. Levee's instincts told him to be cautious.

He walked around the outside of the house. He stopped at the broken window. He peered into the house. On the carpet, mixed in with other glass fragments, was a little glass ballerina. Then he saw not far from it, a little beyond a corner, a man's open palm.

And then another car pulled up. It was the new sheriff, having been called by the operator. He was followed by the U.S. marshal and two deputies. Out of habit, Levee put his gun away and picked up his black doctor's bag.

The marshal was first to enter the pale light of the house. They were all nervous, and the invading fog, sliding in through the broken windows, didn't help. It made the inside of the house seem to be disappearing before their eyes, like a cloud of smoke drifting off.

The parrot flew away south.

For days Nola slept, curled up like a child. Michael Horse sat beside her. He sang one of the old songs, a deep-voiced sound that resembled gentle thunder. As he watched her, he thought of the events that had fallen over their lives in the last year.

It seemed like everything had turned around, had swirled into an ever-tightening circle of danger. Fire, which had meant warmth and light, had come to mean death. Wealth meant poverty. And for Nola, love had turned into loss.

Horse looked at her face. She slept without moving. He watched her chest rise and fall gently.

Horse continued to sing beside Nola and the people at the fire heard the gold-toothed man's soothing voice. It calmed them. They became still, but they were preoccupied with what they would do about the many changes that had come over the settlement. They argued and quarreled among themselves now; they needed to find a new way to keep peace. And what was worse, as the young people learned about the people in town, they became sad and afraid.

Finally, one night of the full moon, Nola stirred from her long sleep. Horse offered his hand to help her up from the bed. He led her out of the hut and toward the people's two fires. She walked with a wide and swaying step.

She went to the oldest woman. "I think the baby is going to be born," she told the woman. "It's time."

That night as Nola went into labor, Horse was inspired to finish writing *The Book of Horse*. He rolled the last page of paper out of Grace Blanket's typewriter. It began with simple rules for life: Take care of the earth and all her creatures. Do not be too afraid. Do not be too sad. Do not be too angry. Then he went outside, to the edge of the settlement, and looked out across the vast landscape.

The Hill Indians had kept their distance from the world outside, the world that was going empty. The settlement was a far cry from the red and black automobiles, silk hats, the jazzmen, and the guns. Horse felt peaceful there, in spite of

all that had happened. He wanted to remain. He could hear
the owls. He spoke to them. The low song of an owl was
close to him when suddenly he heard the sound of breathing.
It was Redshirt. He was sure of it. His heart speeded up. He
stood up and listened hard, closing his eyes, cupping his ears
with his hands. It was him. It was Redshirt. Horse listened.

That night, too, Stace Red Hawk walked through the
moonlight toward the settlement. He carried a lasso with
him. He wanted to find his mare. He was guided, not by the
path, for he could not see it, not even when he was on it, but
by the sounds of the owls and what had to be Michael Horse's
unmistakable voice hooting back at them. The moon was full
and yellow. By its light, Stace could see the cairns and the
bushes, a tumbleweed caught against a tree.

As Stace walked he thought about the recent trials. Hale,
sent to prison, was lost to time. Yet his presence had changed
the world. And Stace was not yet certain the crimes were
over, or that all of the culprits were locked behind bars. He
thought it possible that the crimes ranged all the way to the
higher official offices.

It was dark as Stace neared the sound of the owls. Then,
up in the hills he heard the drumming. He was close. Up in
the hills they were drumming. It made him feel good, feel
almost whole again. The smoky scent of cedar hung in the
air. He felt the spirit world. It was thick there, strong as the
smell of smoke. Then he felt something else. The horses. He
felt, yes, Redshirt and the black mare just beyond the brush.
Yes, it was them. He stopped breathing and listened.

Horse's voice startled Stace. "He's out there, all right. You
can feel him."

Stace looked toward the voice. "I can feel it too. What do
you think we ought to do?"

Horse sniffed the air. "They're real close." He gnawed
on his own lip. "We better leave them. If we let them think
they're safe from being caught, they'll return. If we try to
rope them now, we'll never see them again."

But then they heard the horses, heard the hooves clop on
the ground.

"Do you think they understand us?" Horse asked.

"Probably."

Just then, from down the hill, a rooster crowed. It was

somewhere behind them. The two men turned toward the sound.

"A rooster at night?" Stace wondered aloud.

"It's the moon," said Horse. "It's like daylight."

And then they saw the black and white figure of the priest walking up the path, carrying a rooster in a basket. It was a big orange rooster with red wattles and it looked around nervously, jerking its head and making a soft clucking sound. They smiled.

The priest had come back to tell the people that they were the land. He knew this by now. He was certain.

By the time the three men reached the settlement, Nola had given birth. The sky held a rain cloud. He didn't know for sure, but Horse felt as though the bat medicine had wakened.

"Horse," said the oldest of the women. "Tell us what it is you have written."

He looked hesitant, but he went inside and took papers from within the cedar trunk. Some of the words were written neatly in the script Horse had learned in China. Other pages were typed.

"First, I have to tell you about the book they call the Bible. It is a holy book for the European people, like those who live in the towns. It carries visions, commandments, and songs. I've added what I think is missing from its pages."

One of the younger women interrupted him. "Why can't you just speak it?"

"They don't believe anything is true unless they see it in writing."

Then he explained to the many listeners, "You know all this. It's very simple. That's why it took me so long to write it."

He began reading, "Honor father sky and mother earth. Look after everything. Life resides in all things, even the motionless stones. Take care of the insects for they have their place, and the plants and trees for they feed the people. Everything on earth, every creature and plant wants to live without pain, so do them no harm. Treat all people in creation with respect; all is sacred, especially the bats.

"Live gently with the land. We are one with the land. We

are part of everything in our world, part of the roundness and cycles of life. The world does not belong to us. We belong to the world. And all life is sacred.

"Pray to the earth. Restore your self and voice. Remake your spirit, so that it is in harmony with the rest of nature and the universe. Keep peace with all your sisters and brothers. Humans whose minds are healthy desire such peace and justice."

An old man interrupted. "Say, isn't that what Peacemaker of the Iroquois Nations used to say?"

Horse looked at the man. "The creator probably spoke the same words to him. It wouldn't surprise me at all."

He went on, "This is the core of all religion. It is the creator's history, the creator who spoke to a white man as clearly as he spoke to me, and said to him, 'As you do unto the least of these, my brothers, you do unto me.' The creator said this and we abide by it."

"Now," Horse continued, "the people will go out of their land. They, like the land, are wounded and hurt. They will go into the rocks and bluffs, the cities, and into the caves of the torn apart land. There will be fires. Some of them will be restored to the earth. Others will journey to another land and merge with other people. Some will learn a new way to live, the good way of the red path. But a time will come again when all the people return and revere the earth and sing its praises."

Father Dunne argued with Horse, "You can't add a new chapter to the Bible."

Horse furrowed his brow and looked at the priest. "Hmmm, do you think I need more thou shalts?"

They were all quiet for a while. The owls hooted in the distance. The oldest woman said, "He's a philosopher. He was always like that, even when he was a boy."

Ona Neck said, "I have something to put in the book."

"What's that?" asked Horse.

"Give me liberty or give me death." Her face broke into a wide grin. Then she laughed out loud.

For several nights Horse and Red Hawk heard the horses. They were ready for them. Stace carried two good lengths of rope tied around his waist, in case the horses should come close enough to lasso.

And then he saw the red stallion. Redshirt had come out of the night's shadows. He stood before the men. He whinnied softly. Stace moved slowly. Carefully, so as not to startle the horse, he removed the rope from his waist. He tried to breathe evenly, but he was excited and tense. "Easy," he said to the red horse. "Easy now." His voice was soothing.

In the bright moonlight, he saw that the red horse was growing a thicker coat, preparing already for the coming change in seasons. He stepped toward him. Stace was ready for a struggle, and though he tried to sound calm, his heart raced. He moved forward. He held the rope open with his hand as he moved.

But Redshirt did not bolt. The stallion stood firm, his black eyes gentle in the moonlight, his muscles without their usual tension.

Stace Red Hawk slipped the rope over the horse's long neck and Horse approached the stallion, ran his hand through the long thick mane. He walked around the front of the horse, looking it over, patting the dust from the red coat. The fresh smell of dried grass, of hay and horse, was thick. The old man stood back and looked at the stallion's dark eyes. He saw himself reflected there, then Horse turned toward Stace. "Let him go," he said.

Red Hawk stared at the old man as if he were crazy.

"Go on now, let him go." Horse stood aside.

"But I just caught him," Stace said. His mouth hung open as he looked at the old man.

"No, he let you catch him." Horse himself looked stronger, prouder.

Stace was dubious, but he said, "All right. Anything you say." He loosened the knot and pulled the rope over the red horse's fine-boned head. He stood back and waited.

Redshirt nuzzled the old man, then turned slowly and walked away. The red stallion stopped once, looked back, and then he was gone.

"What's gotten into you?" Stace asked Horse, but the older man had already vanished into the cover of night.

* * *

In Watona, the people were relieved. The trials were over. The red glow of autumn had worked its way back into the woods, and the rainy season was under way, and Belle Gray-cloud with her shocking white hair had returned home alive and without so much as a limp.

One morning she broke the few surviving ears of yellow corn from the stalks and put them in a basket. Moses hitched the two last horses to the wagon. The women of the household were going to the Hill settlement, to visit Nola. They were taking the corn, a golden jar of last year's honey, and a bouquet of red roses for Nola and for the naming of her new baby. Belle was cutting the roses when the chickens grew alarmed and scattered, flapping their flightless wings. She straightened up to see what frightened the hens, and then she heard a low hum in the distance, growing nearer. The bees. They were returning. The land filled up with the sound, a slow vibration.

"It's my bees!" Belle cried out. "They're coming home. Get some pans." She dropped the roses and ran into the kitchen. Indoors, everyone was in motion. Outside, the chickens cackled louder. Then they saw them, the half-round swarm shaped like a dark cloud flying in through the ruins of burned trees. And in the great tumult, Belle ran back outside, banging the metal pan with a metal spoon, screaming at the top of her lungs as she ran, and the swarm was startled by the racket, the great clamor and clang, and the hum dropped down a note, then stopped. As if they were all one body, one mind, they lighted and hung together, swarming over the tree like a shadow.

While they were stopped there, Louise rang the dinner bell. Belle gave Rena the kettle to hit. The noise held the bees motionless.

Belle ran inside pulling on her gloves and veil. Her hands shook. She didn't want to lose the bees and when she went back outside, she moved slowly. First, she set up the hive. Then she went over to the branch and plucked the queen out of the colony. Carefully, she put the queen in the hive. As she walked away, the other bees, obediently following their queen, flew into the hive. Belle couldn't tell for sure if this was the outlaw swarm that had killed the sheriff. They were bees who, like everything else, wanted only to live. That was all they wanted, to live and continue. Belle loved them. She understood them.

One day, right after Nola's baby was born, John Tate dropped Ruth off at the Graycloud yard. Belle, her daughters, and Rena were going up to the settlement to visit Nola and meet the new child. Ruth wanted to stay with Moses, to care for him, she said, but Moses knew how unhappy she was with the little man who was nervous and moved all the time.

That day, Moses hitched the horses to the wagon for Belle and the wagon rattled across the land. From the settlement, Silver spotted the Graycloud women. He and Okeena came down the bluffs to show them the path, then walked with them the rest of the way.

From the top of the path, Belle saw Nola. She sat in a circle with the older women. They were passing the baby around, each of them holding her, trying to make her dark small eyes smile into their own. Nola wore traditional clothing. She was changed. She looked older, but at the same time, she had a softer, more quiet look about her. When she saw her friends, she jumped up. Weeping, she embraced Rena and Louise and Lettie, then Belle. "Your hair! What did you do to it?" Then, reminded of the town by the women's presence, she changed the subject and began to cry about Will. "I couldn't help it," she said, without covering her face or hiding her tears. "He was one of them."

The women listened, but they remained silent. The shadows of day turned long and violet. They sat quietly, Lettie held the child.

"But I loved him," Nola cried. She dabbed at her eyes.

After a while, Rena asked, "What's the baby's name?"

Nola smiled through her sorrow. "Moses."

Rena laughed. "But a man's name? A girl called Moses?"

"Yes, why not?"

Then Belle told her about the shooting incident, her temporary death, and her white hair. "I was at death's door, the top step, and with a hand held out to knock."

Nola laughed. She wiped away her tears.

"It's good to see you smile," Belle said. It seemed like a long time since the death of Grace and the long, hard wave of misery that had washed over them afterward.

Later, as they rode the rickety wagon back home, Rena asked her grandmother, "Why didn't you tell her Will was innocent?"

Belle answered. "It would be worse for her. Think of how she would feel to have killed an innocent man she loved."

In the Graycloud kitchen, Lettie boiled water. Ruth and Moses both stirred sugar into their tea. The older man said, trying to hide his pride, "So, they called her Moses."

It was a cool but sunny day when Stace Red Hawk set out to find his black mare. He was on foot.

He walked through the dry leaves. Autumn had a rich, earthy odor of decay. And then he saw her. She was in an oak grove, standing still beneath red leaves and almost hidden by the dark shadows of tree trunks. When she saw him, he nodded at her as if greeting a friend. She lifted her head. They understood each other; she knew he wanted to harness her and he knew, in no uncertain terms, that she would run if he tried to pursue her, so he sat on a rock and waited for her to come, curious, to him.

Unlike Redshirt, she was a trusting horse, and after a while she walked close enough to Stace that he thought he might reach out, grab hold of her black, thick mane, and slip the halter over her head, but he didn't. He knew her well enough to know that she would triumph over him that day. She had the advantage. She lived without fences or constraint. She would bolt, her hooves thundering over the ground, leaving Stace with nothing but a handful of dry, bristly mane. And it wouldn't do for him to let her go. If he caught her and she escaped, she would be in charge and he would never have the chance again. So he sat quietly and let her eye him, and as he watched her, he decided to build a trap to corral her. He would need a horse if he was going to succeed at driving her into the trap, and he thought he knew just the horse, the red one that belonged to Moses Graycloud. Nola's gift. Redcoat. It was a quarter horse; chasing down and trapping another animal was in its blood.

He turned away from the mare and walked the dirt road to the Graycloud home. By the time he reached the turnoff to the old house, it was evening and there was a feeling of frost in the air.

The house had a dark, closed look to it. It was in need of paint and other care. Stace thought he could trade labor for the use of Moses's Redcoat.

When he knocked, Belle came to the door. "Come in," she said as she opened the door and stepped back, but she said little more to the young man. She only watched him with her sharp eyes.

"Is Moses here?"

She nodded. "In the kitchen."

Moses was at his usual place at the table, but instead of sitting, he was standing, lathering and soaping a saddle that was hanging over the table.

At first, when Red Hawk asked to borrow the horse, Moses eyed the young man with suspicion. None of the Grayclouds except Lettie believed they could trust the Sioux man. But Moses looked at Stace's boots. They were becoming worn and scuffed. He studied the man's hands, hands that had once worked hard, but now were too soft and Red Hawk's shoulders were slumped, tired. But it was the face of the young man that finally swayed Moses. It was the deep-eyed face of a good man. A man rooted in life.

In a calm voice, Moses said, "So you need a cutting horse?" He looked down, then back at Stace's face. "Tonight it's going to frost. I feel it in my leg. You should stay here." He sipped his coffee and wiped the saddle with a cloth. He looked out the window. "It's too dark, anyway. Tomorrow," he said, "tomorrow I'll go with you to catch your mare. You'll need help."

Lettie, who had been listening from the other room, went into the kitchen where the men were sitting, sat down, and looked at Stace. Her face turned rosy, as if she were embarrassed to be in his presence. She smiled for just a moment, but then she grew serious and looked directly at him. "Did you know about the confessions? Were they forced?"

Stace remained quiet. Only seconds passed, but it seemed longer. "I don't know." He shook his head. "I hope not."

"Well, it's done anyway." She stood up and looked at him. "You look tired. Come, I'll show you where to sleep."

As before, he followed her up the dark, musty-smelling staircase. He carried his bag with the medicines, and when she showed him the small bed at the end of the hall, he remembered the macaw feather. "Wait," he said as he placed the bag on the bed and opened it. "I forgot this. I'm sorry. Your mother gave it to me when I was on my way to Guthrie."

As he watched her take the blue feather from his hand, turn it over and examine the other side, he thought, yes, she was a kind woman, she would care for people, maybe for him.

"It was the feather of Osage Star-Looking," she said. "It was all I ever wanted of our life here. It's my inheritance, the only thing I wanted to be passed down to me at the end of the old people's lives. Mama must have thought she was going to die." Her eyes filled with tears, and without another word, she went to her room and closed the door, leaving Stace still standing awkwardly beside the open bag of his medicines.

That night Lettie was unable to sleep. She thought about Stace Red Hawk asleep in the hallway, not far from her. And she thought, what would happen if I went to him in the night, if my bare feet walked across the cool wood floor and stopped beside him? But she remained behind the closed door, and toward morning she fell asleep.

Early the next morning, Stace and Moses set out for the place where the black mare had been seen. There was a white layer of frost on each dry blade of grass. Moses shouted out, holding a lead rope with Redcoat at the other end. He walked alongside Redcoat, not wanting to wear her out before they reached the black mare. Besides, there were several heavy lengths of rope draped across her back. But his leg ached from the cold weather, and finally, when it was late morning, he had no choice but to have Stace help him up into the freshly soaped saddle.

"We need a plan," he said as Stace gave him the boost. "I think we should tie this rope to trees, make something like a fence. Then we chase her into it. Then you can get a rope about her neck. What do you think?"

Stace didn't tell the older man that he'd already made exactly that plan. Instead, he said, "I don't know. I think if we talk about it too loud, Redshirt will hear our plan and tell her what we're up to and we'll never catch her."

"I've heard of horses doing that before."

"Yes, people don't give them enough credit for being smart."

Soon they were at the place where Stace had seen the black mare. There were a few strands of her mane on the branches of one tree. Moses saw it, too. "Here," said Moses. "This is where we should begin to tie the ropes." With some difficulty, he dismounted, took a length of rope in hand, and tied it around the trunk of a tree. Stace, with the other end, walked away, pulled it tight, and tied it to another trunk.

Soon they had a corral, and once they got the mare in the center of it, they would be able to catch her, to get a lasso about her neck, then to slip on the halter, maybe even get the metal bit into her mouth. They were both tense with anticipation of the struggle, and as they waited, they were silent, watching for signs of the horse, but Redcoat sensed their anxiety and whinnied at the shadows.

It wasn't long until the mare appeared, black as the coals of the fire old man Horse carried with him. Black like Raven, the tricking one.

She approached the men carefully, as if she sensed there was a kind of deception. But in spite of her misgivings, she took a few steps into the trap, then stopped as she saw Stace walk away from her, move behind her slightly, forcing her to step forward. And Moses tried to throw his leg over Redcoat, and failed, then managed to swing his leg behind him and get on.

At first, the black mare put up a fight. Stace yelled and waved his arms. She charged him. But he stood his ground and she stepped backward and then Moses turned Redcoat to the left, and with the cutting horse in her blood, she crowded against the black horse.

But in reality, even though she had followed Redshirt, the black mare was a practical horse and was not against being caught. Winter was coming on and it was going to be cold, so when Redcoat crowded her against a tree trunk, and then against the rope fence, she let Stace Red Hawk slip the lasso about her neck and let him also dig in his heels and pull at her, leaning as she backed up a ways. She stretched her neck toward him while she pulled her body away. But she did this only halfheartedly. Still leaning, Stace walked the rope to-

ward her, carrying the halter, and slipped it over her head.
She was completely still. And Stace knew that it was the
mare, not him, that had made the decision to be caught. She
knew it was going to be a hard, cold winter in the Osage
hills. It would be more convenient for her to be caught, to
have food and a warm blanket covering her on the chilly
nights.

It was late when the men and horses returned and saw the
dim lights of the house. Along the way, they'd heard every
now and then, a rustle of dry leaves, and knew Redshirt
followed. They looked for him as they went inside the fence
to the barn. They listened through the autumn darkness that
smelled of drying herbs.

The next day, Stace Red Hawk and the night-colored horse
set up camp on Belle's land down at Mill Creek. Stace looked
at the sky and the clouds moving across the blue bowl above
him, then went out to gather firewood. In spite of the chilly
nights, it was where Stace wanted to be. The sound of water
offered comfort and peace. And he would not find Lettie
Graycloud in every corner of his mind.

Belle was solaced by the presence of Stace. Dark nights,
she could see his little circle of firelight from out in the field,
and one evening, just before dark, she walked down to the
creek. She carried some chicken and an extra blanket to the
place where Red Hawk and his mare had made camp.

Stace was sitting by the water when he heard Belle approach. He looked up at her startling white hair, the whiteness of it surrounded by the old dark sky with its few early
stars.

Belle stood, looking down at him. "I brought you this
blanket."

He thanked her, but he was full of that dry, coarse silence
of one who has been too much alone.

"Is there anything else I can bring, anything at all you
need?" she asked him.

He thought about it a moment. "Yes, I need hope." As
soon as he spoke those words, he realized something else
had spoken through him, a wiser part of himself, and his
words made real that need. He felt overcome with a sadness.
He wanted hope.

That night, after Belle left, Stace Red Hawk put out his

fire and rode the black mare to the Blue River. He was going there to sprinkle tobacco on the water and ask for hope. He thought the creek was not wide enough or deep enough to fill his well of despair.

Not far from the water of the Blue River, Redshirt, loving the black mare, came out of the thick brush to follow alongside them.

Stace greeted him, "Hello, old fellow." Redshirt was calm as he followed the black mare.

Stace watched the moon rise, and when they reached the river, he saw it reflected on the water. He sprinkled tobacco across it. Around him the foxfire was shining on the limbs of dead trees. He thought hope was like that foxfire, alive and bright and growing out of decay.

All that night, he sat before the water, thinking, listening to the occasional whinny of the horses. All around him was alive. A star fell down the blackness. And then, in the east, the sky began to pale, and after a while there was a reddening day and he was cold.

In the morning his clothing felt wet. But it was beautiful dawn.

When Stace returned to his camp that noon, Levee was there. He wore a dark coat and work gloves. Stace didn't ask him what he was doing there.

"I'm leaving," was all Levee said. He looked around at the sunny hills and plains.

Stace said nothing.

"I think I was afraid," Levee said. "I was afraid of medicine. It seemed like so much failure, to fail at healing, to see people die. I thought it would be more." He stood up. "I didn't even find compassion." He sat back down.

Stace turned to look at Levee. "And now? Is it different?"

"Now the world's been turned upside down. Now I don't know the truth from the lie. I'm going back. I lost something, but I found something else. I don't even know what to call it, except I feel something like love for those sick and dying people now."

Stace nodded. "Yes, I lost something, too."

Levee relaxed and looked around. "It's a pretty place, isn't it?"

"Yes. It's a good place."

"Where did you find the horse?"

"Moses helped trap her. She was on to us, though. I think she really trapped us. She wanted a wool blanket for winter and lots of feed. She's like some women, she'll take up with anyone who offers oats and hay."

"Me, too. I was hoping you'd offer me a place to stay for a few nights."

Stace smiled and shook his head. "I'm out of oats."

"So that's why you've gotten so thin, Red Hawk." But Levee didn't say that Stace looked stronger, like a man who knew who he was and where he was going.

That night, still searching for the quiet center of himself, Stace went into the woods.

Levee went silent. He was listening to the sounds of the dark Oklahoma world. He heard a raccoon entering water, an owl cracking a branch.

For some time, Moses had been feeling uncomfortable, as if something was not right. It was a strong feeling he couldn't shrug off. He thought Belle must feel that way when she knew something was wrong. It was real, something he could almost touch with his hand, something cold and cruel.

He slept lightly while the rest of the household was peaceful, relieved to be out of danger. And that night, when he dozed lightly, Moses thought he heard his sister's voice, low and distant as if in a dream.

He sat up on the edge of the bed. He was restless. He pulled on his pants, and from far away he heard Ruth screaming and it was outside, he thought, or imagined, by their mother's barn. Quickly he took the pistol from the drawer. There was no time to lose. His hands fumbled. He was certain Ruth was in danger. He didn't bother to put on his boots. He heard her again, down the road this time. He ran barefoot down the stairs and rushed into the barn and took hold of Redcoat. The workhorses were afraid, seeing the man's bare chest, sensing his fear, and they stamped the floor with their hooves. Quickly, with shaking hands, Moses slipped the cold metal bit in the mouth of Redcoat. The workhorses showed the whites of their eyes. Moses pulled the bridle up over Redcoat's ears, took the reins in hand, jumped onto her bare back and rode out, riding on fear, on the fast heartbeat of the running horse. He rode past the pasture, past the trees that were black as the derricks beneath the staring moon. He rode through the whisper of dry grass, the gun in his hand, his bare feet and legs hitting against the horse, already sore, both of them breathing hard. He could not see his way. A branch hit him across the face. He had to trust the horse. He hunched forward over the neck of Redcoat, racing, slapping the horse with his hand.

From the forest, Stace heard the hooves, turned and ran back to his camp. "Levee!" Stace said in a hard whisper. "Someone is at the Grayclouds!"

Levee jumped up.

Disturbed, Belle turned over in bed. She lit the lantern. She took her shawl from a hook, wrapped it around her shoulders, and walked across the bare, cold floor to the window. It was a beautiful night, and she thought how wonderful it was to look out without fear, to stand in the warm lantern light before an open window. She looked at the distant hills, then a movement caught her eye. She saw a man, below, on the ground. She thought it was one of the watchers returned. But then she saw Floyd. There was a commotion, and then she saw Floyd run up to the man, begin to fight him and push against him. She heard the yelling, heard Floyd screaming at them, telling the family to get out of the house. She tried to think, but then she heard the sound of a horse pounding fast on the ground, and Moses calling, "Get out! Now!" She pulled back from the window and went for the pistol inside the drawer. It was gone.

There were the sounds of the fight, and Floyd again screaming.

Belle rushed into Lettie's room and began pulling at her arms, pulling her to her feet. "Get up. We have to get out!" She was crying. Lettie woke wide-eyed and she, too, went into action, breathing hard, fast.

Belle looked again out of Lettie's window then and heard Floyd say they had set a charge. She ran into the hallway. She heard a gunshot. It filled her with dread that Floyd was slain.

Ben heard the noise and was standing in the hall.

"Get Rena. Get her out!" Belle yelled. "Louise, wake up!" The old woman ran into her other daughter's room, but Floyd's boots already clattered up the stairs. And his voice, yelling out, "Lou! Get out! Now!"

And then the pounding down the stairs.

"The dog!" Belle screamed.

"He's out!" Floyd lied.

Then a shadow passed over the moon and it went dark.

From the creek, Red Hawk and Levee heard the gunshot. Red Hawk, on the horse, galloped toward the Graycloud house to see what was wrong. Levee ran through the thickets.

Stace felt as if his heart would give out, he was so full of fear. When he neared the house, Moses was running wild and out of breath. Moses went inside the barn. The sounds of excited, fearful horses were knocking against the wood. Moses was trying, desperately, to harness the frightened workhorses. Stace jumped down and ran inside the barn, began to help Moses take the horses to the road. All the time, Moses yelled and sobbed. His hands were shaking, and he was sweating and cold.

Levee lifted Louise into the back of the wagon. "What's wrong?" she kept asking. "What's going on?"

Only moments had passed before they were all outside, but it seemed like forever, the sheer terror holding them all, pulling them along in its tight grip.

And then they were quiet, as if they were suspended. Those moments became centuries.

Moses lifted Rena into the wagon and he climbed on. Lettie sat beside him, Belle on the other side of her, both looking at their home, clutching at each other as Moses began to drive the horses away from the farm. Belle saw the dead man on the ground.

Moses drove away from the house, then stopped to wait for Stace.

Red Hawk, on the black mare, stepped out of the dust. Levee moved into step beside the mare. "Where are you going?"

Stace reined in the mare, turned her a bit, and he said to Levee, "With them." He nodded toward where the wagon was moving slowly up the rise. "I'm going with them." He was already riding toward the Graycloud wagon. It was moving in soft light as a cloud passed away from the moon.

And suddenly darkness became a flash of light. It was daylight. The land was red and bright. The wagon was fully visible. There was screaming and the house rose up in flames, wood flying outward, the place collapsing, the broken glass catching the firelight for an instant as the fire ascended in a blast of heat. Even from that distance the explosion lifted the manes of the horses, the hair of the women. In the hot wind their faces burned. The blazing roof of the house seemed to fall inward, to collapse on itself. In the light, there was the startling white of Belle's hair. And in the light, also, they could see the fence that had held in the sad buffalo, the empty land.

The world roared and broke. Smoke billowed up across the sky. It started other fires in the dry autumn fields, and they could see the fireline begin to move outward, like blood of the wounded earth. Through the smoke, Stace rode toward them.

Moses drove on a ways, away from the fire, driving into the night, toward the darkness, then he stopped and put his face in both of his hands, and he was suddenly aware of his nakedness in the chilly night. Belle covered him with a blanket.

"Ruth," he said. "She's dead. Tate shot her. He was one of them. I had to shoot him. I had no choice."

The fire roared behind them.

"What about us?" Belle asked.

"We have to go. I shot him. I'll be arrested. They'll be looking for me."

They looked back once and saw it all rising up in the reddened sky, the house, the barn, the broken string of lights, the life they had lived, nothing more than a distant burning. No one spoke. But they were alive. They carried generations along with them, into the prairie and through it, to places where no road had been cut before them. They traveled past houses that were like caves of light in the black world. The night was on fire with their pasts and they were alive.

Acknowledgments

I am grateful for the help, friendship, and support of the following people:

Eric Ashworth, Marilyn Auer, Michael Cohen, Jean Fortier, Lee Goerner, Becky and Joe Hogan, Pat Hogan, Tanya Hogan, Jackie Peterson, Connie Studer, Sigrid Ueblacker, and my mother and father.

The National Endowment for the Arts provided me with financial assistance for the writing of this novel.
The following people provided me with parts of this story:

My father, CHARLES HENDERSON, for our shared history and for the many stories he told me about oil, land loss, and grief.
CAROL HUNTER, who introduced me to these particular events.
BETTY LITTLE, whose family left Oklahoma in the middle of the night.
DIANE FRAHER, who shared names for the characters of Belle and Lettie from her own Osage Indian family, and provided some information about the character of Nola. As an Osage woman, Fraher has said about this story:

The flaws in the U.S. legal system that allowed murderers and thieves to profit from American Indian land have yet to be righted. Many tribal nations and Indian people are still separated from what is rightfully theirs.

In the case of the Osage, the U.S. federal government was

sorely remiss in protecting Indian rights, and only became involved when monetary gain was the issue. Non-Indian shareholders still receive Osage Indian annuity checks, shares in the Mineral Trust, and unwarranted benefits as shareholders.

Our Indian elders teach us to maintain tradition and survival of spirit, and to begin to let go of the hurt and anger that has resulted from injustice. We know we are all only visitors in this world, and that no matter what has happened, we have refused to let the strength of spirit be taken from us. Out of love for my family, I wanted to share this love and spirit and let it find its way into this story.

The many other people I met in this traveling.

Information about John Stink was added from *Hah Tah Moie: The Story of John Stink* by Kenneth Jacob Jump, a self-published book. Another story of John Stink is written by Anna Mae Walters, a Pawnee-Otoe writer, "The Resurrection of John Stink," in Walters' book, *The Sun Is Not Merciful*, Firebrand Press.

Additional readings may be found in books by Osage writer John Joseph Matthews, in Angie Debo's book *And Still the Waters Run*, and from the people who remember, such as Carter Revard, Osage poet and teacher; and from the many elders who pass the stories on.

About the Author

Linda Hogan is a Chickasaw poet, novelist, and essayist. She is the author of several books of poetry and a collection of short fiction. She has received an American Book Award from the Before Columbus Foundation. Hogan is the recipient of a National Endowment for the Arts grant, a Minnesota Arts Board Grant, a Colorado Writer's Fellowship, and the Five Civilized Tribes Museum playwriting award. She is an associate professor at the University of Colorado, has served on the NEA poetry panel for two years, and is involved in wildlife rehabilitation as a volunteer.